ISLAND WOLF

RACHEL ARMSTRONG

Pink Paws Publishing

First published 2025
Print ISBN: 978-0-6453555-8-1
Ebook ISBN: 978-0-6453555-9-8

Published by
Pink Paws Publishing
Rachel Armstrong

For permissions, please contact:
Rachel Armstrong
PO Box 688, Aitkenvale QLD 4815
Australia
E-mail : rachelarmstrong_author@outlook.com

A catalogue record for this book is available from the National Library of Australia
www.librariesaustralia.nla.gov.au

For Ian

*Thank you for being intrigued by the idea of
wolf shifters on Magnetic Island*

Prologue

Rain's muscles bulged and strained as he leapt up the rock grains and onto the boulders bordering Gustav Creek. Desperation overpowered his weary body and the hopelessness inside his heart. He wanted his brother back. Needed him to return. Rain could sense Sly's pain and shared in his loss, but he couldn't take it anymore. It was too much.

Leaping over the boulders, Rain plunged into the scrub. The vegetation grew denser as he ran up the slope towards the peaks. No bushwalkers lingered this late at night and with the rock band playing at Luna Views Resort, Rain doubted anyone would hear him.

Rocks grated between his toes as he continued to climb. Avoiding the stinging trees, he lifted his face and sniffed. A slither caught his eye and Rain shot his gaze towards the death adder curling into itself, flicking its tongue in warning. Rain's lips quirked as he flashed his teeth at the snake, then powered on through the trees until he reached The Pinnacles.

Mount Aurora.

Heart pounding, he eased out onto the flat rock over-looking the dark bushland of the island he and his brother called home. Hair prickled along his spine. His jaw clenched. He'd never emitted a Call. It was a sacred act. A plea. A cry for help used only at the most desperate of times.

But Rain had run out of options. Sly's trauma darkened with every moon and if he wouldn't listen to reason from his own kin, then Rain needed reinforcements. The help of someone with no affiliations, no connections, and no stake in the situation.

A lone wolf.

A Warrior.

Standing on the edge of the cliff, Rain lifted his face to the light of the full moon. His nose twitched and knees locked as he took in a lungful of air.

Then he threw back his head and howled.

Chapter 1

If it wasn't for Finn's supernatural strength, he'd have a sore ass. Five days riding the waves up the Australian coast on the back of a Sea-Doo was bound to cause some bruises. Not that it hadn't been exhilarating bouncing over the swells and dodging rough currents. Finn lived for the thrill. But nonetheless, he welcomed the sight of Magnetic Island's mountainous terrain emerging in the distance beneath the light of the waning moon. A sane man would have stopped for the night six hours ago and set up camp on a remote Whitsunday Island.

But where was the fun in that?

Twisting the throttle, Finn leaned over the handlebars and shot the jet ski forwards. To his left, the lights of Townsville stretched up the coast, the skyline consisting of a major international shipping port and a dozen multistory buildings that made up the regional city. Red and green lights flashed across the water, marking the channel into the port and towards the island. The cool ocean breeze blew through his blond hair and the waves lapped dangerously as midnight loomed, but Finn rarely knew fear. A growl emanated from his chest. Or his stomach. He wasn't sure which. The tiny towns he'd stopped at along the way might have refueled the Sea-Doo, but they'd done little to replenish his appetite and he'd kill for a steak. Luna Views was a five-star resort and therefore had twenty-four-hour room service, and surely it wouldn't be too much of an inconvenience when he liked his meat rare.

Finn shot through the channel, ignoring the marina as he powered towards the stretch of beach and the glistening white resort rising over the rocky outcrop. Luna Views, the first and only resort of the Moonrise real estate moguls who had made their fortune building magnificent high-rise apartment buildings in major cities across Australia.

And home to Magnetic Island's famous Full Moon Party.

Smirking, Finn slowed as he approached the beach, hit the shallows, and cut the engine. He dropped the anchor, then leapt into the warm water. Shells crunched beneath his bare feet and weeds squished between his toes, which left Finn grimacing. Tropical paradise? He didn't know about that.

Wading through the water around the jet ski, he unclipped his backpack, tossed it over his shoulder, then unzipped the mesh carrier secured onto the back. The small gray snout and long black ears of his Maltese-Shitzu emerged, her tiny nose sniffing the cool air.

"Ride's over, G.B." Finn unclipped the dog and tucked her beneath his arm. "Let's go find the guy who called us, then we'll get some food."

He took the stairs from the beach up onto the deck two at a time. Wind rustled the palm trees in the softly illuminated gardens otherwise, all else was quiet. Not that Finn was surprised. Even tropical resorts didn't party into the wee hours on a Thursday night.

He padded across the deck and sank his feet into the cool grass, not stopping to admire the majestic views beneath the Goddess's soft light. But his little dog was keen to explore and after being holed up in her carrier all night, she needed to relieve herself. Finn placed her down and shoved his hand through his long, windswept hair as she sniffed the garden and squatted.

Glancing around the resort, Finn inhaled, caught the scent, and continued towards reception. The patter of tiny paws followed him through the lush, beautiful gardens before he strode into the airy atrium and to the empty desk. He slapped his hand on the bell.

"One minute!" a muffled voice called. Papers shuffled, a chair squeaked as weight lifted, then a lean, muscular man strode through the open office door. Blue eyes locked onto Finn's, and the man stilled.

Finn inclined his chin. "I received your Call."

Broad shoulders deflated as the man shoved his hand through his chin-length dark hair. "Thank fuck. I'd been wondering." He extended his hand over the desk. "Welcome. Name's Rain. Rain Blackwood."

"Finn Cassidy."

"You just get in?"

Finn nodded. "Came straight here."

"Took the last ferry?"

"Brought my Sea-Doo."

Rain slipped his hands into his pockets. "From Townsville?"

"From Tasmania."

"Shit." Rain's eyebrows shot up. "That's a long ride."

"Yeah, but a man can't leave his beloved toys behind."

He smirked. "I understand that. We're hot into water-sports around here."

Finn nodded, having discovered that when he'd researched the resort. Luna Views might have a reputation for their Full Moon Party, but they'd also boosted tourism on Magnetic Island by bringing an exceptional array of thrill sports and tours, activities that would suit Finn just fine.

"And that's why I think the Goddess had me hear your Call."

"Indeed." Rain moved out from behind the desk. "I could do with a man like you around here. How about I—" His gaze dropped to Finn's feet. "That's your dog?"

Finn glanced at the Maltese-Shitzu as she scuffled backwards, huffed, then sat on his bare toes. Spine steeling, Finn met Rain's frown. "Problem?"

"Nope." Rain's head snapped up with a grin. "We love dogs around here. They're always welcome. They're just not usually so ... small."

Pressing his lips together, Finn bent to scoop his dog up. She might only be eight kilos of solid fluff, but after surviving the loss of her pack, G.B. had proved herself to be as tough and loyal as any dog ten times her size. "She's more than she appears."

"I'm sure she is." Rain clapped Finn on the shoulder. "Thanks for coming. Let me take you through and I'll show you where you can stay."

"Appreciate it."

Adjusting his backpack over one arm and the dog beneath his other, Finn followed Rain out of reception. Wind rustled the manicured bushes as they wandered up the garden path illuminated by soft glowing lights while waves lapped on the beach only meters away.

"Nice resort you have here."

"Thanks. It was always our dream to ..." Rain shot Finn a look over his shoulder. "What do you know?"

"Not much. I heard the Call, so I responded." As a Warrior of the Goddess always did.

"Thank you." Rain started up a slope in the path, passing dark triangular huts that suspended over the outcrop to provide generous views of the ocean. "I'll fill you in on the details of our situation over breakfast, but basically, we're having trouble protecting our territory from the rogues in Pallarenda. They've infiltrated the youth and crime is out of control on the mainland. When we arrived five years ago, there wasn't much trouble. But you know what rogues are like." Rain's mouth twisted as he lifted his shoulders. "They're threatened by those of us who believe in Fate."

Finn ground his teeth. Rogues were the bane of his existence. He'd dealt with hundreds, killed many, and had saved a dozen packs from the threat of the unnatural creatures.

Yet not one of those grateful Alpha's had invited him to stay.

"Bats have also taken over the city and are in cahoots with the Alpha." Rain lowered his voice. "He uses them as spies."

Finn frowned. That was interesting. Bats were cunning creatures and usually kept to themselves, haunting major cities outside of any wolf's territory. Finn had little experience with them since they rarely mixed with rogues, but he never backed down from a challenge.

Rain stopped at the top of the hill outside the final hut. "You and your little dog can stay here. It's one of our deluxe suites with a spa bath, lounge, and uninterrupted views of the ocean. If there's anything you need, don't hesitate to ask. We have room service and yes, the steak is to die for." Rain grinned as he pushed open the door.

"I'll have to take you up on it," Finn said as he stepped inside. Deluxe, indeed. A small lounge and king-sized bed dominated the main room before a large glass wall welcomed the uninterrupted view of the ocean. After camping for four nights and five days straddling the Sea-Doo, a king bed with an ocean breeze was exactly what Finn needed.

"I'll have a meal sent up." Rain hovered by the doorway and pointed his thumb over his shoulder. "You also have direct access to the bushland on the outcrop. You'll have to cross the road to get to the national park, but it's quiet around here.

The island's seventy percent bushland, so there's plenty of room to run."

Finn dropped his backpack onto the floor and placed the little dog on the lounge. "Sounds tempting. Thanks, Rain." Finn strode to the man and extended his hand. "You've been more than accommodating."

"Of course. I asked you to come." After a firm handshake, Rain backed towards the door. "I'll talk to you in the morning."

"Sounds good."

"Excellent. You'll like the island, Finn. Lots of creeks, lookouts, and wildlife, so feel free to explore. There is just one rule." Rain's gaze narrowed as he stepped out into the night. "Don't eat the koalas."

Chapter 2

Ava Hart's knuckles whitened around the wheel as she sped down the tight turns of the Paluma Range towards Townsville. Heart pounding, she hardly dared to blink as she fixed her gaze on the narrow strip of asphalt in her high beams. She hated this road with its twists, U-turns, and blind corners, the impossible narrowness winding its way through the rainforest on the edge of the mountain. It terrified her in the bright light of day, never mind at night in a car that wasn't her own.

But she needed to escape. If Blair charged her with car theft, so be it. Stolen cars were an everyday occurrence in these parts. Though with her luck, her charges would be the ones that stuck, unlike the hooligans who got away with it on a nightly basis.

Ava turned the sleek V8 sedan through the S-bends. She tried focusing on her breathing, but it did little to alleviate the goosebumps on her skin, the sting in her cheek, or her shattered pride. She had damn well known better. She never fell for the bad boy. Ava liked men who were sensible, who had steady jobs and a fierce sense of loyalty. A man she could trust to be kind and passionate. She hadn't thought Blair particularly kind or patient, but she'd given him a chance based on his charm in the hope that maybe she'd misjudged him.

But she hadn't. He was just another arrogant brute who thought his way was the only way. A man who hid his toxic masculinity behind his handsome face and a badge. A man with an insecurity complex and a twisted soul.

A man who only wanted her for her body and who didn't like to be told "no."

Slowing the car, Ava rounded a hairpin turn and grappled with the wheel as she twisted around the bend that followed. Blair had no right to her body. She put her heart and soul into looking fabulous, and she did it for herself. For the health of her heart, muscles, and mind. Not for a man to look at her like a plaything. To take advantage and claim ownership of her body.

And that's certainly what Blair had thought he'd do when he'd "surprised" her with a night at his cabin in the rainforest after only two dinner dates. When she'd said no, he'd flown into a rage, grabbed her by the shoulders, and shoved her onto the bed. Terrified, she'd kicked, yelled, and hadn't stopped even after he'd slapped her with fury contorting his dark face.

I brought you here. If I want to fuck you, I'll fuck you!

A shudder coursed through her, and Ava flickered her gaze to the blood-smeared silver ring on her right hand. She still didn't know what had happened after her fist had collided with his nose. Sure, her ring was big, but she'd never thought it would cause a man to scream bloody murder and roll off her as he clutched his bleeding face.

Not that she'd stuck around to contemplate it. Ava had grabbed his keys and ran.

Turning the car around the last corner, she descended onto flat ground and put her foot to the floor. As soon as she was on the highway, she slumped into her seat.

But as quick as relief came, fear caught in her throat. Blair might not have a car, but he would still come after her. That's what happened now, wasn't it? She'd gotten herself caught by a possessive man, and he wouldn't let her go.

"Shit." Biting down on her lower lip, Ava blinked back tears and tapped her fingers on the steering wheel. What was she going to do?

Hands shaking, she reached for her phone and broke all sorts of laws as she called Eden. It might be getting late, but her friend would understand. As a vet, Eden was awoken at all hours and while Ava might not have an animal that needed tending, she'd certainly been hurt by one.

"Ava?" Eden answered sleepily. "You okay?"

"I need your help."

"Where are you?" Alarm filled Eden's voice, followed by the rustle of sheets. "What happened?"

"I'm leaving Paluma. Blair—"

"What did he do?"

The ache around Ava's heart softened, but it didn't make it any easier to force the words out. "He demanded sex, then hit me."

Silence. A truck roared past Ava, lit up like a beacon.

"Come straight here. I'll put the kettle on."

HALF AN HOUR LATER, Ava arrived at her friend's house in Hyde Park. She climbed out of Blair's flashy Ford Falcon as Eden stepped onto the porch and opened her arms. Ava went to her and clung.

"Are you okay?" Eden whispered.

"I hate men. I'm sick of their bullshit." She drew away and exhaled. "I don't know what to do."

Eden's eyes narrowed as she lifted her finger to Ava's cheek. "It's still pink."

"Don't worry about that." Lowering her gaze, Ava strode inside. Eden latched the doors behind them and applied the deadbolt and chain. A woman living alone could never be too careful in this city.

"I'll make you a cup of tea," Eden said, rubbing Ava's arm as they entered the kitchen. Ava plopped onto a stool at the breakfast bar while Eden took two mugs from the cupboard. "You need to go to the police."

Ava scoffed. "He *is* the police."

"I know." Eden slipped a tea bag into each mug and reached for the electric kettle. "But there are other cops who—"

"His father is the superintendent of Townsville."

"Yes, but—"

"I know how it sounds!" Ava shoved her fingers through her hair. "And I hate it too. I never thought I'd be the girl who lets a man get away with hitting her, but there's something about Blair. He terrified me tonight, Eden. Something isn't right. He's twisted inside. And with cops like him on the force, I'm not surprised that the city is overrun by crime."

Eden grimaced as she passed Ava a steaming mug. "Surely there's someone who will help you."

Ava's stomach twisted. Thankfully, the hospital where she worked as a physiotherapist had forced her to take annual leave, so at least she had time to figure out a plan. "Even if there was, it doesn't change the fact I can't go home. We live in the same apartment complex. I could hardly avoid him before, let alone now. He's going to come after me for sure."

Eden reached across the bench and squeezed Ava's hand. "We'll get you somewhere safe. Why don't you go visit your parents?"

Ava's parents lived in Collinsville, a small town three hours south. She wouldn't mind seeing them and her brothers, but how would she explain her sudden visit or the bruise on her face? "I don't think that's a good idea."

"Then come with me to the island. It's not terribly far away, but you can stay with my mum or at Eucalypts Grove."

Ava considered that as she sipped her tea. Eucalypts Grove was the bush retreat on Magnetic Island that Eden's mum had managed since she was a little girl. "It is nice there. And I could have breakfast with the koalas every day." As a sanctuary for the furry marsupials, the koalas were a major attraction for international tourists.

"And if you want, you can help me at the hospital. I have a koala who requires daily mobilization after hip surgery."

Ava's lips quirked. She could spend her forced vacation in worse ways than volunteering her physiotherapy skills at the Koala Hospital. "I could do that."

"I'd really appreciate your help. Then you can spend the rest of the time having a little holiday. There's plenty to do, Ava. Maggie Island is more than you give it credit for."

That was true as there were many bays she'd left unexplored, hikes left unconquered, and yoga she'd finally have the time to enjoy. Not to mention she might check out what all the fuss was with the Full Moon Party everyone raved about. She wasn't sure which music sensation the billionaire playboys who owned the five-star resort had scheduled to perform this month, but her and Eden's popstar best friend, Isla, was headlining in September.

"All right. I'll go to the island."

"Good." Eden smiled softly over the rim of her mug. "We'll grab your things, and you can come with me on the ten o'clock ferry."

Chapter 3

Finn woke to the usual sensation of an eight-kilo female on his chest as the first rays of dawn seeped through the windows. He'd lowered the blinds over the glass wall as the thought of sleeping in had been bliss after camping on the beach for the past few nights.

His little dog, however, didn't do sleep-ins.

"*Gruff.*"

He peeked one eye open to find her fluffy white paws in the scruff of his chest hair. "Grr ..."

Her feet danced. Nose twitched. "*Grrr-uff!*"

Finn bared his teeth. "Grrrrr-oooowl!"

Her legs locked, and she threw back her head. "*Aaa-rooo!*"

Snorting, Finn tucked her under his arm and tossed his legs over the edge of the bed. "All right, Gracie Belle. I'm up." He rubbed his eyes, then ran his hand down his scruffy face, his beard longer and more unkept than usual after days at sea. Placing Gracie on the ground, he stood and raised the blinds, baring his nakedness to the sapphire ocean twinkling beneath the rising sun. Finn's lips quirked. He'd traveled far and wide around Australia in search of a home, particularly along the coast of Victoria and New South Wales. Occasionally, he'd ventured inland, and he'd spent one freezing winter in the Kosciuszko National Park. But it was always when Finn found himself by the sea that he felt the most settled.

Turning, he found his backpack and grabbed a pair of boxers. "Better find you a nature spot, G.B."

She trailed behind him, still unsure about their new surroundings as she eyed the furniture suspiciously. Gracie was as loopy as they came. She hated change, objects being out of place, and her epic tail chasing was shameful for all canines. But her mother had loved her, and she'd been kind to Finn. The night his neighbor hadn't come home, Finn hadn't been able to bear the thought of Gracie finding herself in a shelter and going to a new house with people who didn't understand her special needs.

He opened the door, scooped Gracie up, and walked her down the three stairs to place her in the garden. Thanks to the money-hungry breeders who had over-bred her mum, the poor little dog had Perthes disease and had been undergoing treatment since she was eight months old to manage the degeneration of her left hip. With a combination of steroids and anti-inflammatories, Gracie had grown into it and her hip was functional and strong. The little girl would never be able to jump up or climb stairs, but Finn didn't mind having to lift or carry her everywhere.

He turned away as she squatted, giving her privacy as he scratched his chest and glanced down the rock-lined path between the triangular shaped cabins. The white-painted wood glistened in the glow of the sunrise while birds squawked in greeting. The abundant foliage enhanced the paradise appeal and, with the tropical location, August didn't bear its normal chill. Though after spending most of his life in the southern states, Finn could get used to the balmy air and sunshine. He wasn't sure how he'd cope come summer, but he might not be there to find out if he didn't form the bond that he'd spent fifteen years searching for. The life of a lone wolf was just as it sounded—lonely. Sure, the Moon Goddess had bestowed upon him a great honor when he'd started hearing a wolf's Call a decade ago. He'd helped many packs overcome various territorial invasions, prevented wolves from rebelling, and had even rescued kidnapped young pups. But when one job ended, there would always be another. Whether that be a few weeks or a few months, Finn never knew. Nor had he minded, as moving from place to place was the best way to stay hidden. His latest stint in Freycinet Bay had been one of his longest at ten months and despite his trauma associated with Tasmania, he'd quite enjoyed the lush landscape of one of the world's most beautiful beaches.

But deep down, a wolf needed a pack. A man needed a home. And he couldn't help but hold on to hope that one day, the Goddess would alter his fate and he could give up his nomadic lifestyle when welcomed into a pack.

Though if this was his chance, he needed to learn what had called him to this mission and the threat he had to face.

Finn glanced down. Gracie sat and flipped her long black ear as she looked over her shoulder, indicating that she was finished. He carried her back inside, fished around in his backpack for her kibble, then drew her meloxicam into a syringe. She hated the stuff and tried to fight him, but he won the battle every time as he parted her jaw and squirted the medicine into her mouth. She smacked her jowls, huffed at him, then turned to her breakfast. Finn left her to it, his own stomach rumbling as he rifled through his meager belongings. He would find Rain, get the run of the land, then go hunting for clothes and other necessities he hadn't bothered to stow inside the Sea-Doo.

He squeezed into a white T-shirt, pulled on a pair of black shorts, then rubbed Gracie's ears before striding out of the hut. Catching a whiff of breakfast from the restaurant, Finn lifted his nose and sniffed. Human ... bacon ... ah. Rain. Following the scent of ozone, salt, and eucalypts, Finn padded barefoot down the ramp and onto the floating pontoon. He found Rain aboard a black jet boat with the toothy grin of a wolf painted on the hull.

"Does she only run beneath the power of the full moon?"

Rain's mouth curved as he brushed his dark hair out of his face. "She certainly runs faster."

Finn snorted. "I bet. With this beast, Luna Views, and the Full Moon Party, it's a wonder no one's connected the dots."

Rain jumped off the boat and onto the pontoon. "What dots? That people shift into wolves? Please."

"A theme never goes astray. I like your jet skis." Finn moved down to admire the Yamaha and stand-up Sea-Doo, two of the best performance skis money could buy. "You do freestyle?"

"Sometimes, just to show off. You?"

Finn shrugged. "I know how to handle my skis."

"You should show me what you've got. Later today, we'll put on a show for the ferry."

"You do that often?"

"Only for the special ones." Rain slipped his hands into the pockets of his board shorts. "I'd do the fun shit all day, but running the hotel comes with responsibilities. And paperwork." He spat the last word.

"You run this place alone?"

"I do now," Rain muttered, anguish lacing his words as they stood and observed the majesty that was Luna Views.

Scratching his beard, Finn resisted the urge to shuffle his feet. He wasn't the greatest conversationalist at the best of times and preferred to avoid social situations. But he'd always be a loner if he didn't try to make connections. "Must be tough."

"Yeah, but I've got a good team. The general manager runs

the day-to-day operations, and the head office at the Moonrise Corporation handles all the business aspects, so I do get to spend most of my mornings focusing on thrill sports. Skydiving is my thing."

Finn nodded. He'd been skydiving a few times and while the sensation of tumbling through the air was a thrill unlike any other, it was the rush of leaping waves on the jet ski and the peaceful silence of scuba diving along the ocean floor that truly awakened his soul.

"What's the problem, then?"

Rain blew out a heavy breath. "I'm not the Alpha."

But Finn had already sensed that. "Where is he?"

Rain's eyes dulled with hollow desperation. "That's why I called you. My brother has abandoned us and if we don't save him from himself, he'll be lost forever."

OVER A FEAST of steak and bacon, plus a platter of fruit to nourish their human souls, Rain filled Finn in on the situation as they sat on the covered balcony of Rain's three-story mansion overlooking the picturesque Picnic Bay.

"Sly and I knew we weren't cut out for the corporate world. Dad and Grandpa might have made a mint building skyscraper apartments throughout Australia, but Sly and I didn't want to take over the Moonrises. Sure, we will inherit them one day and uphold the family name, but we wanted something of our own and were both obsessed with extreme sports. Nothing beats the thrill of jumping out of a plane or skimming over the waves."

Finn nodded as he chewed his steak. He couldn't agree more.

"We had a holiday home here as kids and always loved Magnetic Island, so we pitched the idea of a resort to Dad, and he thought it would be an excellent way to expand the company. Sly and I built Luna Views five years ago and brought new tourism to Magnetic Island by drawing the elite and providing activities for thrill seekers and families who want to have fun. The locals weren't all that happy with us infiltrating their sleepy suburbia, especially when we installed the runway at Horseshoe Bay. But we couldn't very well run the skydiving operation out of Townsville."

"Wouldn't have been practical," Finn agreed.

Rain speared mango with his fork. "Besides, the island's benefited with the opening of new shops and restaurants. The other major resort, Eucalypts Grove, boomed too."

Finn cocked his eyebrow. "They the competition?"

"No, friends. Though they cater more to backpackers than the five-star clientele."

"Right. So, why did any of that bother the rogues?"

"Why does anything bother the rogues? Power. They want to cut ties with the Moon Goddess and gain control over all territories. Sly was—*is*—a powerful Alpha. When we built Luna Views, it posed a threat to the Alpha of the Pallarenda Pack with Fated wolves lurking across the bay. Plus, he thinks the island's his too."

"He can't claim it when separated by such a vast body of water." It was the lore. Wolves were diabolically territorial, but elements of nature easily separated pack lands, which was why islands were luxury territory. The Pallarenda Pack couldn't possibly claim Magnetic Island. "Is this Alpha a true rogue or a Fated rebel?"

"Rebelling against Fate, for sure."

Finn's mouth twisted. Dirty bastard. Finn had little time or care for anyone who turned their back on the Moon Goddess and the fate they'd been born with. The power that flowed through a shifters' veins needed to be cherished and contained, hence the magic of the pack and mating bonds.

The Goddess controlled the power of the wolf, and wolves born of Fated mates were powerful, stable, and belonged to this world. They had a calling and would continue to embrace the potential of the natural elements.

Wolves had lived that way for thousands of years, until the first rebels had fought their bonds to their unwanted Fated mates, turned their back on the Moon Goddess, and bred with humans. Rogue wolves had been born and with no ties to the Goddess, they grew up as out-of-control bastards who wreaked havoc in society. With little sense of loyalty, compassion, or right and wrong, most Unfated rogue wolves had one agenda—to exterminate Fated wolves.

Wolves like Finn and Rain.

"How many rogue and rebel wolves are in Townsville, you think?"

"A few dozen. Most believe in rebelling against the Moon Goddess, others are there because they have nowhere else to go."

"So, what happened to Sly?"

"He found his mate." Rain's eyes dulled, and Finn's heart began to race. "Shelby was a stunning woman. Inside and out. Sly fell for her the moment the bond triggered and loved her fiercely."

Finn's jaw tightened. At least Sly had been lucky there. Wolf shifters were only male and could only mate with special females who had a shifter in their lineage, but their mates rarely knew anything about the paranormal world and accepting the wolf was usually what they had the most difficulty with. Fate didn't necessarily guarantee a happy, loving relationship, and Finn had witnessed that firsthand. Even a wolf had to work to gain the affection, trust, and love of his mate. It's what made finding that person and creating that bond something to crave. And fear.

"They were together for three years," Rain continued.

"But Fated mates breeding more Fated didn't sit well with the Pallarenda Pack. They murdered Shelby."

Finn's knife bent as his fists clenched. "Fuck, Rain. I'm sorry."

Rain's hair curtained his face as he nodded at his bacon. "Thanks. She was the good sort. Kind. Cared about others. Hardly batted an eye when she learned what Sly and I really were. They were perfect together."

Envy prickled Finn's neck. Sly had been lucky to find such a mate. Finn might have faith in Fate, but he'd also seen far too many cases of bonds going wrong and the cynic inside him would rather live content with a pack bond and remain unmated than face rejection.

Love? Was there even such a thing?

Lowering his ruined cutlery, Finn reached for a grapefruit. "Where's Sly now?"

"In the bush."

Finn frowned. "What?"

Rain thumbed behind him, indicating the land at the back of the house. Finn's throat tightened. Finding a mate might be one of the scariest moments in life for a wolf, but losing one …

"How long?" he asked softly.

"Two years."

Finn's eyebrows shot up. "Two years?!"

Rain nodded solemnly. "Yep. We buried Shelby and when the full moon rose the following night, Sly shifted and outran us into the bush. I chased him for three nights, but he wouldn't listen to reason. For weeks, I tried to comfort him, but he continued to give into the wolf. And he didn't shift back. Weeks turned into months and beneath every full moon, his pain peaked and his howls could be heard from every corner of the island. Tourists stopped hiking and rumors started to circulate. That's when I realized they needed a distraction, so I threw the first Full Moon Party. It lifted everyone's spirits, and they stopped talking. I began inviting bigger artists, and the party has become one of the most famous in the world."

"But Sly's still in the bush."

"And I'm running out of time. The pack bond is weakening and without an Alpha, we're vulnerable to the rogues."

Finn blew out his breath and slumped into his cushioned chair. Rain could say that again. To give into the wolf was the one thing a shifter needed to resist. They were first and foremost human. They weren't meant to let the beast take over.

But humanity was laced with pain and turmoil, and it fucking hurt. Animals ran free.

"How many are in the pack?"

"Me and three young scouts. Nate, Kai, and Chad."

"Has Sly officially abandoned you, or—"

"No, but he rarely communicates. I leave him fresh meat every day, but he won't come until I leave. Nate and Kai have been with us for years, but Chad only arrived eight months ago. Sly came to welcome him and give him his pack stripes, then he vanished again."

Finn scratched his chin. "He's not neglecting his duties if he's still welcoming wolves into the pack."

"He can't ignore Fate, though. He has a role as Alpha to welcome wolves and protect his pack. His territory. And no matter how deep his pain, Sly will never turn his back on the Goddess."

The unease inside Finn softened, glad to hear that as perhaps he still stood a chance. He'd wanted to find a pack for so long, he could barely remember a time when he'd felt any sort of kinship. Connection. Not since his mother had been so cruelly ripped from his life. He'd tried before to no avail, but this time, something niggled deep inside him.

Could Rain and the young men he'd yet to meet be the pack he'd been searching for? He was willing to take a chance and this was a different kind of mission, for sure. Finn had never worked without an Alpha before, or to save one. But defeating rogues was his specialty, so he would devote himself to aiding the Magnetic Island Pack and put himself to the test.

Finn shot his hands through his hair. "All right, Rain. I'll do my best to help you, man."

Gratitude lightened Rain's eyes. "Thank you, Finn. I'm not sure where we will start, but Fate allowed you to hear my Call, so we can't deny you're here for a reason."

Finn stood and grabbed their plates. "I guess you'll be offering me a job?"

"Sure." Rain helped clean up. "I need a new man on the water. But first, I want to see how you handle the jet ski, so we better get our tails back to the resort. Our audience on the ten o'clock ferry won't be far away."

Chapter 4

The hairs on the back of Ava's neck prickled as she wheeled her two suitcases down the gangplank and onto the catamaran ferry. Blair hadn't stopped calling her all morning, leaving one voicemail after another.

"Babe, I'm sorry. I didn't mean to lose my head. I was just upset you didn't like my surprise because I wanted to spend the night with you and I hate it when my plans are ruined."

Ruined because he'd *assumed* she'd want to have sex with him after two dinners and his relentless persistence in asking her on a date. Why had she even agreed? Had it been a moment of weakness? The smile he'd flashed her at the time? Fear?

She swallowed. The last one, definitely.

"I suggest you come back, Ava. You need to bring me my car. Don't make me report it as stolen, because I will."

Like a stolen car would be anything new in this town.

"Ava, answer your fucking phone! I hadn't taken you to be such a prude. You strut around the pool in your bikini in front of everyone with no shame. Why the fuck did you expect I wouldn't want a taste of that?"

Ava had shuddered at that one. So what if she enjoyed

swimming at night in her bikini? What right did Blair have to claim her like that? He should be able to control his urges. He wasn't an animal.

"Let's sit up top," Eden said, turning towards the stairs leading up to the open deck.

"It'll be easier to stay inside with my luggage."

"Trust me." Lifting one bag, Eden grabbed the handrail and started up the steep, narrow stairs. "You'll feel better with the wind in your hair."

Ava didn't know about that, but she lifted the suitcase and followed her friend. With the sun hidden behind thin clouds on a tropical winter's day, it would be quite pleasant up on the open deck.

They secured her suitcases by the railing, then Ava slumped into her seat and dropped her head into her hands.

Eden rubbed her back. "It'll be okay. We'll talk to the police on Maggie. Constable Hall is a reasonable man. He'll make sure Blair is charged."

"What if he doesn't believe me?"

Eden glanced at Ava's cheek, then at her forearms, both marred with forming bruises. "He has no reason not to."

"But Blair's father's a bloody tyrant, Eden. Even if the police do all the right things, I doubt the superintendent will let his precious son be charged with assault."

"We just have to do our best." She said the words with confidence, but Eden's eyes gave her away. She knew just as well as Ava did it was a hopeless case.

Ava straightened as they pulled away from the marina, lifting her face to the sun and breathing in the fresh air. The idea of taking forced leave from the chaotic nature of the hospital rehab unit had grown more appealing now that she had a plan. After all, it had been so long since she'd relaxed on the beach, hiked to lookouts, or helped Eden at the Koala Hospital.

Sinking into her seat, she didn't open her eyes again until after they'd idled out of the marina and gunned the engines. The breakwater and casino lay behind them, and the international shipping port spread out to their right as they cruised towards the island. Eden sat upright, craning her neck as she gazed out over the ocean.

"Why are you so excited?" Ava asked with a small laugh. "You come over here every week."

Secrets sparkled in Eden's eyes. "Just wait. You'll see."

Ava admired the view but saw nothing to cause Eden's anticipation. A few boats were out pleasure sailing, and a large cargo ship approached the port. Townsville grew smaller behind them as Ava watched Maggie Island's mountainous terrain draw closer, the granite boulders and hoop pines growing more distinctive as the ocean brightened.

Then movement caught her eye and Ava frowned as two dots approached.

Not dots. Jet skis.

Eden bounced in her seat. "There he is! Wait ... who's that with him?"

"You know them?"

She nodded, then shook her head. "He doesn't usually have a friend," she said, turning in her seat, gripping the back of her chair and the one in front as she stretched her entire spine to get a better view. "But this will be great, Ava. He has pure skill on the jet ski and can pull off some amazing tricks."

Confused, Ava glanced at the black jet ski zooming over the water. "But who is he?"

Eden broke into a grin. "That's Rain."

"Rain? Seriously?"

"Yeah. Haven't I mentioned him?"

"I think I'd remember you talking about a man named Rain."

"Huh. Well, just watch. He's a bloody amazing jet skier."

"And the other guy?"

She shrugged. "Don't know who he is."

The black ski spun in a tight hairpin at a speed Ava was sure should make a man fall off, but Rain powered on. Ava rolled her eyes. She didn't know why anyone would put their bodies at risk traveling at such speed, but as the other yellow ski started spinning donuts, Ava couldn't tear her eyes away from the brainless daredevil.

The ferry came alongside the skiers and other passengers started to look, point, and cheer. The guy on the black ski—Rain—stood straddling the seat, his naked torso exposing a long, lean, corded figure.

The other man, though, had a physique that rivaled anything Ava had seen in the gym, his bare calves bulging as he stood *on* the seat and pulled the jet ski up into the air, bouncing over a swell with every muscle of his arms and broad chest bunching.

Ava's heart flipflopped, and her stomach roiled at the notion. What the hell was wrong with her? She carried bruises from another man, yet there she was, ogling the next one.

But it seemed he wanted to be ogled as, moments later, he skimmed over the water, placed his head on the seat, and threw his body upright into a spectacular headstand.

Eden shot to her feet. "Wow."

"He's bloody insane," Ava muttered, standing too, and gripping the railing as she leaned over for a better look. Weren't you supposed to wear a life vest on a jet ski? Not just shorts? "I can barely do a headstand off the wall in yoga."

Rain shot up beside his friend, gripping the handlebars behind him as he lifted his feet and suspended his body in the air.

Eden laughed. "That's new."

"You see this often?"

"Rain practices every Friday."

Ava raised her eyebrows and turned back to the show. "For the ten o'clock ferry you always take? Are you sure he's not showing off for you?"

Eden scoffed. "I doubt it. Rain's just a friend."

Up ahead, Rain turned a quick one-eighty and sped back towards the ferry before slowing and lifting his hand in a wave. Eden cheered and waved both her arms in the air like a loon.

Ava swallowed a snigger. Just a friend, her ass. A friend Eden had neglected to mention and who also happened to be sin on a ski. They'd certainly be talking about Rain later. But right now, Ava just wanted to watch. Rain and his friend might risk breaking their necks if they came off their jet skis, but at least they were entertaining.

They were passing the jetty at Picnic Bay when the guy on the yellow ski signaled to Rain and shot his hand through the air. Rain replied with a thumbs up, and the yellow skier sped away. Ava watched as he zoomed up behind the boat, stood, and shifted his weight over the handlebars. Then he lifted his body into the perfect prone position before shooting one fist out in front of him, giving her the perfect impression of Superman. Or considering the long blond hair blowing behind him, perhaps he was more Norse god cruising over the tropical reef.

Coming up alongside the boat, he turned his head. The moment their gazes locked, a strange pull wrenched from her belly, and Ava gasped. Her knees crumpled as she sank into her seat.

Then she screamed.

FINN'S BLOOD pounded while his wolf howled with glee. Rain had been right. The ferry made a great audience. A crowd had gathered on the rooftop deck and kids pressed their faces to the salt-sprayed windows. Rain had mad skills too, turning donuts so tight that an ordinary man would have flipped the ski.

But Rain was no ordinary man, and neither was Finn.

He signaled to Rain, shooting his fist out in front of him. Rain nodded and gave him a thumbs up. Gunning the throttle, Finn zoomed down behind the ferry, then chased it, matching its speed as he pulled himself up over the handlebars, activated his core, and lifted his legs. Gaining his balance, he extended one hand out in front of him and assumed the superman position. The ski vibrated beneath him, but he remained steady, his grin widening as the wind rushed in this face and blew his hair down his neck.

Turning towards the ferry, he lifted his brows in a "how's that?" expression, even though he doubted anyone would see.

Then his eye caught the wisp of blonde hair up on the deck, and the air pulsed. Finn stilled as blue eyes connected with his. His heart lurched and wolf howled. The world exploded in a kaleidoscope of color that hit him deep in the gut.

Gasping, his hand released the handlebars, and the Sea-Doo disappeared from beneath him. Finn hit the water with a splat, the impact smashing his abdominal organs through his spine and out his back. At least, that's what it felt like. Swearing into the water, he spat out the salty sludge and let himself sink, pain ricocheting through his body. Until instinct took hold and he kicked towards the surface.

Though Finn would rather embrace the bottom of that deep blue void if what he suspected had occurred was true. Surfacing, he flipped his hair back and gulped in a breath. Fuck. Fuck, fuck, fuck! This couldn't be happening. He'd come to the island for a pack, not a ... a ...

"Finn!" Rain's shout carried above the rev of his jet ski as he raced towards him. "You okay, man?"

No, he was not fucking okay. He'd totally stacked it and she ... that woman ...

"Fuck!" Finn smacked the water as Rain drew his ski up beside him.

"Dude, what happened? You look like you've seen a ghost."

A ghost? More like a fucking nightmare. "I'm fine."

"Yeah, all right." Rain extended his hand, and Finn took hold of his forearm in a monkey-grip as Rain hauled him out of the water. "Mighty fine belly flop, though. Would have done some serious damage to a man."

Settling behind Rain, Finn felt every bruised kidney, rib, and lung, but nothing hurt more than the bruise to his ego. "Where's my Sea-Doo?"

Rain chuckled as he turned the Yamaha around and Finn spotted his Sea-Doo floating up ahead, drifting in the ferry's wake.

"Didn't go far. The crowd screamed, though, and you sure gave me a shock." Rain slowed down and Finn leapt over onto his ski. "But your superman was fucking epic. What happened?"

Raking his hand down his face, Finn didn't want to acknowledge it. Saying the words would only make it real. He might have to do something about it, and he didn't want to.

His wolf snarled in disagreement.

"I was distracted."

"By?"

"The ferry." The words spilled from his lips before he could stop them. "I looked across and ... I saw her."

Rain's eyebrows shot up. "No ..."

"Yep." Finn's forearms corded as he gripped the handle-bars and almost snapped them clean off the ski. "I fucking mated. And stacked it right in front of her."

Chapter 5

By the time they returned to Luna Views, Finn felt like he'd been ripped in two. After years of solitude, everything had changed in less than twenty-four hours. He'd responded to many Calls and while he hadn't yet discovered why he'd heard Rain's, the last thing he'd expected was that this mission would have anything to do with him finding his mate.

Finn growled as he tied the Sea-Doo to the pontoon. He'd rarely hoped for a mate. During weak moments, he'd considered it could be a nice way to escape his loneliness, but forming a mating bond was fucking hard work with three levels needing to be achieved before it was sealed. Fated mates needed to connect on an emotional level—getting to know one another to gain trust and respect. A physical level, which while he liked sex, was a lot more than simply losing himself in the soft heat of a woman. Then finally, the paranormal level, and that was the hardest of them all when the paranormal world was vastly considered a legend.

"You taking off then?" Rain asked as Finn followed him off the pontoon.

"No. Why?"

"Thought you'd want to go find that woman," Rain said as though it was the obvious thing to do.

And it should be, which was why Finn ground his teeth. "Nope."

"Nope? What do you mean 'nope'? Don't you want to meet her?"

Of course he wanted to meet her. His wolf clawed inside him, desperate to sniff her out, learn her name, mark her with his scent, and protect her from all harm.

But he wouldn't let his wolf take control. *He* was the boss. *He* said when and where. And just because his wolf wanted her, and in time Finn hoped he would too, that didn't mean she would want anything to do with him. Her body would, and she would experience an attraction she would struggle to understand, but all of that was physical. A desire based on nothing but pheromones and Fate.

He needed her to like him, and Finn had never been good with people.

"Yes, but not right now. She saw me go splat. She'd probably wonder where the bruises are and why I'm not aching or resting up in bed."

"Fair call. But we could always do recon. Did you get a good look at her?"

Finn exhaled as they stopped by the gardens and gazed out over the ocean. "Sort of. It was weird, man. Our eyes met and then ..." Grimacing, Finn rubbed his bare chest. He couldn't say the words aloud without sounding like a total tosser.

"The world flipped upside down?" Rain suggested. "Everything shifted? She became larger than life, and everything around you disappeared?"

Finn's brow lowered. "You've mated?"

Rain snorted. "Sly told me what it was like."

Of course. Stupid question. "Right. Yeah, it was kind of like that. Bloody shock to the system."

"Hence you stacked it."

Finn's face flamed. "Don't remind me."

Chuckling, Rain clapped Finn on the shoulder. "Don't worry, man. I'm sure one day the two of you will laugh about it."

"If we're lucky."

Rain's eyes narrowed as he stepped around to face Finn. "Any reason you think you won't be?"

"What do you think?" Finn poked his thumb over his shoulder in the general direction of the bush where Sly lurked, brokenhearted. "Fate can be cruel, and mating doesn't always end happily-ever-after. Nor does it start that way."

Rain sobered, his throat working as he swallowed. "Yeah. I know." Exhaling, he turned back to stare out at the ocean.

Finn crossed his arms over his chest, unable to ease his turmoil. "Our mates are human. The fact they're descended from wolves might make them stronger and more capable of accepting the paranormal, but unless they're the daughter of a shifter, they know nothing of our world until they enter it. And once the bond is formed, we put them at risk."

"You don't need to tell me." Rain slipped his hands into his pockets. "With the Unfated out of control and trying to destroy us, our mates are in more danger than ever. We need to put an end to the rogues in Pallarenda, get Sly back, and strengthen our pack if we want any chance of living in peace."

"Yep." And that needed to be Finn's focus. His mate would have to wait, at least until the shock of her entering his life had worn off and he could face her with a level head. He'd need one if he had the slightest chance of ensuring they built a friendship. If there was anything he'd learned from his parents' disastrous mating bond, it was that. Finn would *not* be like his father. If this woman rejected him, he would take it like a man and suffer the pain of a rejected wolf. But he didn't have an Unfated child in tow and Finn's elder brother had been a rogue wolf worth fearing. He shuddered to think about what the man was like now.

Or his father.

But Finn had faith and hopefully when he faced his mate, it wouldn't end in disaster.

"I should shower and change," he said, dropping his crossed arms. "Check in on G.B."

"Come see me for lunch and we can and talk about that job."

"All right."

But before Finn could turn, the scent of strawberry and pine on the salty breeze filled his lungs and warmed his chest until he could barely breathe. His muscles corded in his forearms, shoulders, and neck. His pulse spiked, and the wolf inside him howled.

Rain spun around as a soft, feminine voice called his name.

"Eden ..." he breathed, his shoulders sagging a moment before his eyes lit up. "Hey!"

Finn took a deep breath, fists clenched by his side as he dared a glance over his shoulder. A gorgeous long-legged woman approached, her dark hair cascading down her back while sunglasses shaded her eyes. She moved towards them with haste, and the blonde woman at her heels.

His mate.

Every muscle in Finn's body hardened. Fuck, she was beautiful. Short and small with delicate features that belied her toned, powerful body. Honey blonde hair draped over her shoulder in a long tail, brushing her pert, handful-sized breasts swelling beneath the pink fabric stretching across her chest, hugging her flat belly, and swishing around her thighs. Shapely, athletic legs ended with sparkling toenails cushioned by her slip-on sandals. His wolf salivated, aching to taste those toes. Calves. Thighs. To bury himself between them.

Finn growled. Fuck, she was stunning.

"I know we usually catch up later," Eden said, laying her hand casually on Rain's chest. Finn heard his friend's sharp intake of breath, but Eden didn't seem to notice as her gaze shot to Finn. "But we saw what happened and Ava wanted to make sure you weren't hurt."

Ava. *A-vaaa*. Finn shivered. Such a beautiful name, and a sweet, honeyed voice as she hastened to say, "No, I just ... well, it looked like an awful accident ..."

Finn's cheeks flamed. Thank fuck he hadn't shaved as the scruff should hide most of his embarrassment. He still couldn't believe he'd taken that tumble. The Goddess was being cruel, determined to make a joke out of him and to remind him who was in charge. He hadn't been ready for Ava, but there she was, twisting the end of her ponytail while her teeth nibbled at her suckable lower lip and pink rose in her rounded cheeks that—

Finn stilled. No, her cheek wasn't pink. It was red. And not from flush, but from contact. Heavy contact. Finn drew in a breath, but he didn't need heightened senses to recognize the blood clots forming beneath her delicate skin.

A red haze flashed across his vision and his fists clenched so hard he feared he'd shoot claws through his palms. Someone had laid their hand on his mate. Had hit her. Hurt her. Scared her.

Before he could stop himself, Finn inhaled, searching for any scent she wore. He caught a whiff of musk he found strangely familiar, and his body convulsed with blinding rage.

He knew that smell.

Wolf.

Chapter 6

Ava's feet rooted to the spot as the broad, bare-chested beast of a man stalked towards her. His damp blond hair hung in clumps to his shoulders and his jaw hardened beneath a full-faced beard that was a touch too long to be considered neat and trim. Everything about him screamed powerful. Extreme. Dangerous. Warmth flooded through her vessels until she wanted to slap herself.

What was wrong with her?

Not that a woman would *not* be flushed by such a physique. He was just ... wow. As a practitioner of the human body, she admired a strapping, muscular man, but this guy was something else. Her mouth salivated and knees trembled, her hands itching to reach out and touch the wide breadth of his bulging pectorals. Two hard slabs of concrete muscle with a sprinkle of wet, golden chest hair spreading from his sternum towards the dark round discs of his nipples. All eight segments of his rectus abdominis bunched as he advanced, tapering into a super tight V highlighted by his transverse obliques beneath the waistband of his red boardshorts. His serratus contracted and forearms rippled. Every inch of him was a valley or hill she ached to touch. To feel. Lick.

But before she could completely embarrass herself with the pink in her cheeks or the tremble in her thighs, a flash in his dark blue eyes anchored her. A flash of what? Of anger? Hostility?

Her spine stiffened. Wait a minute. What had she done wrong?

He halted before her, close enough that she formed a more intimate, unwelcome relationship with his glorious heaving chest. Ava drew in a breath and everything inside her turned to molten liquid. Her stomach lurched, like a magnet dragging her towards him.

That wasn't good.

"I've survived worse than a belly flop."

His deep baritone shivered through her, sending her heart sliding down into her stomach like ice cream on a hot day. She swallowed, but her throat wouldn't clear. What the hell was wrong with her? Had she not learned anything after last night? Another attractive male stood before her and she was swooning beneath his brooding glare.

No. This would not happen. Shaking herself from her stupor, Ava took half a step backwards. "Good. Good. But ... you should probably get yourself checked out. How fast was that jet ski going? It doesn't matter. At that speed, you're likely to have damaged more than just your skin." Though there didn't seem to be a mark on him at all, just warm golden skin stretched over his Adonis figure. "You could have internal bleeding. Liver or bowel damage. Are you sure nothing's broken?"

Eden's hand clamped around her forearm and Ava stumbled back a step, fortunately ending her ridiculous rambling.

"Sorry. Ava's a physiotherapist and is terrified of people injuring themselves."

"I'm not terrified! I just know what damage—"

Eden squeezed her arm and Ava shut up. Rain's lips

quirked beneath the dark scruff shading his jaw, his blue eyes glittering. But his friend remained frozen, the perfect imitation of a statue carved in golden marble during the renaissance.

The darker man cleared his throat and stepped forward, extending his hand. "I'm Rain. You must be a friend of Eden's."

Ava's shoulders relaxed as she accepted Rain's polite handshake. "Yes. I've ... I've come to stay for a while."

Rain's grin broadened, dimples flashing in his right cheek. "Excellent. Hear that, Finn? Ava's staying."

He elbowed his friend in the ribs, and a grunt escaped the corner of his taut, full lips. Ava frowned as his eyes darkened further.

"You should come by the house with Eden this afternoon," Rain continued. "Any friend of Eden's is a friend of mine."

Ava's eyes narrowed. So did Finn's. Eden, however, rolled her eyes and batted Rain's bare shoulder. "Oh, stop it."

Laughing, Eden angled her body closer to the fine form that was Rain. He wasn't as broad as his friend, but his shoulders bunched in all the right places and his torso tapered down to strong hips and thighs. The wind blew his lanky, dark hair across the sexy scruff on his face and into his piercing blue eyes.

Yeah, she could understand why Eden had been keeping him a secret, and Ava would extract all the details the moment they were alone.

"We'll be a bright, merry party, especially with the added company." Rain clapped Finn on the shoulder. "My old friend here arrived last night and he'll be sticking around for a while, too."

"Excellent." Eden beamed. "It's a pleasure to meet you."

Finn's blazing eyes unlatched from Ava as he glanced at

Eden and inclined his head. "You, too, Eden. Does Rain put on a show when you leave too?"

"Not always," she said with a laugh, while Rain placed his hands on his hips and scowled. "He's usually skydiving, but I enjoy watching him practice on my trip over. It was fun having both of you today, though. I'm glad you weren't hurt."

"I'm not hurt," he said, and Ava resisted rolling her eyes. Only because he and his macho pride were lucky. Pulling stunts like that at high speed without safety gear or a life vest, the fool could have drowned.

And why did she care?

Swallowing a groan, Ava turned to Eden. "We should go."

"Yes." Eden lifted her hand in a wave. "We'll see you two later."

"Nice to meet you," Finn said, but his gaze remained on Ava. She shivered and backed away, a strange part of her not wanting to leave. But then Eden grabbed her hand and Ava turned her back on the men as she followed her friend out of the resort.

Slipping into the passenger seat of Eden's ute, she clicked on her seatbelt. "So ... how come you've never mentioned Rain?"

Eden turned out of the car park. "What do you mean?"

"Oh, come on! He's sexy as hell and you haven't said a word about him. To *me*. Your best friend!"

Eden blushed. "Yeah ... I know. I'm sorry."

"So, spill!"

"There's nothing to spill. Rain's a friend. I met him when I came back from Lone Pine two years ago when he brought a koala in from way up near the Pinnacles. I was shocked he'd carried it all the way down the mountain, but then I took a good look at him and, yeah. It made sense. Because yes, he's sexy as hell, and he hasn't asked me out."

"Why haven't you asked him out?"

Eden dismissed the notion with a wave of her hand as they curved up past Hawkings Point and down the hill into Picnic Bay. "We're past that. I tried making a move once, but he gently took my hands and said that we shouldn't, so we're just friends." Eden sighed, her shoulders slumping. "Men suck."

"Sure do," Ava muttered, her lips twisting as the blond Norse god popped into her head. "I can't say I care much for Rain's choice of friends. You, clearly, are awesome. But Finn ... Did you see the way he was looking at me?"

"Ahuh." Eden's grinned. "I think he was turned on by your concern about damage to his chiseled abs."

"No, he wasn't! I was a total spazz! Although he's lucky he only splatted a few feet off the water. And that he's apparently a strong swimmer."

"Muscle mass would have helped," Eden added, and Ava's insides warmed. "Pity I can't get stupid Rain out of my head because Finn is bloody hot."

Ava's jaw clenched, her chest constricting with a strange sense of possessiveness as her eyes narrowed.

Eden laughed. "I knew it."

"Knew what?"

"You like him."

"I do not! That man couldn't stop glaring at me with such ... such ... distaste. Hell if I know what I did to him."

"Looking delicious in your pretty pink dress? Made him salivate? Shattered his ego knowing you saw him stack it?"

Ava snorted. "I think he has too big an ego to be shattered. Remember?" She lowered her voice an octave. "He's 'survived worse than a belly flop.'"

Eden's smile broadened. "I think he was a bit embarrassed, Avs. And you have to admit, he is *hot*."

Ava wrapped her arms around herself. Hot didn't even begin to describe Finn. He was magnificent. Pity she hadn't seen the back of him as while a man's anterior torso was more often revered, Ava had always loved the long lines and musculature of a man's back. A strong triangular trapezius branching out from long deep grooves of a spine was Ava's guilty pleasure. That and a round, taut ass. She bet everything she owned that Finn's was worth sculpting. The thought of wrapping her arms around his waist and dipping her hands to squeeze those two perfect glutes ...

Ava clenched her thighs and shoved the thought from her mind. For fuck's sake, she needed to get a grip!

"He wasn't that hot," she muttered.

Eden laughed as she slowed, indicated, and turned off the road. "Tell yourself that all you want." She pulled on the park brake. "So ... are we going in here?"

Ava glanced out the window at the blue and white checkered logo of the Queensland Police, and the warmth inside her vanished. She recalled the previous night, the fear, the pain, the ache that continued to burn in her flushed cheek. The complete disbelief that she'd been so stupid. Sure, she hadn't done anything wrong and Blair had had no right to hit her. He deserved to be charged. Deserved to be reprimanded and to lose his job. A man couldn't be charged with assault and continue to work as a police officer.

Which was exactly why her statement would get lost in the system and charges would never be laid.

"No ..." Guilt knotted in her belly for letting down every other woman who'd been abused, but in her situation, what was the point? "I hate this, Eden, and if Blair wasn't a police officer, I'd make a statement in a heartbeat. But right now, he doesn't know where I am and I can't risk him finding out. I'm safe."

Eden nodded slowly before reaching over to take Ava's hand. "Okay. I respect your choice, Ava. And I understand that you're scared, so I'll help you lie low and if you change your mind—"

"I can come back." Releasing a deep breath, Ava tore her gaze from the station. "Now, let's get some lunch because I'm starving."

Chapter 7

Finn stretched out his legs as he sat at a table overlooking the resort pool, sipping a flat white while he waited for lunch. His foot tapped on the hard patio, his wolf restless inside him, longing to break free and run. Hunt. To chase down the monster who had laid his hand on an innocent woman and marked her so cruelly.

Growling, he sipped the hot, caffeinated milk. The scent left on Ava swirled inside his head. Not the pine or strawberry, but that musky, woodsy smell. It was so familiar, lurking on the edge of his consciousness, but he couldn't put his paw on why. It might come to him, though it wouldn't make any difference. If Finn ever found that wolf, he'd teach him a lesson about hitting a woman. Those men were weak. Insecure. And for a wolf, they were out of touch with their power. They'd lost sense of their purpose and their connection with the Moon Goddess.

Men like his father.

Finn's jaw clenched as the image of his mother curled up in on the floor flashed before his eyes, her golden hair curtaining her face as she wept and clutched her belly. For days after his father's visits, she'd wince and groan as she moved about their small house. His father had never hit her anywhere that was obvious. In his job, he couldn't have been seen as a wifebeater and his mother had never stood a chance of standing up to him. He might have been a rebel wolf, but he was still Fated and his power flowed strong.

It had taken Finn almost too long to realize that. His childhood hadn't been a happy one when filled with fights, tears, and his father's favoritism shown towards his elder brother. But one thing that Finn had known for sure, and what had helped him through life to this very day, was that his mother had loved him.

And fuck, he missed her.

He tossed back more coffee, the scalding in his throat numbing the ache inside his chest and fueling the fire in his belly. Was that why Ava was on the island? Was she on the run? Did his mate know it had been a wolf who'd attacked her?

No. Wolves only revealed their identity for two reasons. One, they told their mate to solidify their bond and exercise common decency. A woman needed to know what she was signing up for and the reason for the animal magnetism they felt towards their mates. With any luck, after the shock and fear, she would accept the truth and find comfort in the fact she was loved by the ultimate protector. A man who was willing to die for her.

Finn had never understood that feeling, until now. Whether Ava was in trouble or not, he would do everything to ensure his mate was safe. And if he were to take the steps to secure their mating bond, which he'd need to do if he were to maintain his sanity, he would ensure he had laid the foundations so that she would accept the truth about him with ease.

The other wolf, likely a rebel or an Unfated bastard, wouldn't have told her the truth until it was too late. Wolves only revealed themselves to an Unfated mate when he was about to kill her, usually after the birth of their Unfated pup.

Finn's hand fisted and popped the lid off his coffee, spilling hot liquid over his jeans. "Fuck!"

"Careful, man." Rain dropped into the chair opposite Finn. "I see you're still worked up over Ava."

"I wasn't thinking about her," he muttered, brushing the liquid from his leg.

"Yeah, right."

"It was that wolf. The one who almost clawed her eye out."

Rain's mouth thinned. "I saw that too. You think that's why she's here?"

"Could be. She reeked of fear."

"Maybe that's because you advanced on her like a predatory Alpha. Seriously, dude. She's been hurt."

Finn's spine straightened. "I didn't scare her!"

"You were a bit standoffish."

"I was trying to control myself," he said through gritted teeth. "All I wanted to do was grab her and demand she tell me who I had to kill."

"Well ..." Exhaling, Rain leaned back in his chair and ran his hand down his jaw. "I'm afraid that his is a scent I could recognize anywhere. Blair Thorne."

Finn froze, every muscle inside him cording as his wolf snapped and snarled. No. It couldn't be. "What did you say?"

"The rogue. Blair Thorne. Nasty, twisted bastard. And his father—"

"Tyrone." The name left his mouth before Finn could stop himself.

"Yeah." Rain's eyebrows drew even closer. "You've come across them before?"

Finn's chest expanded, his fists curling as it took all his self-control not to leap to his feet and shift with an aggravated howl in front of the entire restaurant. All the rage he'd bottled up fizzed and erupted. That bastard Blair had hit his mate. And Tyrone ...

"Nope," he muttered, thanking the perfectly timed arrival of his steak sandwich. "Heard of them, though."

The lie rolled off his tongue as Finn sank his teeth through the bread, salads, and meat, but it did nothing to soothe the bile rising in his throat. Because Finn had more than heard of Tyrone and Blair Thorne. He'd spent half his life trying to escape them. He'd laid low and mastered multiple battle techniques to become a warrior who specialized in killing rebel wolves.

Tyrone Thorne was his father.

And now, after all these years, those two dark wolves were there, across the bay and causing havoc. Trying to control a city and, apparently, doing a good job. There was a saying for it—the city has gone to the dogs.

And the Moon Goddess had called him to Magnetic Island to fight them.

Finn drew in a deep breath. Typical. He wanted to belong to a pack, had heard the Call and formed a connection with Rain unlike any he'd felt with a wolf before. Optimism had led him to believe the pack bond was already forming. He could feel it.

But it never would if Rain learned the truth, and to get what he'd always wanted, Finn would need to face the wolves who'd betrayed him the most.

Finn ate half his sandwich before finding his next words. "The Thornes. They were the ones who—?"

"They killed Shelby," Rain confirmed, and Finn's sandwich churned in his gut.

Rain glanced in the general direction of the mountain, no doubt thinking about his brother. Sly roamed with a broken heart, unable to face humanity after losing his love while his wolf howled for his mate. Finn's gaze flickered in the same direction, his chest tightening. At least he now knew why he'd heard Rain's Call, and he wanted nothing more now than to bring Sly back to himself. Tyrone had a lot to answer for, and Blair ...

Finn's fingers speared through the toasted bread, sauce seeping under his nails. Blair had hurt Ava, and Finn needed to know why. How did she know him? Had they been dating?

Fuck, he didn't want to know the answer to that.

"It was brutal," Rain mused, tapping his fingers on the table. "Tyrone got what he wanted and broke us. But we're not defeated." His jaw hardened as his gaze returned to Finn. "We need to end Tyrone and his rogue pack, Finn. He's a mean old bastard, but I think together, we can take him."

Finn swallowed the knot in his throat. He wasn't so sure.

Rain powered on. "Then we can bring Sly back and you can make it work with Ava."

The mention of her name flicked a switch and left his wolf panting with longing. "I'm certainly down for helping you with Sly, but Ava ... I don't know, man."

"Trust me." Rain snatched a fry off Finn's plate. "You don't want to resist the mating pull for long."

"Like you resist with Eden?"

Rain froze with half a fry in his hand. "What?"

Finn cocked his eyebrow, his spine relaxing at the change of subject. "She's your mate."

"I don't know what you're talking about."

"Don't bullshit me. You know it's the truth."

Rain's eyes flashed as he leaned over the table. "But until we end those bastards in Townsville, I can't do a fucking thing about it, can I? Else she'll meet the same end as Shelby."

"A-ha!" Finn pointed his steak sandwich at him. "I knew it. I could smell you all over her the moment she strolled through the gardens."

Rain snarled. "I know. It was wrong of me, but she only comes to the island a few days a week."

"Where you have regular drinks and you perform a jet ski stunt cock show. Shit, man. How long has it been?"

"Two years."

Finn winced. "Fuck, I don't know how you do it."

"To protect her," Rain snapped. "Just like you will do with Ava. Though, I guess that will be different as one day, the Thornes will come for her."

Finn's fingers speared through what was left of his sandwich again. Fuck. Was he ready for that? He'd spent half his life running, cutting all ties, and vowing never to see Tyrone or Blair again.

But if it meant keeping Ava safe, Finn would do what a wolf had to do.

"Let him try," he growled. "If Blair lays a hand on her again, I'll kill him."

And he would like it.

Chapter 8

Arriving at the Picnic Bay Hotel, Ava slumped onto the stool at the high table as she admired the historic jetty stretching out over the glittering blue ocean. She wished there was more that she could do, but the system was against her and she needed to think about her safety first. The moment she made a report, Blair would know she was on the island and he'd come after her. And she couldn't have that. When no one else was there to protect her, she needed to protect herself.

Eden arrived at the table with two menus. "We'll have lunch and form a plan. I can't leave you here alone, Ava. I know you'll be surrounded by people at the Grove, but I'll still worry about you."

Ava sighed. "It's the way of the world, Eden. If a man wants to come after a woman, there's little anyone can do to stop him. He'll only end up behind bars after he kills her." And Ava bet Blair would escape that, too.

"You could stay at Luna Views."

Ava frowned. "What? Why?"

Eden lowered her menu and leaned in close. "Look, I don't know what it is, but there's something about Rain. I trust him. He has this dark, dangerous, and mysterious aura about him, and money. Lots of it. I mean, a man doesn't jump out of a plane multiple times a day because he's not badass. If we told him, he would help you."

Ava shook her head. "Are you insane? I'm not going to tell some guy I don't know that I'm hiding—"

"But *I* know him. He's my friend, and so are you. Come on, Ava."

"No. I'll stay at Eucalypts Grove and ... well, let's see how the next two days go. I need time before I make any plans. Maybe it's not even worth staying here."

"Where else will you go?"

Ava's shoulders slumped. "I don't know."

"Exactly. Stay here, Ava. Look after the koalas for me and maybe ... spend *some* time at Luna Views?"

Ava rolled her eyes. "And do what?"

"Read by the pool. Have lunch. Lust over hot man-candy."

Ava's hands tightened around the menu as her insides warmed. "That is *not* what I need right now."

"Why not?"

"Because I obviously have a horrible taste in men! I choose those who are bad for me, and I don't jump from one to another."

"Well, it's not like you really knew Blair. You had two dinners together and then he tried to kidnap you."

"Exactly! I make terrible choices!"

Eden smiled kindly. "We all do sometimes, but that doesn't mean you can't look."

"Are you kidding? Looking at all of *that*?" Finn's god-like body, piercing blue eyes, long scraggly hair and a beard that usually wouldn't do anything for her swam in Ava's mind until her toes curled. "You can't expect a girl to look and not touch when a man is that fine."

"Then don't just look." Eden grinned and Ava playfully swatted her menu at her. "You never know, Avs. He could be the one."

"A girl can't be that lucky."

"True." Eden's shoulders slumped. "He probably has a girlfriend. Or hoards of them. Or he's gay."

Ava snorted. "He's not gay."

"How do you know? Don't they say all the best ones are?"

"Yeah, but ..." Remembering the possessive way his eyes had absorbed her and the rage that had bulged his muscles, Ava highly doubted that Finn liked men. Though it sure would be helpful for her if he did. He might be hot as sin and her body had reacted to him in a way she'd never experienced, but she did *not* need a man in her life. Especially the big, imposing, dominant alpha type like Finn.

Grimacing, she glanced at the menu. "I'll have the Cobb salad."

"All right, I'll drop the subject," Eden said as she stood and gathered the menus. "I'll have the Cobb salad too."

After ordering, Ava and Eden sipped their Diet Cokes and then spoke of everything they hadn't had a chance to as Ava shared stories from work and Eden updated her on some of her regular patients at the vet clinic in Townsville. The tension in Ava's shoulders eased a fraction as she enjoyed her lunch and laughed with her friend. When a familiar tune played over the sound system, they both gasped as Isla's voice serenaded them with her latest number one hit. They sang along, dancing in their chairs and tapping their feet without a care in the world that other patrons eyed them strangely. No matter how popular Isla grew, Ava would never tire of having a popstar best friend. She missed her dearly, but Ava was proud of how far Isla had come from the introverted bookworm she'd met on the first day of high school when the three of them had been browsing the library's fantasy novels. Not that

Ava had read much fantasy other than the classics like Harry Potter and Twilight, but she'd certainly expanded her horizons with Isla's recommendations. The three of them had been inseparable since, except for the times Isla's obsessive stage mum had dragged her away for singing competitions, travel, and performances.

But knowing she and Eden would be reunited with their friend in a matter of weeks when Isla arrived to perform at October's Full Moon Party, Ava left the pub with hope in her heart. Isla had made her dreams of stardom come true, Eden was making progress on improving the health of Magnetic Island's koalas, and Ava would soon achieve her goal when she'd saved enough money to put a deposit on a house.

Which couldn't come soon enough now that returning home was virtually impossible.

EDEN STREAMED Isla's music as she and Ava drove across the island to Eucalypts Grove Koala Retreat. Nestled in the foothills of the Forts Lookout by an expanse of native bush-land, the Grove had always been popular and was now the only backpacker retreat on the island after the Moonrise Corporation had bought the old hostel and turned it into the five-star resort that was now Luna Views.

But while the new, flashier hotel might offer an array of water sports, fine dining, and world-class accommodation with uninterrupted views of Cleveland Bay, Eucalypts Grove brought its guests back to nature with peace, tranquility, and quiet bungalows nestled among the gum trees. The access to wildlife set the Grove apart from any other accommodation on the island with not only the sanctuary, but the wildlife often spotted outside the cabin doors. After the Koala Hospital had opened two decades ago, Eden's mother, Jane, had befriended the vet and had jumped at the chance to establish the sanctuary for Australia's iconic creatures, which now included echidnas, wallabies, and a very lazy wombat who couldn't return to wild. Eden had grown up caring for koalas, learning from the vet Vicky, and had never wanted anything other than to take over the hospital and sanctuary herself, which had occurred when Vicky had retired earlier that year.

Ava stepped out of Eden's ute and onto the dirt of the shady parking lot. The most colorful residents, the rainbow lorikeets, screeched in the palm trees as Ava followed her friend into the open deck reception area.

They found Jane in her office.

"Hello, darling," she said, hugging Eden. "Ava! How lovely it was to hear you want to stay."

Ava smiled as she hugged the woman who had been a second mother to her. Having spent her high school years boarding in Townsville, she'd missed her mum terribly and had grown close to Jane. Eden's mum had taken her out on shopping expeditions on the weekends and Ava had spent the Easter school holidays with them once.

"I'm sorry for the inconvenience but thank you for finding a room for me."

"There's always room for family, and I've given you the best one. Though are you sure you don't want to stay at the house?"

Ava shook her head. "I wouldn't want to intrude."

"It wouldn't be intruding. I'm going on a cruise in two weeks anyway, but I understand you want your privacy." Jane reached for a key on a koala keyring. "I've given you bungalow twelve, right at the end of the pathway where no one will bother you."

Ava accepted the key. "Thank you, Jane."

"I'll help grab your bags," Eden said, "but then I need to get to the hospital. I'll see you later tonight, Mum." Eden stayed with her mum for the two nights she spent on the island.

Ava followed her back to the ute.

"I'll leave you to settle in," Eden said as they lifted the suitcases out. "I should be finished by four if you want to come to Rain's place for drinks?"

"I think I'll skip it. I wouldn't want to impose on your Rain time."

Eden rolled her eyes. "Like it would matter. But I understand, you've had a big day. Will you at least come to Mum's for dinner?"

Ava nodded. "That, I can do."

"Good. Do you need help, or—"

"Go see the koalas." Ava waved her off with a smile. "You've given up too much of your time for me already, and I can make it to the room myself. Thank you, though."

"Always."

Eden hugged her, squeezed, then climbed into her ute. After she'd left, Ava pulled up the handles of her suitcases and strode through reception, past the tree-shaded pool, and along the wooden boardwalk through the bush towards the bungalows. Breathing in the fresh air, she glanced up at the sun peeking through the dense trees. Apart from the rattle of her luggage, all was quiet, and perhaps this was just what she needed. Time away from her ordinary life and the never-ending pressure of work to relax and reassess. She didn't want to spend her money on frivolous adventures around the island when she planned to use the leave-loading to add to her house deposit, but hiking, walking, and swimming were free and would keep her occupied while she worked out how she could return home without running into Blair.

Shuddering, Ava lugged her suitcases up the three steps to bungalow twelve and pushed open the door. The double bed took up most of the space in the small room, but she had her own bathroom, a desk, and would head to the supermarket later to buy food to cook in the communal kitchen.

Tension eased from her shoulders as Ava locked the door behind her, slid open the flyscreened window, and headed for the bathroom to relieve herself of the too many Diet Coke's she'd enjoyed with lunch.

Washing her hands, she assessed her reflection in the mirror. Her face remained a touch red where the blood vessels had broken beneath her skin, but otherwise, it didn't seem so bad. With the ice that morning and some gentle massage later, she might avoid any major bruising.

Exiting the bathroom, Ava sank against the head of the bed, tucked her feet up, and hugged her knees to her chest. Glancing around the tiny bungalow, her heart sank like a lead weight into her belly.

How had she ended up here? How had she become this woman? She didn't deserve this, to feel like she needed to run away or to fear returning home. She should have known better. She hadn't wanted to date Blair, but he hadn't let up. Unable to avoid him, Ava had given him a chance. The two dinners they'd shared had been enjoyable enough, despite his comments about her vegetarian eating habits, and she loved Crystal Creek and hadn't wanted to turn down a day among nature.

Then he'd tried to hold her against her will in an isolated cabin tucked away in the rainforest village of Paluma, and now she was hiding and scared because some animal of a man couldn't control his temper.

And the people who were supposed to protect victims like her were powerless to help.

It wasn't fair.

Pressing her face to her knees, tears filled Ava's eyes as her strength vanished and she wept quietly.

Chapter 9

Finn spent the afternoon preparing for his stay on Magnetic Island and ignoring the whimpering of his wolf. Every primal instinct urged him to seek Ava out and ensure she was okay. To keep one eye on her and the other on the ferry terminal for any sight of Blair Thorne, even though theoretically, Ava should be safe on the island. But the rogues rarely obeyed rules, and Finn wouldn't put it past Blair to venture into Sly's territory, especially when the Alpha wasn't present to protect his pack.

So, Finn remained on guard and while he ached for his mate, he couldn't watch Ava for every second of the day. She deserved her privacy. His wolf didn't agree, but Finn needed to listen to his human side, which told him that Ava was a strong woman not only in her body, but in her heart and mind. She had to be if she'd escaped Blair with her limbs intact and for that, he respected her.

But Blair had a death wish if he dared step foot on the island. Finn had a sixth sense for rogues and would know about it in an instant. And would have the bastard's head. Only then might Rain trust him when he learned exactly how Finn knew the devious Thornes.

Snarling, Finn snatched up a shopping basket and strode into the supermarket. Rain had insisted that he could order anything from the kitchen, but Finn didn't want to take advantage and right now, he needed to stock up on snacks for himself, and apples for his little dog. He filled his basket with fruit, bread, peanut butter, beef jerky, and some essential toiletries. After piling the groceries into the back of the Jeep Wrangler that Rain had loaned him, a courtesy car from the resort, Finn set off in search of the other stores his new boss had suggested he visit.

Nearly everything a person needed was on the island, though he wouldn't have much choice of clothing if he were to shred the clothes he'd brought with him. But he found a few T-shirts and a plush dog bed for Gracie before taking the opportunity to familiarize himself with the island. He'd studied maps the night he'd heard the Call and understood the appeal Sly and Rain had felt for the tropical paradise. Magnetic Island was fifty-two square kilometers of mountainous ranges and twenty-three stunning beaches, making it the perfect place for a wolf to stretch his paws. Hoop pines decorated the outcrops where rock had eroded along fracture lines to create a landscape featuring rounded boulders—some larger than houses—perched spectacularly and giving the illusion that they'd topple into the ocean any second.

Leaving Nelly Bay where the supermarket, ferry terminal, and Luna Views were located, Finn marveled at the aquamarine ocean stretching out before him as he crested the headland and wound down the road into Arcadia. Filled with guest houses and holiday homes, the village boasted a long stretch of beach, as well as a pub, shops, and what he'd read was a popular theater restaurant. Exploring a few back roads, he noted the petrol station, bakery, and newsagent. Arcadia seemed like a pleasant spot to be, and he'd enjoy a swim in the cute cove of Alma Bay at some point.

Then he continued along the road, weaving his way over the mountain and through the majestic bush by the historic World War II Forts that had been built to defend Australia in the Battle of the Coral Sea. Another road led to more secluded beaches, but Finn decided to explore those later as he descended into Horseshoe Bay. The north-facing bay was the largest on the island and had been the original home of water-sports before Luna Views had opened.

Finn was halfway to the beach when a magnetic pull tugged at his heart and his nostrils constricted.

Ava. She was close.

Slowing the Jeep, he inhaled again. He wasn't a wolf to ignore Fate, so perhaps the least he could do was discover where she was staying. After all, he couldn't protect her if he didn't know where to find her.

But he'd do that under the cloak of darkness, once again ignoring his impatient wolf as he bought himself a coffee and strode along the beach. With the wind in his hair and cool sun on his face, Finn welcomed the sense of belonging and the stirring inside his soul. He hadn't had many friends and while packs he'd helped before had welcomed and thanked him, he'd never had a mission like this.

To belong to and save this pack, he needed to protect his mate from the man who had killed the one person he loved most and burdened him with the ache of loneliness.

Finn's toes curled into the sand as he downed the hot coffee.

The Moon Goddess wasn't being subtle. First the mating bond, now the Thornes? What had she been fucking thinking?

FINN LUGGED his shopping up the garden path towards his hut, unloaded the groceries, then pulled the tag off the dog bed.

"What do you think of that, Gracie Belle?" he asked, placing her down and almost losing her among the fluff. "Comfy?"

She sat and huffed, her black ears swishing in front of her face. Finn shrugged. It took her a while to adjust to new things, so he rubbed her head, then headed for the shower. After scrubbing away the day, he sat on the veranda and shared an apple with Gracie until well after the sun had set and thousands of stars lit up the night sky, the waning half moon not due to rise until the wee hours after the peak of the low tide.

He ordered room service and enjoyed his rib fillet, basking in his solitude with the cool ocean breeze. Rain had invited him for drinks with Eden, but Finn had politely excused himself. Rain might have resisted the urge to claim his mate, but Finn wouldn't want to intrude on his friend's quality time with her.

Only when the resort had quietened and his neighbor a few meters away had shut off his lights did Finn settle Gracie into her bed and leave her with the crinkly butterfly toy she adored.

"Going for a run, Gracie Belle. I'll be back."

Pulling the door closed behind him, Finn ignored the beckoning of the bush at the end of the path. He'd explore Rocky Bay and Hawkings Point another night as right now, a different part of the island called to him. So, leaping into his red Jeep, Finn drove down the dark road into Nelly Bay, passed the marina, and curved up the headland into Arcadia. After the twists and turns towards Horseshoe Bay, he pulled into the Forts parking lot, stepped barefoot onto the bitumen, and tucked the keys beneath the wheel rim. Ignoring the path to the historic site, Finn strode into the unmarked bush. The leaves crunching beneath his feet over dry land that hadn't seen rain in months wasn't a sensation he was used to, but not having stretched his legs since the full moon, Finn dropped his shorts, then ran into the darkness. In a twist of matter, his bones morphed, and hair pierced through his skin. He leapt over a rock to land on all fours, his claws catching him, and raced through the bush.

Finn's mouth opened in a wolfish smile. Everything was heightened in this form, his sight, his smell, his hearing. His claws crushed the fallen leaves as he leapt onto a granite boulder and down the mountain. He longed to explore the famous Forts Walk, as a wolf or man, but tonight, he had a more important mission.

Standing spread legged on a rock, Finn lifted his snout and sniffed. Strawberry ripped through him. Shampoo. Of course. Salivating, Finn plowed into the thicket, the ground soft beneath the dense vegetation as he stuck deep to the outskirts of Horseshoe Bay. Ava was close. The stronger her scent grew, the faster his heart pounded as Fate drew him towards her.

He crept through the bushes as lights flickered in the distance. He must be close to Eucalypts Grove. Was that where Ava was staying? He'd have thought she'd be staying with her friend.

Then he saw her striding along the dark boardwalk. Finn stilled, ducking his head even though he remained hidden in the trees. She wore a different dress than earlier, this one brushing her calves in a swishy blue skirt. Her hair hung long, tumbling over her shoulders as she fished for her key and strode up the steps onto the porch of the bungalow isolated at the end of the path.

Finn's lips peeled back. The bungalow was too exposed. Easy to access and difficult to protect.

Ava slipped the key into the door, paused, and turned to glance over her shoulder, almost in his direction. He hunched down further, though Finn doubted she'd catch sight of him in the dark. Her eyes narrowed, then she pushed open the door and stepped inside. Lights illuminated the bungalow, and he crept closer. Fuck, he wanted her. He hadn't the first clue what he was going to do about her as he knew he'd need to give into the bond eventually. But there would be a lot of groundwork to lay first and if he wanted their relationship and bond to be a successful one, he needed details.

Who was this woman the Goddess had determined would fill his soul? This woman who saw a stranger belly flop into the ocean and came rushing to his aid. He understood part of that, of course. The Goddess had started to wield her power over Ava and she'd have been driven to check on his well-being. But Finn sensed there was more to her and that she housed a deep, loving soul.

So how had she gotten caught up with Blair?

Baring his teeth, Finn snuck closer yet again. Catching a whiff of her scent, he shivered as everything inside him ached and tightened. He longed to be near her, to hold her in his arms and tell her she would always be safe. That no man or wolf would ever mark her fair skin again. That he would always protect her and that for as long as he lived, she would never need to be afraid.

But how could he? Sitting back on his haunches, Finn's shoulders sank. He didn't know the first thing about romancing a woman. Sex was all he'd ever cared about, meaningless relationships that had no strings attached considering none of those women had been his mate. Finn had been alone for too long, and he was good at it.

Besides, what did he have to offer Ava? He was a nomad with little to his name and a creature she believed only existed in stories. No wonder the mating bond was feared as much as it was coveted. Finn would rather face a thousand rogues than the challenge that lay before him with Ava.

The lights of her bungalow went out and, heart sinking, he dropped his gaze to the leaf littered ground.

He should give it time. She'd just been hurt by one man, the last thing she needed was another making advances on her. Especially one like him. Ava needed a gentle touch and kindly spoken words, and he was good at neither. Besides, he had a job to do, and he couldn't let Rain down by diverting his attention at the whims of his libido.

A howl cut through the air, and Finn's head snapped up. Standing, he cocked his ears and turned towards the national park. The howl hadn't been one of pain or warning, but it held a solemnness that made Finn's heart shudder.

Yes. Sly was his priority and if he was welcomed into the pack, then he might give Ava more thought. After all, there would be no point forging their bond if he couldn't stay.

So, with a final glance at the dark bungalow, Finn turned and scampered back up the hill towards the Jeep.

Chapter 10

Ava brushed light powder on her cheeks. She rarely wore makeup, but she'd rather avoid comments and staring when she arrived at the hospital. Not that she was ashamed. Despite what Blair said in his messages, it had not been her fault. *He* needed to learn how to control his temper.

Ava smacked her compact closed and shuddered. Now that she'd had time to sleep on it, she had to admit she'd been lucky. How had she managed to escape him? Her love for the gym and yoga might have toned her body and strengthened her delicate limbs, but she couldn't overcome basic physics and biology. Blair was bigger than her in height, width, and weight. As a man, he possessed a natural advantage in strength. She was small. It didn't make sense. But as she'd washed the dried blood off her silver ring, she'd considered that perhaps the broken nose really was what had made him scream and wail like a baby.

Ava stifled a laugh. Now see how handsome he thought himself with a crooked nose and the constant reminder that it'd been broken by a woman.

Yet there wasn't any real satisfaction in that as it wouldn't stop him from coming after her.

Gripping the basin, she took a deep breath and blinked back the tears that pooled in her lined eyes as she stared into the mirror. "You will be okay. You stood up to him once, you can do it again."

Besides, maybe the fact that he was a cop would be to her advantage. He'd hardly dare kill her if it meant losing his job. Bruises you could hide or deny, but murder? That didn't seem likely.

Although as she tied her shoes, Ava recalled the scandalous headlines from a few years ago. Rumor claimed that the police had covered up the violent death of that young woman. A woman who, if Ava wasn't mistaken, had been connected to Luna Views. The wife of the owner, who'd left the island shortly afterwards. He must be Rain's brother. It had been the biggest news story at the time, yet hardly surprising considering the crime that ran chaotic through Townsville with violence, car theft, and vandalism occurring every night. Now that she knew there were cops like Blair on the force, Ava wasn't surprised the city was out of control. Was his father as crooked as he was?

Ava grabbed her purse. She didn't want to think about it. Right now, she was safe, and she wanted to enjoy what she had left of her leave before she returned to the exciting chaos of the hospital rehab department. Already, she missed it—mobilizing patients, walking them around the wards, and assessing their lung function after heart surgery. Working in acute care meant she rarely had long-term patients, but she loved her job, seeing people recover and helping them discharge home safely. It hadn't been the reason she'd studied physiotherapy as sports physio had been her goal. But alas, that field was tough, and she found great satisfaction in her career at the hospital. She helped many people a week with various conditions, and they were usually grateful for her help. She couldn't wait to go back.

But for the next few weeks, she'd use her skills to help sick and injured koalas return to the wild, and there was no greater joy than helping creatures who couldn't help themselves.

Grinning, Ava pulled the door closed and skipped down the steps onto the boardwalk, striding through the resort towards the parking lot where she climbed behind the wheel of the pink topless Mini Eden had arranged for her. Minutes later, with her hair suitably windblown, she pulled up outside the Magnetic Island Koala Hospital.

As home to the largest free-roaming koala colony in North Queensland, Magnetic Island had become a haven for the iconic marsupials when they'd been introduced to the island in the 1930s. Isolated from the mainland, the theory had been they could live without threats and have the chance to populate and survive. Too many koalas were dying due to the rapid rate at which their natural habitat was being destroyed thanks to deforestation, the development of needless farmland, and the threat of bushfires. Hospitals and foundations across the country dedicated themselves to studying and saving the koala, and Eden had committed to the cause before she'd even started school. As her best friend, Ava had developed a soft spot for the adorable creatures. Her thirst for scientific knowledge had helped her learn about their unique physiology, and she thoroughly enjoyed caring for them.

Though koalas wouldn't be endangered at all if humans hadn't once hunted them and continued to cut down their homes.

That was another mission for the sanctuary, which worked to protect their habitat by planting more eucalypts while Eden managed the koala's welfare. The biggest threat to the koala's survival were domesticated dogs, being hit by cars, or the males fighting with each other, but they were well protected on the island considering the extensive national park. Most locals were educated and protective of the koala, and tourists came from all over to go koala spotting along the Forts Walk.

Yet they still got sick or injured, so the hospital was always busy. Ava pulled open the glass door and strode into reception. Caleb, one of the regular volunteers, greeted her at the desk.

"Morning, Caleb. Is Eden in yet?"

"She's in the enclosures."

"Thank you."

Ava pushed open the door to the secure, open-aired enclosures overlooking the scrub and mountains towards Arcadia. The hospital was small compared to others in Australia, but thanks to government grants and the generous donations of their supporters, Eden had expanded to six outdoor enclosures, three ICU rooms, a surgery, and had all the basic equipment required to run the center. On occasion, Eden took a koala with her to Townsville if she needed to do further investigations or keep it under close observation. But otherwise, she and two part-time vet nurses took a tiny wage from the grants and the hospital was run by various volunteers in admin, clean-up, tree planting, leaf cutting, and homecare for orphaned joeys.

Ava found her friend examining a small koala sitting on a branch crossbeam while munching on the harvested leaves.

"Morning." Eden flashed her a smile. "How was your night? Sleep well?"

"Yes, it's lovely at the Grove, though very quiet. I could hear every twig crack and branch rustle, so the wallabies must be on the move." Ava nodded towards the koala. "What's wrong with this cutie?"

"Green ants attacked her eyes and nose."

Poor thing. The koala's nose should be long, smooth, and black, but this little girl had pink splotches near her mouth and in the fur around her eyes.

"Is she's going to be okay?"

"Yeah, she's just getting some treatment and should be released soon. I've named her Tammy."

Ava rubbed Tammy's scratchy ears. "Hello, darling. I hate green ants, too. They can be nasty." She glanced at Eden. "Functionally, she's okay?"

"Oh, yeah. She just needs time to heal before being released. I'll update you on our inpatients and what you can do this week."

Leaving Tammy to eat, Ava followed Eden to the next enclosure, but they didn't go in.

"This is Grady. He's an orphan, surviving the dog attack that killed his mum. He was in homecare with Jill and is now getting ready to be released into the wild. He needs more practice climbing, though. I also have another orphan in care with Barb at the moment." Eden's eyes dulled. "I had to euthanize her mum last month after we found them in the national park. She was dehydrated, and we tried but ..."

Ava's heart sank as she squeezed Eden's shoulder. "I'm sorry."

"Yeah, it never gets easier, but Gemma is thriving with Barb. I checked on her yesterday. She's nine months old, so her chances are good."

She'd have been out of her mother's pouch at nine months, but since koalas stayed with their mums until they were a year old, Gemma was still too young to be alone.

"Her mum had pneumonia. It's too dry out there, Ava, and the leaf quality isn't good, so the koalas haven't been in the best shape lately."

Add to the fact that the population suffered from koala retrovirus, a dry environment wasn't helpful for their survival and unfortunately, it rarely rained in Townsville. "I'll keep an eye out when I go walking and note any that seem to be in distress."

"Thanks." They moved from the enclosures and into the hall by the ICU rooms. Eden pushed open the first door, where a koala lay sleeping among towels in a laundry basket on the floor. "This is Marco. He was hit by a car last week and had hip surgery. He's still weak and sleeps a lot, but he's taken some leaf and he'll need mobilization to stay strong."

Nodding, Ava knelt by the little man, his long arms flopped over the towels. The skin around his shaved right hip was pink and seemed to be healing nicely, but he'd need to put some weight through it if he was to climb trees again.

Smiling softly, she stroked the bristly hair on his gray head. Ava had rehabbed many broken hips in humans, so keeping in mind the difference in physiology, she could help Marco out, no problem.

"Don't you worry, buddy. We'll have you out of here and up on that branch in no time."

Chapter 11

Unease trickled down Finn's spine when he arrived at Rain's house to meet the scouts on Saturday. Letting himself in as instructed, he took the elevator up to the next level and strode into the open plan living space where concertina doors opened the kitchen and dining room to the breeze and expansive patio. Rain greeted him with a back slap, and Finn smiled politely before Rain introduced him to the young men, all who looked at him like they'd never seen a Warrior of the Goddess before.

They probably hadn't.

"Finn, meet Kai, our hiking guide. He's passionate about nature and studied geology at university, so he takes people on hikes, four-wheel-drive adventures, and bird watching when the birds flock into Horseshoe Bay every season."

Finn shook Kai's hand. He sure looked like a nature lover with his long auburn hair, five o'clock shadow, and beachwear that almost screamed "hippie." "Nice to meet you."

Rain nodded at a tall young man, almost too slender to be a wolf, with dark chestnut hair spiked on top of his head. "Chad is my right-hand man and skydives with me. He's currently studying for a helicopter license so that we can run chopper tours around Maggie, over to Orpheus Island, and out to the reef."

Then he turned to the blond man leaning on the island counter. "And this is Nate. He's been running the water activities."

"But I belong in the water, not on it." Nate took Finn's hand in a slapping shake. "I take people on diving and snorkel tours."

Kai snorted. "And speaks to the fish."

"Like you can talk, bird-lover." Nate backhanded Kai in the biceps, then turned to Finn. "Nature boy rescues every wounded animal you can think of."

"What would you rather me do?"

Nate replied by running his tongue slowly around his lips, and Kai shoved him.

"You know I'm joking!"

"Indeed." Rain cleared his throat. "But this is a pack meeting, gentlemen, so pay attention."

The soft authority in Rain's tone straightened the young men's spines and sobered their expressions.

Rain glanced at Finn. "I'm putting you in charge of the aquatic activities, so you'll be working with Nate. Nate, you now report to Finn."

Nate nodded. "No worries, boss."

"Finn will run the jet boat and jet ski tours, which will allow you, Nate, to focus on the diving. But everyone needs to help him settle in. I'll brief Finn on what he needs to know, then on Wednesday, he'll start operating the JetWolf. Now, we're not sure how we're going to bring Sly back yet, but Finn is a pro in helping packs like ours and there's a reason he heard my Call. He's our best shot at ending Tyrone's rule once and for all."

Finn cleared his throat, his wolf growling as the young men gazed at him in awe. "Reasons why will become apparent," he muttered. "But first, I'd just like to say I'm sorry to hear about what happened to Shelby. And your Alpha."

Kai's eyes softened. "She was a lovely woman."

"Terrible tragedy," Nate agreed, crossing his arms.

"I wasn't here then," Chad said, "but I'm just as keen to avenge her."

Finn nodded. They might be a small pack, but their belief that they could defeat the rogues couldn't be doubted as their eagerness to protect their territory flowed equal to those Finn had helped before.

Which only made his gut churn harder as he squared his shoulders. "Me too. I've heard of the Thornes. I know what they've done in the past and am keen to end Tyrone's tyranny, which is why I believe Fate had me hear Rain's Call."

Rain's eyebrows narrowed, and Finn powered on before questions could be asked. "I've been fighting this fight for a long time and helped many packs win their lands back from the rebels. Every dark Alpha I've faced has been a vile creature and out of touch with the Goddess, and Tyrone is no differ-ent. We will defeat him. The most important thing is that you all maintain a strong pack bond."

"But our Alpha has fucked off," Nate said, shooting an apologetic look at Rain, who merely shrugged. "How is your presence going to lure Sly out of the bush and convince him to take down the rogues?"

Finn slipped his hands into his pockets. He'd pondered that question all night, resulting in restless sleep and much huffing from Gracie when he'd gotten up to pace. And still, he had no answer.

He couldn't tell these young guys that though, so sharing a look with Rain, Finn shrugged. "We're working on it. But for now, it's best we keep my presence here quiet. The last thing you want is for Tyrone to learn you've brought a Warrior into your midst."

FINN CLIMBED aboard the aptly named JetWolf late Sunday afternoon for his introduction to the bays and sights he would take tourists to during his forty-five minute jet boat rides.

"The island has many splendid features, but not many people get to see the southern and western sides," Rain said as they cruised towards Hawkings Point, the setting sun casting a glow over the mainland. "I usually gun it around here and do a few donuts, then we take a spell overlooking Picnic Bay Jetty, where I give them a bit of history about settlement on the island. The jetty has always been impressive and is on the Queensland Heritage Register. Tourism on the island began in 1877 when the Butler family established a small dairy, orchard, and mixed farm in Picnic Bay. They experimented with planting pineapples and after building some huts, the island became a favorite weekend and holiday destination for people on the mainland. So, the Butlers established a ferry service and began their tourism venture."

Finn surveyed the long wooden jetty as they came around the headland. "You're going to give me a script, right?"

"Yeah, but you don't need to go into detail. I just tell them about the first settlement, the first jetty, and that the ferry used to dock here before they moved the terminal to Geoffrey and then Nelly Bay. But do make sure you point out the *George Rennie*."

"The what?" Finn frowned as Rain pointed towards the water, then saw what looked like the bow of a ship poking up out of the water. His eyebrows lifted. "A shipwreck?"

"Not a very interesting one, but well intact and easy to walk to at low tide. It used to transport coal from West Point to Townsville until 1902 when it was scuttled to serve as a breakwater. But it drifted away and they left it there."

Rain was right, it wasn't very interesting. But a shipwreck

was still a shipwreck, and Finn was intrigued. "Do you have many wrecks around here?"

"Yeah. In fact, that's where I'm taking you. The *SS City of Adelaide* is the highlight of this tour. You won't see another wreck like it." Rain stepped aside and offered Finn the wheel. "Want to take the JetWolf for a spin?"

Grinning, Finn didn't hesitate. At Rain's instruction, they cruised past the village of Picnic Bay, then gunned the jet boat along the west coast towards the small island Rain pointed out a few hundred meters offshore.

But as they approached, Finn realized it wasn't an island but the great hull of a ship rising above the water and overflowing with mangroves.

"The *SS City of Adelaide*," Rain announced.

Finn blew out his breath. "Fuck me. That's amazing."

"Yep. The most important thing is to keep a safe distance to protect the mangroves, but it's difficult to access without a boat so I like to bring people out here and share its history. I'll give you a brief to read, but the *SS City of Adelaide* sailed the seas for over fifty years before running aground. It was launched in 1863 from Glasgow and originally shuttled passengers between Sydney, Melbourne, and Honolulu before it became a cargo ship. In 1912, it caught fire and burned for several days. Then it was purchased by the Butler family to create a breakwater for the jetty. But when it was being towed to the island in 1916, it ran aground here on the reef. It's sat here for over a hundred years, rotting away, and forming its own island."

"Wow." Fascinated, Finn's heart sank as he admired the magnificent hull. His mum would have loved this. When he'd been a young pup, on the nights it'd been just the two of them in their tiny house on Flinders Island, she'd tell him bedtime stories about pirates and ships and the wrecks off their Tasmanian shores. He often wondered now if they were true, but shipwrecks had been his mother's passion and her stories had riveted him.

Finn cleared his throat. "I'll have to learn more about it. And the other wrecks. Are they easily accessible?"

"Some are. You can snorkel over the *Moltke* in Geoffrey Bay, but most are better diving sites, especially those north of the island. I'll give you a map and you can see for yourself."

"Appreciate it."

"No worries." Rain ran his hand through his hair. "But that's pretty much it. Stay off the main part of Cockle Bay Reef and give the riders a bit of fun. I usually do the ride, then stop at the *Adelaide* before jetting it back to Luna Views."

"Sounds easy enough." He inclined his chin towards West Point. "Can I?"

Rain nodded and gripped the hold rail. "Be my guest."

Finn floored it, zooming over the water offshore from the mangroves. He hadn't driven many jet boats, and never for tourists, but the JetWolf handled like a dream and taking holidaymakers out and hearing them cheer and scream sounded like the perfect job.

He practiced twists and turns, spun a donut, then came to a still near the sandy beach of West Point where a dozen or so four-wheel-drives parked along the shore.

"It's common to come out here to watch the sunset," Rain said. "It's not exactly over the ocean, but close enough."

"Would still be a sight to see," Finn muttered as his gaze drifted to the long stretch of beach towards the mountainous headland that was Cape Pallarenda.

His jaw clenched. Somewhere up there, or along that bald stretch of land towards the city, Tyrone Thorne roamed, drawing rogues into his web of chaos and destruction. Wolves who didn't know any better but who were criminals nonetheless. Twisted, soulless, and not meant for this world. Wolves stuck inside men who couldn't control them, especially come the full moon. They couldn't wield the power of the Moon Goddess, and she had no hold over them while she cried her anguish over their existence. As feral, unwanted creatures of darkness and a rebellion who bred quicker than rabbits, the Unfated answered to no one.

But at least a male rabbit didn't slaughter the female.

Finn gritted his teeth. Rogues were barbaric creatures, and Blair had targeted his mate. It didn't matter that Finn's bond with her hadn't triggered, Ava had been destined for him since birth and no matter how hard he tried, he couldn't get her out of his head. Even now, her strawberry scent lingered on the air, and his wolf whimpered.

Rain elbowed him in the ribs, and Finn scowled. "What?"

Rain nodded behind Finn, and he knew without turning what he would see. Drawing a deep breath, Finn dipped his head and shot a look over his shoulder.

Ava stood from the driver's seat of a hot-pink topless Mini and rested her forearms over the top of the windshield. Her blonde hair blew in the breeze while the thin straps of her dress left her shoulders bare. Finn's gut tightened as she lifted her hand to shield her eyes. Fuck, she was beautiful.

"Fate's been kind to you, man."

Finn's hands tightened around the wheel. Yeah, maybe Fate had been kind in the mating aspect, but nothing would be made any easier about the task just because she was pretty. What if Ava didn't like him? He hadn't made a good first impression. Besides, she needed time. And so did he.

Finn cleared his throat. "Why's she alone? Where's Eden?"

"Eden will be on her way back to Townsville by now," Rain said, resignation in his tone. "But Ava's staying for a holiday."

"Seems as good a place as any."

"Yep. So, what are you going to do about her?"

Ava spotted them. Finn knew it not just because she

glanced their way, but by the tug around his heart. Bloody hell. His knuckles whitened as her lips curved, and she lifted her hand in a tentative wave. Finn felt rather than saw Rain wave back, but he couldn't do the same.

Instead, he reached for the throttle. "Nothing. Let's get out of here."

He turned his back and sped away from the sunset.

Chapter 12

Tyrone Thorne marched into his son's office and slammed the door behind him. "What's this crap I hear about you reporting your car stolen?"

Blair leaned back in his desk chair, a smirk twisting his face. "I took that fucking bitch to Paluma, and she stole it and left me stranded there."

"Your car's in the fucking parking lot outside!"

"I know. She returned it and then vanished, but I'm not letting her get away. There's something"—Blair's nostrils flared as he drew in a deep, predatory breath—"alluring about her. Something I need to sink my teeth into."

"Your hormones are screwing with your head. Fuck the woman and discard her. What's so hard about that?"

Blair's eyes flashed as he shot to his feet. "I tried, but the fucking bitch had a silver ring on, okay? She fought back and cut me. You don't need to rub it in my face. One moment of weakness, and she tore out of there like Lucifer himself was on her heels."

Tyrone growled and advanced, narrowing his eyes at his son. His pride and joy. But the brainless fucker continued to let him down with his relentless pursuit of women and failure to produce him a grandpup. "And now you're making false accusations to get the constables to search for her?"

"They're not false accusations. She *did* steal my car."

Tyrone slammed his hands down on the desk. "You have your precious car, so forget the woman. Find another to fuck. We have bigger concerns brewing right now."

Blair frowned. "What concerns?"

"Something is happening on the island. One of our spies saw a new wolf with Blackwood, and we need to investigate. He's up to something."

Blair snorted and crossed his arms over his chest. "Please. The man is focused on nothing but saving his brother. What makes you think he'll take a stand?"

Tyrone's lips twisted. "Have I taught you nothing, boy? Never underestimate your enemy if you want to win."

"They're not our enemies, Father. They're scum who need to be squashed. And I'm not afraid. I'll go over there. The Island Pack are broken and don't scare me."

"That might be, but until we know more about this new wolf, I won't send you in unprepared." Swallowing the ball of emotion in his throat, Tyrone clapped his son on his broad shoulder. His fearless boy possessed a thirst for blood that Tyrone had proudly used in the past, but the kid could also be reckless and on occasion, needed to be reeled in. Blair was all Tyrone had left in this world, and he had big plans for his heir. His *true* heir, not the one Fate's twisted sense of humor had forced upon him. And if Tyrone stood any chance of squashing Fate and setting the wolves free, he couldn't risk anything happening to his beloved son.

But he had allies he could call upon. Allies that were expendable.

"A leader needs to take a back seat and use the tools at his disposal, Blair. I've sent the bat, and he'll return with a report before dawn."

TYRONE PROWLED BACK and forth atop the brick bunker, glaring into the blackness beneath the waning moon. No wonder the troops had used this spot in World War II as it offered the perfect view of his enemy occupying the mountainous landmass on the other side of Cleveland Bay. Though tonight, his hackles rose as he sensed the unrest in the waves breaking on the rocky shores of Shelly Beach. His senses had always been heightened near the sea, hence he'd spent his life trolling the coast and marking his territory in places like Jervis Bay, the Sunshine Coast, and had housed his "family" on Flinders Island. It's why he needed to gain control of Magnetic Island. Just because he didn't live there permanently, it didn't mean those rich Fated assholes could swoop in with their private planes and luxurious resorts and take over his turf. The island was a fucking suburb of Townsville, and he owned this city.

Blair raced up the track from the beach, rounded the front of the fort, and clambered up onto the roof from the slope behind. "*He's coming.*"

"*I can see that,*" Tyrone snarled, having spotted the wings gliding through the sky moments ago. The bat drew closer and flapped into the small tree beside the bunker. Tyrone and Blair looked down their snouts, watching as the bat dropped from the branches and shadows twisted to form a man. The vampire rose to his full height, his pale skin glowing in the darkness. Tyrone and Blair shifted too, but maintained their height advantage on the roof of the fort.

"What did you find out?" Tyrone demanded.

The spy, Eric, brushed his hand through his long dark hair, his lips twisting in a sneer. "This new wolf is strong, boss. Stronger than I've ever seen—after yourself, of course," he hastened to add as Tyrone bared his teeth.

"Where did he come from?"

"I don't know, but Blackwood isn't taking any chances with this new recruit. He's no scout, that's for sure. In fact, he has a presence." Eric's pointed canines flashed. "A lone presence. You know what I'm saying?"

Tyrone's wolf bulged against his skin, bursting to escape as his heart thundered against his ribs. No. It couldn't be. Surely if Blackwood had sent out a Call, Tyrone would have heard it. A lone wolf couldn't have come to his aid.

But as he glanced at the silhouette of the island, Tyrone knew it to be true. It's why he could sense the change. The imbalance. Rain had called in reinforcements. A Warrior.

The Goddess had sent this new wolf to bring him down.

Tyrone resisted a snort. Let the fucker try. A Warrior of the Moon Goddess was just one more enemy he would take pleasure in killing. The Alpha grew weaker and wouldn't last much longer in the bush. Once the wolf took over, the Island pack would break, and no Warrior was going to change that.

But who was this wolf who dared to oppose him? Did the bastard know what he would face? *Who* he would face? Tyrone had already cut Sly's fate and would destroy Rain's soon enough. He wouldn't hesitate to do the same to this newcomer.

He shot his gaze to Eric. "Return to the island and keep an eye on this wolf. Find out who he is and where he came from. But be quick. Time is of the essence."

Chapter 13

Finn spent the rest of the week in battle with his conscience and insatiable wolf as he settled into his new job, learned the ropes, and took his first group on a thrilling jet boat ride to West Point. He'd read everything he could about the *SS City of Adelaide*—which admittingly wasn't much—but while it hadn't been the most interesting ship, its wreck was a bloody freak of nature.

Despite the clawing inside his chest, Finn was in his element as he spent his days on the water and his evenings venturing into the bush with Rain to leave food for Sly. The Alpha moved around a lot and Finn had yet to get a good read on him, but they brought the raw cuts of meat, stayed until Rain was satisfied that Sly was approaching, then left again.

"He won't come if we're there," Rain said as they climbed back into Finn's Jeep. "He used to, but now he rarely speaks to me."

"He's retreating more into the wolf," Finn said as they drove out of Arcadia.

"Yeah. But all hope isn't lost. I don't sense any animosity about your presence, and he would know you're here."

Finn's hands tightened around the wheel. Sly would

certainly show animosity if he knew the truth about Finn's connection with the man who'd killed his wife. In fact, Finn was quite certain he'd need to make another dramatic escape on his jet ski once he fessed up his secret, that's if he managed to outrun the Alpha to safety.

Shame oozed down his spine, leaving him with the sickening sensation of self-disgust. He hated not being honest and if he was to prove his loyalty and be welcomed into the pack, he needed to come clean.

Because Finn had never wanted to belong to a pack more. Magnetic Island had captured his heart with its majestic landscape, tropical beaches, and year-round warm climate. He liked Rain and hoped they could become good friends as they worked together to bring Sly out of the bush. A pack was what he needed. So, after another day of wrestling with his conscience, Finn approached Rain's office door on the upper floor of Luna Views. He'd almost revealed his story earlier when he'd tried talking his way out of performing for the ten o'clock ferry, but Rain hadn't taken no for an answer. So, he'd kept quiet and supported his friend by showing off his mad skills while Eden waved from the rooftop deck. And even though Finn thought Rain mad, he had a newfound respect for him. How the fuck did he resist Eden? And how could Finn do the same with Ava?

Perhaps he would ask him if he was welcomed into the pack. But despite all the signs indicating that Finn had found his place in the world, he couldn't get his hopes up.

Gritting his teeth, he slapped his hand on the door jamb of Rain's office. "Got a sec?"

Rain looked up from his laptop, the chair squeaking as he leaned back and interlocked his fingers behind his head. "Sure. What's up?"

Finn stepped inside, closed the door, but remained standing, spreading his feet as he slipped his hands into his pockets.

"I haven't been honest with you. About why I heard your Call. I know why the Goddess sent me here, because I lied when I said I knew Tyrone and Blair by reputation only."

Rain blinked slowly before his eyes narrowed into a frown. "You know them? Personally?"

"I do." Squashing his guilt, Finn straightened his spine. "Tyrone Thorne is my father."

Rain's eyebrows shot up so fast Finn swore they'd flown off his head. His chair snapped upright, and a growl rumbled from his chest. "He's what?"

"My sire," Finn repeated, purposely using his preferred term this time. "It's not something I'm proud to admit—"

"Nor would I!" Rain sprang to his feet. "Are you fucking with me, Finn? I thought—"

"Whatever you thought, it was right," Finn said, forcing his tone to remain calm. "My blood might be tainted, but that's all that connects us."

"This is fucked up." Rain spun to stare out the floor-to-ceiling windows offering a generous view of the darkening sky. "Here I thought Fate had sent us the help we needed, a Warrior, and I got the bastard son of a rebel wolf."

Baring his teeth, Finn crossed the room in a flash, grasped Rain's shoulder, and spun him around. "I am *not* the bastard son. *He* is!" He pointed in the general direction of nowhere. "Blair. Blair the Heir. Blair, who could never put a foot wrong, never mind that he was the product of Unfated breeding and I was the cast-off Fated son of the woman he loathed."

Fire coursed through Finn's veins as the rage he'd been bottling up this past week poured out, his wolf pacing. Snarling.

Rain blinked, then shoved him off. "You should have told me, Finn."

"I know." Finn drove his hand through his hair. "And I'm

sorry, but it was a shock to learn they were here. That it was Blair who hurt ..."

He couldn't finish that sentence without choking. Or breaking something.

"Then tell me now and tell me quick."

Finn blew out his breath. "What do you want to know?"

"Start from the beginning." Rain crossed his arms over his chest. "And if you want me to trust you, don't leave anything out."

Finn sank into a chair, giving Rain the advantage as he remained standing. "Tyrone Thorne is a bastard. Not in the breeding sense, he's just downright twisted, as you know. Nasty. He was the second son and hated not being the Alpha. Thought Fate had gotten it wrong, so he turned his back on the Goddess and rebelled. He had Blair to prove that he didn't need to be beholden to Fate. Then, three years later, Tyrone mated. With my mother."

Leaning back in his chair, Finn rubbed the ache in his chest. "My mother was an amazing woman. Tough and fearless. She was a marine archaeologist and was studying shipwrecks in Tasmania when they met. I think she'd have found herself attracted to him, but Tyrone wasn't going to put in the effort of creating a solid mating bond, so ..."

Rain's shoulders deflated as the fire vanished from his eyes. "Oh."

"Yep." Finn cleared his throat. "Tyrone marked her. Imprisoned her and used her as he felt fit." Finn took another breath to calm himself before continuing. "I think having me saved her life for a while. I gave her something to live for, and she loved me fiercely."

Rain's lips quirked in a small smile.

"But Tyrone was determined to make her life hell and, in return, make mine hell too. I was ten when she decided we needed to run. I was too young to know it would be impossible, so I was relieved when she told me we'd go start our lives without Tyrone and Blair. But of course, on the night we were supposed to leave ..." Dark memories flashed before his eyes, and his childhood wolf whimpered. Finn didn't want to go into the details of how his father had arrived. Not now. "She told me to run. Promised she would catch up. And when my mum promised, she never failed. So I ran, a scared pup with his tail between his legs."

Rain shoved his hand through his hair. "Shit, man. You were ten. You can't blame yourself."

Finn dropped his elbows to his knees, gazing at the floor. He had blamed himself. For a long time. Sometimes, he still did. "I didn't go far. I waited in the trees, listening. They yelled. Screamed. When all was silent and she didn't come, I ran back to the house and ... and ..." Finn choked back a curse and squeezed his eyes shut. After all these years, he still couldn't say it. "It was a nightmare."

Silence fell as Finn fought the images that had caused years of broken sleep. His father hadn't killed his mother. The wolf had slaughtered her.

Rain's hand fell to Finn's shoulder. "I'm sorry."

After an age, Finn glanced up. "Tyrone kept me after that. I spent years suffering Blair's bullying and torture until one day, I stole some unsuspecting bastard's jet ski and took off with nothing but the clothes on my back. I was fifteen and free. So if you want to know if I'm on your side ..." Finn rose to his feet. "You'll find no one more willing to bring those bastards down than me."

Rain nodded slowly, then clapped him on the shoulder. A strange ripple moved through the air as they met in a backslapping hug.

"Sorry I doubted you, man."

"It's fine. I might have doubted me, too." Finn drew away.

"Though ... it makes sense. I mean, I always knew Tyrone was a cruel bastard, but I didn't think a wolf could ..."

Finn swallowed. "Kill his mate?"

Rain's gaze lowered. "Yeah. Sorry, if that's—"

Finn waved the apology away. "I've wondered that myself. He has always been cruel, but I can't be sure if the murder changed him or not. He didn't show any signs of being twisted by it in the years that followed, but he was already so nasty that it was hard to tell. I just assumed that if you don't love your mate, then you don't feel her death as deeply."

Tyrone had claimed her without consent, defying the laws and purpose of the traditional mating bond. How could he have grieved her loss?

"Hmm ... sounds reasonable. To mark your mate with a bite is despicable. Although—" But Rain didn't finish that sentence as his shoulders tensed and he whipped around to face the window. He lowered his head, his ears twitching.

Finn frowned. "What happened?"

"Shh." Rain held up his finger, listening for a moment before his head snapped up. "We need to go."

He swept past Finn and out the door before Finn could even turn. Swearing, he followed.

"Who was it?" he asked as Rain headed for the fire stairs, though Finn already knew the answer.

Sly had called.

Chapter 14

Their feet pounded down five flights of stairs as they sprinted out of the hotel and into the resort. Finn didn't dare question Rain as he followed him through the gardens towards the parking lot. Rain checked the various supplies he kept in the back of his Jeep, then jumped into the driver's seat. It wasn't until they were tearing out the resort towards Picnic Bay that Finn asked, "What happened?"

"Sly called in another attack."

"Attack?" Finn's wolf stood to attention. "You mean the rogues?"

It couldn't be. He'd have sensed if Blair was near the island.

"No," Rain growled. "Bloody bats."

Finn's lips twisted. "Fucking pests, those vampires. Should be exterminated."

"Yep. I fucking hate bats. Not the flying foxes—it's not their problem that their natural habitat is being destroyed. Deforestation is out of control in this country."

"True."

"But the vampires only make them look worse, adding to their numbers in the cities and wreaking havoc at night."

"Like I said. Exterminate them."

"Yeah, but they're slick, bloodthirsty creatures, and Tyrone has them under his thumb."

"Which is definitely concerning." Finn mused over that, then frowned. "Wait. Did the bat attack Sly?"

"No, Sly can take care of himself." Rain turned the car away from the beach and headed west. "It attacked a koala."

Finn's eyebrows lifted. "A koala? Why?"

"To piss me off."

Rain tore through Picnic Bay towards West Point Road, speeding past the mangroves and into the dying sunset. Finn remained silent as the dirt road narrowed and wove through the bush. The Jeep found all the bumps, bouncing along the track until they arrived in the small village of West Point beneath the shroud of darkness.

Rain pulled over beneath a dense cover of trees.

"What's the plan?" Finn asked as Rain grabbed wooden stakes from the back of the Jeep and shoved them into a hessian sack. "Are we killing the bats?"

"Nah, the bat will be long gone."

"Then why the stakes?"

"To mark the koala's home trees so that we know where to return it."

Finn scratched the back of his neck, confused. "Right. But I'm not sure if—"

Rain's eyes flashed. "The koala will be fine, as long as we find it quickly."

Finn decided it was best not to argue. "Where is it?"

"Sly said not far from Rollingstone Bay. If we cut through those hills, we should find it." Rain pointed with his chin as he tied the sack closed, secured the tools, and pulled off his shirt.

Finn did the same, tossing his shirt into the Jeep before following Rain into the bush. The moment they were out of sight, they dropped their shorts and shifted. Finn arched his spine and dug his claws into the dirt as Rain, in his midnight black wolf form, clasped the bundle of wood and hessian in his jaw.

Together, they ran into the darkness.

Finn's hind legs bunched and stretched as they leapt and scampered over rocks along a creek running between two hills, venturing deeper into the bush in silence. Wolves could communicate in wolf form, but only if they were pack or blood bound.

After a few minutes, Rain slowed and sniffed the leaf-littered ground while cicadas buzzed around them. A bush rustled and Finn glanced over his shoulder to watch a wallaby hop away.

Rain's soft howl drew Finn's attention, and they continued on. Then Rain stilled, his tail lifting, and Finn saw the lump of gray fur lying crooked at the base of a gum tree. The koala's long claws stretched out over the dirt, its eyes closed as two puncture wounds seeped blood over its tiny shoulder.

Rain shifted and skidded to his knees as he bent to examine the bite. "Bloody leeches," he muttered venomously.

Sensing his anger and compassion for the innocent creature, Finn shifted and knelt beside him. "What can I do?"

"We need to mark the territory. It probably fell out of this tree, so paint a cross on it and plant a stake so we know where to return her. We'll need to go back to the car in wolf form, so I'll tuck her into my bag and—" Rain lifted his head, his nose twitching. "There's a joey."

"How do you know?"

"I can smell it. The fear. It couldn't have gone far." Rain grabbed the bag and extracted the stakes. "I'll take care of this. You find the joey."

Leaving Rain to it, Finn stood. He didn't understand why the bats would have come for the koala, but lifting his nose to the chilly air, he smelled it too. Young fear. Loss. Desperation. His wolf yowled, but Finn shoved the memory down as he dropped to his hands and knees. Sniffing the earth, he used his supernatural senses to scan the dense undergrowth.

Where are you?

A shuffle sounded, and Finn turned his head, connecting with large wide eyes crouched beneath a fallen log. A small black nose poked forward, followed by two fluffy, white-rimmed gray ears and tiny claws.

Finn's mouth curved. "There you are, you little cookie." The babe scuttled backwards. "It's okay. I won't hurt you."

The big black eyes blinked. Finn inched forward. Then, before it could move again, he grabbed the joey. Sharp talons dug into his hands as he brought the baby koala to his chest.

"Got it?" Rain called.

Finn nodded. "Yep. Seems to be okay." He gave it a quick look over. "I don't see any blood or injury. Has a tight grip."

"Good. Joeys are usually adept at escaping while mum takes on the predator."

Finn's throat tightened as the memories surfaced. His tiny hands clutching at the tree, his breath heaving in tiny white puffs as he waited, terrified. Hearing his mother's screams. Wood and glass breaking. The silence. Waiting for the footsteps that never came.

Shaking himself like a dog, he hugged the koala close and peered into the bush. But before he could return to Rain, another set of eyes rooted Finn to the earth. A long, dark snout followed the piercing stare as the wolf crept through the trees.

Finn's heart lurched. "Sly ..."

Leaves scuttled as Rain spun around, but he didn't speak. Neither man moved as Sly's eyes remained glued on Finn. His breath caught. What was Sly doing there? Had Rain told him who he was? Would he—

Then the dark wolf lowered his head. "*Welcome.*"

The air pulsed, knocking the wind from Finn's chest as he clutched the koala between the groove of his pecs. His shoulders slouched and it took a moment for him to catch his breath.

But when he glanced back into the trees, Sly was gone.

"Did ... was that ..."

Rain's hand fell over Finn's shoulder and squeezed. "Pack bond. You're one of us now."

Finn blinked. Really? "But ... but how? He doesn't even know me!"

"Does it matter?"

"Yes. He doesn't even know I'm Tyrone's unwanted heir. He'll—"

"Sly believes in Fate, Finn. You've come to our aid. Trust me, he wouldn't have made that choice lightly."

"Yeah, but—" That couldn't have been it. His bloodline aside, he'd dreamed about this moment for half his life and knew what it was meant to entail. The pack bond was more profound than a simple nod and a shiver on the breeze. What about the initiation ceremony? The run? Sure, it wasn't full moon, and the bond didn't always need to be completed under the Goddess's full light. But tonight held no moon at all, and that wasn't how things were done.

Frowning, Finn ran his hand down the koala's back. Something wasn't right.

"The Goddess knows what she's doing, man, and now we're one step closer to bringing Sly out of the bush. But first, we need to save these two."

Finn wasn't so sure about the Goddess, but Rain was right. They had a job to do.

"Will she be okay in there?" Finn asked as Rain slipped the mama into the hessian sack.

"I'll keep her safe, and you can take the little joey. She'll clutch to your back while we return to the car, then we'll get them to Eden."

"Eden?"

"Yeah. She's the vet who runs the Koala Hospital."

Finn shuddered. "You're mated to a *vet*?"

"I know, right?" Rain smirked. "But like you said, Fate can be cruel. Now shift and I'll secure the joey."

Handing the little cookie over, Finn shifted. His heart pounded as he glanced over his shoulder at his long golden fur, then sank in disappointment. "*Where are my pack stripes?*"

"I don't know. But that wasn't exactly an initiation ceremony."

Finn grunted. The fact Rain could hear him as a wolf was promising, but he'd worry about the poorly executed pack bond later as Rain placed the joey onto Finn's back. His long, soft fur might not be what she was used to, but she dug her claws into his ribs and held on.

Then Rain shifted, gathered the sack carrying the injured mother into his jaw, and they ran back to the Jeep.

Chapter 15

Ava lowered from plank position into a push-up, then rose into cobra and filled her lungs with the crisp night air. Her week of hiking the trails, taking in the glorious sunsets at West Point, and strengthening Marco's hip had brought her peace and eased the tension in her spine, but she was glad to have Eden by her side again as they pushed back into downward dog. The hospital volunteers had been welcoming and helpful, but Ava rarely socialized well and had spent her nights curled up in her bungalow with Mozart playing while losing herself in the spicy sports romances she'd downloaded onto her e-reader. It was, after all, the only place happily-ever-after's and multiple orgasms existed, but a girl could find herself too lonely.

Eden sighed contentedly as they rolled up their mats. "That was just what I needed. Though damn, Ava, you worked me hard."

"You'll thank me when you're on your feet all day in surgery."

"Probably," she said as her phone rang. Snatching it off the table, pink rose in her cheeks as she answered. "Rain?"

Ava lowered her head to hide her smile. Eden had forgone

drinks with the billionaire tonight so they could catch up, and she would have felt bad except—

"Shit! Where are you? Ahuh. All right. I'll meet you there." Eden hung up. "We have to get to the hospital."

Springing to her feet, Ava tossed their mats into the bungalow. "What did he say?"

"He found a mum and joey. Mum's been bitten, though he couldn't tell me what by."

Slipping on their shoes, they grabbed their purses, then hurried through the retreat towards Eden's ute.

"Is he waiting?"

"Said he'd be twenty minutes."

It only took two for Eden and Ava to arrive at the hospital.

"I'll call Dee," Eden said, switching on the reception lights. "You prepare a basket for the joey."

Ava nodded and strode towards the storeroom. They wouldn't know how badly the koala was injured until Eden assessed her, but if she needed to be euthanized, as most of them were, then Ava would much rather be setting up a playpen for the joey than watching an innocent life slip from this world.

Grabbing a laundry basket, she dropped two fluffy white towels inside it and stomped into an empty examination room. Flicking the lights on with her elbow, Ava dropped the basket onto the table with a thud, her heart breaking. The poor koala had probably been injured through another act of human carelessness, another dog owned by an irresponsible asshole who let it roam free. Wandering dogs were out of control in Townsville, though people on the island should know better. They'd been educated about the dangers dogs posed to koalas as even the smallest puncture wound could be fatal to the thin, pliable skin of the unique marsupial.

"How are you going?" Eden asked, poking her head into the room.

"Good. I'll grab some leaves in case the little one is hungry. How about you?"

"Yeah. Dee's on her way if we need to do surgery."

"Do you think it was a dog?" she asked, following Eden back into the hallway.

"Maybe. Rain said the joey's fine, but I'll get you to check it over to make sure. We'll need to contact the carers and see who can take it on."

"I can do that." Even if Eden did save the mum, she wouldn't be fit to look after her baby. "Do you want me to set up some formula?"

"That'd be great," she said as Dee strode through the front doors.

Ava left Eden to speak with her nurse and went outside to grab some pre-cut branches of eucalyptus leaves for the bub to snack on, then mixed up some nutrient. By the time the doors opened again, Ava was all set up for her patient. She caught Eden in the hallway and together, they strolled into reception.

Where Finn, in all his golden glory, stood clutching a tiny koala to his bare chest.

Ava stilled, her heart fluttering as the blood drained out of her chest and pooled into a molten puddle deep in her belly. Fuck, she'd forgotten how hot he was. She'd seen him in nothing but boardshorts twice, but was still pissed at the way he'd snubbed her when she'd waved to him at West Point. Then again, they didn't know each other, and the Nordic god-like surfer dude was hardly the friendly type.

But tonight ... hot damn, he was a mess. Dirt smeared his chiseled abs, a scratch marked his forearm, and twigs twisted in the scruffy hair along his jaw. He looked downright danger-ous. Wild. Dirty. Which only fueled her insane urge to throw herself around him and never let go.

But his arms were currently occupied with the little koala nestled against his sternum, her claws clutching his bulging pecs. Ava's mouth twisted. Never had she been envious of a joey.

"Bring her in here." Eden's voice drew Ava out of her stupor as she turned to Rain cradling a lumpy sack. He, too, was shirtless and just as filthy as he carried the injured koala into the room Eden had prepared. "What happened?"

Rain laid the hessian on the table and helped Eden and Dee remove the small, listless body. "Found her at the base of a tree. She has these bite marks."

Eden slipped on some gloves and examined the wound. "It doesn't look like a dog bite. Where did you find her?"

"West Point."

Eden's gaze flickered to Rain. "West Point?"

The twig in his hair flicked back and forth as he nodded.

"What were you doing at West Point?"

"Fishing."

"Fishing." This time, Eden wasn't asking a question, and Ava didn't blame her. She didn't believe Rain either. "At this time of night?"

The two men nodded.

"Yep," Rain said. "Fishing."

"In a boat," Finn added.

Ava and Eden exchanged glances, their eyebrows lifting.

"At sunset?" Eden asked.

"Best time for fish," Finn said, his large fingers stroking the joey's back. "It's quiet."

"But—"

"Are you interested in my nighttime pleasures, Eden?" Rain asked, his mouth curving as he moved towards her. "Or would you like to save the koala?"

Eden straightened, unhooked the stethoscope from around her neck, and listened to the koala's chest. "Breath sounds are shallow. Heart rate's not great." She examined the bite again, then pinched the koala's back. "She's not bleeding anymore, but she's very dehydrated. You didn't see what bit her?"

Rain shook his head a little too quickly. "She was like this when we found her."

Ava didn't buy it. "While you were fishing, in a boat, you found a koala at the base of a tree."

The sinfully gorgeous men stilled. Seconds ticked by as they exchanged sideways glances in an attempt to align their lies.

Then Finn said, "We went for a hike."

Ava rolled her eyes while Eden scoffed.

"You're just as bad a liar as he is," she said before turning to Rain. "Will you ever tell me the truth?"

Rain's smile slipped. "Maybe one day."

Eden blew out her breath. "Fine. But I have to check these wounds in surgery and get her fluids up. Ava, get these two so-called fishermen out of here and look over the joey for me, please."

Chapter 16

Finn strode into the waiting room unable to shake the tension bunching between his shoulder blades. He'd kept the little cookie snuggled close since shifting back and had nursed her mama in his lap while Rain had driven like a madman from West Point to the hospital on the opposite side of the island. Mama's breath had labored, but she'd hung in there. Hopefully Eden would save her as he couldn't bear the thought of the adorable little cookie losing her mum.

"Um ... if you could bring the joey up this way?"

Ava's voice did nothing to ease his tension, her long blonde ponytail swaying over her shoulders as she looked anywhere but him.

Sighing louder than necessary, Rain lowered himself into a seat. "I'll wait here. You know? Three's a crowd."

Finn's jaw clenched. Bastard.

"All right. Finn ... follow me."

Uncertainty laced her tone, and Finn's wolf snarled. She didn't want to be alone with him. Not that he could blame her. Friendliness wasn't his virtue and after the way Blair had laid his unnatural paw on her, she had every right to be skittish.

But as he followed Ava and her tight, lycra-clad ass down the hallway, he forced his anger down. He couldn't fuck this up. This was his chance to make amends and while he might not be ready to be alone with her, at least he understood the magnetic pull between them. She didn't.

Ava gestured him into the exam room. "Place her in the basket and we'll take a look."

Finn eased the joey off his chest and settled her into the soft, towel-lined basket where she immediately recognized the plush koala as kin and clutched to its back.

An ache spread through his chest. Poor little mite.

"Did you notice any injuries?"

He shook his head, keeping his gaze fixed on the cute koala and not the beautiful woman fussing over her on the opposite side of the table. "Nope. She's fine. Strong. Clung to me the whole drive here."

Ava ducked her head, but not quick enough to hide her blush. "Where did you find her?"

Forcing down his hankering wolf, Finn cleared his throat. "Like I said, we were—"

"Fishing, I know. Then you grew bored and took a hike."

"The fish weren't biting."

"Right." Sarcasm as sweet as honey rolled off her tongue as she examined the little cookie's claws. "But was she with her mum, or—"

"She'd hidden under a fallen log."

"The joeys usually escape if mum's being attacked."

Finn's chest tightened. "That's what Rain said."

"A mother's protective instincts, I guess. But she looks fine."

Ava straightened, her blue eyes sparkling as a smile curved her plump pink lips. Fuck, he longed to taste her, to lean across the table or stalk around it to pull her body close and claim her mouth as his.

All of her as his. Because she was. *His*.

Yet even after a week, she still reeked of Blair.

His wolf growled and Finn glanced at the cutie in the basket. "Good. She'll have to be tough. Especially if her ..."

He couldn't say it. Stroking the joey's back, he hoped to the Moon that her mother would pull through. The bloody vampires had a lot to answer for.

"Eden's a great vet," Ava said, turning to the bench behind her. "She'll do all she can to save her mum."

Finn nodded, unable to draw his gaze away from Ava's body as she gathered supplies. Her swirl-patterned lycra pants hugged her finely shaped thighs, ass, and nipped in at her waist while her tight white singlet exposed her lean shoulders.

"How long have you two been friends?"

"Eden and I met in high school, so about ten years now." Ava turned, a syringe of white liquid in her hand.

Finn's spine tensed as he reached for the joey. "What is that?"

"Milky nutrient. She looks about ten months old, so she's probably off milk and onto gum leaves, but it's just a little something to keep her going while mum's recovering."

Finn nodded, trusting Ava knew what she was doing as he lifted his hand from the little cookie's back. Ava bent down, her hair swishing over her shoulder as she held the formula to the joey's mouth, and she gobbled it up.

Ava grinned. "Yummy, isn't it?"

Finn's heart warmed, his wolf shivering as his belly tightened and cock stiffened. Fuck, she was gorgeous.

His hands tightened around the plastic basket. The Goddess might not be showing herself tonight during the height of the new moon, but Finn figured it was a good opportunity as any to lay some groundwork. "You been helping Eden for a while, then?"

"Yeah. Any time I come to the island I end up helping where I can."

"And you enjoy it?"

"There's nothing more rewarding than helping others. Especially animals who can't fend for themselves."

The heat inside him ignited and his wolf clawed to get out, aching to claim her. Cherish her.

Finn glanced back at the joey. "She is very cute."

Ava's grin could have lit up the moon. "We'll have to give her a name."

"Cookie." It left his mouth before he could stop it, and his wolf slapped his paw over his eyes.

Ava's eyebrows lifted. "Cookie?"

Fuck, would he ever stop embarrassing himself in front of this woman? "It's what I've been calling her."

"All right." She smiled at the koala with all the tenderness in the world. "Are you finished, Cookie?"

Ava withdrew the empty syringe and reached for a cloth to wipe the drops of formula from Cookie's mouth.

Finn rubbed his fist over the ache in his chest. "You're good at that."

"Yeah, well ..." She shrugged and tossed the syringe into the trash. "She's not my first joey. But she seems to like you."

Finn had reached into the basket and Cookie had clutched his arm again. "We had a good run out of the bush, didn't we, little one?" She'd clung to his wolf's back without the slightest hint of fear.

"Hmm ..." Ava bit down on her lower lip, and warmth shivered through Finn as her glittering eyes roamed over his arms, chest, then locked with his. For a moment, he held her gaze, and the world slanted. His wolf preened.

Ava's shoulders lifted as she inhaled and crossed her arms

beneath her pert breasts. "So, it doesn't look like you have any bruising."

Finn frowned. "From the koala?"

"No. From the jet ski."

He scoffed. "Like I said, it wasn't so bad. And I've had plenty of time to recover."

"Indeed. But you had a cut when you came in. It looked nasty. Would you like me to clean it for you?" She moved around the table. "A little bit of iodine and ..."

Her delicate fingers wrapped around his forearm and Finn's breath caught. Heat slammed through him like he'd been submerged in a jacuzzi, his muscles tensing as the scent of her strawberry shampoo made his head spin. She turned his arm over and it took every inch of his self-control not to place his hand on the small of her back, draw her close, and bury his nose in her sunshine hair.

"Huh." She flipped his arm back over, then let go. Finn's wolf whimpered at the loss of her touch as she examined his other arm. She frowned. "I thought I saw ..."

Finn's thumping heart screeched to a standstill. Shit, he'd been bleeding after cutting himself on a branch. It'd only been a scratch so he hadn't concentrated on healing it quickly, but his wolf abilities would have caught up since and sealed the wound by now.

Ava shook her head and moved to the other side of the table. "I thought you were bleeding."

"I don't think so."

"My mistake." She picked up the gum leaves and placed them beside Cookie. "We'll see if she likes these."

"Doesn't look like it." His words came out gruffer than he'd intended as Cookie sniffed the branch, then turned her head away.

"Maybe later. She's had a rough night." Ava moved around adjusting the leaves, plush koala, and Cookie. But when she glanced at his forearms, Finn shivered and folded them across his chest.

He needed to distract her. Keep her talking. But fuck, how did he do that? Learning more about her was vital if he wanted to pursue the mating bond, which he needed to do else risk going insane. Rain might have gotten away with ignoring his mate since Eden was rarely on the island, but Finn sensed Ava everywhere he went and every day it had grown harder to resist the pull that compelled him to seek her out.

And now ... what the fuck was he supposed to say?

"Ahh ... how was your first week of vacation?"

"I've kept myself occupied helping around here." Her shoulders slouched as she adjusted the gum leaves. "Are you on holiday too? Visiting Rain?"

"Nah, I came to do a job for him."

"Oh. What do you do?"

He flashed her a grin. "Jet ski instructor. And more recently, jet boat driver and tour guide."

"Yes ... I saw you on the jet boat." Her eyes dulled, knocking a hole in his gut. He wasn't proud of how he'd snubbed her. "Looks like fun."

"Then you should come along."

Ava shook her head. "No, I don't like extreme things."

"The jet boat isn't extreme. We only twist, turn, and spin. No one's fallen out. Yet."

She rustled the gum leaves at Cookie, but didn't meet his eye. "I'll think about it."

"Do." He planted his hands on the table and leaned forward, well aware of the flex and bulging of his arms and shoulders. "What are your other plans while you're on the island?"

Her gaze flickered to his body, cheeks pinked, then she glanced back to Cookie. "Hiking, probably. I like walking and have taken the track over to Balding and Radical Bay a few times. It's a bit of a hike, but a good a place as any to read. If the water wasn't so cold, I'd love to go snorkeling as I've always wanted to see the shipwrecks."

Finn's eyebrows shot up. "Yeah?"

"Yeah. The only one I've seen is the *George Rennie* and that's because it's—"

"On the beach in Picnic Bay." Finn smiled as she looked his way. "I've just learned of the shipwrecks myself. Maybe we could go together?"

Shit. There he went again, his wolf seizing control of his head. Stupid bloody animal.

Ava blinked her big sapphire eyes, then lowered them, her teeth clamping over her bottom lip. "I dunno ..."

Bloody fool. Just as he'd feared, she wasn't ready, and she didn't need an oaf like him making advances on her.

Yet he remained compelled to tilt his head and ask, "Why not?"

"It's just ... I'm not ..."

The door opened behind him. "Sorry to interrupt," Rain said, and Finn's jaw clenched. "Is the joey settled?"

Ava nodded far too quickly for Finn's liking. "She's doing well."

"She's not hurt?"

No, but Rain was about to be. Finn glared at him. "Cookie's fine."

"Good. Because we need to call some wildlife carers and see who might be able to take ... Cookie."

Chapter 17

va welcomed Rain like a person did in a drought. "Yeah, I'm supposed to do that. You two watch Cookie."

Goddammit, Ava could barely catch her breath. She'd spent half an hour alone with Finn and every inch of her ached for him until she no longer felt like herself. She didn't understand it. Her hands tingled, toes curled, and her heart felt like it wanted to leap from her body and attach itself to his. Her brain had officially liquified into molten mush and unleashed desire that prickled over every inch of her heated skin.

Attraction like that wasn't normal, especially for a man who'd snubbed her. Twice. Then asked her out.

He *had* asked her out, hadn't he? It certainly sounded like it. The idea of snorkeling with Finn, seeing the waves lap against his rock-hard chest and sunshine glitter off his wet body ...

Rain stepped aside, allowing Ava to slip out the door and leave the two unlawfully sexy shirtless men with the baby koala. Alone, her shoulders relaxed and pulse slowed, but an ache lingered as she felt the loss of Finn deeper with every step she took away from him.

Bloody ridiculous.

She found the volunteer list in the office and since Barb was already taking care of an orphaned joey, she called Lois.

"I would, dear," Lois said, before breaking into a coughing fit. "But I can't shake this terrible cold and can barely get out of bed, let alone take care of that little lass. Is Paula available? Otherwise—"

"No, don't stress yourself, Lois. I haven't called Paula yet."

"Oh, good. I'm sure she can take her."

Ava wished Lois well, then called Paula, who agreed to take the joey but was currently in Townsville and couldn't collect her until the morning.

"That should be fine." Ava and Eden would likely stay tonight with the mum, so they could take care of Cookie until Paula collected her. "Thank you. We'll see you in the morning."

Ava hung up and dropped her head in her hands.

"You found someone?"

She spun around in the desk chair. "What are—what are you doing?" Ava leapt to her feet as Cookie turned her head from Finn's chest, blinking. "You're not supposed to be cuddling her!"

He tilted his head, both he and the koala looking at her as though asking, "Jealous?"

Yes.

"Why not?" Finn asked.

"She needs to remain independent and free from human attention so she can return to the wild."

"But you just called someone to care for her."

"Yes, but you're still not supposed to cuddle her."

"What's the harm in a cuddle?" The words came out gruffly otherwise would have risked sounding far too sweet as his sinful mouth curved beneath his beard. He glanced down at his chest, rubbing Cookie's fuzzy ear between his thumb and forefinger. "She misses her mum."

Ava tore her attention from his long, thick fingers. "I should check on her."

"Rain's checking in with Eden now. You think they'll be okay?"

Sighing, Ava couldn't tear her gaze from Cookie's tiny body curled against such warm, tanned skin. God, if only she were a koala. "Eden will do her best for the mum and Paula will look after Cookie."

"But won't give her cuddles," Finn muttered.

Ava sighed with resignation. "Koalas aren't pets, and they shouldn't be treated like one."

Although the fact that this big, strong, wild man couldn't seem to let go of the baby made Ava's insides warm in all the best places. She wanted to snatch Cookie from him so it would *just stop*.

Thankfully, the door opened and Eden strolled in.

"Well, mum's a fighter. She's going to need a good, strong name."

Ava's chest lightened. "She's going to be okay?"

"I'm fairly confident. The bite didn't sever any major vessels and I have her on IV fluids. Once she's hydrated and starts eating again, she should recover nicely." Eden stepped aside as Rain walked into the office behind her. "Dee's watching her now and we'll move her into the ICU once her sedation wears off. How's this little one?"

Eden stroked Cookie's shoulder. The joey lifted her head off Finn's chest and sniffed.

"She looks fine to me," Ava said. "Likes Finn, though."

"Of course she does. He's the brave, handsome hero who rescued her." Eden flashed Ava a smile, her eyes twinkling as Finn's chest expanded.

Ava crossed her arms. "She *should* be in her basket."

"Yes." Eden sobered and glanced between the two men. "Now, I need to know. Where *exactly* did you find these two? The *truth*."

"Just like we said, Eden. Not far off West Point and inland from Rollingstone Reef."

Eden's nose twitched. "Well, it's quite unusual. The puncture wound looked like a snakebite, but that doesn't make sense. It looks … it looks …" Eden waved her hand in a circle, unable to find the word.

Finn and Rain exchanged looks, and Ava frowned as a silent conversation passed through their eyes.

"Oh, I don't know." Eden's hand dropped. "I guess it could have been a dog bite, though dogs usually maul."

"I doubt dogs venture that deep into the bush," Rain said. "There were flying foxes, though."

"*Pfft*, flying foxes don't hurt koalas."

Finn's brows lowered. "I heard they were pests."

"No, they're not." Eden's sigh barely masked her frustration. "They're just not popular in the cities because they suck the life out of trees, cause a ruckus, and don't smell very nice. But it's not their fault that land clearing and drought has forced them out of the bush. They're just like that little girl there." She nodded at Cookie. "If humans stopped destroying their habitat, they wouldn't need to invade ours."

"Exactly," Ava said. "And we only have a few bats on the island, so they're hardly pests."

"And they're the only mammal who can pollinate certain types of eucalyptus, so they're essential to the survival of koalas. We need them here. Besides, flying foxes eat nectar and fruit. They wouldn't attack a koala."

Finn glanced down at Cookie, then back at Eden. "Maybe they were vampire bats?"

Rain elbowed him in the ribs. "Dude!"

Eden, however, simply laughed. "Vampire bats don't live in Australia. They're native to Central and South America. We do have the ghost bat, but they're a false vampire that eats invertebrates, lizards, and other small animals. I don't often see them in Townsville, though, and they still wouldn't hurt a koala."

Rain shared another long glance with Finn, then shrugged. "If you say so. You're the expert."

Eden nodded, ending that discussion as she drew in a breath and gestured towards Cookie. "So, what are we doing with this little one?"

"Paula's collecting her tomorrow morning when she gets back from Townsville."

"Excellent. In that case, we should put her back in her basket and let her rest. Finn? Hand her back to Ava."

The big man peered down at the little bundle, hair brushing over his shoulders as he stepped towards Ava. "Cuddle time's over, Cookie. These ladies will take care of you until your mum is better, okay?"

After a brief hesitation, he placed Cookie in Ava's arms. The joey's sharp claws dug into her chest as Finn's large, hot hand came to rest over her shoulder, and she froze. He brushed his hand down her bare arm, leaving a tingle in his wake as Finn scratched Cookie's ears goodbye. Then he drew in a deep breath. A shiver coursed through Ava that both delighted and terrified her. But before she could make sense of it, Finn stepped back and clapped his hand on Rain's shoulder.

"We gotta go."

"Yep." Rain nodded at Ava and Eden. "Thanks, ladies. Do let us know how the koalas fare."

In a flash, they were gone.

Eden turned to Ava, her eyes wide. "Did Finn just *sniff* you?"

Heart pounding, Ava pressed her lips together. "I think so?"

"Oh, girl." Eden grinned. "He likes you."

"He does not!" Though she couldn't deny the shiver coursing up her spine.

"Oh, I think he does. He looks at you the same way Rain sometimes looks at me. Like he owns you."

Ava blinked. "And you *like* that?"

"Hey, Rain can own me any time he wants, but the stubborn idiot seems hellbent on ignoring what's between us. But that's his loss." She shrugged, though Ava didn't miss the disappointment in her friend's eyes. "Now, let's get this joey ready to go into care. What did Finn call it?"

Ava's lips twitched. "Cookie."

"Cookie." Eden nodded slowly. "Right ... seems like our big bad wolf has a soft side."

"Seems that way," Ava agreed, following Eden down the hallway to where she'd left Cookie's basket. "But I have to say, you're right about Rain and Finn. There's something shifty about those two."

Chapter 18

Finn scrubbed his hands over his face, soaping his beard and washing the dirt, sweat, and sea breeze from his tension riddled body. He couldn't believe he'd sniffed Ava like some hungry predator. Like he wanted to run his hands over her body, lick every inch of her creamy skin, and bury his nose in her soft, luscious hair. Against her toned belly. Deep in her hot core. His wolf had relished it, but the man—

"*Fuck!*" He slammed his fists against the tiled wall. His hard, throbbing cock ached for release as even his human side couldn't deny she'd smelled like heated promises and forever. He'd never realized how much he liked strawberries until he'd caught the scent on her, the sweetness mixing with the salty sweat from the workout their emergency call had clearly interrupted. His wolf prickled at his skin, desperate to claim her.

But Ava was not his to claim or keep, to control or fuck. She wasn't his unless she wanted to be and even though she had barely stopped ogling his body tonight, Finn was no fool. Looks were shallow and attraction was meaningless unless a deeper connection could be formed. Fate might have bonded them, but it took more than the magnetic pull of their mating bond to seal the deal. Ava needed to feel it too, to want him, and to accept their fate. She needed to open her heart and embrace love.

But she didn't even want to go snorkeling with him. And why? Because Blair had hurt her and tainted her trust in men.

Finn slammed his fists against the wall again and thumped his forehead for good measure. "Fucking bastard."

His brother would pay for what he'd done to Ava. Finn would make sure of it. But until he was ready to come out of hiding, Finn had to focus. On Ava, and on Sly.

Drawing away from the wall, he rinsed his hair and turned his thoughts to the earlier perk of the evening. He had pack bonded. The Alpha had welcomed him, and his sense of belonging had solidified. The landscape seemed brighter, hope filled his belly, and he was within reaching distance of every-thing he'd ever wanted.

Though he was concerned about his lack of pack stripes. A wolf wasn't truly accepted until he'd been marked with stripes that matched the Alpha's fur. But surely the oversight was down to poor timing. Finn was confident that Sly would take care of his initiation at a more suitable moment, so he finished washing, then shut off the taps. He dried off, pulled on his black boxers, and strode out of the bathroom. Gracie Belle lifted her head from where she lay stretched out in the middle of the polished wooden floor.

"Why don't you sleep in your bed?"

She dropped her head and shifted onto her side, stretching out her little legs. Finn resisted a chuckle as he snatched a bottle of water from the fridge. Yeah, sometimes a smooth, hard surface was just the ticket, but as a man, he preferred a bed. So, he flopped onto the mattress, settled the pillows behind his back, and grabbed his iPad from the bedside table. He'd read plenty of local history and geology this week, but if he wanted to persuade Ava to go snorkeling with him, then he better brush up on the Magnetic Island shipwrecks. He'd already read about the *SS City of Adelaide* and the *George Rennie*, but there were twenty-three wrecks around the island, most within the intertidal zone having run aground or sunk on the reef. The Maritime Museum in Townsville had created a shipwreck trail that circled the island with buoys marking the location of the wrecks and information boards on land for those who didn't want to get wet. Since boats had plied between the mainland and island for over a hundred years, the maritime landscape reflected upon a history that he was keen to explore and learn more about. Not just on Magnetic Island, but hopefully he could join Nate on a day trip to dive the *Yongala* sometime. Over a hundred lives had been lost when the ship had sunk during a cyclone in 1911, and the wreck had become one of the world's most famous dive sites since being discovered in 1958.

But that adventure would need to wait for another day, after Sly was saved and the Unfated were defeated.

In the meantime, Finn concentrated on learning all he could about the Magnetic Island shipwrecks as his need for discovery was an ache he'd never been able to shake. Nor would he want to as it was one trait he shared with his mother.

Heart clenching, Finn recalled the time he'd spent exploring the West Australian coast littered by the debris of the ill-fated Dutch East India Company ships with the stories his mother had told him echoing inside his head. He'd always begged for more knowledge, more tales of the unforgiving ocean and the brave, fearless men who'd sailed the seas when she'd put him to bed all those warm, cozy nights. The nights they had been happy, just the two of them.

Until his father had destroyed his childhood and tried to turn him into a monster.

Finn ran his hand down his scruffy face. Fuck, what if Ava rejected him? Failed to fall for him or accept him as the man he truly was? What if he turned out exactly like his father? This possessive need inside him to keep her close and protect her overwhelmed every one of his senses. If he had to, would he be able to let her go?

"*Pffft.*"

Finn dropped his hands and glanced down to where Gracie tapped her front paws on the wooden floor. But as he went to pick her up, she scampered out of his reach. He sighed. "Do you want up or not?"

She tentatively stepped towards him, and he scooped his hand under her belly. Bloody loopy dog. Placing her on the mattress beside him, Finn shook his head. Gracie sat, sneezed, and tilted her head, her long black ears twitching.

"What?" The doubt inside him eased as her tail thumped against the mattress. Grinning, he rubbed her head. "What is it, G.B?"

She moved towards him and pressed her snout against his cheek. Then huffed again.

"Yes, I know I need to shave. You need a tidy up, too. You're getting scruffy again."

Although he preferred her scruffy. Her mum used to take her to the groomers every few weeks and she'd return home with a long fluffy tail and short body hair with her ears and face trimmed to look like a neat, pretty little girl. One time, she'd even had bows in her ears, but Gracie had quickly pawed those out. Bows and clothes were one of the many things Gracie Belle would not tolerate, and Finn didn't blame her. He thought her cuter when her hair was long and curly as it gave her a wilder, wolfier look.

Though given her breed, she needed regular grooming, so he'd clip her feet and backside, trim around her eyes and chin, and brush her ears whenever she needed a touch up. She didn't like it, but despite what she might think, she was not the Alpha of their little pack.

She was, however, his confidant.

"What do you think, G.B?" He scratched her back. "Do you think it's worth trying this thing with Ava?"

Mating still terrified him, but if he waded in and found trust, comfort, and mutual respect with Ava, then their bond would grow, his fear would subside, and they'd solidify the strength that his goddess had destined them to have.

But before he did anything, he needed to make himself a little more presentable. Even he thought himself wild and fierce with the inch long hair around his face, and it was far too hot in North Queensland to sport such a look.

Tossing his legs off the bed, Finn jumped to his feet and strode into the bathroom. Grabbing his electric razor, he slid on his preferred clippers and began shaving. Hair fell into the sink and within minutes, he looked more like his normal, trimmed self with short whiskers along his jaw and a groomed, circle-style beard around his mouth.

He walked back into the room and Gracie thumped her tail in approval.

"Feels better too," he said before grabbing a band and tying back his hair. That was something he preferred to hang to his shoulders, and he didn't care what anyone else thought. Besides, women liked it these days after some of the latest blockbusters had made long hair sexy again.

Feeling refreshed, he lay back on the bed, picked up the iPad, and opened his email to find the many notes Rain had forwarded him. Finn had worked for many people while moving from place to place, but this past week at Luna Views had been the first time he found something he truly enjoyed. Taking tourists out on the boat was fucking awesome, and he got along well with the young scouts, too.

Was that why Sly had welcomed him?

Frowning, Finn opened the document on the shipwrecks. He wasn't sure. But during that moment in the bush, Finn had sensed Sly's turmoil. His pain and agony. And the Alpha's respect.

Finn would help him. They'd bring him back, restore the pack, and end Tyrone's power in the region. His father and Blair had already taken so much from him, Finn wouldn't allow those bastards to take his pack too.

Chapter 19

Finn started his day with a brisk run to exercise his human form and alleviate the heated tension coursing through his body. Seashells cracked beneath his bare feet while weeds squelched between his toes. Any sane man would have worn shoes, but what tosser wore shoes on a beach as picturesque as Nelly Bay?

Clear water lapped at his feet as he pounded along the sand. His chest heaved with effort, but his breathing didn't labor. Fitness had always been a core part of Finn's soul. He'd been building and maintaining his strength and stamina since the day his father had dragged him off Flinders Island and the ability to run had been vital to his survival. As well as the ability to fight to keep Blair off his back and put the bastard down when he'd needed to.

Blair might have been older and meaner, but Finn would always be more powerful with strength enhanced by the Moon Goddess. Finn had knocked him out a few times and despite the punishment he endured from Tyrone, every moment had been worth it.

He reached the breakwater that protected the marina at the northern end of the beach, then turned and jogged back to

Luna Views. Estimating the foreshore was about a kilometer, Finn completed a dozen laps before climbing the stairs onto the deck and strolling back to his hut. He took Gracie out to use the garden facilities, then settled her inside to enjoy the cool breeze through the open veranda doors while he hit the shower.

He let the warm water wash over his body and lifted his face to the spray. He had jet boat rides to conduct this afternoon but until then, Finn was a free man, and he couldn't continue to ignore the ache burning deep inside his gut. Ava called to him, and after last night, he was desperate to learn more about her. He wanted to see her again, see her smile, and revel in her scent. But most of all, he wanted to gain her trust. And though diverting his attention from his mission to save Sly pissed him off, he couldn't ignore Fate's call. He wouldn't have found himself tasked with completing a mating bond if he wasn't ready for it. Right?

Cursing, he switched off the shower, sprayed on deodorant, and dressed in his best jeans and a white T-shirt. He brushed his hair, pulled it back with a black band, then grunted as he tied on a pair of sneakers.

"I'll bring you next time, G.B." He rubbed her head, then stood. "But I don't think dogs are allowed at the Koala Hospital."

Gracie didn't seem fazed as she curled up in her snuggle bed. Strolling through the resort, Finn's wolf preened and ignored the dread itching up his spine. Good sense told him he should stay away from Ava. She'd hesitated at his invitation to go snorkeling and would have turned him down if Rain hadn't interrupted them. Only a week had passed since Blair had hurt her and she wasn't ready to move on. Finn understood that.

"Where are you headed?"

Finn turned to find Rain behind the reception desk. There

was no accusation or question in his tone, only a gentle tease to match the gleam in his pale eyes.

"Nowhere."

Rain folded his arms. "You feel the pull, don't you? Of the bond?"

"No. I'm just ... going for coffee."

"And to check on Cookie?"

"She had a fright last night. We bonded."

Rain chuckled. "Right. Well, if you want to woo a certain blonde, I'd suggest grabbing coffee for the vet crew at Café Nourish. They're big on soy milk at the hospital."

"Thanks for the tip."

"Any time, man."

Turning his back on the cheeky devil, Finn strode out of the hotel, jumped into the Jeep, and took off into Nelly Bay. Wind blew through his hair as he rested his elbow on the door and glanced out at the still, aquamarine water. No wonder Sly and Rain had ached to claim this territory. With its dense national park and hidden bays, it was the perfect place for a wolf. He would be happy to call the island home and protect it with his life.

A vow that ventured his thoughts to last night as he maneuvered the Jeep into Horseshoe Bay. He didn't know what the bat shifters were up to or why one had hurt a koala, but he'd kill them himself if Cookie's mum hadn't survived the night. Hopefully Ava and Eden had given her a name, a strong one to help her fight. Arti, maybe? After Artemis, the Greek Goddess of the Hunt? Of the Moon? Was that going too far?

Maybe.

He arrived on the esplanade where cafes, restaurants, and multilevel holiday units overlooked the beach, parked the Jeep, and strode into Café Nourish. Even if the ladies didn't drink coffee, he hoped the gesture would show Ava he wasn't a dominant alpha male who acted purely on his animal instincts.

He took Rain's advice, ordered half a dozen cappuccinos on soy milk, unsure how many volunteers would be at the hospital, took his own on regular milk, then jumped back into the Jeep.

As he approached the hospital, his pulse settled into a steady, even beat.

Ava was there.

Balancing the tray of coffees in one hand, Finn set his shoulders and strode inside. A young man greeted him at reception.

"Morning. I'm looking for Ava."

"Ahh ..." Seeming unsure, he glanced behind him into the office. "Hey, is Ava here?"

Finn's jaw clenched. Yes, she was there. He could smell her.

"Who's—" Eden poked her head out of the office and spotting Finn, broke into a glittering grin. "Hel-*lo*, Finn."

Fuck, Rain was one lucky dude. And fucking crazy for resisting such a beauty with her tumble of chocolatey hair, big dark eyes, and a long, willowy body.

"Morning, Eden. I brought you all coffee." He placed the tray on the reception desk and slipped his hands into his pockets as nerves scurried up his spine. For fuck's sake, he could do this. "Rain said to get soy cappuccinos, and I wasn't sure how many people would be here."

Eden accepted a cup. "That's very thoughtful, Finn. Thank you. It has been a long night, but both Cookie and Xena are doing well."

Finn resisted a cringe. "Xena?"

"Ava thought she needed a warrior name, so what better than the Warrior Princess?"

Many, but he wouldn't say that. If that's what Ava wanted

to name the koala, then he was sure it suited Cookie's mum. "Fair enough."

Eden nodded at the coffees. "You can take one to her, if you like? She's in ICU room two, just down the corridor."

Finn's throat tightened at the twinkle in Eden's eye. Bloody hell, was he that obvious?

He picked up his coffee and took one of the soy cappuccinos for Ava. "Thanks."

Anxiety rippled through him as he strode down the corridor, his wolf clawing at his ribs to escape. But the man remained in control as he straightened his spine, found the ICU room, and peered through the window in the door. Ava knelt on the floor, her shoulder to him as she bent over the koala resting on a pillow.

Taking a deep breath, he entered the room. Ava glanced up, then straightened with a jolt. "Finn."

She had changed her clothes since last night, but still wore a pair of tight-fitting yoga pants that hugged her thighs to her knees. A pale pink T-shirt covered her creamy shoulders that he'd resisted kissing last night, and his wolf grinned. The color suited her.

"I brought you coffee." He held out the cup. "Soy cappuccino, I was told."

"Thank you." She reached up to accept the cup, then settled back on her bum, crossing her legs in front of her. "It was one hell of an evening."

"You stay here all night?"

Her ponytail swished as she shook her head. "Dee grabbed us dinner, then Eden and I stayed until ten. Dee monitored Xena until Eden and I returned at dawn. It's been a busy morning with the other patients, though."

Finn looked at the immobile koala slumped over the pillow. "Do you have a lot of patients at the moment?"

"Yeah. Marco had surgery a fortnight ago and is in rehab.

Reggie fell out of a tree this week and needs close monitoring, though he's essentially okay. Tammy's still recovering from her green ant attack, and we've got a few joeys in, too. Thank God Eden's got days off and is staying until Wednesday as it's been hectic."

Sure sounded like it. "And how's Xena?"

Sighing, Ava stroked the koala's back. "She's all right. Just needs plenty of rest and help with her lungs while she recovers."

Finn sipped his coffee. "What's wrong with her lungs?"

"Well, everyone needs help with their lungs after surgery, but the koalas on the island all suffer from KIDS. It's the koala equivalent to human AIDS and makes them more susceptible to infections."

Wincing, Finn ran his hand down his beard. "Shit. That sucks."

"Yep."

"How did she get that?"

"We're not sure, but losing your home and habitat causes a lot of stress. The landscape's changed, the soil and trees have changed, and koalas don't have the same home they did three hundred years ago."

Wasn't that the truth? The animal inside Finn raged for the poor creatures as he tossed back a gulp of coffee, then sat across from Ava by Xena's side. Only then did he notice the koala was awake, looking at him with exhausted dark eyes. "Humans for you, hey?"

Ava nodded and placed her coffee on the floor beside her. "Eden does the best she can to keep the koalas healthy and to maintain the natural landscape. The biggest problem we have is dogs. And whatever it was that bit Xena."

"Hmm ..." Finn placed his coffee beside Ava's and rested his forearm on his bended knee. "So, what are you doing with her?"

"Mobilization. She needs to remain strong so she can return home, but she's tired and weak, so I'm taking her joints through passive range of movement."

She lifted Xena's back leg and gently moved the limb in a natural pattern.

Finn's lips twitched. "You're good at that."

"I've had plenty of practice."

A memory niggled at the back of his mind. Hadn't Eden said ... "You're a physio, right?"

She lowered Xena's leg. "Yeah."

"And you work on koalas?"

She stifled a laugh and heat flared in his cheeks as his wolf facepalmed.

"Not exclusively, but I had a lot of leave accumulated and work told me I had to take it."

"So, you came to help Eden?"

"It wasn't the original plan," she muttered as she leaned over Xena and moved her other leg. "But I'm happier being here than with that ... well ... I enjoy helping the koalas."

She pressed her hand against Xena's foot, then lowered it back onto the towel. Xena's ears twitched.

"She liked that."

"Movement is medicine even when you don't have the energy to do it yourself. So yes, she should like it. It'll improve her circulation and therefore speed up her recovery. Soon, she'll be up on this tree branch." Ava placed her hand on the crossbeam that currently sat on the floor. "When she starts feeding, we can move her outdoors until she recovers."

"Sounds like Xena's in good hands."

Ava smiled and lifted her coffee. "Eden's fantastic."

"I meant you."

She stilled, then took a long sip, her gaze fixed on Xena. "I like what I do."

"And what do you normally do when you're not rehabilitating koalas?"

"I work in acute rehab at the hospital, keeping people mobile and getting them up after surgery."

"Like joint surgery?"

"Sometimes, but any surgery, really. Or acute illness. I work mainly on the cardiac ward, so they might have just had heart surgery or been hospitalized for heart failure or a respiratory illness."

Finn cocked his eyebrow. "That's impressive."

Ava shrugged. "It's my job. People need help to get back on their feet after surgery, especially bypass, and they need the confidence to do so. That's all I do, and that's all I'm going to do for Xena, too. Now, I'm going to help her sit up and put some weight through her bum, then we'll leave her to rest."

Finn shuffled out of the way as Ava maneuvered around the basket, shifted Xena's IVs, and slipped her hands under the koala's armpits. Xena blinked sleepily as Ava sat her up, exposing her white belly and the shaved area around her shoulder.

Finn's teeth cracked. Bloody bat shifters. What the fuck had they been doing on the island and why the hell were they roosting in Townsville?

"Look at you, girl!" Ava's cheerful praise drew Finn from his thoughts. "How does that feel?"

Xena made a yawny sound, her claws trying to clutch at each other as Ava held her up.

"Just a little longer, darling. Then I'll go check on your baby. She's doing very well."

Xena's head drooped, and Ava laid her down gently. She drew a blanket over the top of the basket, covering but not touching Xena.

"We'll let her rest." Ava grabbed her coffee and stood. Finn followed her to his feet and into the corridor.

Chapter 20

va ignored her thumping heart and focused on the job at hand as she led Finn down the hallway. She hadn't been able to get the man out of her head all night. Her first evening on the island had been bad enough with images of his glistening torso and bulging biceps maneuvering the jet ski keeping her awake all night. As she'd fantasied about licking the salty water off his ridiculously defined abs, raw, uncontained desire had successfully shoved aside most of her fears about Blair.

Then he'd snubbed her at West Point and her fantasies had vanished. Until last night when Finn had stridden into the hospital with his wild hair, dirt-smeared forearms, and Cookie nestled against his golden chest hair. Ava wasn't a fool. She knew where her attraction stemmed from. The man was fucking hot. Sinfully so. The fact he'd shaved only ignited her cravings as while she'd liked the untamed scruff he'd sported last night, his neat, circular beard and trimmed cheek lines did wonders to highlight his full, kissable lips. Lips made to pleasure a woman. And she longed to know how it would feel to have his gorgeous face nestled between her thighs, his stubble brushing against her sensitive flesh as he licked her, sucked her, and made her cry out his name.

Ava downed the last of her coffee. "Cookie's down here. She's a cheeky little thing but is stressed being away from her mum."

"A baby shouldn't be taken from its mum too early," he said, a slight crack rippling through his deep voice.

"That's true. But we're supplementing her feeds, and we'll get her to try climbing as that's what Xena would be teaching her to do."

Ava pushed open the door and Cookie's ears twitched as she peeked up from her towel-lined basket. Her long claws gripped the plush koala as she opened her mouth and released a mix between a squeak and a cry. Ava lifted the basket from the floor onto the table, and Finn reached out to scratch the joey behind her ears. Damn, his hands were as big as the koala.

"How'd you go last night, little one?"

Cookie tilted her head, watching him as he continued to scratch, and Finn's face broke into a wide smile. Ava turned her back, her breath catching as she opened the small fridge and gathered Cookie's nutrient. She needed to get a grip. Finn didn't seem half as standoffish today as he had after falling off the jet ski, and he'd been genuinely worried about Cookie last night. Ava shouldn't have been surprised that he'd come to check on the joey. Perhaps she had misjudged him? It said a lot about a man when he cared about wildlife. Finn might have all the appearance of a badass, but Ava couldn't deny that there was a heart inside that sculptable chest of his. Cookie had sensed it and now, she did too.

She drew the milky liquid into the syringe, then offered it to Finn. "Do you want to feed her?"

"Really?" She nodded, and his ridiculous smile widened. "Thanks."

Her knees weakened and she sank against the cabinets.

"Just be gentle," she instructed as Finn slipped the tip between Cookie's tiny lips and slowly pushed the plunger like a pro. Cookie's claw wrapped around the base of his thumb as she drank like any hungry baby.

His eyes lit up. "She sure does like it."

He emptied the syringe and Ava held out the cup of formula. "She needs two more doses."

He refilled the syringe and continued to feed Cookie. After the third lot, Ava handed him a towel. "Dry her mouth off."

The baby koala opened and closed her lips as Finn wiped around her mouth, his hands slow and gentle. Cookie released another little squeak as he placed the towel down.

He glanced at Ava. "What now?"

"We place her back on the floor so that she can't hurt herself if she climbs out," she said, swallowing the lump in her throat as Finn lifted the basket and placed Cookie down. "Paula will be by to collect her shortly."

"When does she get to practice climbing?"

"Paula will have a small tree for her. It's more like a sturdy branch in a pot, but I'll get her to bring Cookie in for practice during the week. Right now, we want her to rest in case she did fall last night."

Finn nodded as he offered Cookie the gum leaves. "I think you should be eating these yum yums."

Ava's pelvic floor drew up tight as heat flushed through her core. "Yeah, she doesn't seem to like those leaves. We might need to swap them out for another type."

Finn's thighs strained against his jeans as he stood. "How many types are there?"

"Hundreds, but koalas can only tolerate those from their natural habitat. She has red gum and white gum there, but she hasn't fancied either. I think she's just stressed, but if we can't identify a leaf she likes soon—" Ava's eyes snapped to his. "Do you know what tree you found her in?"

"No. But I can find out."

"Eden didn't want to ask since you accessed the area by boat, but if you can find out, that would help Cookie a lot."

He nodded. "Leave it with me."

"Thank you, Finn." Ava hid her smile as she reached down and plucked the leaves from the basket. "These are getting dry though, so let's swap them out and see if we can tempt her."

They left the treatment room, strode past ICU, and out into the yard where Ava opened the large shipping container that housed their freshly cut eucalypts.

"Shit, that's a lot of food. Where do you get it all from?"

"We have a conservation site where we've planted many types of eucalypts to harvest for the koalas in care," she explained, stepping inside the container where the coolers and irrigation system kept the cut leaves cool and moist. "Bob and Jimmy are our volunteer leaf cutters and one of them is out here every morning replenishing the stock as needed."

"I guess a lot of work goes into an organization like this."

"Yes, there are a lot of things to consider." Ava selected a clump of leaves. "This gum is abundant at West Point, so we'll see if she likes it."

They returned to the consult room where they found Cookie asleep in her basket with her head snuggled against the plush koala. Ava smiled, doubting she'd ever get past the cuteness of the koala as she placed the gum leaves down, and they left the joey to nap.

Ava turned to Finn in the hallway. "I'm heading to the Forts now as Eden wants me to check on some koalas up there. So ... thanks for the coffee. I'm sure—"

"Can I come?"

Ava blinked. Shit. She'd been hoping to escape his wild manliness, not go trudging around the bush with him sniffing at her heels. "Ahh ... I'm just going to be walking around. It's nothing exciting. And don't you have to work?"

"Not for a few hours." His lips quirked as he angled his body closer to hers, the scent of salt, sand, and earth swirling dangerously inside her head. "I like talking to you, Ava. And I haven't been to the Forts, so if you wouldn't mind ..."

Her breath hitched. Shit, this wasn't good. The attraction she'd tried to subdue rose and tugged at her belly, drawing her towards him. The urge to press herself close, wrap her arms around him and sample a taste of his wicked smile was almost too strong to resist.

But while part of her managed, the other uncontrollable part of her brain overpowered her better judgement as she shook her head and said, "No. I don't mind."

But she did mind. She minded a lot.

As though he could tell exactly what she was thinking, his wicked mouth stretched into a grin. "Good. So, what do we need to do up there?"

"We just need to find them and see if they're okay, but I hope you have your good walking shoes on." Thankfully, he wore runners today unlike last night and his curiously bare feet. "The Forts is not an easy walk."

Finn shrugged, his T-shirt catching at his pecs. "I used to roam the wilderness of Tasmania, Ava. Magnetic Island has nothing on it."

"I'll have to trust you there."

He quirked his eyebrow. "You've never been to Tassie?"

"Nope. Let's check in with Eden, then we'll go."

They found her friend in the treatment room checking on Tammy's green ant wounds. "All good, Ava?"

"Xena and Cookie are sleeping. I'm going to the Forts now and am taking Finn."

Eden's smile was far too pleased. "Are you now? All right, then. Have fun."

Finn chuckled and Ava's hand tightened around the door handle. "Is there anything in particular you want me to check on while we're up there?"

"Yes, Hallie has a joey. It should be seven months old, so can you see if it's peeking out of the pouch yet? Gumnut and Prickles I released a month ago, so please check that they look healthy."

Ava nodded. "Can do."

She closed the door before her friend could offer any more remarks to match the tease in her eyes. Though any remark would be justified as Ava glanced up at Finn and lost the instinctive ability to breathe.

"Let's go, then."

Finn beat her to the front door and held it open, gesturing for her to precede him.

Ava's belly fluttered. "Thank you."

He lowered his sunglasses over his eyes, adding to his delicious rebel appeal as he twirled the car keys around his finger. "Let's take my Jeep."

"But I—" She eyed her topless Mini, then Finn as he strode towards the bigger, bulkier Jeep Wrangler. Yeah, he'd be squished in the Mini.

She followed him, blinking as he opened the passenger door and held his hand out for hers. What the hell? Was chivalry not dead where he'd come from?

But Ava didn't comment, choosing to go with the flow as she placed her hand in his. Fire coursed through her veins and then, she could barely speak at all. "Th-thanks."

He nodded and closed the door with a thunk. Ava reached for the seatbelt as Finn climbed in behind the wheel. Tossing his brawny arm over her backrest, he turned to look behind them as he reversed out of the park.

She drew in a breath, then let it out slowly. Not that it helped much. He smelled dirty and delicious.

"So ... how come you haven't been to the Forts?"

"I've been busy."

"Oh." He had been settling into a new job, after all. "This your first trip to the island?"

"Yep. First trip to North Queensland."

"How are you liking it?"

He smirked, blond hair that had escaped his ponytail whipping over his dark sunglasses. "It's warm. But the island's nice and I'm keen to see a bit of the reef."

"The reef is beautiful, but like everything else, it's dying off, too."

Finn's lips twisted, and Ava agreed. It was tragic.

He pulled into the Forts car park and cut the engine. Ava unclipped her seatbelt but didn't move as she opened the GPS app on her phone. "Let's just check where the koalas are ..." She spread her fingers over the screen to zoom in, tapping on the first green dot along the track. "There's Tommy."

Finn appeared at her side, opening her door. "Is he easy to find?"

"Should be." She accepted his hand and hopped down from the Jeep. If he offered her an excuse to touch him, she would take it, though she couldn't explain why. "We've tagged all the koalas we've released and have a few living around the Forts as it's one of their favorite habitats. And it's a lovely walk."

"I'll follow you, then."

He gestured for her to take the lead but remained by her side as they ventured along the path. The beginning of the walk consisted of mainly flat terrain, but steeper hills, steps, and narrow tracks would feature further along the path. Ava eyed Finn as he strolled leisurely beside her, his blond jaw twitching as he observed his surroundings and shoulders stretching his T-shirt as he lifted his hand to shield his eyes.

Gut clenching, she turned her attention to the trees and swallowed hard.

She hadn't found herself this curious about a man in years. If ever. She might have dated, but it had never been serious. Especially since most of the men she'd gone out with turned out to be alpha, dominant jerks, Blair the worst of them all.

But while Finn appeared to possess some kind of dominance, something told her he was different. And maybe if she got to know him better, this strange need growing inside her might ease.

Ha. As if.

"So, where were you living before you came here?"

"I was in Freycinet Bay. In Tasmania."

"Do you miss it?"

"Not really. I move around a lot."

"So, you don't have an actual home?"

"Not since I left Flinders Island."

"Where's that?"

"In the Bass Strait." Finn's jaw hardened beneath his blond bristles, his gaze glued to the trees. "It's very remote, mostly bush, and has a population of a few hundred people."

"Sounds peaceful. Are your parents still there or ..." Ava trailed off, sensing rather than seeing the pain in his eyes.

"No. My mother was killed when I was ten."

Ava glanced at her feet as an ache speared through her chest. Killed. Not died or passed away. "I'm sorry, Finn."

"Not your fault," he muttered. "And I have nothing to do with my father, so no. I have no family."

Ava's heart sank further. She might not see her family often, but her parents and two brothers were alive and only a short drive away. She could visit them any time she wanted and couldn't imagine them not being there.

"Must be lonely," she whispered. "Who do you spend Christmas with?"

"I don't celebrate Christmas."

"Really? Who doesn't—" Ava shut up before she put her foot in it any further. Many people didn't celebrate Christmas. "Oh. Sorry."

"It's not that I'm not a Christian. I'm not, but it's just another day. Same as birthdays and other holidays. I usually let the day pass by."

What a sad, lonely life he must live. Did he not have anyone to turn to?

"At least you have your friends," she said, trying to think positively. "Like Rain."

Finn's mouth quirked. "Yeah. I have Rain."

"Friends can be the family you choose." She studied the GPS as they continued along the path. "There should be a koala up ahead."

They paused at the site of the green dot and searched the surrounding trees. It took her a few seconds as she twisted and turned, then Ava spotted the ball of gray fur curled up in a branch. Smiling, she elbowed Finn lightly and pointed. "Do you see him?"

"Yeah. I—" Finn stilled, the tension she'd sensed in him earlier radiating from his skin tenfold.

"What is it?"

Finn's throat worked as he swallowed. "Bat."

"A bat? Where?" Then she saw it, the black triangular animal dangling from a branch near the koala. "Oh. I see." Her gaze shifted to Finn. "You don't like bats?"

"Not particularly."

Resisting a sigh, Ava opened the koala's file in the tracker and typed in a brief note about their sighting. "First of all, they're flying foxes. Not bats. And while I know they haven't been welcome in the cities, they're just animals trying to find their place in this changing world."

Finn growled. He actually growled, causing Ava to peek

up from her phone. And even though she couldn't see his eyes past his sunglasses, she sensed his anger.

"That might be true of flying foxes, but ..."

She waited for him to continue as he glared at the flying fox, fists clenching.

When he didn't elaborate, Ava finished typing the note. "It's one bat, Finn. I doubt it'll cause any harm. Now, we still need to find Hallie, Gumnut, and Prickles. Tommy here seems to be doing just fine."

Chapter 21

Finn followed Ava up the rocky steps towards the sign that read "The Forts Circuit." Noting the distance, he swore under his breath. Eight hundred meters? Of course, that was nothing. But the further they ventured into the bush, the more concerned Finn grew about the bat shifter.

Fucking slimy asshole. He'd been enjoying his time with Ava, relishing in her smile and her passion for koalas. She was a remarkable woman and after rescuing Cookie, he was beginning to feel a connection with the endangered marsupials and wanted to help the joey and her packmates any way he could.

Turning right at the sign, Ava paused and surveyed the tree, shielding her pretty eyes with her hand. "There's Prickles! Aww, he looks so happy."

Prickles sat nestled in the V of a gum tree munching on some leaves so yeah, he looked like a happy koala. Finn smiled softly, then scowled as he spotted the bat shifter swinging from a branch in a nearby tree. His spine prickled. Wolf snarled. The fucking bat better leave Prickles alone. It or a member of its coven had already hurt Xena and almost orphaned Cookie.

But while he didn't want a koala massacre on his hands, it wasn't what worried Finn the most. The bats were in cahoots with Tyrone. And therefore, Blair.

Had this bat been sent to spy on Ava?

Finn's chest expanded until he all but howled with rage, resisting the urge to shift, leap up the tree, and kill the bat with one smooth bite. Inhaling, he smelled the asshole's glee mixed with its disgusting odor. The bloody creature almost cackled with it.

Ava lowered her phone after making a note and taking photos of Prickles. "Come on, the first bunker is up this way."

As she moved on, Finn glared at the bat and bared his teeth. He'd get the little fucker. But first, he needed to make it through the rest of this walk and sure enough, they soon came across an old brick bunker. Or a powder keg, as the sign described it.

"This was the reserve magazine," Ava said, studying the sign. "They'd carry the ammo up here. Forty-three kilos each." She whistled. "Screw that. But look!" She pointed and Finn leaned over her shoulder, the strawberry scent of her hair making his head spin as he glared at the drawing of a bat. "'*Today the store serves a more peaceful purpose, providing a cool dark daytime roost for northern broad-nosed bats. On occasions, clusters of about two-hundred babies of this microbat species huddle here as a creche while the adults fly out at dusk to feast on midges and mosquitos. The rough cement walls also make a good base for mud wasps to build their nests.*' See Finn?" She turned her head, blonde ponytail whipping over her shoulder. "Nothing to worry about. The bats live here."

Her smile floored him, her eyes gleaming with satisfaction of proving him wrong. Finn's jaw tightened. How he wished she was right and that the bats who lived on Magnetic Island were only the broad-nosed variety and not blood sucking demons from Hell.

But as his gaze dropped to her beautiful pink mouth, he vowed he wouldn't let the bat harm her. He'd shield her body with his if it came to it.

Ava's smile faltered and realizing he'd moved closer and risked penetrating her personal bubble, Finn cleared his throat and stepped back. "I'm sure it's a nice home for bats."

"I wonder if there are any babies in there?" She lifted her foot onto the step, but Finn grabbed her arm.

"Let's not disturb them."

This time, Ava's smile was far too teasing. "Aww, are you scared of the itty bitty bats?"

His spine tensed. "No."

"Then, come on."

She leapt up the few steps into the open entry of the bunker. Exhaling, Finn followed. He wasn't scared of the bloody bats and wouldn't want her thinking otherwise. But like hell was he going to let her go in there alone.

Thankfully, they found nothing but a dark, empty bunker and with Ava's curiosity satisfied, returned to the path. They located another koala on the GPS, then arrived at the old gun emplacement, a concrete circular depression where guns would have been placed to fire at any attempt of invasion by the Japanese during the war. It certainly was an advantageous location as the view was magnificent. They read the sign telling them that within a week of the Japanese Armistice Day the guns had disappeared, never to be found.

"I wouldn't say I'm particularly interested in World War Two history," Ava said as they strode around the perimeter of the sunken circle. "But I do think the Forts are pretty cool."

"I can see why they're a popular attraction," Finn said, standing beside her as they admired the view over the dense bushland and clear blue water. "Interested in war history or not, the views are spectacular."

"Breathtaking. This is what I love most about the island. The hikes and views."

Finn watched her as she brushed away the hair blowing in her face. "The hikes are pretty excellent," he agreed, having done a few of them himself. "Maybe later in the week, we could go on another?"

She flicked him a glance. "Maybe. But right now, we need to find Hallie, and there's another gun circle with a better view." She hurried away. "Come on."

The bat shifter glided out of the tree, practically cackling. Finn snarled and followed Ava back up the path. Tension niggled at his spine and his wolf prowled restlessly inside him, but Finn couldn't deny that he was enjoying himself.

Ava paused on the goat track steps and examined at her phone. "Gumnut's around here somewhere."

Finn peered into the scrub. Unable to see past the canopy of trees, he stepped off the path and clambered up some rocks. He sniffed, turned, then spotted the ball of gray. "There he is."

"You see him?" Ava's shoe squeaked as she slipped on the boulder and grabbed a branch.

"Careful!" He bent and extended his hand. "Here. Let me."

Ava steadied herself on the tree, then accepted his help. His hand closed around her tiny fingers as she stepped one foot up onto the rock.

"You good?"

She nodded and he hoisted her up beside him. Ava released her grip and while his wolf grumbled at the thought of letting go, the gentleman inside him won. Slipping his hands into his pockets, Finn observed Gumnut.

"He looks sleepy."

"But healthy. His fur is thick and he seems to have good muscle tone."

He wasn't sure how she could tell, but Ava was the expert. As she made notes in the app, Finn leapt off the boulder. The gravel slipped beneath his feet, but he took it in his stride as he turned to wait for Ava. Her thumbs raced over the screen, then she slipped her phone into her pocket and crouched.

"I've got you." He reached for her waist and her hands fell to his shoulders without hesitation. Finn's pulse spiked, his gut clenching as he pressed his fingers into the taut muscles of her back. Heat corded through his forearms, driving the urge to pull her against his body and ravish her beautiful, plump lips.

But he couldn't. He wouldn't. Yet every time they touched, the hesitation in her eyes grew dimmer and dimmer and hope bloomed in Finn's chest.

Lifting her off the ledge, he turned and placed her on her feet. Ava's grip loosened on his shoulders as she brushed her fingers down the front of his T-shirt.

Finn shivered.

"Thank you," she whispered.

He nodded, words escaping him as he let her go and she stumbled through the scrub back onto the path. They walked the final meters to the gun emplacement in silence, emerging from the trees to another sunken concrete circle that offered uninterrupted views of the dense bush below and the headland that separated them from the endless stretch of deep blue ocean.

He and Ava stepped up onto the boulders and marveled at the sight, the cool wind blowing in their hair. He wondered if the pack ever celebrated the full moon here as it would be a delightful place to stand and bask in the Goddess's glory as she rose over the glittering ocean.

"Wow."

"Beautiful, isn't it?"

"Yep. Almost as good as hiking the Great Ocean Road. There's nothing like a good walk."

"I thought you were more the watersports type?"

"I am," he said, flashing her a grin as they turned their backs on the view and rounded the concrete circle back to the track. "But that doesn't mean I don't like hitting the trails."

"You like jet skiing more though, I bet."

"Of course." He couldn't deny that.

"I guess they look like fun."

"You've never been?"

She shook her head as she preceded him down the steps. "No, but last time my brother visited, we did rent standup paddleboards."

"I'll have to take you, then."

She glanced over her shoulder. "Promise I won't fall off?"

Her teasing smile knocked the wind out of him, the flirtation in her eyes making his cock twitch and wolf stand on its hind legs in a celebratory howl. Hell yes, he wanted to take her on the jet ski. To show off and hear her laughter or screams of pleasure as he sped and spun them across the ocean.

Her screams of pleasure as he relished her beautiful mouth and plunged inside her.

Finn gritted his teeth. "I promise."

But again, she made no commitment to do so as they returned to the main path. Ava studied her phone.

"Does that tell you where Hallie is?"

"Yeah. She's near the command post."

They explored the signal station, then approached the command post. At three stories tall, it was easily the largest fort with stairs that led up to the modern steel railing rooftop. But first, they needed to locate Hallie.

After glancing through the trees, Finn spotted the koala munching on leaves while a little head peeked out of the pouch low in her belly.

"Wow," Ava breathed. "Aren't they beautiful?"

"Sure is pretty cool." Koalas living independently in the wild and enjoying their natural food in a safe habitat. Exactly what Xena and Cookie would have been doing when the bat shifter had felt the need for a snack.

Narrowing his gaze, Finn scanned the various branches and spotted the pest dangling in the wind. It screeched and bared its fangs.

Ava's head whipped around. "What was that?"

"Just the wildlife," he muttered, glaring at the bat. "But Hallie looks good, so why don't we head back?"

"You don't want to see the command post?"

Finn resisted a sigh. He didn't want his time with Ava to end, but now that they'd completed their mission, he wanted to tuck her away at the hospital, hunt down the bat shifter, and demand to know what the Thornes wanted.

But a minute to poke through the ruin wouldn't hurt, so they climbed up the steps and entered the dank, concrete building where a long gap less than a foot in height provided a view of the water. Finn had to bend almost in half to see through it.

"So, the war didn't come to Townsville until 1942," Ava said, reading the information signs on the opposite wall. "They identified Townsville as a strategic port and military base and moved the Kissing Point guns up to the new battery at Cape Pallarenda."

Finn's shoulders tightened as he strode across the bunker. "Pallarenda?"

"Yeah. They have forts too, though not as nice as these ones."

Finn frowned. "What's it like?"

"Pallarenda? It's nothing special. There's a small suburb of houses, but it's just a stretch of beach between the Cape and Kissing Point. There's the Town Common, which is nice if you want to get in touch with nature. A lot of wildlife live there."

Not to mention rogue wolves.

"And it's not too far from the island, is it?"

"Not really. Cape Pallarenda is the closest point to Maggie. You'd have seen it when you were fishing last night."

"When I was ... oh, right." He nodded. "Yeah, I guess I'll get to Townsville and familiarize myself with the place soon."

But not while Tyrone and Blair continued to rule and threaten their way of life. What did they want with Magnetic Island anyway? And why was Ava important enough to send the bat to spy on her? Was it just Blair's wounded ego and possessive instinct to claim her? Finn knew it was inevitable; Blair would come for Ava. But was Finn ready to face him? He wasn't sure. All he knew was that the only way to protect Ava would be to stand up to Blair and the moment he did, the bastard would know she was his Fated mate and would be more determined to kill her.

"Hey, look at that!" Her delight snapped him out of his dark thoughts as she pointed at the board. "It's about the plane wreck."

Finn angled his body against hers as he viewed the picture of the coral-covered aircraft engine. "Yeah, I need to see that."

"Over two hundred wreck sites have been mapped, apparently, with a concentration around Maggie Island. This one's in Geoffrey Bay."

"On the snorkel trail." He remembered reading that. "You know ... you never said if you wanted to check it out with me."

"No ..." Her lips quirked and Finn's breath caught as her eyes darted from his, to his mouth, then back again. "But you know ... I am free on Monday."

He stilled. "Yeah?"

"And it's not the smartest idea to go snorkeling alone."

"No. So ... it's a plan?"

"Sure." She smiled softly, then stepped away. "But right now, I should probably get back to the hospital. And don't you have to get to work?"

"Yep." But it wasn't jet boating he had in mind as he followed her outside and glared at the tree where the bat shifter waited, teasing him. "I sure do."

Chapter 22

Finn eased his tension by asking Ava about her job as he followed her along the rocky path back to the Jeep. But while her clinical knowledge impressed him, he listened with half an ear, watching the bat every time they stopped to tell the neck-craning tourists where the koalas were hiding.

As he drove back into Horseshoe Bay, the slimy shifter glided in and out of his rear vision mirror, fangs flashing as he teased Finn. Taunted him.

Finn gritted his teeth. *Game on, little fucker.*

"So, you'll call me about snorkeling?" Ava asked, unclipping her seatbelt as he pulled up outside the hospital.

"I will. I'm quite booked up tomorrow, but I'll check the tides and—wait! I don't have your number."

"Oh. Silly me." She blushed as he opened his phone and handed it to her. She typed in her number, then handed it back before climbing out of the Jeep. "I can be free any time."

"I'll call you. And Ava?"

She turned to him and raised her eyebrows. "Yeah?"

He flashed her his best smile. "I enjoyed our walk."

Ava's lips quirked. "Me too."

She closed the door and backed away, lifting her hand in a wave. Finn's wolf whimpered, heat scorching through his belly as he returned the gesture. Then she spun on her heel and strode into the hospital, her hips and blonde ponytail swaying.

Finn dragged his hand down his face. Fuck, Fate had been kind. Ava was a true treasure. One he would die to protect.

Slowly, he turned his gaze through the windscreen and eyed the bat swinging on a branch in front of him. Finn's hands tightened around the wheel. If the fucker wanted to play, they would play.

The bat dropped from the tree, spread his wings, and swooped over the top of the Jeep, its claws barely missing the roll bars. Peeking quickly behind him, Finn shoved the Jeep into reverse, did a quick one-eighty in the parking lot, then took off down the road east towards the national park.

The bat glided left and right, screeching with glee. Finn doubted he'd catch the gnat as bats were super speedy and while he had many abilities, Finn could not fly. The bat could have gone by now if it'd wanted to, but its taunting would be its downfall.

Finn would find out what the bat wanted. What Tyrone wanted.

He sped past acreage lots, a small mango farm, and the conservation site. Suddenly, the bat shot upwards, and Finn's head lifted. Then he ducked as it swooped up behind him.

The bat screeched.

"Bloody asshole."

Finn reached the end of the road and braked in a cloud of dust. Cutting the engine, he leapt over the windscreen, onto the hood, and hit the ground with a thud before racing into the bush. His muscles tensed, bulged, and as he vaulted over a log, he twisted his body, shifted, and landed on four paws.

He ran, trailing the disgusting scent of the bat as it glided ahead of him, darting in and out of the scrub. Finn bared his teeth, longing to sink his canines into the pest.

Springing over the rippling creek, he dodged boulders and logs. The land slanted as he ascended. Finn's heart pounded. The bat cackled again as it glided around the tree to circle over him. The muscles corded in Finn's hind legs, then he leapt and swiped his claw at the pesky shifter, but the bat was too quick.

He landed and continued to give chase, until the smell vanished. Finn skidded to a halt, his paws digging into the leaf-littered dirt as he lifted his nose and sniffed.

"Give it up, little wolf."

Finn spun around. The vampire stood in a massive gum tree, draping his thin, pale body over the thick branch, conveniently hiding his pelvis as his toes wriggled on the branch below. Dark hair swished over his wide forehead as his eyes twinkled with mirth.

Finn growled and shifted, kneeling one knee in the dirt as he glared up at the filthy creature. "Why are you here? What does Blair want?"

The vampire's crimson lips stretched wide. "Little wolfie is so angry."

Finn bared his teeth. "Quit playing with me. You obviously want to talk." He wouldn't have led Finn this deep into the bush otherwise. "Tell me, what does Blair want with Ava?"

"The same as you, I'd say. To sink his cock into her and pump her full of wrigglys."

Finn roared, his quads clenching as he leapt up the tree. His claws sank into the bark as his hind legs scratched at the trunk, but he didn't possess the koala's efficiency at climbing. Growling, he slid back to the earth and shifted. The bat snickered.

"She's not his."

"She will be once I tell them she's here."

Finn stilled. "You weren't sent here to spy on her?"

"No." Cackling, the vampire flashed his fangs. "I'm here to spy on you."

Finn froze. Of course. Tyrone had probably sensed the shift in power. He might not know Finn's identity, but any wolf worth his soul could smell another from miles away.

"Yes, little wolf. And Blair will be very interested to know that you're mated to his whore."

Finn sprung to his feet, fists clenching. "Blair touches her, he dies."

"Ooh, such strong words for a little wolf!"

Finn snarled. *Call me little one more time* ...

"I don't know who you are," the bat continued, "or where you come from. But you are no match for Blair Thorne."

"He's a half-breed, twisted fucker. I can take him."

"And his father? Is the little wolf strong enough to take on one of the most revered dark Alphas out there?"

Finn didn't dignify that with a response. The vampire sniggered, taking his silence as surrender.

"Tyrone Thorne rules this town, little wolf. You and your rich friends need to remember that. You will never defeat Tyrone and he will endeavor to end your fate until—"

A growl echoed as a black flash leapt off the rocks behind Finn and clamped around the shifter's forearm. A blood-curdling cry pierced the air and Finn watched in horror as the wolf fell and dragged the pale man over the branch to the ground with him.

But only the wolf landed, hitting the earth with a thump. The bat shifted, fluttering his uninjured wing before falling too. Struggling to maintain the shift, he morphed and convulsed until he lay in his vampire form in the dirt. The wolf rose to his feet and leered over the struggling creature, drool dripping from his elongated canines.

"Fucking beast! I was just teasing the little wolf! Please! Let me go!"

The wolf lowered his head, muscles cording as he sniffed the vampire's neck. Finn's breath caught, sensing the Alpha's pain and hatred as he shifted.

"Sly, wait! Don't kill him. He might have information that—"

Shadows swirled as the vampire disappeared and the bat shot up with one good wing to catch the branch. Sly's back legs coiled as he leapt after it, but the slimy bastard was out of reach.

The vampire shifted back, panting as he clutched the tree with his uninjured arm.

"You think you're so tough," the vampire spat at Sly. "But look at you, hiding in the woods and leaving your brother to call for a Warrior on your behalf." He glanced at Finn. "You won't succeed, little wolf. This Alpha is broken. There's only one way to save the pack now."

Then without another word, he shifted and shot up through the trees. Sly's muscles corded and Finn almost leapt ahead to give chase. That bat knew Ava was on the island and if he didn't stop him—

Sly spun around and flattened his gums over his teeth. *"He was the first one I'd caught,"* he snarled, his deep voice echoing inside Finn's head. *"I've been trying to catch them for months, but the pests keep coming back. Spying on us."* His eyes narrowed. *"You should have let me kill him."*

"I know." Guilt coursed through Finn's veins as he pawed at the ground. *"I understand your anger. Trust me."*

Sly's spine straightened as he narrowed his eyes. *"Who are you?"*

"Name's Finn. I heard your brother's Call. He's worried about you and wants you back."

"I'm not coming back." Sly spun around. *"Tell Rain to stop denying the truth. The pack needs an Alpha."*

Finn bared his teeth. *"You are the Alpha."*

Pain shivered through the bond as Sly jumped onto a boulder. *"Listen to the bat, Finn. An Alpha needs his mate. And I'm broken."*

Then Sly vanished into the bush. Finn almost ran after him as the urge to help pulsed through his veins. He needed to get to the root of Sly's pain. To understand why he'd given up. To gain his pack stripes.

But his fur remained one hundred percent golden.

Heart sinking, Finn sauntered back towards the Jeep. He'd truly fucked up, had let Ava down, and now—

There's only one way to save the pack ...

What did the bat mean by that? Had Sly truly given up on them? Was he too far gone?

No. Impossible. Sly had welcomed Finn into the pack without even knowing him, and after sensing his pain, Finn knew the man in Sly still lived. He would help bring him back.

Somehow.

But first, he needed to protect Ava.

Reaching the edge of the bush, he nosed the remains of his busted sneaker. Fucking great. They'd been his only pair, too. Glancing up, he huffed at the strips of his favorite jeans clinging to a tree branch.

Such was the life of a shifter.

Poking his head out of the trees, Finn sniffed. Dog. Kookaburra. Snake. No humans. Not that he had a problem with nudity, but he didn't want to become "that man" as he shifted and dashed naked to the Jeep. He grabbed a pair of shorts, pulled them up his legs, then slipped behind the wheel.

Turning the keys he'd left in the ignition, he spun around and sped away.

Chapter 23

"Hey! Just in time. I've locked in the final artist for the Full Moon Parties next year." Rain grinned as he rose from his desk, the sapphire water of Cleveland Bay stretching behind him through the floor-to-ceiling windows. "We're going to have a stellar lineup."

"Great." Finn spread his bare feet wide and crossed his arms over his chest. "There are bat shifters on the island."

Rain's grin vanished. "How many?"

"Not sure, but one was following Ava and I around the Forts just now."

"What were you doing at the Forts?"

Breaking down her barriers and trying desperately not to kiss her. "Koala spotting. The filthy pest was teasing me after I dropped her off, so I chased him into the bush. I tried to get information about Tyrone, but all he said was that we wouldn't defeat him." Finn's lip curled. "And he knows about my bond with Ava."

Rain blew out his breath. "Fuck. And the bastard got away?"

"Unfortunately. Sly almost took him down, but—"

"Sly?" Rain's eyebrows shot up. "You saw him? Is he okay?"

"As good as you'd expect. He clipped the vampire's wing, but the fucker will probably survive." And it was his fault as while a wolf's bite could kill a vampire, a nip on the arm wasn't enough to finish the job. It would wound, but a fatal bite needed to be made to the jugular, and Finn had distracted Sly before he'd had the chance to do so. "The bat shifted and flew away. But not before tormenting Sly."

"What did he say?"

"Nothing important, but he won't be flying back to Townsville any time soon, so he's either still here or waiting to stow away on the ferry." Finn had stopped at the terminal before returning to Luna Views, watching and waiting until the ferry arrived, dropped off passengers, and departed again. But he hadn't managed to catch a whiff of the shifter, bat or vampire. "But apparently, he'd come to spy on me, so Tyrone knows I'm here."

Rain straightened. "Knows *you're* here, or—"

"Probably not me, his Fated, unfavored son. But he knows a lone wolf has come to your aid."

Rain ran his hand down his dark jaw. "Shit."

"And he'll also know Ava's here and that she's my mate."

Pulling at his hair, Rain turned to the window. "Fuck. He'll know we're rebuilding. Gathering reinforcements. And if he finds out who you are ..." He spun back around. "Do you think he will?"

"I wouldn't doubt him." And when the time came, Finn would be ready. He'd make sure of it.

"Fuck. Can it get any worse?"

Finn drew in a deep breath. "Sly says the bats have been spying on you guys for months. So, I'm thinking that if they picked up on the bond between me and Ava, then ..."

Rain froze. "They'll know about Eden."

"I think so."

Murder flashed through Rain's eyes. Finn didn't blame him. He felt the same way.

"Well, there's a simple solution to that," Rain said, his chest deflating. "Eden cannot leave the island."

In a few swift strides, he approached the exit, but Finn blocked him. "Dude, calm down."

"No."

Finn flung his arms across the doorway. "What do you plan to do? Walk up to her and demand she can't go home? You can't do that!"

Rain's glare could have frozen fire. "Watch me."

He elbowed Finn in the ribs, but Finn didn't budge. Grabbing Rain by the shoulders, he spun the man around and held him against the wall. "You'll scare her, you idiot! She doesn't know about any of this. You can't just capture her and—"

"She's in danger!"

"I know! They both are! But the mating bond is there for a reason. If you hold her captive on the island—"

"If I let her go, she'll be killed!"

"You mated with Eden two years ago! If they wanted to kill her, they'd have done so already!"

Rain bared his teeth, grabbed Finn's arm, and shoved him. Sensing the man had regained control, Finn stepped aside.

"Then what am I supposed to do?" he asked, pacing back towards the desk. "We abide by the lore. Tyrone doesn't. He roamed Pallarenda and laid claim to all the northern suburbs, but the river was meant to keep us safe. Taking the barge to the south side of Townsville had meant to be safe. But ..."

"That's where they got Shelby."

Rain nodded. "Tyrone thinks he's above the lore."

"He thinks he *is* the law." Finn's fists clenched. "It's why he hit, raped, and murdered my mother and got away with it."

Rain sank onto the edge of the desk. "He needs to be stopped."

"He does."

"We've been without Sly for too long. Been vulnerable for too long and now, we can't even protect our mates."

Finn bristled. "We *can* protect them. We just can't capture them and force them to our will."

Rain's lip curled. "I know."

"So, why do you resist, man?" Finn frowned as curiosity got the better of him. "Why haven't you forged the mating bond?"

"Because I thought Tyrone didn't know. I thought I was keeping her safe. But now ..." Finn waited for him to make some kind of declaration, but instead, steel filled Rain's eyes as he straightened. "If we're going to bring Blair and Tyrone down, we need to strengthen the pack. And I think that means you and Ava need to complete the mating bond."

Finn's heart catapulted into his throat. "I don't know how that'll help stop Tyrone."

"Think about it." Rain rounded the desk. "There's a bigger reason why you're connected to all this, Finn. About why *you* heard my Call. A reason that Blair became obsessed with Ava. Because as much as you might want to forget it, you *are* Tyrone Thorne's son. His flesh and blood and one true heir."

Finn's lips twisted. Fuck, Rain was right. He'd tried to deny it, but fear had been clouding his judgement. And Finn refused to be afraid of Tyrone and Blair. "I need to be the one to take a stand."

"You do. So, what can I do to help you with that?"

"Actually ... I need time off to take Ava snorkeling on Monday."

"Sure, man." Rain grinned and gripped Finn's shoulder, squeezing in encouragement. "You go get your girl."

Finn exhaled. He might have enjoyed his time with Ava today, but it didn't ease the dread in his gut. Or his guilt. He should have killed the fucking vampire.

But he couldn't do anything about that now, so instead, he'd just have to do all he could to protect her. Which should be easy considering that's what he'd been born to do.

"All right," he said. "And just so you know, Eden's staying on the island until Wednesday."

Rain's shoulders sank. "Thank fuck."

"Yeah. But I'll see if Ava can convince her to stay for a little longer. I don't know how, but I can try."

"Thanks, man. I appreciate it. Because if not, I'm sure there will be a major koala crisis that I might or might not be responsible for."

Chapter 24

Tyrone steepled his fingers as he leaned back in his chair while Blair draped himself in the seat opposite him and Lucas, the only vampire Tyrone had any patience for, paced slowly on the other side of the desk, his hands slipped casually into the neatly pressed pockets of his dark suit. The bat was no doubt itching to return to his haunt of Night Bite, the underworld nightclub he owned where he and Tyrone often conducted business and took their pleasures, but Lucas was keen to learn about the new wolf as much as Tyrone. He didn't particularly enjoy working with bats, but they had a power that Tyrone lacked, so he'd forged a mutually beneficial arrangement. One which Tyrone controlled, of course.

With an unnecessary sigh—the bastard didn't need to breathe—Lucas turned and heel-toed across the carpet, then paused as the door squeaked open.

Tyrone glared at Eric. "You're late."

"Sorry, boss. My lord." Eric nodded the latter address towards Lucas as he limped into the room and held up his bandaged forearm. "Bloody wolf clipped my wing and it took me a while to get to the ferry."

"The wolf bit you?" Lucas asked, his voice Mediterranean silk.

"Sly," Eric snarled. "Fucking beast. Not a mortal wound, thank fuck, but it hurts like a fucking bitch."

Tyrone's lip curled. Any other creature and Eric would have healed by now, but a wolf bite was a different matter. A wolf bite could have killed him if done correctly. Not that Tyrone would care as Lucas had more bats at his disposal to replace Eric as their spy.

"I don't care about your bloody arm. Tell us what we need to know."

"The newcomer? It's not just his presence, boss. He harbors a power I haven't seen before. And he doesn't even know it. But that's not all." Eric's gaze shot to Blair. "He's mated. To your whore."

Blair shot to his feet, the chair crashing to the floor behind him. "What?"

Eric's eyes gleamed. "Your woman is on the island."

"Fuck," Tyrone breathed, standing as Blair shoved his hands through his hair.

"I have to get her." Blair's face twisted, baring his teeth as his fists clenched by his side. "Father—"

"Hold on." Tyrone held up his hand. "Don't go rushing into anything. Eric, tell us more."

"They haven't completed the mating bond yet, but he's trying to claim her. It's sickening." The bat shifter shuddered. "But she's staying at the koala sanctuary and is helping her friend look after them."

"I should have known," Blair spat. "She mentioned a friend who saves koalas."

Tyrone's fists clenched as he rounded on his son. "Ava Hart is friends with the koala vet?"

"Apparently."

Air hissed between Tyrone's teeth. "That woman is the mate of Rain Blackwood!"

"And you know this?" Blair's eyes flashed. "Fuck me. Why is she still breathing?"

"Don't question me, boy. That woman is currently of little concern as the rich cunt is fucking smart. He hasn't secured the bond, afraid we'll do to his mate what we did to his brother's."

But Tyrone's plans for the koala lover were far darker than the slaughter of Sly's slut.

"He should be afraid," Blair said. "I say we kill her anyway."

Eric grinned. "It would be my pleasure—"

"Not yours, you fool!" Lucas snapped. "Remember your place."

Eric recoiled. "Yes, my lord. I know. I was just saying—"

Lucas's dark eyes flashed towards Tyrone. "I am ready. If you want me to deal with this problem, I can do it."

Growling, Tyrone turned his back on the vampire's hungry gaze and glanced out the window. It wasn't much of a view from his office at the station and the city was quiet at this late hour, the locals too afraid to venture out at night. But this was his territory. His city. It was a place where wolves could roam free and didn't need to tie themselves to the ridiculous notion of Fate. Where bats could be unleashed to do what they did best by wreaking havoc and destruction. Townsville was a big enough city for both creatures to have their fun, but far enough from the capital for the higher human authorities to care about how he controlled it. Or, in his case, didn't. The stealthy bats made the perfect partners in crime by slipping easily into the native flying fox community and providing dark, underworld services. Tyrone had an endless supply of meat, sex, and espionage, which was all a wolf needed.

And to kill the Fated living on his doorstep.

"What else did you learn about the wolf?"

"That's it, boss. But there was something familiar about him. I'm not sure what. Might have been his scent? But if you want to prevent their mating bond, you will need to act fast. The bitch is ready to spread her legs for him."

Blair growled. "Not if I have something to say about it. I don't care what the blasted Moon thinks, that woman was meant to be mine."

Tyrone turned to his son. "I agree. You need a legacy, and given she's a Fated mate, this woman will be the perfect vessel to carry your heir."

Lucas cleared his throat. "And the other woman?"

"We will take care of Rain's whore when the time comes," Tyrone said, glancing at the bat. "But right now, Blair needs to finish what he started. Go claim that slut as your own."

"I will." Blair's spine straightened, his chest puffing as the wolf inside him prepared for the hunt. "I'll get her back, Father. And I'll remind Blackwood who ran these shores first."

Chapter 25

Going snorkeling with Finn might not have been the brightest idea she'd had, but Ava refused to back out as she hadn't explored the ocean in such a long time. When she was little, her family had often taken weekend trips to the Whitsundays where they would cruise the islands, swim in the crystal-clear waters, and snorkel over bright coral reefs and colorful fish.

At least, that's how her young mind had remembered it, so she'd been bitterly disappointed when she'd returned during university. Coral bleaching and climate change couldn't have destroyed the reef that much in fifteen years, but the bright colors had vanished and the aquamarine water had dulled. Ava expected that the coral today would look somewhat the same. Magnetic Island had beautiful reefs, but it was sunlight and the high-tec cameras that gave coral its colorful appearance. She'd enjoy watching the fish though, searching for rays, and observing the giant clams as she flippered across the water.

With the sexiest man she'd ever met.

Grinning, Ava placed her hat on her head and grabbed her beach bag. Warmth filled her chest as she left the bungalow, rainbow lorikeets squawking in the palm trees shading the boardwalk. She wasn't proud enough to deny that she'd misjudged Finn, or that she'd enjoyed every minute of her walk with him at the Forts. She hadn't stopped thinking about him in the two days since, stirring the ache inside her that built with every breath.

She liked him. Yes, he'd snapped at her the day they'd met, but she'd forgiven him for that. The man might portray the image of a macho, bad boy, don't-mess-with-me-and-my-super-cool-Jeep type, but beneath that bulk of muscle, he had a heart. And she wanted it. She craved his affection and his fucking sexy body, his sardonic smile and unshaven face that she hadn't stopped thinking about kissing. Or having him kiss her. All over.

Shivering, Ava strode through reception and spotted the sleek red Jeep waiting for her. Finn rested against the side door, his ankles crossed and hands in his pockets, his blond hair tied back in a short tail.

Her knees weakened. Fuck, what was a girl to do?

Taking a deep breath, she mustered a smile and strode towards him. "Morning!"

"Hello, Ava." His lips twitched. "You look nice."

Her gaze dipped to the plain blue T-shirt she wore with her swirling purple and aqua boardshorts that hardly covered her bottom. If only she were brave enough to expose the canary yellow bikini she wore underneath, but this was North Queensland, she had fair skin, and she'd rather not be laid up with sunburn for days growing melanoma. "Thank you."

Ava accepted the hand he offered as he opened the passenger door and she climbed into the Jeep.

"How've you been?" Finn asked as he settled behind the wheel.

"Good. Worked with the koalas yesterday and Marco is getting stronger. What about you?"

He started the Jeep. "Work was busy, then I took the Sea-Doo out to get my dog some fresh air."

Her eyebrows shot up. "You have a dog?"

Finn nodded. "Maltese-Shitzu. I adopted her a few years ago. She's five."

"I love dogs. What's her name?"

"Gracie," he replied, and her eyebrows rose even higher. "Don't look at me like that. I didn't name her."

"Yes, but you kept her name when you took her in." Damn, would this man ever stop surprising her?

He shrugged one bulging deltoid. "It was her name. You can't change a dog's name. And her mum liked it."

"Her mum?"

"The lady I got Gracie from. She adored that dog."

Ava's stomach clenched. "What happened to her?"

"She was my neighbor in Batemans Bay. Nice lady. Early fifties. Divorced. We talked over the fence every now and then. One night, I came home and Gracie was whimpering. It was late and Noelle's car wasn't there. Made a few calls and eventually found out she'd been killed in a car accident."

Ava winced, her heart hurting for the little dog. And Finn. "So, you took Gracie?"

"I couldn't bear the thought of her ending up in a shelter. She has OCD and a deformed hip, so she needed someone who understood her."

A fresh wave of lust washed through her. God, this man ... "That's lovely, Finn."

He shrugged again. "Dogs are pack animals. She couldn't be alone."

"That's true. But wait, did you say you took her on the jet ski?"

"Yeah." Finn flashed her a grin. "Gracie loves it."

"But ... how?"

"She has her own carrier on the back."

Ava clenched her knees together. "Oh my God, that's way too cute. I'll have to meet her."

"Sure. You should come jet skiing with us. It's the best way to reach the secluded bays."

"Yes, it is."

They crested the hill by the Forts and caught the beautiful sight of Cleveland Bay glistening beneath the sun as it stretched towards the coast. Minutes later, Finn pulled up by the beach outside the Arcadia Hotel, and Ava jumped out of the Jeep. Excitement bubbled through her belly as she gazed out at the still water. Then Finn grasped the back of his shirt, pulled it over his head, and she froze.

Bloody hell. How was she supposed to enjoy herself when she had to be up close and personal with all of *that*.

"I got you a pink snorkel." Finn handed her the goggles and a snorkel pack that still had the tags attached. "And I borrowed these flippers from the resort. We also have these swim cards that Rain gave me."

The card mapped the trail and included information about the types of coral and fish they might see. Ava hoped they'd give her something to focus on besides Finn's ripped body. Glimmering in the sun. Wet.

She snapped the swim card's rubber band around her wrist. "Thanks, Finn. And you know what? I do like pink."

"I figured. You wear it often enough." His mouth curved as they strolled over the nature strip and down onto the beach. The water would be freezing beneath the spring September sun, but it was a risk she had to take as she sat by the lapping waves and slipped on her flippers. Finn plopped down beside her, flashing her an impressive view of his bunching serratus anterior as he hunched over his solid legs and snapped his own flippers on.

Ava's tongue darted between her teeth. Damn, he'd have

been useful to have around when she'd been studying anatomy.

"All right." He extended his long legs and reached for his goggles. "Ready?"

Nodding, she picked up her face mask, loosened the straps, and slipped it over her head.

"Hold it in place, Ava, and I'll adjust it for you."

He knelt behind her, her skin warming at his proximity as he pulled her ponytail through the split strap and adjusted it behind her ears. Closing her eyes, Ava took a deep breath. Then another. But nothing could reduce the lust simmering inside her.

"Feel secure?"

No. She was in terrible danger of falling for him, of throwing away all her inhibitions and straddling him right there on the beach. "Yep. Thanks, Finn."

Needing distance, she pushed herself onto her jelly legs, then ungracefully flipper walked into the ocean. Yep, the water was freezing, but Finn didn't seem to mind as they waded in thigh deep.

She shivered as his large hand caressed her lower spine. "It's best we just dive in. Get it over with."

Finn dove beneath the wave, then surfaced a few meters away, his back emerging from the ocean like Poseidon as he flipped his wet, golden hair off his face. Turning, he flashed her a grin. The man could even make goggles look sexy.

"Come on, Ava!"

What had she been thinking when she'd agreed to this? Not that she could back out. Heart racing, she took a deep breath and dove. Her vessels constricted as the cold enveloped her, but she frogged her arms, kicked her legs, and eyed Finn's solid abs ahead of her before rising beside him.

"Not too cold?"

"Bloody freezing," she replied, and his chest heaved as he laughed.

"Better get moving, then." He extended his hand, and she took it, intertwining her fingers with his. Perhaps she wouldn't need kinetics or the sun to keep her warm when she had Finn by her side. Was it just her, or did he run hotter than other men?

He popped the snorkel in his mouth and blew water from the black tube. Shaking off her lusty thoughts, Ava did the same. Then they slipped into the water.

Peace enveloped Ava as she breathed solely through her mouth, flipping her feet in time with Finn's as they swam to the first buoy that marked the snorkel trail. It was almost four hundred meters, shorter maybe at low tide, and there wasn't much to see other than the sandy ocean floor. And after a few minutes, Ava realized that while she kept herself fit by swimming laps in the pool, she'd underestimated the strength of the ocean.

By the time they reached the buoy, she felt like she'd swum a marathon as she treaded water and popped the snorkel from her mouth.

"You good?" Finn asked, his cheeks crinkling into a smile.

"Yeah," she breathed, her chest heaving. "Just not used to swimming with the current, I suppose."

His smiled dropped. "You're not a strong swimmer?"

"I am. But turns out, only in a pool."

He exhaled softly. "Then we'll take it at your pace. Stop whenever you want and if you get too tired, you can hold on to me."

Ava blinked. Did he realize what he'd just said? He must have if the smile he flashed her was any indication. In that case, maybe she'd feign drowning.

Finn inclined his chin. "The next buoy doesn't look too far, and that's where I believe the giant clams are. But the

Moltke is at the last one." He pointed and Ava turned in the water. Surely, she could make it that far.

"Where's the propeller though? It's somewhere all the way out there." She glanced out to the unmarked ocean. "Do you think we'll find it?"

"I'm sure we will. If you're up for it?"

It would be an awfully long swim if they had to search for long. Then again, it might give her the perfect excuse to clutch to Finn.

Fuck, the salty seawater had gone to her head. "How about we just do this part first? Are you ready?"

He nodded and after popping her snorkel back between her teeth, she took Finn's hand and lowered her head into the water. After a few kicks, the reef came into view in a long shelf of whitened coral. Clumps of seaweed and algae moved with the current and small fish darted in and out of hidey-holes. Ava looked left and right, not wanting to miss anything. Her breath whooshed in and out of the snorkel as they fought against the lapping waves, and the salt coating her lips wasn't all that pleasant. But the company sure made up for it as Finn's large, calloused thumb stroked back and forth over her hand.

He tugged gently and pointed out a stingray gliding across the sandy floor. Ava smiled and seawater seeped between her lips. Disgusted, she blew it out of her snorkel.

They swam on. The reef grew larger and soon, a rope appeared as they arrived at the second buoy. But rather than surface, Finn led her on until they spotted the two large clams. Blueish in color, they sat with their wriggly shells open and breathed through the hole in their center.

Finn pointed his thumb upwards, and they surfaced. "Shit, they are cool."

"I've never seen clams before."

"They're quite rare. Clams are endangered as much as your koalas, and these giant clams are even more so."

Ava's heart sank. "That's sad. Too many animals are endangered."

"Sure are," he muttered, nodding to the next buoy. "I believe there are more over there."

She stuck her snorkel back in her mouth as he did the same, and they continued to swim. It was then that the reef fully emerged, and she could almost reach down and brush her fingers over the seaweed and stag coral. Now and then, the sunlight caught the water to create flashes of blue, red, and green over the coral, and Finn squeezed her hand to point out another colorful fish.

Before she knew it, they arrived at buoy three, and two more giant clams greeted them.

"You ready to find the shipwreck?" he asked when they surfaced. "Or do you want a break?"

She shook her head. "No, I'm good."

Though her body began to tire as they headed for the fourth buoy. The reef disappeared, the water grew murkier, and the waves rougher. Ava tried not to panic as water lapped over her head. She could barely see anything.

Then Finn squeezed her tingling fingers, pointed, and the wreck emerged from the gloom in a swarm of tiny, silvery fish. Ava's eyebrows shot up as her kicking slowed with wonder. Wow. There it was, the *Moltke*. She couldn't identify what part of the ship she was seeing, but it was a magnificent sight. Coral had taken over the wreck, providing a home for the thousands of small fish and other plant life. Unable to stop staring, Ava kicked lightly as Finn led her around in a circle, pointing out aspects that looked interesting. She smiled at the sight of a black-and-white striped angel fish. Then Finn tugged on her hand and surfaced.

She lifted her head and removed her snorkel. "Wow. Did you see all that coral? It hardly looks like a ship!"

"It'd be an amazing dive. Might try that another time. Now, where do you think this propeller is?"

He lifted the swim card, then surveyed the bay. Ava took a moment to float on her back and catch her breath. She needed to build up her stamina and a tolerance to seawater. She hadn't swallowed any, but the taste on her lips alone was enough for her to crave sugar.

"Hey, are you okay?" Finn asked, touching her shoulder.

Ava opened her eyes. "Yeah. Just resting. Do you know where the plane is?"

"I think so ... but it is a bit of a swim." He frowned with concern. "You sure you're up for it?"

Nodding, Ava flipped back onto her belly and paddled. She hadn't come all this way for nothing. "Yeah, I'll be okay. But you might have to tow me."

"That is not a problem."

The propeller of the World War II plane was not marked by a buoy, so Ava put her trust in Finn's sense of direction as they continued to swim. The waves grew rougher, the water murkier, and after a few minutes, Ava wondered if they'd ever find it. She could just make out the sea floor and continued to focus on the fish dancing in and out of her vision. Then Finn's hand squeezed hers and she saw it—a hunk of metal lying on the ocean floor and making a new home for the coral. It was obviously a bi-wing propeller from the plane that had been brought down during the war, but where the rest of the aircraft was, no one knew.

They circled the wreck, then surfaced. Glancing over her shoulder, Ava couldn't believe how far from shore they were. Chest heaving, she lifted the goggles from her face and drew breath through her nose and mouth. She didn't know how long they'd been swimming, but it was certainly enough as she turned onto her back. Her flippers moved slowly through the water as Finn reached out and lifted the goggles off her head. Then he removed his own, his long golden hair clinging to his neck and shoulders.

Ava stilled.

"Come here." He tugged her hand and pulled her upright against his body, shooting any chance of her pulse settling straight to hell. He wrapped his arm around her waist, and her hands dropped to his chest.

His hot, naked, wet chest.

Ava wasn't sure she'd ever breathe again as her fingers pressed to his hard flesh and she brushed her thumbs through the hair over his sternum. His pecs expanded and contracted against the water, droplets glistening on his golden skin. Warmth pooled inside her and Ava clenched her pelvic muscles tight as his hand circled her hip. Their knees knocked and flippers tapped as they treaded water.

Well, while Finn treaded water. She could barely move as she trailed her gaze over his wide shoulders and the hard column of his throat where muscles tensed and contracted. His lips pressed together in the center of his beard, water droplets glistening on the short fibers along his jaw. His nostrils flared. Then she met his darkened blue eyes and everything inside her clenched. His gaze absorbed her with the same hard possessiveness that she'd witnessed the day they'd met. A look she had thought had been one of anger. Of frustration. But now that she'd gotten to know the man beneath the steel, Ava knew she'd been mistaken.

It was a look of desire. Hot, barely controlled, raging desire. For her.

"Finn..."

His arm wrapped around her, their masks and snorkels knocking into her back as he drew her flush against his body. Ava shivered, her nipples pebbling against the warmth of his chest as she grasped his shoulders. Every hard plane of his body pressed against hers, including the rod of steel against her thigh. Gasping, she dug her fingers into his back as they stared into each other's eyes, water lapping around them. Finn moved nothing but his flippers and Ava didn't move at all.

Fuck, she was going to drown them, but Finn continued to hold them up. How, she didn't know, but nor did she care as his fingers spread across her lower back. Ava cursed the existence of her T-shirt and her responsible need for sun protection as her gaze fell to his mouth. The mouth she hadn't stopped thinking about since the first time he had scowled at her. Now, his full lips twitched into a smirk, and Ava stopped thinking.

She pulled herself upright and kissed him. Warm, salty lips greeted her, surrounded by the prickly but surprisingly hot sensation of his beard brushing her skin. His arms tightened, lifting and crushing her to him as his mouth opened to welcome her. Ava whimpered as their tongues touched, swirled, then he sucked her lower lip between his. She barely had time to draw breath before his mouth claimed hers again and passion surged.

Breathing was no longer necessary. Kissing Finn was all that mattered. All that would keep her alive. His hands slipped down her back and over her butt before gripping the bare skin of her thighs. With strength she couldn't fathom, he lifted and wrapped her legs around his waist. She didn't hesitate, squeezing his hips with her thighs as he held her out of the lapping water. A growl vibrated from his chest and shuddered straight to her core, her muscles clenching and aching, longing for the erection teasing her through the frustrating barrier of their shorts.

Like the rest of him, Finn was huge.

A thrill of both excitement and terror shot through her as his hands clutched the back of her shoulders. Drawing on her lip, he nipped lightly, then lathed it with his tongue. Her eyes fluttered open to meet the insatiable look in his. He changed angles, his nose brushing hers as they drew breath and plundered again. Ava surrendered to him, taking in every sensation. The cool water, the fever of his tongue, power of his lips, soft wetness of his beard, and the strength with which he held her when she certainly had no strength at all.

Not until she was almost dizzy with oxygen deprivation did they draw apart. Her eyes flickered up to his and she found herself captured in his dark, hooded gaze as his chest lifted against hers.

His mouth stretched into a grin. "I thought you needed to catch your breath."

"I did, but ... but I ..." Heat crept up her neck as she bit down on her lower lip, but Ava couldn't suppress her grin. "I've been dying to kiss you."

He chuckled, the deep sound rolling from his chest as he lifted his thumb and tugged her lip gently from her teeth. "Dying, have you?" he asked, brushing his mouth back against hers.

"Mmm-hmm." She clenched her thighs even tighter and lifted her hand to stroke his jaw, the bristles tickling her fingers. "There was a twig here and a koala clutched to your chest, but I knew. I wanted you."

His broad shoulders softened. "I want you, too."

"You do?" she stupidly asked, pressing her thumb against the speck of hair beneath his lower lip.

Finn pulled her pelvis closer to his and she gasped. "You feel that?"

"Bit hard to miss."

"Only one thing will get rid of that, Ava."

Smiling softly, she lowered her hand as a brazenness she'd never felt before surged through her veins. Finn's arms twitched as though he wanted to stop her, but he didn't get the chance as her fingers stroked his hardened cock through his shorts. "This?"

Finn hissed between his teeth. "Fuck, Ava. Stop that."

She released him and slid her hand slowly up the bumps of his tight abdomen. "All right. But I could really enjoy that."

"And you can, when we're not bopping in the middle of the fucking ocean."

She stifled a laugh and dropped her head against his shoulder. "I'm sorry. It's not funny."

"You'll pay for it," he growled, running his teeth over the top of her ear. "But right now, I think we should swim back to shore. If you're ready."

Nodding, she unhooked her legs. "Yeah, I'm—shit! I'm sorry! I've been clinging to you like a life raft."

His lips curved. "It's fine."

"But you must be exhausted, holding me up. We could float for a while."

He shrugged and took her hand. "Superhuman strength," he explained, humor flashing through his eyes.

Ava snorted. "No one's that strong."

Even with that body of his, he had to be tired. But Finn simply laughed as he nuzzled her neck and inhaled. "You bring it out in me."

Ava's toes curled inside her flippers. Yeah, they had to get back to shore before this man made her drown.

He refit her goggles and snorkel, threw his own back on, then took her hand to make a beeline back to the beach. Ava didn't know how Finn did it—superhuman strength indeed—but she was positively panting when they swam into the shallows. Dropping to her knees, she ungracefully lifted her mask and kicked off her flippers. Finn gathered their equipment, tucked it all beneath his arm, then took her hand and pulled her to her feet.

"Thank you," she breathed, leaning into him as he

wrapped his arm around her waist. Her heart pounded as they strolled out of the water, her knees wobbling with exhaustion. "Sorry. I thought I was stronger than this."

"Don't apologize. It was a big swim."

And she felt every inch of it as they headed for the cool shade of the trees, sand coating her wet feet. "We'll have to do it again."

"Absolutely," he said, brushing his hand up and down the side of her ribs. "The Nelly Bay trail is supposed to be easier."

"Now you tell me." She flashed him a smile as she looked up. And up. Damn, he was tall. Not ridiculously so, but she barely brushed his shoulder. "I had fun, though."

His eyes flashed, though with what, she didn't know. Wonder, desire, or something more primal. But then his lips curved and he pressed a kiss to her hairline.

Ava almost melted into the sand.

"Me too, Ava. Now, what do you say we get out of these wet clothes and grab some lunch?"

After their passionate moment in the ocean, she'd have suggested they skip lunch and get out of their wet clothes somewhere more private. But even though she wanted nothing more than to explore Finn's body and feel the full length of him plunge inside her, Ava's desire for food outweighed that for sex. And she'd never been the kind of girl to jump straight into bed with a man.

Hence why Blair had hit her.

But Finn? He was different and for the first time in her life, Ava wondered if perhaps she'd chosen right.

"Lunch sounds great."

Chapter 26

Only by sheer force of will did Finn maintain his self-control as Ava peeled her wet swim shirt from her lithe body, revealing inch by gorgeous inch her tight, toned torso and her perfectly rounded breasts cupped in a yellow bikini. He'd been pretending not to look as he scrubbed a towel over his head, but after the woman had palmed his rock-hard cock when he'd had no intention of using it, fair was fair.

Ava shimmied her wet shorts down her thighs, which had felt so right clenched around his waist, and kicked them off with a wet plop. Only then did she reach for the towel, but not before providing him with the perfect view of her sculpted ass.

Finn blew out his breath and rubbed the towel harder over his head. His mate was fucking hot and his wolf had been howling to claim her since the moment her taste had knocked him breathless. Kissing her had felt better than any run beneath the full moon ever had, tasted better than the finest steak, and sent more thrill through him than a headstand on the jet ski. He would fucking lose it when he finally sank himself into the warm depths of her. When she gave herself to him heart, body, and soul. When he finally got to claim her as his.

Forever.

After he gave himself too. His whole self. Which meant revealing his wolf. And while they might be mated and she might even grow to love him, that didn't guarantee that she'd accept the paranormal.

Finn tossed the towel over the side of the Jeep and reached for his T-shirt, tugging it over his head as Ava finished buttoning her floral beach dress over her yellow-clad breasts.

She flicked her hair over her shoulder. "What do you want to eat?"

You? Finn inwardly growled at himself. "We're on an island, so what about fish and chips?"

Her adorable button nose twitched. "I don't really care for takeaway. The pub does a good lunch."

Finn couldn't agree more. He'd rather quality sustenance too, especially after that swim. "The pub it is."

He offered her his hand, she took it, and they crossed the road to the Arcadia Hotel. Settling onto the alfresco patio overlooking the swimming pool, they sat adjacent to each other and studied the menu. Of course, his wolf only wanted one thing, but even Finn grew tired of red meat, so he stuck with his cravings and chose the catch of the day. Ava decided on the broccoli pesto penne with spinach and toasted pine nuts, and he ignored her protests when he insisted on paying.

"A gentleman shouldn't let a lady pay," he said when he returned with two glasses of icy water.

"Maybe if it was a date."

He quirked his eyebrow. "This isn't a date?"

She smiled around her straw. "I don't know. Is it?"

After the way she'd clung to him, kissed him, and handled his cock, Finn didn't know how else to describe it. "It should be. And I think for our next one, I'll take you out on the jet boat."

"I thought we were going to jet ski?"

"Another day, when we can take our time and circumnavigate the island."

Ava smiled. "I'd like that."

"Good. I'm busy tomorrow, but I'm running jet boat rides on Wednesday. Maybe I can take you for a spin when I finish?"

"I can come out with the group."

Finn placed his hand over hers on the table. "Maybe I want you all to myself."

Her smile broadened. "Maybe we shouldn't be alone on the jet boat."

"Why?" He raised his eyebrows, blood pumping through his primitive vessels. "Afraid of what might happen?"

"No. But ... we should take it slow, Finn."

"You call what we did in the ocean slow?"

Her cheeks pinked. "That was me losing it in the moment."

Finn leaned closer. "You can lose it any time you want, honey."

Her blush deepened, but she didn't look away. "Finn ..."

His heart pounded as the air whistled between them. People chatted and music pumped from the speakers, but he saw nothing except Ava as her smile slipped slowly from her face.

"I've made bad choices."

Finn frowned. "What bad choices?"

"With men. In the past."

His thumb brushed hers. "We all make bad choices sometimes."

"Yes, but I never have any luck. And the last guy ..."

The hairs on the back of Finn's neck stood up. He didn't want to hear about the last man she'd been with, especially since that man had been Blair. The bastard deserved to be ripped limb from limb for what he'd done to her and Finn would be the first in line to relish that task.

Ava's shoulders slouched. "I'm sorry. I shouldn't be telling you this."

"You can tell me anything." The words growled from his chest. "And it's okay. I know he hurt you."

Her head snapped up. "You do?"

"I saw your bruised cheek the day you arrived on the island."

"Oh. Yeah ..." Her hair curtained her face as her chin dropped. "I'm glad that faded fast. I should have known better—"

"It wasn't your fault."

She blew out her breath. "I know. And I wanted to report him, but the man ... he's a cop himself and I doubted my complaint would be processed. Plus, I figured he'd find me faster if I went to the police."

Finn ground his teeth. He wasn't surprised that Blair had become a cop like their father, but Ava had no way of knowing how twisted Blair really was. That he was a wolf shifter who reveled in power and chaos. That he abided by no one's law and he was so consumed with his kind's mission to end Moonbound shifters like Finn so that the wolves could run wild and free.

Ava had no idea how lucky she was to have escaped with her life. But while he longed to know how she'd done it, now was not the time to ask.

Instead, he fought all his natural instincts, reeled in his anger, and reached for her hand. "I'm sorry you had to go through that."

She smiled sadly. "Thank you. But the thing is ... I don't know what I'm supposed to do now. I can't stay on Maggie Island, but I can't go home either."

No, she couldn't, but not for the reasons she thought. That bat shifter would have returned to Townsville and told Tyrone about his and Ava's bond, which would only put her in more danger. She'd either be killed immediately upon return or Blair would have his sickening way with her first.

She gasped and Finn realized he'd squeezed her hand too hard. "Shit, sorry." He softened his hold and forced calm into his eyes. He had to play this cool. "You think he'll come after you?"

"I *know* he will. He was just so ... predatory. Obsessive. I showed no interest in him and declined going to dinner with him a few times, but he wouldn't let up. I know that should have been a warning sign, but he was nice about it. So eventually, I gave in."

Finn nodded slowly. Wolves were talented hunters who wore down their prey until they had little energy left to keep running.

But it also begged the question: why *hadn't* Blair come for Ava? It'd been two days since Finn had let the bat shifter escape and while Magnetic Island might be Blackwood territory, it wasn't like the Thornes cared for rules.

That was a thought to ponder later though as right now, he needed to focus on Ava. He needed to be the caring, compassionate man that she deserved and ignore the wolf that rattled in its cage desperate to be unleashed and tear some bodies apart.

"How long were you together before he hurt you?"

"We weren't."

"What do you mean?" he asked, raising his eyebrow. Even his wolf calmed. Then growled when they were interrupted by the waitress.

Finn and Ava drew apart as he indicated he'd have the fish and the waitress placed the large bowl of green pasta in front of Ava. It looked good, but his fish looked better. Cutting into it, he took a bite and resisted a moan as the flaky flesh fell apart in his mouth.

"Good?" Ava asked, and he nodded.

"You want a bite?"

She shook her head. "I ... ahh ... don't really eat meat."

Finn stilled. "It's fish."

She quirked her eyebrow. "Is that not meat?"

Finn glanced at the fillet, then back at her. "It's ... fish. Which I suppose is meat," he muttered after her prolonged stare. The poor thing had been alive once.

She nodded as she speared the green speckled penne onto her fork. Finn ate his fish and silently cursed Fate. She'd played her first hand, tying him to a mate who didn't eat meat.

What was a wolf to do?

Not make a big deal out of it, that's what. Ava's diet wasn't an issue. But Blair was.

"Before lunch arrived, you were saying ...?"

"Right." She paused to chew, then swallowed. "I went to dinner with this guy twice and met up for a walk along the river after work one day. Since I was going on annual leave, he invited me for a day trip to Paluma, a small village tucked away in the rainforest north of Townsville. It's beautiful and I agreed to go. But then ..."

Finn's hands tightened around his cutlery, waiting for Ava to continue as she delayed her story with another bite of pasta. He saw where this was going, Blair taking her away to the secluded rainforest.

"It's okay, Ava. I think I get it. You don't have to tell me."

"I just think I should have seen it coming, is all. It's embarrassing."

"Don't be embarrassed." He placed his hand on her forearm. "You did nothing wrong."

"I know." She brought her gaze back to his. "He took me to his cabin there. It was isolated and quiet. He thought he'd surprise me with a night away, but I wasn't ready for that. When I told him and asked if we could go home, he ..."

She shuddered. Finn let her go for fear of clenching his hand and snapping her forearm.

"The change in him happened so quickly. One second, he was a man excited about his ill-thought-out plan, then the next he ... I don't know how to describe it."

She didn't have to. Finn knew what would have happened, the rage Blair would have felt and the primal urge to claim, mate, and pump into her like a savage beast. It bordered on what he could feel. What he almost had back in the ocean. What he would when he finally had Ava naked in his arms.

Except Finn would savor it. He would honor the bond his goddess had bestowed upon them and control it. Even with his other lovers, he had the ability to exercise care, passion, and respect.

But Blair and his twisted existence could only feel the need to possess. Taking no for an answer? Impossible.

Trusting his temper, Finn gently squeezed Ava's wrist. "I'm sorry you had to go through that."

She dropped her fork into her bowl and interlocked her fingers with his. "Thank you, Finn. And for listening. I thought it'd be hard to talk about, but with you ... I don't know. Maybe I've just talked it through with Eden enough already, but you're a good listener."

Finn's chest swelled. He'd been called many things, but rarely that. "It helps to have people listen without judgement. Although ... can I ask how you got away from him?"

Her shoulders sagged. "That's a good question. I don't know. I mean, I was lucky. He slapped me once, then grabbed me. It was terrifying, but I managed to punch him. In the nose. Blood spurted and he screamed in agony. It sounds strange now, but I didn't stop to think about it. I grabbed his keys and ran."

Finn grinned. He couldn't help it. He might have broken Blair's nose himself—twice—but to know that Ava, too, had plowed her fist into the bastard's face made his wolf chase his tail in glee.

No wonder they were meant to be.

"Good on you, Ava."

"Thanks. I was a little proud of myself, though I still don't know how I did it. It wasn't a good punch as I'd never hit anyone before. I guess when you're scared, adrenaline takes over. But I'd say the ring helped."

Finn frowned. "The ring?"

"I was wearing a dress ring Eden gave me for my birthday."

"Gold?" he asked, knowing that was the wrong answer.

"No. Silver."

His gaze darted to her hands. She wasn't wearing it now and he didn't recall her wearing a ring since, but his spine relaxed nonetheless. Not that she could hurt him anyway. Everyday silver wasn't deadly to wolf shifters as that would be incredibly inconvenient, but that didn't mean silver couldn't hurt them when used correctly. When her ring had connected with Blair's blood, the sting would have shot through his body in agony.

"Why aren't you wearing it now?"

She shrugged. "Took it off to wash it and just haven't put it back on."

Hmm, he'd fix that. But for now, he bit into a chip and flashed her a smile. "Still must have been one hell of a punch."

The dullness in her eyes brightened. "Must have been."

"And you stole his car, too?"

"Borrowed," she corrected, pointing her finger. "But yes."

He nodded, though none of that explained why she felt she couldn't go home. *Finn* knew, and she would leave Magnetic Island over his dead body. But Ava was only worried that the man who'd hurt her might not let her go.

"But you need to return to work soon," he said conversationally, "so why don't you think you can go home?"

"Because we live in the same apartment complex."

Finn's chest tightened. Fuck.

"So I'll have to move. And even then, he's a cop. He'll find me."

Finn brushed his thumb over her knuckles, unsure of how to comfort her. "You said you have another week of leave?"

"Yeah. But I thought I'd stay with Eden when I go home. He doesn't know about her."

Finn swallowed a snort. There was no telling what Blair and Tyrone knew about Eden and Ava with the bat shifters in their back pocket. They'd probably been spying on Ava while Blair had been stalking her. They knew Finn was on the island and it was only a matter of time before Tyrone and Blair discovered his identity.

Remembering his promise to Rain though, Finn took a chance. "Maybe Eden should stay here? Just in case."

Ava frowned as she finished her lunch. "Really? But I doubt—"

"The cops have access to more information than we know." He wasn't sure if that was true, but he didn't care. "As you said, this ... man pursued you. He's obsessive. Are you sure he doesn't know about Eden?" Finn quirked his eyebrow as doubt rose in her eyes.

"I don't ..."

"What if he went to Eden? What if he hurt her?"

"Stop it!" Cutlery cluttered into her bowl as she lifted her hands, palms out. "He wouldn't go after Eden. He ... he just wants ..." Her shoulders slouched and she dropped her elbows onto the table, her head in her hands. "Shit."

Guilt clawed in Finn's gut. "Sorry. I didn't mean to scare you."

"No, you're right." Her fingers scraped down her face as

she looked at him. "I don't know what Eden can do, but she might be able to stay a few days longer. I'll talk to her."

"I think that's a good idea."

Though the words tasted bitter in his mouth as he hated instilling fear inside Ava. But he'd promised Rain and more sacrifices would need to be made before they lured Sly out of the bush and exerted their territorial power over the Thornes. Ava and Eden giving up their lives would only be the beginning, as well as vital if they were to succeed. These two women were the key to Finn and Rain's survival. The only way the Thornes could bring them down, like he'd brought Sly down.

Their mates were their weakness and had to be protected, but they needed to remain on the island of their own free will. So hopefully, Ava could convince her friend to stay because Finn couldn't let Rain risk his soul by holding Eden captive.

Or hurting innocent koalas to make her stay.

Chapter 27

Ava stared absently into the bush as Finn weaved the Jeep up the hill on their way back to Eucalypts Grove. She hadn't planned to tell him about Blair and hopefully she hadn't ruined their "first date" with her poor choice of conversation, but Finn had listened with a sharp ear and without judgment. An element in his aura cemented her trust in him, pulling at her so wholly and allowing her to open up to him in a way that Ava wouldn't even know where to start analyzing it.

"What's the plan for Xena this afternoon?"

She turned to face him, watching his golden hair whipping in the wind. "More mobilization. She's getting better and is feeding so we hope she'll be independent by the weekend. But it'll take some time before she's climbing trees again."

"Seems like such a long recovery for a little bite."

"Yeah, but koalas have a unique physiology. Eucalyptus leaves are full of fiber and lack nutrition, so they have a very slow metabolic rate to maximize their energy. It's why they sleep for eighteen hours a day, so it also takes them longer to recover from injury and illness."

"Sounds like a hard life, all that sleeping. When do you think Xena and Cookie can return to the wild?"

"Eden thinks it'll be a few weeks yet."

"What happens if a koala's sick and she's in Townsville?"

"Depends. If it's an emergency and she's available, she'll come to the island as soon as she can. Otherwise, she relies on her volunteers."

"Why doesn't she run a vet clinic on the island?"

"It's not viable as there are only two thousand permanent residents. But she hopes to expand the hospital and get funding that'll allow her to work here full time so that she can also be a vet for local pets. But for now, she enjoys her job in Townsville."

And it would be difficult to get to stay. Ava tapped her fingers on the door of the Jeep as she contemplated how to go about that. Eden had already taken three days leave as her mum left for her cruise tomorrow, and she planned to return late Wednesday to work the weekend shift. Finding someone to cover that would be impossible.

"What does she need funding for at the hospital?"

Ava frowned. "Everything. The equipment, the drugs, the facilities—"

Finn waved his hand, halting her. "Sorry, that's not what I meant. I know she operates as a charity, but doesn't she have a backer? Regular government support? Donations?"

"She gets grants, but she only applies for certain ones since it's the government who are destroying the koalas' habitats. Sometimes she hosts fundraisers and she has a few regular donors who help keep the doors open. One gives a large sum every month. She calls him the Cheeky Wolf."

Finn snorted, then threw back his head and laughed. Ava's heart warmed at the deep, rumbling sound.

"I know. It's a ridiculous name, but that's what the money comes in under."

"That explains a lot. But you know ... Rain's stinking rich."

"I mentioned that, but thankfully, Rain denied it. Eden's a proud woman and doesn't want to accept large donations from her friends, but he does give a small amount that they agreed upon."

"And Rain's an honorable man, so he wouldn't donate more behind her back."

"Yeah, I think so. I mean, I only met him last week, but ..." Ava trailed off as Finn arched his eyebrows over the top of his sunglasses. "Are you being sarcastic?"

"You tell me."

Ava frowned. Finn had a point. Rain was filthy rich, owned a five-star beachside resort, and had built his own airstrip to operate his skydiving business. It wasn't that far-fetched that he'd anonymously donate a shitload of money to the Koala Hospital every month if he so desired. She and Eden had already established that Rain was a master secret keeper and talented at spinning tales. Just like Finn, if their story about how they found Xena and Cookie was any indication.

"I think their friendship is too strong for him to do that to her," she said as he turned into the parking lot at Eucalypts Grove.

Finn shoved the Jeep in neutral, lifted his sunglasses onto his head, and took her hand, gazing at her with wicked blue eyes. "You're probably right. But what about us? Are we friends?"

"I think so. Maybe ... a little more?" Her nerves coiled, liquifying her insides as the words escaped her mouth.

Finn's eyebrow quirked. "Was that a question?"

Ava cheekily threw his words back at him. "You tell me."

The tendons in his throat worked as he swallowed and tightened his hand around hers. "I'd like to see you again, Ava. Try to be more. And I meant what I said earlier. In the ocean."

Recalling the sensation of his thick, hard cock in her hand tenting his boardshorts, Ava shivered. "How you want me?"

"Yes, but not just like that. I'm not like the bastard who hurt you."

Ava blinked as his eyes flashed and a growl echoed from his chest. "I never thought you were."

"Good. Because how I want you … it's more than you can understand." He brushed his large, calloused fingers down her face, and Ava stilled, waiting for him to elaborate. But he didn't. "Will you come out on the jet boat with me on Wednesday?"

She nodded. "Okay."

"Good."

Then he cupped the back of her head and pulled her towards him. Heat clenched in her core as he pressed his mouth to hers and the hot bristles of his beard brushed her skin. Her lips parted and it took everything inside her not to whimper as her hands lifted to touch him. One found his shoulder, the other his rock-hard biceps. His tongue toyed with hers, and she melted. Fuck, this man could kiss.

Ava's neck arched as he took her lower lip between his teeth, then released it gently as he drew away.

"I'll see you Wednesday," he said.

She nodded, ignoring the disappointment in her belly. But they were both busy tomorrow and she needed to get out of the car. No matter how much she wanted to, she couldn't kiss Finn all day. "Let me know what time."

"I will."

He drew her towards him once more, causing her breath to hitch. But his nose simply found her temple, her ear, then dipped to her throat, where he drew in a deep breath and released his hold.

"You better go. Otherwise, I won't let you. You smell incredible."

Ava's brows tightened as she reached blindly for the door handle. "No, I don't. I smell like the ocean."

"That's what you think." His lips quirked. "Have a good day tomorrow. And don't forget to talk to Eden."

"I won't." She hopped out of the car. "Thanks, Finn."

He lifted his finger from the steering wheel, then she turned and strode away, not daring to look back at the glorious sex-god in the super-hot Jeep. Yet, her heart continued to soar as she returned to her room and hopped into the shower.

Finn was everything she'd ever wanted in a man. Sexy, yes, but also kind, exciting, and despite his alpha attitude, he was a man she could easily talk to. One who had listened to her story with rage and compassion battling in his beautiful eyes. And the desire? It was next level. Her hormones were out of control as her imagination ran wild. Biting down on her lower lip, Ava recalled the hard length of him through their clothes running along her cleft. Remembered his girth as she'd caressed him. His stamina as he'd miraculously kept them from drowning in the middle of Geoffrey Bay. It wasn't hard to envision his strong arms holding her as he drove that cock of his into her against this wall ...

Ava's knees buckled. Fuck. She might not want to rush things, but she felt comfortable with Finn and wanted him more than her next breath.

But since she had to wait until at least Wednesday, she turned off one tap and doused herself with cold water. Gasping, Ava resisted the urge to jump out as her skin pimpled. But her desire continued to linger and since she'd hate for it to vanish all together, she turned the hot tap back on, reached for her loofah, and washed quickly.

After drying off, she changed into a pair of shorts, a T-shirt, then raced out to her Mini. A few minutes later, Ava strode into the Koala Hospital to find Eden with Cookie in the outdoor enclosure.

"Hey! How was snorkeling?"

"Fantastic!" Ava bounced on the balls of her feet, unable to contain her grin. "The *Moltke* was awesome, then we swam all the way out to the propeller, which almost killed me."

Eden's eyebrows quirked as she dropped her hands from Cookie, who sat on the cross-branch helping herself to the gum leaves. "And? Don't hold out on me, girl."

"I kissed him."

Eden's grin almost split her face. "Yes! Oh my God, tell me everything!" She grabbed Ava's wrist. "Did he have a shirt on?"

"Nuh-uh." She shook her head, and Eden groaned. "And I clung to him like a koala in a tree."

Ava told Eden everything, shivering as she recalled the kiss, though she left out what had happened below the surface.

"Damn, Ava." Eden blew out her breath. "That is hot."

"I know." She leaned her shoulder against the support beam and studied Cookie. She'd spent a few days in homecare with Paula and had thrived on the leaves they'd matched from a photo Finn had sent. The fact he'd returned to that isolated part of the bush had been another thing that had turned her insides to mush, but there didn't seem to be much that Finn wouldn't do for Cookie. Today, the joey had been brought in so that Eden could assess her independence. "I mean, I wanted to kiss him a few times at the Forts, too." Like when he'd lifted her off the rock, when he'd helped her up the stairs, and when they'd simply stood marveling at the views. "But I wasn't sure, you know?"

"About him?"

"No, I wasn't sure if I was ready. But I don't want what Blair did to hold me back. And I like Finn. A lot."

Eden nodded, her smile holding all the secrets and knowledge that only a best friend possessed. "He's just your type, Ava. You might deny it, but you like the big, strong, alpha male type. They might have hurt you in the past, but you keep going back to them for a reason."

"I suppose. I do like men who take care of their bodies, and I guess that sometimes comes with an ego. But Finn isn't like the others. He might act tough, but deep down, he's a big softy."

Eden snorted. "Don't say that around him. Men like Finn wouldn't like being called soft. But he certainly showed that side of him when he brought in this little girl, didn't he?"

Ava smiled as Eden rubbed Cookie's back. "Yes, he did. And apparently, he has a Maltese-Shitzu."

"Finn? I thought he'd be more the big dog type."

"Me too. But it just proves again how sweet he is. Gracie was his neighbor's dog and when she died unexpectedly, he took her in."

"Wow ..." Eden crossed her arms and sighed wistfully. "Sounds like you've got yourself a keeper."

Ava's heart clenched as she admitted, "I hope so."

"When do you see him again?"

"Wednesday. He's taking me out on the jet boat."

Eden shuddered. "That wolf-looking boat that zooms at breakneck speed and spins over the water?"

"Yep. It's going to be fun."

"If you have a death wish."

Ava placed her hand on her friend's forearm. Eden had been afraid of fast boats, rides, and anything that she deemed "extreme" ever since a traumatic boating accident she'd experienced as a child. "I'll be perfectly safe, Eden. Don't worry."

Eden blew out her breath. "I know."

"Besides"—Ava tried a lighthearted grin—"you certainly have no problem watching Rain perform stunts on his jet ski."

Eden blushed. "Yeah, but you're the one who freaked out when Finn came off his."

Ava winced. She had no comeback there.

"But I'm glad you're not afraid, Ava. Of dating Finn. He's not asking for too much too fast, is he?"

"No, he's quite the gentleman."

"Good. Because I'd hate to see you go through what you did with Blair again. Not just him hitting you," she said before Ava could jump in, "but with his relentless pursual of you. You were terrified to say no."

Ava watched Cookie stand up on her little back legs and reach for a higher branch of leaves. Eden was right, which only solidified Finn's concerns. And hers. "I know." She took a deep breath. "I told Finn about him. It felt good to get it off my chest. And to see the fury burning in his eyes." Ava was woman enough to admit that she'd liked that—the protectiveness and desire to defend her honor. "And while we're on the subject, what do you say to staying here for the rest of the week?"

Eden smiled warily. "I'd love to, but you know I can't. I'm on call this weekend and besides, you don't need me when you have super sexy Finn to keep you entertained."

"No, but ... I was thinking—or Finn wondered—if Blair might use you to get to me."

"Blair doesn't even know me."

"That's what I said, but he's a cop, Eden. Who knows what information he can access."

"They can't access everything, Ava. They have rules."

Ava quirked her eyebrows. "Do you think Blair would abide by rules?"

"Well ... no. But I think you're overreacting."

"Maybe," she agreed. "But you're my best friend, Eden." Ava reached for her hand and squeezed. "I'd hate it if anything happened to you. It's only a couple of days."

"But I'm taking two weeks off when Isla comes next month for the Full Moon Party."

"I know, but I promise we'll have fun. We could even go hiking up Mount Cook way to track koalas?"

Temptation flickered in Eden's eyes as she glanced at Cookie. Ava's spine tingled as the more she thought about it, the more she felt Finn could be on to something. There was no telling what Blair might do to get to her and if Eden got hurt, Ava would never be able to forgive herself.

"I'll think about it," Eden sighed, and Ava smiled.

"Thank you."

FINN'S MOUTH watered at the scent of raw steak as he walked into Rain's house. His wolf growled, starving as neither of his appetites had been satisfied today. Though Finn would rather the sensation of Ava's warm body wrapped around his than the wet, metallic taste of raw beef.

Rain turned from the fridge behind the bar on the first floor of his multistory mansion, looking Finn up and down as he placed the meat in a cooler bag. "Looks like you made progress."

"Some." Finn couldn't hide it if he tried. Ava's scent covered him, and his wolf preened with pride as he placed his hands on the bar. He nodded towards the meat. "Is that blade and chuck steak?"

"Yeah, I kept the best for myself. Sly can have ribeye when he shifts back." Rain grabbed another tray from the fridge and elbowed the door closed. "So, things went well with Ava?"

"We're bonding. Saw some cool fish and the wrecks were awesome. Kissed her a bit."

Rain grinned. "Excellent, man."

He lifted his palm and Finn slapped him a high-five.

"Yeah, and she opened up about that Unfated bastard."

"Shows she trusts you. The emotional connection is supposed to be tough."

Finn snorted. "Yet you've already conquered it with Eden."

"Don't start." Rain yanked open the smaller fridge under the bar and grabbed two bottles of water. "It was a bit hard to avoid."

Finn caught the bottle Rain tossed him. "Yeah, because she sure does trust you. And I think Ava will trust me too, though it almost killed me not to reveal what I knew about Blair."

Rain twisted off the bottle lid. "Do you think she'll accept the wolf?"

"I haven't started to test those waters. But Blair seemed to have revealed enough of his twisted, unnatural side for her to accept my concerns about him using Eden to get to her, so she's going to ask Eden to stay."

Rain's shoulders sank. "Thank fuck."

"I didn't say she'd be successful," Finn warned him. "But she will ask."

"Dunno why she doesn't just stay here and work anyway," Rain muttered.

Finn smirked. "Why don't you just give her more money, Cheeky Wolf?"

Rain lowered his drink with a sigh. "How'd you find out about that?"

"Ava happened to mention the name of Eden's anonymous donor. She truly believes it's not you, doesn't she?"

"Because I told her so. Repeatedly. Swore it on everything I own."

"You lied to her."

"Bloody stubborn woman," he snarled, rolling his eyes. "I offered to give her enough money to build her dream hospital with all the latest equipment, a koala kindergarten, and a massive sanctuary where the koalas could live peacefully, and she said she couldn't accept."

Finn frowned. "Why?"

"Pride." Rain crossed his arms and leaned against the backbar. "She said she didn't want to *owe* me anything."

"So you give her the minimum she'll accept *and* whatever the Cheeky Wolf contributes?"

"Yep." Finn lifted his eyebrow until his friend's shoulders slumped. "And a little bit more."

"How many of her regular donors are you?"

"Dunno how many she has, but I know I'm four of them."

Finn chuckled. "She's going to be so pissed when she finds out."

Rain's eyes flashed. "What was I supposed to do? She wants to work here full time, and I want her out of Tyrone's territory. But the bloody stubborn woman could pay herself a full-time wage five times over and she keeps spending it on the fucking koalas."

Rain's chest heaved, and Finn laid his hand on his friend's shoulder. "I'm sorry, man."

"You reckon Ava will convince her to stay?" he asked, hope filling his eyes.

"We'll work on it. And if not, we'll sabotage every ferry that comes into the marina until no one can leave."

"I'm down for that." Rain swung the cooler bag over his shoulder and grabbed his keys. "But I'm glad things are progressing with you and Ava. What's next?"

"I want to take her on the JetWolf on Wednesday. If that's all right?"

"Sure, man. Whatever you need. But right now, we should take this food to Sly and go for a run."

Finn nodded as he kicked off his shoes and followed Rain

out the door. "Yeah, that steak smells fucking good. You know Ava doesn't eat meat?"

Rain's shoulders slumped. "Oh, thank fuck it isn't just me. Eden doesn't eat meat either."

Finn chuckled. "The Goddess really has it in for us."

"Tell me about it. Though I totally get where Eden's coming from, and I like the bean burgers she makes when I go over for dinner."

"Yeah, but you'd do anything for Eden," Finn said as they jumped into Rain's convertible.

"I know. I'm pathetic."

"Oh, buddy. Mating makes us all pathetic. But I wouldn't worry. When Eden finds out you fund her hospital, I'm sure she'll forgive you." He clapped his friend on the back. "*After* she skins you for your pelt."

Rain grimaced as he backed out of the garage. "I'm more worried about my balls. She cuts them off for a living."

Chapter 28

Ava's heart soared as she pulled into the Luna Views parking lot and saw Finn standing in the open entryway, his legs spread and hands on his hips. With his hair pulled back, sunglasses on, and hard jaw beneath his beard, he looked formidable. Unapproachable. She wanted to climb up his torso, wrap her legs around his waist, and feast on his oxygen until they were both breathless.

Grinning, she hopped out of the car and strode towards him. He lifted his sunglasses and her belly clenched as he watched her with cool, assessing blue eyes. The moment she stepped into the atrium, he reached out and snatched her around the waist.

"Afternoon, Ava."

"Hey." She slipped her sunglasses off and arched back to meet his gaze. Hungry eyes devoured her, sending a thrill straight to her belly as Finn lowered his head and pressed his mouth to hers. His fingers spread around her waist, almost spanning it as she clutched his tight T-shirt. Damn, he tasted good.

But before she could settle into the kiss, he drew lightly on her lower lip, then straightened. He grinned slowly. Seductively. As though he knew exactly what he did to her. "Ready to take a ride on the big bad wolf?"

Ava's knees wobbled as desire blazed through her core. She wanted to take a ride all right, but she wanted him. To be over him. Under him. To scratch her nails down his rock-hard abs as she rode him until he roared.

"I sure am."

"Excellent." Keeping his arm around her waist, he led her through the atrium and into the gardens. "How's your day been?"

"Busy. You should have seen Cookie. Paula said she's moving around the house more, so we encouraged her to climb and now she can't stop. She's a tough little thing."

"That's why I called her a tough cookie. And Xena's okay?"

"Still weak, but Eden's not worried."

Finn's hand firmed on Ava's hip. "Did you ask her to stay?"

"Yeah, she said she'll think about it, but I doubt it's possible. She can't get someone to cover her weekend shifts."

"Hmm ..." Finn's eyes darkened as he scratched his jaw. "We'll see what we can do about that later. First, let's have some fun."

"Yes." Ava skipped out of his hold as he gestured for her to precede him onto the pontoon, the metal clanging beneath her sandals. Finn had already spent the day taking tourists on the jet boat and she'd have been happy to join him on one of those. But as he stroked his fingers along the small of her back, Ava had to admit she was glad he'd insisted on a private ride.

He reached into the boat, black boardshorts stretching over his tight ass, and lifted out a life jacket. "Slip this on," he said, holding it open for her.

Ava didn't insist she could do it herself as she slid one arm through, then turned into him to do the other. As she faced him, he reached for the clips and strapped her in tight. Her nipples pebbled under the pressure.

"I'm not going to fall out, right? You won't spin us too fast?"

Grinning, Finn hooked his finger through the straps and pulled her against him. Ava's hands fell to his biceps and curled around his hard, warm flesh.

"I'm going to spin us so fast that your back will ache and throat will be raw with laughter. So, you better hold on tight."

Her body flushed as she arched against him. She could think of other fun activities that would leave her back aching and throat raw. "All right. Make me scream, Finn."

His hand tightened around her vest, pulling her up onto her toes as he kissed her. Ava knew she deserved the torture and torment of his wicked mouth, of the way his hand spanned the small of her back and pressed her against his hardening groin. But she couldn't help it, he was fun to tease.

His tongue stroked hers once more, then he ripped himself away and snatched up his life vest. Ava rocked back on her heels, barely resisting her grin.

"Right." He clipped the buckles, then extended his hand. "Ready to get wet?"

She stifled a snort. She already was. "Absolutely."

Ava took his hand and stepped into the front row while Finn untied the boat and jumped in beside her. There was no windscreen to protect them from the water, but Ava guessed that was the idea as she grasped the steel bar in front of her.

Finn revved the boat to life, tightened the band holding his hair back, then eased them away from the pontoon. Ava glanced out at the calm blue water, the sun low in the sky on the other side of Hawkings Point to create another lovely spring day.

"Ready?" he asked when they were a few meters out. Ava nodded, and Finn pushed down on the throttle.

Her back flattened against the seat, her forearms tensing as she held on tight. Finn let out a whoop as they sped away from Luna Views. Ava grinned, her hair whipping in her face as he steered the boat south, twisting and turning over the water. Ava rocked from side to side, tingles shooting through her body every time her shoulder bumped Finn's. Her toes curled and she couldn't stop smiling as she soaked in the view.

"Hold on!"

He spun the boat in a three-sixty, slamming her body against his as water sprayed over them. Ava squealed in delight, and Finn laughed as he let the boat idle.

"How was that?"

"Fantastic. Can we go faster?"

"We will once we get around Picnic Bay. I'll take you up to West Point, then we'll come back to the *SS City of Adelaide*." He tossed his arm around her shoulders. "Sound good?"

"Yep."

"Excellent."

He released her, leaving her shoulders cold. But Ava didn't mind as she nestled herself close beside him. Nothing would diminish the heat sizzling between them. This pull and need to be near him, to feel him, touch and taste him, it was not going away. She didn't want it to.

As they approached the Picnic Bay Jetty, Finn spun them in a U-turn, then skimmed the boat back across the water. She grinned like a loon. It almost felt like she was flying.

"Can I put my arms out?"

"Stand up."

She stared at him. "What? Like in *Titanic*?"

He shrugged. "Sure."

"You won't do a three-sixty?"

"No. You'd get seriously hurt."

She exhaled softly, then on wobbly knees, Ava pulled herself upright and spread her feet. She felt steady, but if anything, Finn seemed to increase the speed as her hair whipped back and water sprayed up over the front of the boat.

"Let go, Ava."

Before she lost her nerve, she flung her arms out. The wind hit her in the chest, and she grinned. "Oh my God!"

Finn chuckled. "Now, brace yourself."

Her heart lurched as Finn grabbed the back of her life jacket. "What?"

"I've got you, Ava. Trust me."

She did trust him and as they approached Hawkings Point, Finn gently turned the boat in a wide arch. Ava shifted her weight and leaned into it until they were facing Picnic Bay again. Once he'd slowed, she laughed and fell back down beside him.

"Thank you, that was awesome."

Finn smiled, turning his shaded gaze to hers as he slipped his arm around her waist. "I didn't know you were that fearless."

"I'm not."

"That's bullshit. You're a tough woman, Ava."

"You don't know that." The urge to stand and fly was so unlike her, she wasn't even sure why she'd done it. But it *had* been fun and while she might have told him things she hadn't told anyone else, there was still so much he didn't know about her. She trembled at the sight of spiders, wouldn't dare ride an upside-down rollercoaster, and she gave into favors, pleas, and coercion too often because it was easier than saying no.

If she were truly fearless, she'd never have accepted a date with Blair.

"Oh, but I do." Finn smirked, and she could sense his unsaid words as his fingers brushed her hip. *You told me so on Monday.* "You need to give yourself more credit."

Staring up at this gorgeous, golden man, something inside her loosened. He might be right. But since she didn't want to ruin this moment by thinking about what frightened her, she shoved it all aside and leaned into his warm body. "Can you spin me around again?"

"Only if you admit you're brave."

She drew in a deep breath. She could be brave. Brave enough to embrace what she felt for him. "I am brave, Finn."

"Good. Hold on."

She did, but this time, Ava ignored the bar and wrapped her arms around his waist. Finn didn't say a word as he shot them across the water away from Picnic Bay. They twisted and turned, wind whipping in their hair. Then he spun another three-sixty. She squealed as water sprayed over the hull and laughter roared from his chest. Finn wrapped his arm around her shoulders, and Ava melted. Peeking up at him, she lifted her chin and marveled at his glorious jaw, absorbing the strength embracing her and relishing in his warmth.

Finn might rock the golden bad boy surfer image and the hardened man of steel, but deep down, he was more than that. Finn was dependable. Reliable. Rain had called him and he'd come without question. He cared deeply and protected those he cared about. Like Cookie.

Like he would her. She hoped she wasn't mistaken by adding herself to that list, but he seemed to want her on a physical level, and she wanted him just as badly. Slowly, she ran her hand up his hard oblique, the bumps of his serratus, and the warmth of his pulsing pectoral before cupping his jaw and brushing her thumb through the scruff on his chin.

Finn lowered his head to hers. "How brave are you, Ava?"

"Brave enough to invite you to my bungalow tonight," she whispered without hesitation.

Finn inched closer, his eyes blazing. "Dinner first."

Ava shouldn't be surprised. Finn was always the gentleman. "Deal."

"But I'm down for easing this tension between us." His

lips curved, flashing his ridiculously straight white teeth. "All this touching you're doing makes it hard to drive the boat."

"You shouldn't be easily distracted."

"Your scent distracts me, Ava." Burying his nose in her sunshine hair, he inhaled. "You smell of strawberry."

"My shampoo."

"Hmm. And pine, which I find curious."

She grinned. "I have pine shower gel. Left over from Christmas."

"And peanut butter."

Her head tilted back with laughter. "Oh my God, Finn. Do you actually know what I ate for lunch or is it just your fantastic sense of smell?"

"Can't help it. I was born with it."

Ava moaned as he kissed her, sharing in his hunger. He must like peanut butter too as his tongue tried to extract every taste of it from hers, then he drew away with that sexy nip of her lip that he seemed to favor.

Sick of the barrier between their gazes, she lifted her sunglasses onto her head and brushed her fingers through his beard again. "I like this."

"The beard?"

"Yeah. I've never dated a man who grew his before or understood the appeal. Like with the actors and such. All the girls get hot over Aragorn and Thor and McSteamy." They were her favorites, anyway. "But now ... I get it."

"You like?"

"I like."

His lips quirked. "Good."

He crushed his mouth back to hers, the bristles prickling her skin as his lips dragged hers apart. Ava's blood fired, her head falling back as she gripped his and slipped her fingers into his hair. Her name growled from his chest as he nipped her lips and her core clenched tighter, hotter.

Ava gasped for breath as he released her lips and trailed his rough face over her jaw, up to her ear, then down to the throbbing pulse point in her throat. Her hands clenched around the straps of his life vest. Why the fuck he wore it, she didn't know.

Finn released her flesh and inhaled deeply, brushing his nose up her skin before drawing away.

"Forget your bungalow. We'll have dinner at Luna Views and then I'll take you back to my hut. They have the best restaurant on the island and heaps of vegetarian options."

She couldn't argue with that logic. "Okay. But maybe we should stop talking about it else I'm not going to wait that long."

"If anyone were to lose control, Ava, it'll be me." He released her so quickly she almost staggered into her seat. His hands dropped to the wheel. "But I'm trying to be a gentleman, and you want to see the *Adelaide*, right?"

"Oh, I almost forgot about that. Let's do it."

Finn lowered the throttle and the tension in Ava's spine released as they bounced over the water, the west coast of the island shooting by as they passed what she suspected was the *Adelaide*. But first, Finn wanted to twist and turn her again, making her laugh and squeal as he spun the boat a couple more times before idling back to the wreckage sitting abandoned on the reef.

"Wow ..." The rotting hull peeking up out of the water was almost invisible beneath the mangroves. "It seems like it was put there on purpose, doesn't it? Like some strange work of art."

"Sure does."

Staring at the beautiful sight, Ava thought it a pity it had practically been forgotten. Any time she had mentioned Magnetic Island shipwrecks to her colleagues or patients, they had stared at her with confusion or wonder. Not many people had heard of them and while she would admit they weren't the most spectacular of wrecks, they were still worthy of attention.

After circling the wreck a few times, Finn suggested they head back. He gave her one more run over the water, then pulled up by the pontoon. Powering down the boat, he leapt out and secured the ropes with what appeared to be such ease as his muscles bulged in a way Ava would never tire of admiring.

He extended his hand and she stood, her knees shaking as she climbed out.

"We'll have to do that again."

"On the jet ski." He nodded behind her and Ava turned, spotting the Sea-Doo she'd witnessed him manipulating the day they'd met. "I have Mondays off if you want to take the whole day to circumnavigate the island."

"Monday sounds good, Finn."

"We might even take Gracie."

Ava's heart clenched. "Oh, I have to meet her!"

"Now?"

She nodded and he wrapped his arm around her waist. "All right. She could do with a walk. Let's go."

Chapter 29

"Since it's low tide, we could walk down to Picnic Bay and look at the *George Rennie*?" Finn had seen the wreck from Rain's house but hadn't ventured into the water for closer inspection yet.

"That'll be cool. I have walking shoes in my car."

"I'll fetch Gracie and meet you in the car park, then."

Finn kissed her briefly, glad she wouldn't bear witness to his disorganized room, then backed away until she headed towards reception. Turning up the garden path, he raked his hands down his face. Fucking hell, that woman was hot. His cock still ached from her teasing in the boat and if he wasn't trying to be a gentleman, he'd have seduced her in the front seat of the JetWolf for anyone looking to see. His wolf rattled inside his cage, desperate to complete that physical act of the mating bond. But Finn wouldn't let him out.

Though if she liked his beard, she'd like it even more when he buried his face between her legs and made her scream tonight.

Shivering, Finn shook himself like a dog, then leapt up the steps to his hut. He'd need to tidy up because when they returned after dinner, he planned to use every part of it—the windows, the balcony, the bathroom. The bed. The place wasn't filthy, but he'd rolled right on in after a run in the bush last night and he didn't always pick up after himself. He wasn't a grub, but he was single and Gracie didn't care if he left his clothes on the bathroom floor. In fact, she preferred it as it gave her easy access to his socks. Just his socks. She wasn't interested in stealing anything else.

"Gracie, let's go for a walk."

Her head popped up from her bed by the partially open balcony door, allowing her outside access even though he doubted she'd take it. Unlike him, Gracie hated outside. She said so too when she made no effort to move.

He picked up her harness. "Do you want to meet Ava?"

Her ears twitched, but she didn't get up. Sighing, Finn strode towards her. "Good thing I'm bigger than you and you have no choice in the matter."

But she stood still in protest as he placed her feet through the leg holes and clipped her in. When he scooped her up, she dug her claws into his forearm to hold on, not trusting him to do the job properly. Grinning, he rubbed her scruffy head. "Come on, G.B. You'll love Ava."

I do.

Finn's chest clenched. Shit. Yeah, sure, he'd always planned to love his mate, but feeling the pull inside his gut and the heat in his body ... the ache around his heart and steel in his spine ... to have tasted her, smelled her ... all of that made his feelings true. And the urge to protect her even greater.

Pulling the door behind him, he practically strutted through the resort. Catching Rain's and Nate's gazes at reception, he offered them a two-finger salute, then strode into the parking lot.

Ava gasped at the sight of Gracie, and her eyes lit up. "Oh my God, she's so cute!"

Gracie's front claws dug deeper into Finn's forearm. She

huffed. Ava's grin widened. Finn placed Gracie on the ground where she huffed again in her half bark, half sneeze, her nose twitching as her little paws danced.

"She's a bit of a fruitcake."

Bent over at her waist, Ava's gaze shot up, her eyes narrowing. "Don't say that. She's just a baby."

Finn snorted as Ava extended her hand to Gracie. "She's five years old."

"Still a baby." Ava grinned at the little dog. "And you should be treated like one."

Gracie stopped her huffing, stilled, then looked over her shoulder at Finn as though to say, "Yeah. We keep her." She turned back to Ava and sniffed her hand, her tail wagging.

Ava rubbed Gracie's head. "We'll have cuddles later," she promised, straightening. "Can I walk her?"

"Sure." Finn handed Ava the leash without hesitation. "She's not trained, only walks when she wants to, and she doesn't like the wind on her butt."

"You *are* high maintenance, aren't you?" Ava took a step and Gracie hopped off the concrete onto the asphalt. And stilled. "Come on."

But Gracie refused to budge, probably hating the rough sensation of gravel beneath her paws. Finn sighed and scooped her back under his arm.

"See? Told you. She only likes being carried."

"If she doesn't walk, then why did you say she needed one?"

"Because being cooped up inside all day isn't good for any dog. So come on, let's take in the fresh air and see this shipwreck."

Tossing his other arm around Ava's shoulders, Finn strode through the car park. Ava wrapped her arm around his waist and smiled at Gracie.

"You're right. She is quirky."

"That's why I had to keep her. No one else would understand."

"They might have learned, but like I said. It was nice of you. And she is cute."

Finn's chest swelled. "She is."

"So, what's wrong with her leg?"

"She has Perthes Disease. I don't completely understand it, but the head of her femur is deformed and her hip doesn't work properly."

"Poor thing. I hear it happens a bit in dogs. Usually, it means the blood supply is disrupted and the bone tissue starts to die. Is she on medication?"

Finn shook his head, having forgotten that Ava probably knew all about Perthes disease as it occurred in people too. "She used to be on steroids, but her last x-ray was good and now I just give her anti-inflammatories in the morning so that she's not in pain. She has high quality food and lots of bickies with that glucosamine stuff in them."

"Sounds about right. Does she mobilize well?"

"She runs around and can stand up on her hind legs for a moment when I have beef jerky. But I still carry her up the stairs."

Ava squeezed him around the waist. "Oh, Finn. You can't spoil her. She needs to keep her hip strong and the only way to do that is if she uses it."

"Yeah but ... she doesn't like stairs."

"Probably not." She rubbed Gracie's head, then glanced up at him. "I don't want to tell you how to look after your dog, but honestly, small stairs should be encouraged. And walking."

Ava was probably right, but his gut churned all the same. He didn't want the little girl to be in pain, but nor did he want her hip function to deteriorate either. "But she still can't jump off the bed."

"Hell no. She needs some help, but you have to make sure she stays strong. Else one day, her leg will be lame. Do you get her checked regularly?"

"Yeah, and every vet has been happy with her." Neither of them liked going, but Finn had to be the stronger one to make sure Gracie was looked after. "She didn't need surgery as a pup because her mum got her started on treatment early."

"That's good. So, what are her other quirks?"

"Good thing we've got a bit of a walk," he said before filling Ava in on all his dog's dislikes and OCDs. When they reached the top of the hill, they veered off the road and down the goat track into Picnic Bay. Finn peered into the bush towards Hawkings Point, Rain's preferred stomping ground as it was conveniently located between his house and Luna Views.

"I think Gracie's lucky to have you," Ava said, descending the stairs ahead of him. "Fate knew what she was doing when she stuck you two together."

Finn almost stumbled down the track. "You believe in Fate?"

"Sometimes. I mean, usually things happen for a reason, but others ..." She sighed and waited for him as they arrived at the end of a street in Picnic Bay. "I don't know. There doesn't seem to be an explanation."

"Do things always need an explanation?" he asked, adjusting Gracie in his arms.

"I guess not. At work, they do. I need to know why a patient de-sats or why their muscle isn't activating. But other things? Not really."

The tightness inside him loosened. "There are a lot of things you can't explain in this world, Ava."

"Yeah. I know."

They continued walking through Picnic Bay and soon arrived at the end of the beach, Rain's glorious house looming over them as they strode onto the sand. Finn surveyed the twisted metal lying in the crystal-clear water.

"You've seen this wreck before, haven't you?" he asked.

"Yes, but not for a few years now. It's beautifully intact though."

They kicked off their shoes and Gracie dug her claws in deeper as they walked into the cool water. Getting wet was another thing Gracie did not like, but Finn wouldn't drop her.

They approached the wreck of the *George Rennie*, a steel-hulled ship that had scuttled in the lee of Hawkings Point over one hundred years ago. The base of the hull remained almost intact; a rib-like skeleton covered in coral with the bow poking out of the water.

Finn blew out his breath. "That's pretty neat."

"I know there's no mystery about it, but it's cool to have a shipwreck right on the beach."

"Especially one so beautifully preserved." Careful about where he placed his feet, Finn stepped over the edge and stood in the middle of the ship, glancing towards Townsville as fishermen sitting on the jetty waved to the approaching ferry. Ava waded slowly through the water, admiring the wreck as she tucked her hair behind her ears.

"Have you dived any shipwrecks?" she asked.

"Yeah, a few around Melbourne. The *Ex-HMAS Canberra* was cool, but The Ships Graveyard there is the best. So much to explore."

Her brow furrowed. "A graveyard? Like, where they—"

"Deliberately sink ships. Yep. There are forty-six there alone and it's bloody amazing."

"Wow. And I think *this* is cool." She glanced back at the *George Rennie*. "Is it hard to learn how to scuba dive?"

His lips quirked as he stepped over the wreck and moved towards her. "Not really. Why? You want to learn?"

"Maybe ..." Her eyes glittered. "Will you teach me?"

"Absolutely." He kissed her softly, lingering for a moment. "But you'll need to get used to swimming against currents first."

"I can do that."

Finn slipped his hand into hers as they admired the wreck for a few more minutes, then started to head back. Finn allowed Ava to precede him up the steps out of Picnic Bay, unashamedly admiring her ass as her shorts strained against her tight glutes. Once they reached the boardwalk, Ava wanted to try walking Gracie again and Finn decided to humor her. But his little dog trotted along enjoying the sea breeze with her tongue hanging out as though she had no care in the world.

Little minx.

"So, what time should I meet you for dinner?" Ava asked when they returned to Luna Views.

"I'll pick you up at seven."

"Don't be silly. We're dining here, so—"

"Ava, it's a date. I will pick you up."

She sighed. "Okay. Thank you."

"No worries." It gave him two hours to tidy up, shower, and organize dessert because like hell was he waiting past the main course to feast on her.

Smiling softly, she reached up and brushed her lips over his. "I'll see you then. Bye, Gracie."

Ava picked the dog up, kissed her head, and placed her in Finn's arms before sashaying back to the car. He admired her legs as she climbed in over the lack-of-doors and clipped on her seatbelt. Finn lifted his hand in a wave as she backed out of the car park, watching her blonde hair fly in the wind as she disappeared down the road.

Chest expanding, he glanced at his dog. "Yeah, Gracie. The Goddess has been kind to us."

Yet the hairs prickled on the back of his neck as he returned to his room. Despite the dangers, he wanted Ava. He could keep her safe. She feared going home to Townsville as much as he did, so he'd find a way to keep her on the island. Hell, come the full moon, she might even learn the truth. The mating bond rarely took longer than a moon cycle or two to complete, unless a wolf was an idiot like Rain and resisted it. Once Finn was sure his union with Ava was solid, that she loved him and he her, the only way to complete their bond was to tell her the truth.

Finn kicked his door closed and placed Gracie down with a groan. Ava might believe in Fate, but that didn't mean she'd easily accept that the paranormal was true. That Fate played a role in everyone's lives. That he was a man who shifted into a wolf and that the monster she'd escaped from wanted to do more than get her back.

But that was the last thing Finn wanted to think about as he unclipped Gracie from her harness. He needed to tidy up and get this place into shape, because tonight—

Finn stilled, his wolf's ears twitching as beside him, Gracie released a low growl. Digging his fingers into yesterday's T-shirt, Finn's heart hammered as he lifted his nose into the air and took a deep breath.

He released it in a huff. Gracie barked.

Wolf.

Ava!

Dropping the shirt on Gracie's head, Finn ran.

Chapter 30

A chorus of rainbow lorikeets welcomed Ava's return to Eucalypts Grove, screeching in delight at feeding time and causing quite a ruckus as they flew from one tourist's outstretched hand to another. The birds' excitement almost reflected her own, a different kind of hunger humming through her body as heat simmered in her thighs. Ducking her head to hide her blush, she passed the tourists and skipped up the path. Part of her wished Finn had laid her over the seat and devoured her in the jet boat, but while she liked hot sex, she wouldn't sacrifice her dignity. There was a time and place, and Rain's boat shouldn't be one of them.

But alone beneath the brightening moon with the waves crashing beneath his ocean view balcony? Yeah, she could lose herself in Finn then. Feel the strength in his arms, suck on his abs, and thread her fingers though his golden hair as his beard chaffed her skin.

Ava almost stumbled on the boardwalk. She needed to stop thinking about it else she'd beg him to skip dinner, which wouldn't be the worst idea. But despite the magnetic pull between them, she'd seen the determination in his eyes earlier. *I'm trying to be a gentleman.*

Ava shivered and skipped in delight. Finn *was* a gentleman. He considered her, showed her respect, and that itself was hotter than his rippling pectorals.

So she needed to shower, shave her legs, wash her hair, then figure out what she was going to wear. She'd brought some pretty dresses and matching sets of underwear, but not those made for night games, so the purple lace bra and undies would have to do. She had a simple little black dress and a pair of cute flats, neither of which she would normally wear on a date where she wanted to feel feminine and sexy. Finn wouldn't mind, but she liked to have the confidence boost of her hidden undergarments and heels.

Not that it would matter once the lace was scattered on the floor.

Grinning, Ava turned towards her bungalow. As movement flashed in her periphery, she lifted her gaze from her skipping feet.

And drew to a halt.

Blair turned from her front door, his mouth stretching into a grin as dark hair curled over his forehead. "Hello, Ava."

She opened her mouth, but no words came out. Panic skittled up her spine as her hand tightened around her keys. The metal dug into her palm. Her knees locked.

Blair descended the two steps onto the path. "Miss me, baby?"

Her stomach churned at the slime in Blair's voice. The same malicious gleam filled his eyes that had the night she'd run. His nostrils flared, shoulders tensed. He looked like a lion ready to pounce, and she stumbled back a step.

She had to get away. Get back to the safety of the common areas. Yell for help. Why had she been placed in a bungalow at the back of the resort?

"You ... you shouldn't be here. Please. Go away."

Blair's teeth flashed. "Ooh, Ava. Come on now, you don't mean that."

Her nails dug into her palm. "Yes, I do. I don't want you here."

"You don't know what you want." His eyes darkened as he stood before her, hands in his pockets. "First, you denied me when all I wanted was a date. Then after we go to dinner, you agree to go away with me and denied me sex!" His mouth twisted into a sneer, his breath huffing. "What did you expect a man to do, Ava?"

Her heart pounded. She wanted to retreat, but she held her ground. She could do this. No one else would stand up for her. "I did not agree to go away with you, Blair. It was meant to be a day trip. You never asked me if I wanted to stay the night. If you had, I'd have told you I wasn't ready for that."

"It was a surprise!"

"And it was an ill-thought out, unwelcome one. Now, I will only ask you one more time. Please leave."

"Ava ..." Light ebbed into his dark eyes as he reached for her wrist. "Don't be—"

"No!" She tried to pull away, but Blair's grip hardened, and his lips curled into a snarl.

"What are you going to do?" He squeezed and she whimpered under the pressure. "You can't go to the cops. I *am* the cops! Those bastards you're running with might think they can take this island, but I *own* this town."

Before she could wonder who and what he meant, Blair grabbed her other arm and pulled her towards him. She cringed as her breasts pressed against his lean chest, sludge oozing down her spine as she tried to free herself from his grip. But he was too strong.

"Let me go, Blair. Please."

His face twisted into something even more revolting.

"Aww, she begs. Come on, baby." He lowered his mouth to her ear. "Beg me for it."

Bile rose in her throat. She shoved him again, but he was like granite and wouldn't budge. Then Blair's mouth closed over her ear and he sucked. Loudly.

Crying out in disgust, Ava crumbled. The sludge filled every crevice of her soul, squeezing around her heart as his tongue slivered into her ear. A thousand spiders scuttled down her spine. She couldn't fight him. She didn't know how she'd escaped him last time, and now—

Thundering footsteps echoed behind her, followed by a thump, a grunt, and the vise released from her forearms. Her bones sprung back into place as she gasped and stumbled sideways until her hands found a tree.

"Get your filthy paws off my woman!"

The growl was unlike anything she'd heard before. Catching her balance, her head snapped up to find Blair pressed against a tree with his feet dangling inches from the ground.

And Finn's hand at his throat.

FINN COULDN'T CATCH his breath as fury unlike any he'd ever felt coursed through his veins. His bond with Ava had tugged at his gut and alerted all his senses until only two words had occupied his brain.

Ava. Trouble.

He'd thundered through reception, roared orders at Nate, then jumped into the Jeep. He'd broken every road rule as he'd sped across the island, but he'd had to get to her. Ava. His mate. His family.

The red haze eased from Finn's vision, but his hand

continued to tighten around the bastard's throat. His wolf snarled. *He* snarled.

Blair's eyes widened. "Fuck me, look who finally came out of hibernation. Little Finlay. Thought I smelled a traitor."

Finn's wolf snapped and bared its teeth. His forearm corded. He longed to squeeze the bastard's throat. He deserved it after all those years he'd bullied Finn, after the abuse and calling his mother a whore.

He deserved it for hurting Ava.

But her horrified gasp locked his wolf back in his cage. "You know him?" she cried, her shock ricocheting through the gum trees and drawing Finn out of his murderous haze.

Gritting his teeth, he released the scum and reveled in the mild satisfaction of watching Blair crumble to the ground.

"Touch Ava again and I'll bite your fingers off one by one."

Smirking, the slimy bastard unfolded his lanky form. He brushed dirt from his forearms and heaved a nonchalant breath as he glanced at Ava. "Who are you talking to, dearest? Me? Or my pathetic little brother?"

A strangled cry ripped from her throat, her eyes widening as her hands flew to her mouth.

Finn's fists clenched. "I am *not* your brother." He turned to Ava, her pain cracking their forming bond. "Ava—"

"No! Stay where you are!"

Finn froze, his wolf howling and leaving his heart quivering.

Blair sniggered. "Ooh. Rejection hurts, bro."

Finn rounded on him and bared his teeth. "Get the fuck off this island."

"No."

"Don't test me, Thorne." Finn stalked towards him, barely resisting the urge to shift and sink his teeth into the bastard's jugular. The flash of yellow in Blair's eyes told him he preened for a fight too. "Leave. Now."

Blair lifted his chin. "Make me."

"Our pleasure." Rain's voice rolled down the pathway like a boulder, his footsteps thundering ahead of Nate, Kai, and Chad's. "Get off our island, Thorne, or suffer the consequences of the lore."

Blair's lips flattened, his nose curling as he glared at Rain and the younger wolves. When his gaze returned to Finn's, pure hatred filled his dark irises.

"You can't protect her forever," he snarled.

"Oh, yes, I can." Finn backed up until he stood shoulder to shoulder with his mate. Pain shuddered through him when she flinched, but he didn't show it. "And I will. Especially against monsters like you."

"You little—"

But before Blair could take two steps, Rain and the pack formed a barrier between him and Finn, the veins bulging in their forearms crossed over their heaving chests.

For a moment, nothing moved as Blair shot daggers at each of wolf individually. But his eyes were on Finn when he said, "I'll be back for you."

Then his gaze shifted to Ava, leaving her with a dirty promise before he turned on his heel and left.

"Nate, Kai, see him onto the ferry," Rain said.

The two young wolves followed Blair, then with a nod in Finn's direction, Rain left with Chad.

Finn turned to Ava, his pulse pounding in his throat. "Are you hurt? Did he—"

She lifted her hands, blonde hair whipping over her shoulders as she shook her head, tears glistening in her eyes. "Okay, Finn. You need to explain this because I don't understand. Blair is your *brother*? How is that possible? Wh-what is ...?" Her hands fell and face twisted, her disgust shattering him. "And why the hell were Rain and the others ...? How did you even know ...?" She gestured towards where the men had disappeared, then sank her teeth into her lower lip. "Finn, what is going on?!"

He shot forward and grabbed her wrists before she could stop him, tearing her fingers from her hair before interlocking them with his. Finn understood her confusion and sensed her fear. He couldn't imagine what he and the pack had looked like as they defended their territory against that monster.

But how could he explain it?

"I'll tell you all that I can, Ava. But first, let's get one thing straight. Blair is *not* my brother."

"He's not?"

"Well ... technically he is," he muttered, the truth tasting like dirt on his tongue. "Half-brother. The bastard my father had before ... me."

Ava tried to wrench herself free, but he wouldn't let her go. "So, he *is* your brother."

Bile bubbled in his throat. "He made my life a living hell, Ava. I haven't seen Blair or my father in fifteen years. They are *not* my kin. Not my family. I feel nothing for them. But you are ..." His heart twisted as he observed the disbelief widening her eyes and whatever it was that made her tremble. Fear? Disgust? Either way, he didn't like it.

But he couldn't tell her the truth. He couldn't tell her about the feelings that had captured his heart and infiltrated his blood like a virus. He couldn't tell her about their mating bond and that Fate was stronger than she knew. He couldn't tell her the depths of Blair's sadistic nature. But fuck, he had to say something else risk losing her.

He forced his hands to uncurl from her forearms and stooped to bring his gaze level with hers. "You are important, Ava. To me. More important than anyone else will ever be."

He paused, resisting the urge to touch her and longing for

her to look at him. It felt like an age until the breath eased from her body.

"Is that true?"

He nodded. "Yes, Ava."

She peeked up at him. "Blair isn't your brother."

"Not like yours are. I didn't even know Blair and Tyrone lived in Townsville until I arrived on the island. And I ... I didn't know ..." But it was hard to lie to her, so placing his finger underneath her chin, he lifted her gaze higher. "It was only by some sick twist of fate that Blair's the one who hurt you when I ..."

Her eyes softened. "You what, Finn?"

I'm the one the Moon Goddess tied you to for eternity. But he couldn't say that, so he softened his jaw and said, "I care about you, Ava. And when he comes back—"

Her eyes widened. "Shit! He's going to—"

"Not while I'm here, he won't." Finn didn't care that he sounded like a brute. When it came to Ava's safety, he wouldn't be anything but. "Blair won't lay another dirty paw on you."

Her eyes shimmered, her lashes blinking rapidly as though she struggled between wanting to crumble, or leap into his protective embrace. Either way, he was there to catch her as he pulled her into his chest. She went willingly, her arms snaking around his waist.

Finn's lips quirked and his wolf howled.

"I knew he'd come. That he'd want me back."

"He can want all he likes, Ava. He'll have to get through me first."

Her fingers dug into his spine. "I was scared. I just ..." She lifted her head, her brow furrowing. "Why are you here? How did you—"

Finn touched his lips to hers, stopping the questions he

couldn't answer. "It doesn't matter. I mean it, Ava. I will keep you safe. We'll work out a plan. Rain and I—"

"Yeah, what was with him? And the other guys? Blair seemed to—"

"Come with me to Rain's tonight and we'll tell you everything we can."

"All right. I'll have to talk to Eden, too."

"Bring her. We'll strategize."

"And I'll ask her if she'll stay. I can't bear the thought of her going back to Townsville now."

"We'll convince her." Resisting a smirk, Finn reached up and brushed her hair behind her ear. "Now, I'm not leaving you alone, so grab what you need for the night. We'll figure out where you can go and what we'll do. I'll wait right here."

"I do need to shower," she muttered, cringing as she lifted her shoulder towards her ear. The one Blair had tried to devour. Finn would knock his teeth out for that.

"Take all the time you need."

She backed up towards her bungalow. "You can come in—"

"Best I don't. I'll wait right here."

He jumped off the boardwalk and turned to sit on the edge of her elevated patio, slipping his bare feet into the dry foliage of eucalyptus leaves.

Ava frowned as she ascended the steps. "Do you ever wear shoes?"

"Sometimes." He flashed her a grin. "But on this occasion, I was in a hurry, and it slipped my mind."

"Hmm ..." More questions flashed through her eyes as she opened the door. "You're a strange man, Finn."

"Honey, you don't know the half of it."

His grin widened and she smiled softly in return before slipping inside. She left the door open, but he turned away.

The smile slipped from his face as he glared into the bush and curled his hands over the edge of the patio.

He didn't know why Blair had waited so long, but the rogue had encroached on their territory. Touched his mate. Threatened them.

Finn heaved out a deep breath. If only Sly wasn't hiding in the woods. If only he was willing to face life again and defend his island.

But the Alpha had abandoned them, so it was up to Finn. He would stand up to Blair, to Tyrone, and he would defend their territory. Defend the pack.

And above all, he would protect Ava.

Maybe then, once he'd proven Fated mates could conquer, Sly might be willing to emerge from the bush.

Chapter 31

Ava should have known that the sprawling, architecturally designed house perched onto the side of Hawkings Point was Rain's. He clearly enjoyed flashing with the cash and didn't care about saving on electricity bills when all three floors overlooking Picnic Bay were lit up like a beacon.

"Wow," she breathed as they curved up the driveway. "Wouldn't it be nice to wake up to that view every morning."

Eden leaned forward, resting her elbows on the back of Ava and Finn's seats as she gazed up at the glittering mansion. "Yeah. Gorgeous, isn't it?"

It was bloody stunning. The driveway sloped up to the first floor, which featured a spectacular veranda cantilevering over the beach where Ava, Finn, and Gracie had stood only hours earlier. The next two levels boasted wide verandas too, all three floors and the roof held up by two V-shaped pillars.

"There's more balcony space than interior square footage, I reckon," Eden said as Finn parked the Jeep outside the triple garage. "It's only four bedrooms, with the master taking up the top floor, and he has his own private trail that meets up with the Hawkings Point track."

"That's convenient." Though while she might be impressed, Ava's heart continued to race as she strolled to the door beside Finn. He reached for her hand, squeezed, and her shoulders relaxed.

Rain greeted them at the front door. "Hey, guys."

Ava smiled softly as they strolled into the living room. Rain. No wonder Eden was drawn to him as he was another mystery all together.

The four of them fit comfortably into the elevator—because why would a billionaire bother with stairs?—and rose to the second floor. Arriving in the kitchen, Ava took a moment to admire the view of Picnic Bay, the jetty, and the glistening lights of Townsville across the vast black ocean before turning her back on it all and sliding onto the barstool Rain offered her. Placing her hands on the massive island countertop, she surveyed the two men.

Rain and Finn might have their secrets, but she couldn't protect herself from Blair if she didn't know the truth, and she wasn't leaving tonight without answers.

She'd had plenty of time to think while she'd scrubbed every inch of Blair from her body, but she still couldn't make sense of what she'd learned. So many questions raced through her mind, the biggest being how Finn and Blair could possibly be brothers. They were so different. They even *looked* different. Sure, they had different mothers, but even genetics couldn't make that big a difference in a person, especially two men who shared a father. They might both be tall and strong, but Blair was positively lean beside Finn's bulk. Blair was cruel and calculating, while Finn was kind and thoughtful. Blair had revolted her from the moment he'd flashed his sleazy smile, whereas Finn had done nothing but make her heart sing and insides warm with pleasure.

He made her feel safe.

But he still had secrets she longed to discover, and so did

Rain. What had he meant earlier? *Get off our island or suffer the consequences of the law*. What law? Rain didn't own the island. Well ... she didn't think he did. Magnetic Island wasn't like Hamilton or Orpheus. Most of it was national park while the rest was governed by the Townsville City Council. Rain might own Luna Views, the runway, and had somehow obtained approval to build a house on this point, but it wasn't *his* island.

Though by the frustration huffing from Blair's nostrils at having to obey Rain and his young cadre of daredevils, Ava wasn't so sure.

And that was another question. How had they come to her aid so quickly? How had they known Blair was there? And why hadn't Finn been surprised to see him?

"What would you like to drink, Ava?" Rain asked, opening the fridge. "I have red wine, spirits, or a bunch of non-alcoholic beverages."

"She'll have some of my Diet Coke," Eden said, reaching into the glass-fronted cupboard beneath the island counter and extracting tall-stemmed glasses. "Ava doesn't drink alcohol."

"No wonder you're friends," he muttered, reaching for the bottle of Diet Coke and the wine. "Finn?"

"Water's good."

Eden poured herself and Ava drinks while Rain popped open the wine. "I have lasagna sauce in the fridge if you'd like that for dinner, Eden."

"Oh, yum. Would you like me to make it?"

"If you like. You know I'm hopeless."

Eden gripped his shoulder. "No, you're not. You just like it better when I make it."

"Tastes better," he muttered before throwing back a mouthful of Shiraz.

Eden got to work, knowing her way around Rain's kitchen. Ava smiled softly, then took a deep breath.

"So, what do you two know? Hmm? Who exactly is Blair?" She glanced between Rain and Finn before focusing on the golden man beside her. "Why were you not surprised to see him despite your claim that you didn't know he lived here? And why did you" —she turned to Rain—"appear to be marking your territory?"

Her questions were met with silence. Eden, too, studied men while placing a baking dish on the bench. Rain watched Ava as he sipped his wine, then turned to Finn.

"What I told you is true, Ava," Finn said. "I hadn't known Blair and Tyrone were here, but when I learned they were the ones giving Rain trouble, I wasn't surprised. They've always been nasty, twisted, evil ... creatures."

Ava frowned. She'd think that description was a little over the top if it wasn't, well, true.

"I didn't know Finn was related to them either," Rain said. "Blair and Tyrone form a sort of, for lack of a better term, underbelly."

Ava's eyebrows shot up. Underbelly? Organized crime. In Townsville? Again, preposterous, except it also sounded ... true.

"But they're cops! Tyrone Thorne is the superintendent and—"

"Which means no one can stop him," Rain said. "It's why crime in Townsville is out of control. Half of the cops are part of it while the others have no choice but to knuckle down and keep quiet. They also have other ... nocturnal workers on the payroll."

"Something about the way you say that makes me shudder," Eden said, laying pasta sheets in the dish.

"Me too," Ava said. "But I still don't get it. What do they want?"

Finn and Rain glanced at each other again, and Ava blew out an exasperated breath. "What is with you two? Can you read each other's minds?"

Finn almost choked on his water while Rain lowered his glass with a smile. "Not right this second."

Ava's and Eden's frowns deepened.

"There's something strange about you two ..." Eden said.

Ava shook her head. "Anyway, what do Blair and Tyrone want?"

"What any mob boss wants," Rain said. "Money. Power. Control over their territory."

"They're greedy motherfuckers, Ava. Always have been and always will be unless they're stopped."

Still confused, Ava sipped her drink as she studied Finn and the lines creasing his forehead. How could this evil "mob boss" be Finn's father? "And you haven't seen either of them in fifteen years?"

His blond jaw hardened. "Not since I ran away. I spent five years being tortured by those bastards until I escaped them. I was fifteen and finally free."

Ava's heart clenched. Fifteen. He'd been alone since he was fifteen after losing his mother and—

She gasped, her hand shooting to her mouth. "Oh my God. Did he kill ..." She couldn't say it. It was too awful. But Finn understood her question as his chest expanded, and he nodded. Ava sucked her lower lip between her teeth, blinking back tears. "Oh, Finn ..."

"I can't prove it, but Tyrone killed my mother."

She stood, aching as she rounded the bench, slid her arms around his middle, and nestled into his side, Finn welcomed her in a one-armed embrace as he placed a kiss in her hair.

"I'm sorry, Finn. I don't know what else to say."

"It's fine. She didn't deserve such a death, but one day, I will make sure Tyrone pays."

Ava straightened out of their cuddle but kept her arm around his waist. "I can't believe how small this world is. How your brother and I ended up living in the same apartment block. How he pursued me like he did."

Finn's eyes darkened. "I'll make sure Blair pays for that, too."

A strange heat shot through her, but she ignored it. "You know what? He didn't seem surprised to see you either."

"Blair and Tyrone have their spies," Rain said. "They knew he was here."

"Oh." She didn't know about the crooked workings of the underbelly, but that made sense. "Still ... how could you threaten him with the law on your island?" she asked Rain. "It's not yours. Is it?"

Rain's eyes clouded, and his gaze dropped to his glass. "No, but it's ... my family has had a lot of influence. And the Thornes weren't happy when we came here and made our mark."

"You mean, when you built Luna Views?" Eden asked, opening the oven. "I know many people had a problem with that, but—"

"It's complicated," Rain said, lifting the lasagna dish before Eden could and sliding it into the oven. "The Thornes might *think* they have money and power, but the difference between them and me is that I actually do."

He closed the oven with a thump, and Eden's eyebrows shot up. "Oh, you do, do you?"

"Have you seen my resort?"

"Yeah, and I know you have money. But power?"

"Money is power, Eden. At least, it usually is." Rain reached for his glass and sipped his wine. "We built Luna Views and brought thriving businesses and jobs to the island. Tyrone didn't like that. It undermined him in ways the two of you wouldn't understand. And so ... he murdered my sister-in-law."

Ava stilled, her mouth dropping open with a silent gasp. It was true. The police *had* covered up the brutal murder of that woman. Tyrone and Blair ...

Her fists clenched. "I'm sorry, Rain. I heard about that, and it was just awful."

"It was. And my brother has never recovered."

"Do you still hear from him?" Eden asked, placing her hand on Rain's back.

"Rarely. When I do, he doesn't say much."

"Where did he go?" Ava asked, having heard he'd left after the incident, abandoning Rain and the resort.

"He's out there somewhere," Rain said, waving his hand in no particular direction. "Living as a recluse."

"But he's okay?"

"He's alive, but I don't think he'll ever truly be himself again unless we bring Tyrone and Blair to justice."

"And how do you plan to do that?" Eden asked.

Again, the men exchanged a prolonged glance. Ava wouldn't be surprised if they did have a telepathic connection, if such things existed, because words were certainly passing through their eyes.

"That's for us to work out," Finn said before turning to Ava. "For now, the most important thing is to keep you safe. You were right about Blair. He's obsessive. He's a predator and he will continue to hunt you."

A shiver coursed down her spine. Finn made Blair sound like an animal. Like she was his prey and he wouldn't stop until he sank his claws into her and ... and killed her.

He might have killed before.

"Then what's she supposed to do?" Eden whispered. "The police won't help her, but—"

"We will," Rain said, lifting the basket of bread rolls. "Come sit down and we'll discuss it."

They strode through the concertina doors onto the balcony, settling around the outdoor dining table. Waves lapped below them while the ocean breeze added a salty tang to the rich aroma of lasagna drifting from the kitchen.

Ava sat beside Finn and across from Eden, accepting a bread roll from Rain. "I knew this would happen. How am I supposed to go back to work when—"

"You won't be going back to work," Finn said, biting into his roll.

"I know we talked about it—"

"You can't go back to Townsville. Not until this is resolved."

Ava frowned at the steel in his eyes, the cording in his shoulders. He radiated tension. Anger.

She glanced at her bread. Damn, she hated this. She couldn't argue with him. Despite Blair's presence today, she was safe on this island, whereas if she returned to Townsville, she'd be walking right into the hands of the mafia.

But while Finn might want to protect her, he didn't need to be a jerk about it.

"So, she's just supposed to stay here, then?" Eden asked, refilling her and Ava's glasses.

"Yes, but you can't stay at Eucalypts Grove," Rain said, and Finn nodded in agreement.

Ava's belly sank, though she'd already realized that. Blair knew she was there now and she had nowhere to hide when she was alone on the edge of the bush with only wildlife as her neighbors.

She looked at Eden. "Maybe I should stay at your mum's house with you?"

"Where you're alone?" Rain's lip curled. "I don't think so. You'll stay at Luna Views."

Ava's heart leapt as her gaze shot to Finn's. "I don't—"

"You can have your own room." Finn's eyes narrowed at Rain. "Right?"

Ava didn't know whether to be offended or relieved. If things had gone to plan, she'd be enjoying dinner with Finn alone right now before dragging him back to his room and discovering all the ways he could make her scream and squirm. But Blair's unfortunate timing had destroyed her night of hot sex, replacing her sizzling desire with crippling fear.

But she liked that despite Finn's defense of her and the overprotectiveness bulging in his muscles, he wouldn't put her in a position that made her feel vulnerable. And even though that made him a gentleman, it also made him stupid.

"We have some rooms in the main hotel and Ava will be safe there. But we're booked up next week with the Full Moon Party."

"The main hotel would be lovely, Rain," she said, before turning to Finn. "Or I just stay with you."

His gaze whipped to hers. "What?"

"Are you going to sleep knowing I'm tucked up in the hotel? Or will you be prowling the halls making sure that Blair hasn't snuck back onto the island?"

Rain covered his snort with a sip of wine as Finn stroked his jaw.

"Fuck. You know me so well."

Ava popped another piece of bread into her mouth. It might not be the smartest idea she'd had, but she wouldn't rest if she were alone and based on the primal alpha act Finn had pulled since Blair arrived, Ava doubted he would be satisfied unless he had his eyes on her.

She had to admit, she liked that. She might be scared, but she didn't need to feel it. And it didn't make her any less of a woman to take comfort in the idea of having someone, anyone, there to watch her back.

She was just lucky that someone was Finn.

"It'll be fine." She said it to reassure herself, though she blushed at Eden's suggestive eyebrow wriggle. "And I still think you should stay, too."

"Me?" Eden placed her hand on her chest. "But—"

"She's right," Finn said. "You can't go home."

"But I—"

"Didn't you hear what we said?" Rain growled. "About the Thornes and their rogue ... underbelly ways?"

"Yes, but they don't know—"

"They know about you," Finn said, sharing another secretive look with Rain. "You're Rain's friend and ... like we said. They have their spies."

Eden huffed, clearly annoyed. "So, am I to stay at Luna Views too?"

"You'll stay here," Rain said, staring into his wine. "Upstairs."

Eden blinked. "Why can't I stay at Luna Views?"

"Like I said, we're booked out." But again, Rain didn't look at her.

"Fine," she muttered, ripping into a bread roll. "Hold me prisoner, then."

Rain's nostrils flared. "You don't have to stay, Eden. You have every right to refuse."

Eden exchanged glances with Ava as they had their own telepathic conversation. *Do I?* Eden asked, and Ava's eyes softened as she shook her head.

"No, it's okay. I'll stay."

She sounded resigned, but Ava didn't miss the slight curve of her friend's mouth. Ava almost smiled herself as at least Eden would be safe. This thing she had with Blair now went beyond her own issues with him. Eden was Rain's friend and Blair had history with him, too. She still didn't understand it or why the cops would cover up the murder of Rain's sister-in-law, but the reason any criminal mastermind did anything was often convoluted and didn't make sense to people who weren't psychopaths.

Ava shuddered and sipped her drink. She'd known she'd had poor taste in men, but Blair had taken it to a whole new level. And while she might have overpowered him once, she doubted she'd be able to do it again. Today, she'd been defenseless, fear rooting her to the spot as his mouth had descended ...

She shivered, violation crawling over her skin like spiders. Then Finn's hand fell to her knee and the spiders vanished.

"You okay?" he asked, a cloud of concern passing through his blue irises.

"Yeah. I was just ... something still doesn't make sense. I mean, I know I told you I was worried about going home, but part of me thought I'd manage it. I could take extra precautions and if Blair started to stalk me, then I thought someone in the police would help. But now ..." She shook her head as dread slumped her spine. "What am I going to do? Will I ever feel safe again? When can Eden and I go home?"

Finn massaged her thigh and glanced at Rain. "We sort of have a plan."

Rain nodded. "It's complicated, and we won't lie to you. Our mission to take down the Thornes won't happen overnight."

Eden's brow furrowed. "You can't bring down a mafia boss on your own."

But as Rain poured himself another glass of wine and shared a secret look with Finn, Ava didn't doubt him. There was a lot these two weren't telling them, and Ava wasn't so sure she wanted to know. She'd thought Blair was simply a police officer with a twisted moral compass that didn't include the phrase "no means no", but he turned out to be the son of a mob boss who'd covered up the most brutal murder Townsville had seen in years. The murder of Rain's sister-in-law, a death that had sent his brother running for the hills. Ava didn't blame him for wanting to bring justice to the cops who had killed her.

Then Finn had turned up out of the blue to work for Rain and help him with some personal matters. At least, that's what he'd said, but now ...

"Or can you?" Ava whispered. "Is that why you're here?"

Eden gasped. "Of course! If the Thornes are organized crime, then you two must be here to stop them."

Heart hammering, Ava watched the hard line of Finn's jaw as he sipped his water. It would make sense and answer many of her raging questions. Finn possessed a dangerous aura and strength that seemed to defy even his own perfectly sculpted body. How he'd held her in the water while she'd clung to him proved he had extreme levels of endurance, and he couldn't have pinned Blair to that tree so efficiently if not for specialized defense training.

"Are you undercover?" she whispered. "Are you two government agents?" It seemed unbelievable yet also, so possible.

Rain placed the bottle of wine back on the table. "If we were, we wouldn't tell you."

"It would blow our cover," Finn said with a smirk. "But no. We don't work for the government."

"But trust us when we say that we're the only people who can stop Tyrone and Blair."

"And that you two can forget about returning to Townsville until we do."

"But even so, we need to keep you both safe, because Blair will be back."

Ava's stomach plummeted. "But why? I know I hurt his pride when I punched him and got away, but—"

Finn's hand dropped back to her thigh. "Blair is a

monster, Ava. And yes, you hurt his pride and ruined his plans."

Ava stilled at the fire coursing through Finn's eyes. "What plans? We'd only just met. Do you mean ... oh God. He targeted me, didn't he? The way he pursued me. Pressured me."

Finn and Rain nodded, and she cringed.

"But why? What did he want?"

Finn turned to face her, softening his hand on her thigh as he said, "Blair has one objective, Ava, and only one reason to keep a woman. He'd have used you as a sex slave, then killed you."

Chapter 32

Ava's heart wouldn't stop racing as she strode through the illuminated gardens of Luna Views. Shivers coursed up her spine, and they had nothing to do with the cool ocean breeze blowing through her hair. Finn's heavy footsteps followed her, along with the rattle of her suitcases on the concrete path as they strolled towards his hut.

Despite Eden's attempt to brighten the conversation over their delicious dinner, Finn's haunting words continued to whisper inside her head.

Sex slave. Kill her.

What kind of man *was* Blair?

Finn's hand touched her back. "This one," he said softly, turning her towards the hut. Lucky too, since she'd been about to walk off the path and into the bush.

She preceded him up the step as he slammed the handles down on her suitcases and lifted them up. She hated not helping but had secretly loved the macho "don't you dare think about it" look he'd given her when she'd gone to lift them from the Jeep.

She peered into the dark scrub of the headland. "Do you get wallabies around here?"

"Sometimes."

"I enjoyed Eucalypts Grove and waking to bird calls and seeing the wallabies of a morning. My apartment complex was always so busy."

"Well here, you can wake up to the waves." He slipped the key into the lock, then paused. "I ... ahh ... apologize for the mess. I was about to tidy up when I realized you were ... well, let's just say I didn't."

Ava smiled softly. "It's all right, Finn."

He turned the handle, then hesitated again. "And also know that I don't expect anything from you. For being here. I'm not ... I'm not like Blair." His jaw hardened and eyes flashed beneath the pale porch light.

"I know." She placed her hand over his chest, shivering at the pounding of his heart. "That's something I haven't doubted, Finn."

"Okay." Even so, he didn't move. Heartbeats passed as the wildness eased from his eyes, then he straightened. "Good."

He pushed open the door and gestured her inside. Ava stepped into the hall as Finn switched on the light. Gracie ran towards them with both front paws shooting ahead of her simultaneously, her black ears bouncing until she halted at their feet, looked up at Ava, and wagged her gray tail. "*Ruu-uff!*"

"We have a guest, G.B." Finn closed the door, grazing Ava's shoulder with his pectorals as he slid past with her suitcases. Ava jumped back and tucked her hair behind her ears.

"G.B?" she asked, squatting the pat the little dog.

"Gracie Belle," he muttered, placing her bags down and scratching the back of his neck. "Remember, I didn't name her."

"I know." Ava tickled Gracie beneath her adorable chin, then placed her hands on her thighs to stand. "So ..."

Finn cleared his throat and snatched a T-shirt off the floor. "It's not much, but it's one of Rain's nicer suites. We'll find room for your things, and you can put whatever you want in the bathroom. Just ... let me tidy up in there first."

"I'm sure it's ..."

He reached for the door and pulled it closed. Not that she was going to peek.

"Remember, it's a hotel, Ava. I don't have a laundry hamper."

She grinned. The pink in his cheeks was super cute. "How about I soak in the views from the veranda while you tidy up, then?"

His shoulders relaxed. "Thank you."

"No worries." Though she couldn't see what he had to be embarrassed about as she crossed the room. Two empty water bottles sat on the table and his open backpack spilled clothes onto a single chair while one lone sock sat in what appeared to be Gracie's bed. Having seen the state of her brother's house when she'd last visited, Ava knew it could be worse.

She slid open the door and stepped out into the cool breeze. Gracie followed her but remained inside, her feet dancing.

"Are you coming out, Gracie Belle?"

Her paws tapped quicker, then she leapt over the inch-high steel threshold as though it was an Olympic effort. "Wow. You really are a fruitcake."

But she was an adorable one. Ava scooped the little dog into her arms and cradled her like a baby as she eyed her crossed hind legs. Did her hip give her trouble, or did the little dog just lack confidence? Ava wasn't sure. Sinking onto the patio chair, she laid Gracie along her thighs and examined her little legs. The left was clearly underdeveloped with less muscle definition than the right. The treatment Finn had described seemed adequate, and she clearly had no trouble running based on her greeting them at the door. But she certainly needed to be cared for if she were to remain strong throughout her life.

"Good thing you're only little, hey darling?" Gracie squirmed and Ava lifted her back into her arms. "And I'm sure Finn takes good care of you."

But Gracie did need to learn how to use the stairs, Ava thought as she stood and stared out over the dark ocean. Bushes blocked the light from the hut a few meters beside Finn's, and she could see the marina in the distance to her left. But otherwise, there was nothing but the deep rumbling sea, white crests of breaking waves, and the red and green flashing lights marking the channel.

And somewhere out there was a man who wanted to kill her.

Ava's arms tightened around Gracie. Why? What was wrong with Blair? Finn wouldn't tell her, and she knew that wasn't all he was withholding. Even after tonight's revelations, Finn remained shrouded in mystery. She wouldn't have been surprised if he was a government spy or federal police officer, but he'd denied both and neither of those hit the mark. If Finn were either of those things, he'd have had intel on Blair and Tyrone before he'd arrived, and the operation would consist of more people than just himself and Rain.

"What isn't he telling me, little one? Do you know?"

Gracie lay still, stiff as a board with her front and back paws crossed. Did she even like cuddles? It didn't look like it.

Ava placed Gracie down, then gripped the railing and watched the lights of a cargo ship leaving the port. Breathing in the cool, salty air, tension eased from her bones. Honestly, it didn't matter what Finn wasn't telling her. He could be an undercover cop or the world's greatest assassin. He could be the brawny hero straight out of a blockbuster film or the monster who lived in the darkness. None of it would change the fact that she trusted him. Even without the strange chemistry tingling between them, she'd known for days that he was a man who wouldn't hurt her. A man she could rely on. He'd proven that when he'd magically appeared and knocked Blair into a tree to stop him from devouring her.

Ava closed her eyes as a shudder coursed through her. She didn't want to think about that. Not now. Not tonight. The incident had already vanquished the burning desire that had built earlier in the jet boat. It seemed like days ago, though it'd only been hours since she'd wanted to climb onto Finn's lap at the wheel or have him bend her over the bow. Hours since they'd made plans to ravish each other.

But now, they were alone in his room, and she wasn't feeling the least bit sexy. Which was a shame as his footsteps sounded behind her and she turned to watch him lean his forearms on the doorway. His muscles bulged beneath his black T-shirt and his lips quirked, flashing his prickly dimples. But his eyes had lost their playfulness.

"Bathroom's tidy and there are fresh towels for you to use."

"Thank you. But I showered earlier, so I'll be okay until morning."

"All right." He cleared his throat, his arms flexing as he pushed against the doorframe. "There are snacks in the fridge. Fruit, mainly, but help yourself. I'm sure Gracie will share her apples."

Ava glanced down at the little dog, whose ears twitched as though affronted. "I'll buy her more if I need to."

"Rain's allowed me to order room service free of charge too, so you can use that."

She frowned. "That's kind of him."

His shoulders lifted in a shrug, bulging near his ears in their abducted position. "Staff benefit."

Ava didn't believe him, but let it slide.

Finn dropped his arms and stepped out onto the veranda, leaning his hip on the railing beside her. "So ... are you okay?"

Her gaze dropped back to the waves crashing over the rocks below. "I'm trying to be. I don't like being scared."

His fingers brushed her lower back. "We're allowed to be scared sometimes, Ava."

"I know. But with Blair it's ... different. I rejected his first invitation to dinner based on gut instincts, but after a while ... I think I was more worried about what he'd do if I continued to reject him, so I gave him a chance." She dropped her head, allowing her hair to curtain her face and hide her shame. "I should have known better. He was a police officer and he was harassing me. If that wasn't a sign—"

"We all make mistakes. It's okay."

His hand rubbed along her spine, opening something inside her as she confessed, "But I feel stupid. Stupid and vulnerable. And today when I saw him ..."

She shuddered at the memory of the wicked gleam in Blair's eyes, the flash of his canines and the anger that had contorted his face as he'd raged about being denied sex. Bruises had formed where he'd grabbed her forearms. Then the sensation of his tongue in her ear—

Strength vanished from her knees, leaving her gasping. But before she could crumble, Ava found her head nestled against warm muscle as Finn's arms wrapped around her.

"You're safe, Ava. Remember that. I'll keep you safe."

She believed him, but— "How? How can you and Rain take on a whole criminal gang by yourselves?"

"Because we're stronger than they are. And as long as you're with me ..." His chest heaved and she swore a faint growl echoed from his throat. Finn's lips nestled against her temple and pressed lightly. "Trust me, Ava. That's all I ask."

Everything inside her softened. "There's a lot going on that I don't understand, but I do know that I trust you."

His lips spread in a smile against her hair, then he kissed her again and straightened. Ava took that moment to nestle her chin on his sternum and meet his gaze.

"What I don't know is how you came to my rescue today."

He stilled. "I just ... knew you were in trouble."

She raised her eyebrows and stared at him until his chest deflated.

"You know what you said earlier? About Fate and things you cannot explain?"

She nodded slowly.

"Well ... I feel a connection with you, Ava. I can't put it into words, so let's just call it one of those moments."

Strangely enough, that was one of the first things Finn had said tonight that made sense, because she felt the exact same way.

"All right. Then, I guess all I can say is thank you."

"For what?"

"For feeling that. For coming after me even though you were on the other side of the island. Because otherwise ..."

Sex slave. Kill her.

Ava's breath caught, then Finn's arms were back around her, his beard brushing her brow as he pressed his lips to her hairline.

"No need to thank me, Ava. It's what I'm here for. Though can you do me one favor?"

Her nose brushed his neck as she nodded. "What is it?"

"That silver ring you punched Blair with. Could you wear it?"

She curled her hands over his shirt. "Why? In case I need to punch him again?"

"It worked once before. And while I swear to protect you, I want you to wear it so you can use it again in case I can't be there."

Ava frowned. It seemed an odd request as she didn't know how the ring could be so important, but perhaps it was another one of those things that didn't need explaining. And she could hardly say no if it helped ease his worry as he was right. It had helped her before.

"It's in my suitcase. I'll put it on in the morning."

He squeezed her gently. "Thank you."

Ava splayed her hands over his chest, then ran her fingers beneath his arms, and over the bump of his traps before digging them into his shoulders. And as she inhaled his delicious scent of salt, lasagna, and the tang of the bush, she knew she was a strong wind away from toppling straight into love. Or she was already there, a thought which terrified and thrilled her in equal measure.

Chapter 33

Finn kissed Ava's hairline, afraid he'd squeeze the air from her lungs as he held her to his body. Tonight would be the ultimate test of his self-control as his wolf paced in its cage, grating his nerves and sending shivers up his spine. Fuck, she smelled divine. Sweet, woodsy, and liberating. Bloody delicious.

Mine.

He drew in a breath, then shuddered it out. She was also scared, vulnerable, and in pain, so with a barely resisted groan, Finn pressed his mouth to her forehead once more, then drew away.

"It's getting cold out here." A lie considering he felt nothing but hot. "Let's go inside and get you settled in."

With his hand on her back, he guided her into the room, Gracie having already returned to her bed. Finn slid the door closed and locked it for the first time since he'd arrived before turning back to Ava. His chest tightened as fear continued to fill her eyes, but with her hair tumbling over her shoulders and a sky-blue dress wrapped tight around her waist, it had taken everything he had not to devour her when she'd emerged from the bungalow at Eucalypts Grove. If it hadn't been for the incident that had just occurred, he would have. But she'd still reeked of Blair, despite her horrendously long shower. Sitting on her patio listening to the water on the other side of the thin wall had been the most torturous thing he'd experienced in years. Thinking about the many ways he could destroy, maim, and kill Blair had been the only thing that had stopped him from losing control and going all alpha male on her.

But that would make him no better than the animal that raged inside Blair, and Finn was a million times more than that beast. Ava deserved respect, and that's what he would give her. No matter how much he longed to take that zipper dangling at her nape and pull it down until the dress was nothing but a puddle around her ankles, he wouldn't.

Clearing his throat, he strode purposefully towards the mini fridge. "Are you thirsty?"

She shook her head and sat, her skirt billowing around her knees. "Not really. Thank you."

He grabbed a bottle of water and an apple. "Would you like to do apple time with Gracie?"

She lifted her eyebrows as Gracie ran over and danced at his feet, her jaw dropping open in a happy pant.

"What do I have to do?" Ava asked.

He grabbed a paring knife, then handed it and the apple to Ava. "Cut it up and feed it to her in thin slices. Maybe broken in half."

"Okay." She stood. "Where do I ..."

Placing the water down, Finn took the fruit and knife back and deftly sliced it in half in his hands. Within seconds, he had it in quarters with the core removed and handed the pieces back to Ava. "You think you can handle the rest?"

She sank back into the chair. "I think we can manage."

Gracie sat to attention at Ava's feet and Finn took a long sip of water as he watched her slice the apple, break it in half, and offer the piece to Gracie. The little dog politely accepted it and chewed loudly, her tail wagging.

"Yummy, is it? Let's see." Ava popped the other piece in her mouth. "Oh, yeah. That's a good apple."

Finn swallowed a groan, shuffling his feet as he watched Ava slice another piece. It'd been his suggestion to keep her occupied while he showered, another thing he hadn't managed to do before racing to her rescue. He still smelled of sun, sweat, and ocean, and he couldn't go to bed like that.

Not that he was going to bed. Not *that* bed anyway. Hell, he'd probably wait until she was asleep, then sneak out to roam the perimeter all night, even though he knew Blair had left the island. Kai and Nate had seen him on to the six o'clock ferry and as far as Finn was aware, Kai was still at the terminal, standing guard.

But Finn couldn't leave. The last thing he wanted was for Ava to wake and find him gone.

"She's so cute." Giggling, Ava fed Gracie another piece of apple.

"She is." Gracie might be quirky, little, and not the type of dog he'd have chosen for himself, but she was so fucking cute that he couldn't have helped but fall in love with her.

Though she wasn't as cute as the woman feeding her. For a moment, the room filled with no sound other than the slice of steel through fruit, the snap of the apple, and Ava and Gracie's quiet chewing. Finn's pulse raced as he chugged down his water. When it was empty, he cursed silently and wished he cared for the taste of alcohol as perhaps he needed something stronger to ease his tension.

He placed the bottle down with a thump and ran his hand along his jaw. Shower. That's what he was meant to be doing. Although the thought of stripping naked ...

"Finn? Are you okay with this?"

"With what?"

"Me staying here. I know it was presumptuous of me, and I'm sorry if I made you uncomfortable—"

"You haven't." *Liar.* "You were right, I would have been worried if you weren't here with me."

"So why do you look like you want to murder that water bottle?"

He glared at the crinkled plastic bottle. "I just ..." *Want to kill Blair. Want to help Sly. Want to slip my head beneath your dress and make you scream before ...*

Turning his back to her, he ran his hand down his face again and stared out into the night. Except all he could see was Ava's frown in their reflection as she watched him. Thankfully, it didn't seem like his erection was obvious.

"I just want you to be comfortable, Ava. I know this hadn't been our plan tonight—"

"Me staying here? I thought it was."

Her smile managed to soften his shoulders but did nothing to ease the ache in his throbbing cock. "Yes, but this wasn't what I'd planned to do with you."

"No." She glanced back to the floor and popped more apple between her lips. "And I'm ... I'm sorry, but—"

He took the opportunity of her distracted gaze to cross the room and stand behind her chair. Dropping his hands to her shoulders, he squatted, deserving the pain in his cock for his dirty, ill-timed thoughts.

"You have nothing to be sorry for," he said, brushing his hands up and down her silky arms. "You've had a big night and we both need to sleep it off." Though he doubted sleep would vanquish the murder running through his veins.

She turned to him, her eyes brimming with emotion that made his heart stutter. "I do want to be with you."

"I want to be with you, too." He risked it and brushed his mouth over hers, delighting in her shuddering moan. "But right now, I need to take a shower. You can have the bed."

She frowned as he strode towards the bathroom. "What about you?"

He waved her off. "I've slept in the dirt before, Ava. The floor is nothing."

She stifled a laugh. "We can share a bed, Finn. We're not animals."

He paused in the doorway and shot his gaze to hers. "I'll be fine, Ava."

Then he shut the door, braced his hands on the wood, and banged his head. Softly. Clawing his hands, he spun around and pulled his shirt off with a barely controlled growl. He *was* a fucking animal and it longed to be unleashed. He wanted Ava more than he wanted his next breath. His urge to sink into her warm depth and claim her could barely be contained. It was all he'd thought about on the boat, at the *George Rennie*, and ever since she'd caressed his cock in the ocean.

Then fucking Blair had turned up.

Finn kicked off his shorts, flicked on the taps, and stepped beneath the cold spray. Lifting his face to the water, he closed his eyes and took deep, controlled breaths. He was *not* like his brother. He could contain the wolf. He was Fated to carry this burden and no matter how much he wanted Ava, he would not seduce her after everything she'd been through tonight. That beautiful, adorable, kind, and loving woman out there was his mate. And he would treat her with respect. Forging the physical aspect of their mating bond would have to wait until the fear had disappeared from her eyes and violation no longer prickled her skin. Until the rage that coursed through his veins slowed, which wouldn't happen until the bruises on her arms faded.

So Finn stood beneath the cold water until his flesh goose-pimpled and his balls shriveled up into his body. Only then did he ease his torture, turn the hot tap, and lather himself with soap.

He toweled off, then grabbed the black silken boxers and white singlet he'd placed on the bench earlier while he'd been tidying up. He brushed his teeth, clipped lightly at the hairs beneath his nose and chin, and ran a comb through his hair.

After running out of ways to procrastinate, he gripped the door handle, took a deep breath, and stepped back into the room. Ava had switched off the main lights, leaving the room basking in the soft glow of the lamps on either side of the bed while the waxing moon gleamed through the windows.

Ava rose from beside Gracie's bed, drawing Finn to a halt. She'd changed into a pink slinky night dress adorned with black foliage and what looked like tracings of the Eiffel Tower, the lacy black trim brushing her creamy thighs and barely containing her pert breasts.

"I wasn't sure if she slept in her bed or with you, though I'm okay if she joins—"

"She'll be fine." Finn dismissed her concerns with a wave of his hand as Ava rounded to the closest side of the bed. As she bent over to pull back the covers, he caught the outline of her knickers beneath her nightie and forced himself to remember his cold shower.

He padded across the room as Ava tucked herself in. "Wow. Talk about five-star luxury."

"Yeah, it's comfy," he said, squatting beside Gracie and making a fuss over rubbing her ears. The silence stretched thick.

"Are you coming to bed?"

"Someone needs to keep watch."

She heaved a breath. "Blair's not coming back in the middle of the night, Finn."

"You don't know that," he said, glancing over his shoulder. Her eyebrows lifted and he straightened. "We don't know when he'll be back."

"Okay ... now you're scaring me."

"Good." She flinched and guilt clawed in his gut. Exhaling, Finn sank onto the edge of the bed opposite her. "I'm sorry, Ava. I don't want you to be scared."

Her eyes softened as she patted the spot beside her. "Then hold me."

His fists curled over the covers. "That's not a good idea."

"Fine." She turned her back on him and curled into herself. "Be that way."

Finn raked his hands down his face, rubbing until he all but clawed his eyes out. Fucking hell, what was wrong with him? She was in this position because of him, scared and unable to return home to get on with her life, unaware of the true dangers that lurked in the shadows. And no matter how much he might want to, he couldn't share that truth with her. So many aspects were out of their control.

But one thing he could do was provide the woman he loved comfort, so before he could think better of it, Finn lay down and nestled his head in one hand. Placing his other over the blankets against her belly, he drew her close enough to tuck her shoulders against his chest.

She kept her eyes closed, but a small smile tugged at her lips as she wriggled into the mattress. She took his large paw between both of hers and nestled their hands beneath her chin.

"Thank you."

Warmth spread through Finn's chest, his wolf whimpering as he leaned down and brushed his lips over her temple. "I've got you, honey."

He reached over her to switch off her light, rolled to get his own, then nestled his head back in his hand. Within minutes, her breath softened as she drifted into sleep.

But he didn't let her go as he stared into the darkness.

Chapter 34

Tyrone's head snapped up as the curtains of the private room at Night Bite flung open, jolting the topless dancer currently gyrating her hips inches from his face. And rock-hard dick.

"I'm back, Father."

Tyrone snarled over the undulating spine attached to that gold-spangled ass. "You need to work on your timing, boy." Adjusting himself, he dismissed the dancer with a wave of his hand. Pouting, she left, and Tyrone reached for his whiskey as he studied his son. Blair was not at all pleased. "You've returned alone. Why?"

"Why do you think?" Blair crossed his arms, lips twisting with disgust. "The fucking Fated came for her. Blackwood's scouts practically marched me off the island in their piss-weak, don't-want-to-cause-a-scene manner. And that lone wolf ... Fuck me, you won't believe it."

Tyrone lifted his eyebrows at the growl in Blair's voice. "You know him?"

Blair slipped his hands into his pockets, radiating calm despite the tension pulsing through the room along with the steady *boof-boof-boof* of the techno music. "Of all the wolves to become a Warrior—"

"Blair." Patience wasn't Tyrone's virtue, and his son knew it.

"It's Finlay, Father. Finlay is on the island."

Tyrone's wolf froze as he held his whiskey to his lips. Finlay? After all these years, could it really be ... "Are you sure?"

"I think I know my own brother," Blair snapped. "Bastard's the spitting image of his bitch mother."

Tyrone tossed back his whiskey and slammed the glass down. That fucking whelp. After slipping from his clutches fifteen years ago, Tyrone had spent months trying to track him down, hunting him from the South Australian peninsulas all the way to Sydney. But the pup had been a master at covering his tracks and Tyrone had been forced to stop trying, much to his chagrin. Tyrone Thorne had never given up on anything. He'd always got what he wanted.

Until Finlay had disappeared.

He'd never wanted the pup, but the evils of Fate had wielded its power. Tyrone had tried to get rid of him but no matter how much he'd bashed his mother, the fucking tyke had stuck. Once he'd been born, Tyrone had let that bitch raise Finlay until he became of an age that would be useful to him, then had killed the woman to prove his point to the boy.

The Moon Goddess did not control them.

But despite the horrific lesson, Finlay had held onto the ridiculous notion of Fate and no matter how hard he'd tried, Tyrone had been unable to beat it out of him. Finlay had escaped under Blair's watch, broken their bonds, and had become a lone wolf.

And a Warrior.

Tyrone ran his hand down his face. Fuck. He shouldn't be surprised. Finlay had always had a foolish streak of protective pride, jumping in front of his mother to take a hit or leaping onto Tyrone's back in attempts to pull him off the bitch. He'd hated the pup for it, but he'd never been blind to the fact that the kid was strong. Determined. Fierce and loyal. Tyrone could have used that and had planned to.

But the whelp had dedicated his life to taking down rebels like him, and if Eric had been right about the aura he had sensed ...

Tyrone shot to his feet. "We need to bring him in."

Blair snorted. "Yeah, right. What do you propose? We ask him to come home? Rejoin our pack? Play happy families?"

"Don't be stupid, boy." Tyrone didn't care for the return of Blair's jealousy, not that he knew what his heir had to be envious of. Blair would always be number one. But he couldn't have that pup the Goddess had forced on him running around unchecked, unchallenged, and fighting against him. "We simply need to prove once and for all that he's on the wrong side. Teach him a lesson. Take what means the most to him."

"The whore."

"Right." Tyrone poked Blair in the chest. "So go back and bring that useless piece of shit to me."

Blair's lips quirked. "Yes, Father. Though if he's so useless—"

"Don't, Blair." Tyrone narrowed his eyes. "You know as well as I do the threat Finlay poses. We need to break him. If he retreats into the wolf, that will show weakness on his part, but if gives in and takes our side—"

"We'll be unstoppable," Blair growled.

"Exactly." Tyrone's chest expanded. "So, pleasure yourself with his woman if you please, but she needs to be dead before the glow of the full moon."

Chapter 35

Ava awoke in the darkness of Finn's room. Alert and rested, she glanced at her hands clenched around her pillow, disappointed to find their fingers were no longer intertwined. But as she absorbed the sensations around her, she smiled softly and curled her knees into her belly, then straightened and rolled onto her back. Heart pounding, she turned her head.

Finn lay spread out beside her over the covers, his handsome, hard jaw angled towards her. His pecs rose and fell gently, the hand beside her resting on his belly while the other lay flung over his head.

Ava slowly pushed herself up to sit and stared. He was so beautiful. Handsome. Even now as he lay vulnerable, everything about him screamed strength and power. The way his shoulders stretched beneath the pillow while his white singlet barely contained the flat, square planes of his pecs, blond hair peeking out over his sternum. Both biceps bulged, his cephalic veins defined even in sleep. The hair on his forearms glowed and she watched, mesmerized at the hand laying over his belly. It was so large. Comforting. Smooth, even though she'd bet he'd thrown a few punches in his life. But his knuckles weren't scarred. In fact, for a man who was likely a cop, agent, spy, or whatever it was you called someone who thought they could take on the Townsville Underbelly, she would think he'd have battle scars.

But he didn't. Finn was perfect. At least, what she'd seen of him was and right now, those chiseled abs and lickable obliques were hidden by a white singlet that must be removed. Quickly.

Grinning, Ava shifted onto her knees and took a moment to revel in his vulnerability. Not that a man like Finn could ever let his guard down.

She dropped her gaze to his black boxers and the bulge that satin couldn't hide. A shiver coursed through her as heat poured between her legs. Breath catching, she let her gaze linger over thighs the size of her waist, shins as hard and unscarred as granite, and rough feet consistent with his dislike for shoes.

Then she glanced back at his beautiful face, and everything inside her fired. Finn Cassidy was hers. Deep down, she could feel it. And he felt it too. He might have wanted to prove that he wasn't like the other men who'd hurt her, especially his unfortunate half-brother, but he hadn't needed to keep his hands off her to do that. He'd proven already that he was different. And right now, she didn't want him to be a gentleman.

Sitting back on her haunches, Ava tucked her hair behind her ears and whispered, "Finn." He didn't move. She leaned closer. "Hey, Finn."

His face twitched, then relaxed.

Ava placed her hand on his ribs and poked him. "Finn."

He grunted.

"You awake?"

"No."

Ava huffed out a breath, then poked him harder. "Finn!"

His eyes popped open. "Ava?" He jerked up onto his elbows. "You okay?"

Pressing her lips together, she nodded.

Finn fell back against the pillows, his arms flopping behind his head. "Good. Go sleep."

A chuckle escaped her before she could stop it, and her hand fell to his chest. "I slept it off."

His hooded eyes returned to hers. "What?"

"The fear. I slept it off. And now ..." She ran her hand up his belly, lowering her body until her breasts pressed against the hard planes of his chest. His heart rate spiked beneath her palm as his eyes widened. Ava grinned. "Now you're awake."

"Yeah." His jaw firmed, then his hands lifted to grip hers as he sat them both upright. "Ava, you sure?"

"Oh yeah," she said, caressing his prickly face. "I want what we talked about on the boat. To recover what we can of this night. And I want to feel this sexy mouth of yours between my legs."

Never had she been so brazen, but as Finn's irises darkened, Ava decided she liked it as his hands curled around her ribs and thumbs lifted to caress her budded nipples.

"Your wish is my command," he growled, then he kissed her.

Ava gasped into it, her arms wrapping around his shoulders as he flipped her onto the bed. Finn's hand slipped beneath the flimsy triangle covering her breast and cupped her completely, rubbing her nipple between his fingers. Ava moaned as she arched into his touch. Body to body, they pressed against each other, noses squishing and teeth clashing as she spread her legs to accommodate him. Racing her hands down his sides, she slipped her fingers beneath his singlet and tugged. But she barely managed to lift it an inch over his bulk.

"Finn ..."

His mouth left hers and fell to her throat. "Patience, honey. Must practice patience."

Fuck patience. But she was in no position to argue as his mouth trailed hot kisses down her throat, sucked at her carotid, then nipped at her collarbone, the chaff of his beard igniting the pleasure in her belly. She dug her fingers into his lats and focused on breathing. The strap of her nightie fell from her shoulder, exposing her breast, followed quickly by the other. Then his mouth was over her nipple and sucking her whole weight into his mouth.

Ava cried out as his wicked tongue pressed and flicked at her sensitive flesh. Then he tortured her other breast and Ava's nails clawed thread from his singlet.

Off. It needed to come off. She shoved her hands up over his belly and crumbled at the sensation of his rippling abs.

"Finn. Get. This. Off."

This time, he didn't argue as he reared, reached behind his shoulders, and pulled the singlet over his head. Her fingers fell to his pecs and dragged down his body. When she reached his waist, her eyes widened at the sight of his erection escaping the leg of his boxers. Her mouth watered and heat shot through her as she touched the head of his huge cock.

Finn shivered. "Fuck, Ava. Later."

"Later?" she cried, her eyes darting to his. "But—"

"I want to feast on you." His hands fell to her hips where her nightie bunched. "Isn't that what you want?"

She did. She wanted it all. His mouth, his cock. In her. In her mouth. She wanted everything. She wanted it to last forever. And it would. But right now ...

"Yes."

"Right. Patience, then." His feet found the floor as he stood and drew the nightie down her body, tossing it over his shoulder. Then his fingers hooked around the waistband of her knickers, and he slipped them down her legs too, before dropping his own boxers and leaping on top of her. His hands grabbed her hips as his mouth pressed into her belly at the base of her sternum. Ava's head arched back on a moan, relishing in the sensation of his hot, hungry, and prickly kisses as he worked his way down. She could barely breathe. Her knees fell open. Then his fingers slipped through her sliver of hair to press against her hot, aching clit.

She cried out. Finn was magic. Sinful. His mouth dangerous as his tongue licked over her pubic bone and his finger slid down through her center. Whimpering, she dug her teeth into her lower lip and slapped her hands against his shoulders.

"Yeah, hold on, Ava." His mouth curved against her as his head lowered. And he looked at her. Just looked. His hand returned to hold her hips, then he buried his nose against her and inhaled. "Mine."

His mouth pressed to her hot, aching flesh and she roared, gripping his head. It was everything she'd imagined as his jaw chaffed her thighs and lips kissed and sucked at the same time. Then his tongue speared into her, and she whimpered.

Fuck, it was too much. Whatever she felt for him, it pulsed through her until she couldn't breathe. "Finn ..."

"Patience, Ava." His teeth ground against her as he pressed his hand to her belly, holding her still.

But fuck him and his patience. "You have too much self-control."

"Oh, no I don't."

Then he slipped his finger inside her and she bucked beneath his hand. Holy fuck. He stroked once, twice, and her pelvic floor clenched tight. Then he slipped in a second finger, stretching her and finding that spot that had her coming in a rush of ecstasy.

Ava cried out, feeling Finn's lips curve against her flesh as she tugged at his hair. He ran his tongue along her one more time, then moved up, trailing kisses over her torso until pressing his lips deep into her throat.

"You spiral me out of control, Ava. But I do hope to please."

"Oh, you pleased. But now, let's do this."

She lifted her knees and shoved at his shoulders, rolling him. Finn fell onto his back, a wolfish grin spreading across his face as she straddled his thighs and took his cock in her hands. "You called me yours. Now, I want you to be mine."

His chest expanded and again, he growled. "Yes, Ava." His gaze fell to her hands. "All of that is yours."

She shivered, stroking her fingers up his steel shaft before running them around the large, swollen tip. She knew all men were different and she hadn't slept with many, but Finn ... he was something else entirely. Thank fuck he'd already stretched her as she'd have to take him slowly.

"Did you get condoms?" she asked, not having had the time herself, or expected that she'd need them while she was on the island. Not that it mattered, she'd do this anyway. She was on the pill to prevent pregnancy, but it was better to be safe than sorry.

"In the drawer."

He reached across to the bedside table, but Ava beat him to it, snatching the sealed box from the drawer. Finn slid up the bed and propped himself against the pillows before snatching her around the waist. She fell against him, her knees settling on either side of his hips while his erection throbbed between their bellies. He brushed his fingers over her lower back and her gaze locked to his.

"You like a woman on top, do you?"

He nipped at her lower lip. "I like a woman anywhere."

Ava shivered, moving closer and pressing her breasts against his chest. "And you know what? I'm rather bendy."

She smiled as he bared his teeth. "Fuck, Ava. Stop teasing me."

Good idea, she thought, her breath catching as she tore into the box and grabbed a condom, ripping it from its packet. He lowered his thighs to give her room and helped her sheath him. Then Ava's hands fell to his shoulders and held tight as he guided her hips to help take him inside her. After an inch, Finn's breath hissed out, his head falling back as her eyes closed.

Fuck, it was tight. It was good. She breathed deep, and moved down, reveling in the glorious sensations spreading from their joining up to her heart. The fire, the burn, it was nothing like she'd felt before. She could barely describe it as her thighs trembled and this time, Finn certainly growled as he clamped his mouth around her shoulder, bucked his hips, and she slid on home.

Ava cried out as her body clenched around his, her hands spearing into his long, soft hair. She couldn't move. Didn't want to.

"Aaa-*vva*!" His mouth unlatched and pressed to her throat. Though he hadn't bitten her, her skin burned like a brand as she buried her head against his. Skin to skin, they clung to each other as she lifted herself up, then sank. Again and again. His beard chaffed her throat, chest heaved against her breasts, but they didn't stop, gathering momentum and building friction until the heat inside her exploded in a kaleidoscope of color. Yet still, she couldn't stop, her breath catching as she rode him into oblivion. He thickened inside her, warming until she could take it no longer and came in a cry of relief. Finn clawed at her buttocks and held her tight as he found his own release, the tendons in his neck straining as he roared.

For a moment, Ava thought he would crush her in his embrace. She feared she would break. But then his thighs sank from her back and Finn slid them down the bed until he lay against the pillows. Ava nestled her head against his pounding heart, utterly spent.

It took her a moment to catch her breath, for her head to stop spinning, and her eyes to focus. "Wh-what was that?"

His hand stroked lazily up and down her spine. "What was what, my Ava?"

"That ... that moment." Blinking, she lifted her face to his. "Did you feel it?"

"The orgasm?" He grinned and she palmed his chest.

"No. Well, yes, but ..." It hadn't been an ordinary orgasm as *that* had not been just sex. Or maybe it was just the best sex she'd ever had and she couldn't recognize it.

But she hadn't imagined that moment of connection. Of something deeper forming. Of ... love? Is that what it felt like?

Exhaling, she lay her elbows on his chest and looked deep into his clear blue eyes. "That was fucking good, Finn."

He grinned, positively vibrating. "It was. And yes, Ava." His hand slipped into her hair. "I felt it. It's called a bond."

"Bond ..." she breathed. Wow. Finn was just ... he might be all of *that* in looks, strength, and stamina, but he would never stop surprising her with the depth of his soul. Earlier, he'd talked about connection. One he couldn't explain. He believed in Fate. And now ... "You think we're bonded?"

His mouth twitched. "I know we are. You have a fierce hold over me, and now ... I don't think I'll ever let you go."

She stilled, dazed by the promise in his eyes. But before she could respond, he caught her lips with his and Ava forgot all thoughts of Fate and bonds as she lost herself in Finn's kiss.

Chapter 36

Finn woke with his cock nestled between Ava's firm butt cheeks, and his wolf shivered with delight. Tightening his arms around her firm middle, he buried his face in her pine-scented neck. His blood still reeled from last night and he longed to feast on her again, to slip inside her and stay there forever. He'd had good sex before; he wouldn't deny that. But this mating bond? Why the fuck would those who'd shunned the Moon Goddess give up something so powerful? So meaningful and possessive? He couldn't understand it. Nor did he want to as a moan escaped Ava's throat. She arched against him, opened her neck to his mouth, and reached back to slip her fingers into his hair. Fire coursed through his body as he pressed his tongue to the throbbing pulse in her throat and sucked on her delicate skin.

"That feels *soo* good."

He smiled, then moved down to her shoulder. "I'll always try to make you feel good." Because he sure did. Never had he been more satisfied as when he'd kissed her hot center, or when she'd seized control and taken him into her tight little body. Fuck, she was little. Tiny. Precious. *His.*

Throwing his leg over her hip, Finn dragged her against

him and cupped her breast. She gasped, her hand slapping to his thigh and gripping. Hard.

"Yes. Oh, Finn. Take me."

"Now?" Growling, he moved his hand over her belly and down into her hot, damp curls. He shuddered at her wetness, every muscle contracting inside him as his wolf panted with need.

"Yes." Her hips shifted to take his cock between her thighs. "Now."

Gritting his teeth, he rocked his pelvis against hers, his chest heaving as he slid against her. He tweaked her perfect nipple, pressed against the sensitive spot, and nudged at her opening. He could wake like this every day for the rest of his life. Take her and worship her. He'd staked his claim, she was his, and there was little she could do about it.

Except ...

He grunted, thrust his cock against her, and pressed. Hard.

"Finn!"

His palm flattened over her chest, the thud of her racing heart settling his. No, she would *not* reject him. He could feel it. Sense it. His anxiety could just fuck off as he took her chin, turned her head, and met her lips with his. Moaning, she opened as his tongue sought hers and tasted. Licked. His cock throbbed, aching to sink in home, so he took her with his finger instead. She bucked, her hand gripping the back of his head as she bit his lip. Hard.

Finn's chest exploded as they gasped apart.

Ava's eyes widened. "Sorry," she whispered.

"Don't *ever* be sorry. Bite me, honey. As much as you want."

"I might need to if you don't use this thing properly." Her hand slipped from his thigh and grasped his cock, stroking her thumb over the aching tip.

He narrowed his eyes. "Patience."

"Fuck patience."

Chuckling, he couldn't agree more as he painstakingly slipped his hand from her and rolled away. Condom. He needed—

"And fuck those. Are you clean?"

"Ahh ..." Considering he'd never had an infection in his life, respiratory, wound, or sexual, he rolled back. "Yeah."

"Good." Having escaped the trap of his own legs, she threw her thigh over his and dragged him back. "Now, do as you promised and make me feel good."

Finn didn't need to be told twice. Pressing her to his chest, he held her like the precious person she was and slid into her warmth. His breath shuddered out with barely sustained control. He longed to drive, longed to take her quickly, but she was so small, so tight, and he wanted to torture her. Kindly. And torture himself, it seemed, as he reveled in long, lazy strokes until he finally sheathed himself inside her.

She squeezed her thighs tight, trapping him. "Do not move."

He didn't want to. Couldn't. He was completely at her mercy as she slid her fingers through his hair, pulling as she clenched her core around his cock. He cried out and had no other choice as he moved, and she let him. Finn flattened his palm over her chest and held her against his own, their hearts pounding as they rocked. He squeezed her thigh and she pulled at his hair until they came in a shuddering cry.

Coming down off the high, they lay still, spent. Taking in the soft contours of her shoulder and neck, Finn brushed his nose along her skin and basked in her scent. She smelled glorious. Fresh, feminine, and mated. No wolf would dare touch her now without a death wish. Which, unfortunately, didn't include that Unfated scum Tyrone preferred.

Growling softly, Finn kissed Ava's neck as her knee fell

back to the mattress and he slipped out of her. Drawing in a deep breath, she rolled until she snuggled into his chest and lifted her chin to meet his gaze.

Her smile could have lit up the moon. "Good morning, my sexy daredevil."

Finn couldn't resist chuckling as his own face split in two. "Good morning, my beautiful."

He pressed his lips to her forehead, then drew away to meet her mouth, kissing her long and lazily, though heated with new desire and unleashed passion. Her hands splayed over his chest and pushed until he found himself on his back and her perfectly slender thighs on either side of his. Ava's sunshine hair curtained their faces as she kissed the breath out of him, relishing the bond she couldn't possibly understand.

Her teeth plucked at his lip, and he grinned as she drew it away, releasing his mouth with a soft *plop*. Then she straightened and sat back on his thighs, tossing her hair over her shoulder with a flick of her beautiful head. His abdomen sank with the release of his breath as he admired every inch of her fine body.

The Goddess fucking loved him.

"Last night ..." Her eyes glittered as her sated smile told him everything he needed to know. "And now ... Wow."

"Yeah." He cleared his throat, ogling her pert nipples, pink and aching to be devoured. "You are amazing, Ava." He slid his hands up her sides, loving how fit she was. Her muscles weren't obvious, but they were there when it mattered, and she knew how to use them. Especially that carnal pelvic floor. "Gorgeous. Tiny." Fuck, she was so tiny he was afraid he'd crush her beneath his bulk. Another reason why he'd loved it when she'd taken him on top. "I want to call in sick and spend all day playing with these."

He cupped her breasts and flicked her nipples. Ava leaned closer, bending until he had the weight of her in his hands.

"I would love to play all day, too," she whispered, spreading her fingers over his solid pecs. "I want to examine every muscle in this fucking sexy body of yours. Especially these." Her hands ran down his sides to the dip of his hips. "You know obliques are my weakness, right?"

He shivered. "I thought women liked abs."

"Abs." Her fingers splayed over them. "Pecs. All of it is good." Her hands brushed up the side of his ribs and he hissed. "Ticklish?"

"No." He wasn't lying, but her touch was more tantalizing than most.

Ava merely grinned and continued the exploration of his body. "I also like these. Serratus anterior."

Her hands slid under his back and stuck there, cradling his chest in her arms as he continued to hold her boobs. Hair fell over her shoulders, tickling his neck as his cock twitched between them. But all Finn could do was gaze into her wickedly, seductive blue eyes until he fell and fell and fell ...

After what felt like an eternity and her breath was escaping in short, sharp bursts, he cleared his throat and lowered his hands, her own abs shivering beneath his touch until he cupped her taut bottom.

"Which muscle is your favorite?"

Her teeth sank into her lower lip in the way that made him ache. "I don't know ..." Drawing back, she eyed his body. "There's too many to choose. But on you? You do have sexy abs, Finn."

Her hands fell to his belly and, chuckling, he flexed the muscles. "Thanks, Ava. So do you."

She scoffed. "My Pilates is nothing compared to what you do to keep in such great shape. I want to lick every bump and groove of your belly. Your chest. Your—"

He squeezed her ass. "Stop."

Her eyes fell to his semi, then returned to his. "Too much talking for you, Finn?"

"No. But if you keep going, we'll never get out of this bed. And fuck knows why, but I need to go to work."

"Yeah ..." Her hips sank into his hands. "I have koalas to attend to. But tonight, I'm going to lick your abs."

Grinning, she clawed her nails down his belly.

Finn quirked his eyebrow. "You want chocolate sauce with that?"

Ava burst out laughing, her body shaking as she fell over him. Finn smiled softly as her breath tickled his neck and he brushed her hair off his face.

"Oh, Finn. Chocolate sauce would do just fine. Though I think you'd taste better with caramel."

Cupping her nape, he looked deep into her beautiful, glistening eyes. "I like honey. Strong and sweet, just like you. I would smother you in it, then lick you and suck you and take you over and over all night long."

She shivered, her thighs tightening around him. "I'm going to be in a world of hurt later. All these muscles flexing as you take me hard—"

He pressed his finger to her lips. "I will *never* hurt you, Ava. Ever."

"I know," she whispered.

Finn eased the pressure of his finger, then dropped his hand back to her shoulder and drew her close. But this time, her warmth didn't ease the fear coursing through his body. "Don't be afraid of me, Ava. Whatever happens ... that's all I ask."

Her brow furrowed, but she inclined her head as her hand stroked up to cup his shoulder. "I'll never be afraid of you, Finn."

"Thank you. Because know this ..." His belly clenched,

but he couldn't stop the words spilling from his soul. "I will protect you. With every breath in my body, with every strength I possess, I will throw myself before any harm that comes your way. Because that's what a man like me does. Understand?"

AVA'S BREATH CAUGHT. No, she didn't understand. Not his words or the fierce loyalty flashing in his eyes. The determination in his jaw or the possessiveness of his hold. Nor did she understand the heat coursing through her veins at his words and touch, or the latch upon her heart as it ached to leap out of her chest and join his.

It was insane. They barely knew each other. How could he say such things with that strength of conviction?

But she nodded because, deep down, she felt safe and sheltered in his hold. How could she not when danger lurked across the waterway in Townsville?

"I understand. And I'll protect you, too. From whatever it is you're afraid of, Finn." She pressed her hand over his spine. "What is that?"

"Trust me, and you'll never have to find out."

She frowned. He was such a riddle sometimes. "Bats?"

Finn rolled his eyes. "Bats are nothing but a pest. Hardly worth being afraid of. Speaking of which, you need to get to the koalas."

He rolled away and sat up, abs flexing as he swung his legs off the bed. Ava followed him, kneeling on the mattress. Then she froze. Gracie tilted her head.

"Oh. Hello."

"Morning, G.B." Finn stood and stretched.

"How long has she been awake?"

He shrugged. "She gets up when she wants to."

Ava sat back on her haunches. "Do you think we woke her?"

Finn threw back his head and laughed, his whole glorious body rippling. "Oh, Ava. You're embarrassed we had sex in front of the dog?"

Her cheeks heated. "Well ... she's just ..." She gestured towards Gracie, but Finn grabbed her hand and yanked her off the bed. Ava toppled against his side while Gracie glanced between them with a blank look on her adorable face.

"I don't think she cares, but if it makes you feel better, we'll lock her out of the bathroom."

Ava followed him to the shower. She wasn't embarrassed, she'd just forgotten that the dog was there. But she didn't plan to keep her hands off Finn, and Gracie had nowhere else to go.

They stepped beneath the rain shower head and Finn reached for a bar of soap. But as water plastered his hair to his face and neck, Ava found her arms wrapping around him again and drawing him into a kiss.

"You're insatiable," he muttered against her lips.

"And you're incorrigible."

"Oh, yes, I am." And with the growl that she loved so much, he hoisted her up and Ava wrapped her legs around his waist, clinging to him as water rained over them and he drove inside her.

She cried out, blinded by the pace he set as her nails dug into his flesh. But she met his thrusts, riding him until she shuddered with another mind-blowing orgasm. It was only then that she realized he'd never even held her against the wall.

Chapter 37

They stopped by the restaurant for breakfast, where Ava enjoyed an acai bowl filled with enough wholesome carbs to replenish the energy stores Finn had depleted, then he drove her to the Koala Hospital.

Unclipping her seatbelt, Ava was equally disappointed and relieved to be parting from him, but she needed time to recover. Her pelvic floor had been stretched and worked beyond its limit. So, she blinked when Finn switched off the ignition and unclipped his seatbelt.

"I thought you had jet boat rides to run."

"Yeah, but I need to say hello to Cookie first."

Ava's spine softened. Of course he did.

They strode into the hospital where Caleb greeted them at reception.

"Morning, Caleb. Where's Eden?" She'd messaged her friend over breakfast to see if she needed a lift, but Eden had said she was already there.

"In the ICU with Xena."

"Does she seem ... okay?"

Caleb shrugged. "She hardly looked up when I popped in to say hi."

Ava's stomach plummeted. After the first message, she'd asked Eden how her night at Rain's had been and had received no reply. It didn't seem like she'd been as lucky as Ava, not that she was surprised. Finn was dead keen on her, whereas Rain ... Ava didn't understand Rain.

"Has Paula dropped Cookie off?"

"Yeah, she's in her tree."

"Excellent."

Taking Finn's hand, Ava led him through to the outdoor enclosure. At the sound of the gate opening, Cookie peered over her shoulder, munching on gum leaves.

Finn's face broke into a grin. "Wow, look at her. She's totally independent."

"She still needs her mum," Ava said as she closed the gate behind them. "She's not ready to be on her own yet, but she's learning."

"Sure is. Hey, Cookie! Remember me?"

Cookie turned her back, but rather than reach for more leaves, her little arms stretched around the trunk holding up the crossbar and she climbed around the tree.

"What's she doing?"

Finn stepped towards her, but Ava pressed her hand to his belly. "Wait. Don't move."

Cookie looked uncertain, but Ava trusted the koala as she maneuvered around the trunk, then scampered down. She dropped to all fours and lifted her head, her ears twitching.

"She recognizes you," Ava said.

"Or you."

Ava shook her head, suspecting what Cookie was up to as the joey lifted her little bum into the air and raced towards them on all fours. She stopped at their feet and looked up, but she only had eyes for Finn.

He positively preened as he reached down, but Ava stopped him. "What now?"

"I want to see—"

Then Cookie scratched at his leg, latched on, and lunged up his shin.

"Holy fucking shit." His face lit up as with strength and determination, the joey climbed Finn like a tree. "Hey, Cookie. You do remember me!"

The joey reached his hip, and Ava didn't stop him this time as he scooped his arms under her heavy bottom and lifted her to his chest.

"Of course, she does," Ava laughed, as she stared at man and koala. "You rescued her from a tree."

"From beneath a fallen tree," he corrected her, before gazing at the joey with that same adoring look that had softened her heart on Friday night. "But there was a moment she had to cling to me tight as we raced back to the car. Hey, Cookie?"

Cookie squeaked, sharing a look with him that Ava didn't quite understand as a strange sensation spread through her belly.

"She's been doing great here during the day, but she still needs care at night. Xena's sitting up and eating, but she lacks the energy to climb. We give her and Cookie time together a few times every day so they don't lose their bond, but Eden thinks she'll be strong enough to join Cookie out here next week or so."

"That'll be nice, won't it, Cookie? A little one needs her mama."

Ava pressed her hand to her throat as the truth hit her like a tidal wave. Shit, why hadn't she thought of it before? Cookie might be cute and anyone would love her, but Finn cared about Xena and hoped she pulled through because he couldn't bear for Cookie to be left without her mum. Like he'd been.

Dammit. She cleared her throat, but it did nothing to ease

the lump that had formed. "Would you ... like to restock her leaves? We figured out which ones she liked from your photo, of course, and they're in bucket three. Do you remember where they are?"

He nodded. "And I need to spray them with water."

"Yes. So, can I leave you with that while I check on Eden? I just want to make sure she's okay after last night's drama."

"I think Cookie and I will be fine." He started to return her to the tree, but Ava stopped him.

"Let's try this." She pried Cookie from his chest and latched her onto Finn's back. "There. You go about setting up her enclosure and she'll hold on."

Finn glanced over his shoulder at the koala and laughed. "She's a tough little critter. Sure can hold on tight."

"Koalas have strong claws. You don't mind, do you?"

His grin turned seductive as he wriggled his eyebrows. "Are you kidding? I love a girls' claws in my back."

Ava reached up onto her toes and cupped his sexy jaw. "I already clung to you this morning."

"Oh, I know." He caught her in a kiss, then straightened. "Go find Eden. Cookie and I have things to do."

He tapped her on the bottom, then left, strolling out of the gate with Cookie clutching his traps. Ava blew out her breath and fanned herself.

How had she gotten so lucky? Because damn, Finn could carry a koala any time.

Bouncing out of the enclosure, she headed towards the ICU, where she found Eden sitting cross-legged by the makeshift tree on the floor. Xena sat on the crossbar, holding the branch as she fed herself leaves.

Eden turned at the sound of the door opening and grinned, her eyes twinkling as she looked Ava up and down. "Hel-*lo*. Look at you."

Ava smiled and lowered herself onto the floor. "What? Is it written on my forehead or something?"

"That you spent the night with a hot, hunky man? Hell yes. You're positively glowing. With beard burn."

Ava pressed her hands to her cheeks. "I didn't think it was obvious."

"Oh, yes, it is. Don't hold out on me, Avs. I need to live vicariously. You did have sex, right?"

Ava pressed her lips together, aching at the heartbreak lingering behind the sparkle in Eden's eyes. She wanted to grab Rain and shake some sense into him, or at least demand to know what his problem was. Eden was kind, beautiful, smart, and clearly adored him. And if Ava wasn't mistaken, Rain cared for her too.

But clearly, he had no intention of acting on it. And since Ava, Eden, and Isla had been sharing modified details of their sex lives since Isla had been the first of them to lose her virginity at seventeen, Ava allowed herself to grin.

"Oh, yeah. We did."

Eden squealed, wriggling with glee. "I almost thought you wouldn't after everything that happened last night. He seemed too protective, macho, and insistent on making you fear Blair."

Ava's mouth twisted. "Yeah, he was all those things. And I didn't just go back to his room and jump him. Blair had successfully put me out of the mood. But Finn and I had a nice night and he was all 'can't sleep in the same bed', but I talked him into it. We went to sleep. *Then* I woke up and jumped him."

"Wow. And it was good?"

"Out of this world." Literally, considering the strange connection that had exploded between them.

"And is he ..." Eden spread her hands apart and cocked her eyebrow.

Ava bit down on her lip. "Ahuh."

"And ...?" Eden formed a circled with her fingers and Ava's core clenched.

"Yep."

"How can you still move?"

She pressed her hands to her belly. "I can't!"

"Oh, wow ..." Eden grabbed Ava's hand and squeezed. "I'm so happy for you. And do you ... I mean, he seems so serious about you."

Ava's breath caught as she stared at her friend. "That's the thing. Finn's just ... I don't know. He says strange things, but his words make me believe that he *is* serious. And it's happening so fast it scares me. I barely know him, but it feels so right, Eden. I think we were made for each other, I just don't understand how or why."

"I don't believe there's a reason for soulmates. These things just *are*, and you need to go with it."

"Yeah ..." She watched her friend's eyes dull as Eden turned back to Xena. Shoving her own joy aside, Ava reached for her compassion. "I take it nothing happened between you and Rain?"

Dark hair curtained Eden's face as her chin dropped. "Nothing will ever happen between me and Rain. He showed me to the beautiful master suite upstairs, which he never occupied after his brother left, then he vanished. I honestly don't think he even stayed in the house as I didn't hear him walking around. But I felt his presence, and he was home to drive me here this morning, but he barely said a word."

Ava reached for her hand. "I'm sorry, Eden."

"Doesn't matter. It's not like I expected anything to happen. He was just being nice and he doesn't like me the way I like him. I have to accept it and move on."

But doubt curled in her belly as Ava watched Eden push to her feet. "I wouldn't give up hope just yet."

"I need to else I'll go insane. I'm going to check on Cookie, then I'll get ready to go to the Forts. If I'm forced to stay here, I may as well make the most of it. Are you going to do Xena's physio now?"

"Since she's awake, it would be best. Good luck with Cookie, though."

Eden frowned as she opened the door. "What do you mean?"

"Finn's walking around with her clutched to his back, and I don't think either of them are ready to let go."

COOKIE HAD TALONS ALL RIGHT, but Finn didn't mind as he filled the tubs that held the eucalypts with water. The poor babe still pined for her mum, so he couldn't deny her comfort.

A door closed nearby and a moment later, Eden arrived and leaned over the enclosure gate. "Got a little backpack there, have you?"

Finn grinned as he switched off the tap. "You should have seen her, Eden. She came straight to me."

"Hmm ..." Her pretty brow furrowed. "Strange. I mean, koalas will do that, but usually only those who've had a lot of contact with humans."

Finn twisted his neck to peer at Cookie, then regarded Eden. "Let's just say we share a special bond."

"So, it seems. Do you know what you're doing?"

"I hope so. I was refilling the water and giving her fresh leaves."

"Excellent." Eden continued to watch but said nothing, though he sensed questions brewing as he picked up the leaves he'd left by the wall.

"I'm sorry about what happened, Eden. But I'm glad you decided to stay on the island."

Her shoulders sagged. "You and Rain didn't leave me much choice. I had clients to see today, you know? Now, they need to shuffle around the schedule, my boss isn't happy, and you guys can't even tell me why."

Guilt swirled in his gut, but he quickly squashed it. She could be angry all she wanted, at least she was alive. "We did tell you. Tyrone and Blair are ruthless, and they will stop at nothing to achieve their goal."

She quirked her eyebrows. "Which is?"

Finn placed the eucalypts into the holder, buying time to answer as he arranged the leaves to look appetizing. "They want to destroy what Rain and I care about the most, Eden. The things in life we depend on."

"I don't know what that has to do with me."

Finn took a deep breath. He couldn't say it. He shouldn't. But fuck, Rain needed to be scalped for what he was doing to Eden. He might deny the mating bond, but that didn't mean it wasn't already at play, and his resistance was killing her. Maybe not physically, but emotionally, and it was only a matter of time before the woman snapped.

He understood Rain's motivations, but things were changing now and the only way to get Sly out of the bush was to solidify their strength and stand up to Tyrone.

Finn walked around to the other side of the crossbar and eyed the willowy vet. "Rain cares about you, Eden. And Tyrone knows it."

Confusion and desire warred in her dark eyes. "But ... but he ..."

"It might not be in the way you want him to care," he admitted, regrettably tugging Cookie from his back. "But it's enough leverage for Tyrone to use."

He placed the joey on the crossbar and watched as she

crawled towards the leaves. Smiling softly, Finn stroked her spine before approaching Eden. He wanted to tell her so much more. To ease her suffering. To let her know that the ache she felt was real, that it was strained, and that Rain would release the tension he held over her one day and take her in every way she longed for.

But he couldn't. So instead, he acted like any friend would in Rain's defense as he opened the gate. "Don't give up on him. Okay? Trust him and what you feel in there." He nodded towards her chest where he could almost hear the pounding of her conflicted heart. "You feel it for a reason."

Her long lashes blinked rapidly, then her chest heaved and sank. "Ava's right. You say the strangest things ..."

He smiled softly. "I've always thought I had a way with words. So, is she with Xena?"

"Yeah. I guess you need to go to work?"

"Yep. Jet boat's awaiting."

"You're mad." Shaking her head, Eden strode into the enclosure. "But have fun."

"You, too, Eden. I'll see you later."

She waved politely and he left her to her thoughts, hoping to have instilled a little faith in her as he strode towards Xena's room. But after he'd found Ava, kissed her wantonly, and returned to Luna Views, Finn didn't plan to bestow the same courtesy to Rain.

He strolled into the executive office and found the man stretched out with his socked feet on the desk and head lolled back. Asleep. Stifling a snort, Finn slammed the door closed.

Rain sprang to his feet in a way unnatural to anything but a predator, then relaxed at the sight of Finn.

"Fuck, man. You scared me half to death." He ran his hands up his face and dug the heels into his eyes.

"You shouldn't let your guard down." Finn crossed his arms over his chest. "Restless night?"

"Didn't sleep much."

"Eden too much of a distraction?"

Rain slapped his hands on the desk and bared his teeth. "Could smell her fucking everywhere. Couldn't stay. Had to run."

"You *left* her? Alone?"

"No. I did zoomies in the backyard, then kept watch. All fucking night."

Finn drew in a breath and dropped his arms. "Rain, you can't let this go on. It's not good for you, for her, or the pack. Sly, especially."

Pushing upright, Rain snarled. "Easy for you to say. You're one shift and an awkward conversation away from mating with Ava."

Finn couldn't stop the smug grin from crossing his face even if he tried. His wolf preened. Yes, he was and for the life of him, he didn't know why he'd ever feared mating. The bond was Fated for a reason. It was powerful. It was strength, courage, and determination wrapped into a single surge of energy pulsing through his vessels. Once that bond was sealed, Finn felt he would be capable of anything.

"Yes, I am. And remember why, Rain? To strengthen the pack and get Sly out of the bush. *Your* brother. And don't get me wrong, I'm thrilled to have been welcomed into the pack, but this was your plan and we need an Alpha if we're going to have any chance at defeating Tyrone."

Rain shoved his hands through his hair. "I know. And it's good, you and Ava. Already, I feel the pack bond strengthening."

Hence Finn had been able to call upon his pack yesterday afternoon. "So, I'll keep working on that. But you know what, Rain? A rejected mate is just as destructive as a dead one. Be careful, okay?"

Rain blew out his breath. "I know. And maybe now that

Tyrone knows about her and she's safe under my roof ... it might be worth thinking about."

Finn's lips quirked as he strolled around the desk and slapped Rain on the shoulder. "It is worth it. Trust me. Because this mating bond ... it's the best damn thing that can ever happen to you."

Chapter 38

After spending most of the day hiking through the bush tracking koalas, Ava returned to Finn's hut to stretch out her aching body on the veranda, enjoying the cool breeze blowing through her hair. The tide was out and the sun set quickly on the cool August night, but the cold didn't bother her as she was sure to be warm and snug in Finn's bed. Grinning, she continued to stretch as Gracie walked around her huffing and tapping her feet as though asking, "What the hell are you doing?"

"It's called puppy pose," she said, with her chin on the ground, arms stretched out before her with her bum in the air and knees digging into the wood. "You can do it too."

Gracie *tsked* and stamped her paws. Then with a yawn, she stretched out her front legs, almost mimicking Ava before slumping onto her belly with a happy pant. Ava grinned as she opened her ribs, feeling her shoulder and spine muscles contract and belly open. Damn, if Finn saw her like this it might give him ideas. Ones she would be willing to try.

Ava giggled to herself. She'd never been bold when it came to sex and though she might be bendy, she hadn't experimented with positions. She only preferred to be on top because she'd always felt squashed in missionary, but none of her partners had been keen to try anything interesting either.

Ava groaned as she sank into child's pose. With Finn, she'd be willing to try almost anything and loved that he'd awoken the feline inside her. She felt brazen, powerful, and beholden to his desire. She wanted to try everything, feel him everywhere. She wanted to go down on him and feel every inch of him in her mouth, and that wasn't something she usually liked doing, probably because it'd only ever been demanded of her.

But she'd enjoy Finn. If she didn't choke herself in the process.

Her nails clawed over the wooden floorboards as she eased up onto her haunches, heat pooling in her lower belly. Damn, she would never get enough. Not only was the attraction between them burning, but it was like he'd been built for sex and she'd never tire of worshiping his body. She only wished she had her sexy see-through black and blue bra with matching V-knickers and suspenders to wear as she ate ice cream off his abs.

Ava glanced at Gracie. "You'll close your eyes and cover your ears tonight, right?"

Gracie stared at her blankly. Ava rubbed her head, stood, and called her inside, locking the glass door before heading for the shower to wash the scent of koala, bush, and sweat away.

She was wearing the plain black dress she'd originally planned to wear last night when Finn strode through the door smelling of the sun and sea with his windswept hair and bare feet. With a twist of his full, gorgeous lips, he thundered across the room and slipped his fingers through the sides of her hair, but Ava didn't need the encouragement to throw her head back and catch his sexy mouth with hers. Pleasure snapped through her body, igniting her thighs in an instant. She'd never kiss a clean-shaven man again.

Fuck, she'd never kiss anyone but *Finn* again.

"You didn't wait for me," he growled.

He kissed her jaw and down her neck, leaving her gasping for breath as her fists tightened around his shirt. "Wait for—"

"You're clean."

"Oh. Yeah, I was in the bush all day and got dirty and sweaty. I didn't want to stink—"

He buried his nose in her throat and breathed deeply. "You could never stink. You smell divine. Always." He nipped at her collarbone, then drew away. "Come. Tell me how your day was while I shower."

He took her hand and led her into the bathroom.

"Well, Marco's come a long way and Xena's stamina's improving."

"Excellent." He shucked off his shirt and switched on the taps. "How was the search around the Forts?"

He dropped his shorts and stepped beneath the shower, turning to ensure she got the whole full frontal as he brushed his hands back through his hair. Her knees weakened and she sank back against the vanity cabinet. "What?"

His lips quirked with pure smugness. "Did you find any new koalas? Sick ones?"

"No. But Molly has had a joey."

"Bet it's not as cute as Cookie."

Nodding absently, Ava tried to keep her eyes on his face. But ... wet Finn. Wet hair. Wet chest. Abs. Bulging biceps as he continued to wash his hair, flexing everything at the front.

Ava swallowed. "What is with you?"

He blinked innocently. "Me?"

"You don't have to put on a show. I've seen it all."

"Yet, you're watching." He took his cock in his hand and stroked. "And you're liking it."

"Probably not as much as you." Though she wasn't sure if that was true. She could watch him all day. But keep her hands off? Thank fuck she never had to again.

He's mine.

And she couldn't get enough. Lifting the hem of her dress, she pulled it off and dropped it to the floor, giving him his own show of full-frontal nudity.

"Now, finish cleaning that thing and I'll meet you on the bed."

Ava strode out of the bathroom, ensuring a sexy sway of her hips as she left. But she barely made it to the lounge before footsteps pounded behind her and Finn lifted her into his arms. Hair dripping, he plundered her mouth with his, then tossed her onto the bed. She landed with a bounce, gasping as he stalked towards her.

Ava shot out her hand. "No."

He froze. "Av—"

"You'll drip *all* over the bed."

His eyes lifted and with a huff, he scooped her back up and deposited her in a chair before falling to his knees. Nudging her legs apart, he slid his hands under her thighs and lifted her feet. Ava draped them over his shoulders as he pressed his lips between her legs and kissed her intimately.

She grabbed his hair and threw her head back, her spine arching as his tongue slipped inside her wet heat.

"That's right. You drip right there."

They ordered room service, which Ava agreed was the safest bet since she didn't trust Finn to behave outside the privacy of their room. Honestly, nor did she trust herself as they ate beneath the lone light illuminating the veranda.

Sipping her Diet Coke, Ava admired the rippling sea as the tide came in, faint stars shining around the almost full moon. This was what last night had been supposed to feel like, talking over dinner before ravishing each other into the early hours without the prickle of fear. But while those threats continued to lurk, the danger was easily forgotten inside the warm bubble she'd created with Finn.

She smiled at him across the small table on their deck as she dug into her teriyaki stir-fry. "This is delicious."

"Good," he said, mixing his own Mexican black beans. "I don't mind it."

"You could have gotten something else—"

"I like wholefoods, Ava. It's what keeps me in such great shape." He flexed his naked pecs and she stifled a giggle. "Besides, it wouldn't be polite to gnaw on a T-bone then use my tongue on all the places I want to on you."

Ava's toes curled against the floorboards. "Are you always thinking about sex?"

"Around you? Constantly. Call it my natural instinct."

"Yeah, me too." She pressed her knees together, but it didn't dull the ache. "I'm not usually so horny but with you, I could go all night."

Finn's chest expanded, and she wanted to knock the smug grin off his face. "I could go all night too, Ava. You make me feel young again."

She snorted. "You're hardly old, Finn."

"My ID says thirty-three."

Ava almost choked on her tofu. "I thought you were thirty?"

"I am, but my paperwork says otherwise."

"You forged your ID?"

"Had to, to get a job and a rental, else I'd be treated like a runaway, put into a home or, Moon forbid, returned to my father."

Ava frowned. *Moon forbid?* "And you wouldn't have wanted that. So ... can I ask how you ..."

"How did I escape?"

"How did you live?" she breathed, more interested in his survival story. "You were so young, Finn."

"I grew up fast."

"So, you forged a new identity?"

"I couldn't go by Finlay Thorne anymore. I didn't want my father finding me, so I took my mother's name."

"And he didn't find you that way?"

"Cassidy wasn't her surname, Ava. It was her first."

Her shoulders softened. "That's nice, to carry her with you like that."

He nodded, his throat working as he drank, but Ava didn't miss the emotion brimming in his eyes.

"So, how did you do it? Successfully disappear?"

He lifted his shoulder. "When you know the right people, you can do anything."

A shiver coursed through her. He'd been raised by a mob boss. A criminal. The things he knew would probably terrify her.

Ava mixed noodles around her fork. "I just don't know how someone as kind as you can be related to monsters like them."

His eyes flashed. "I can be a monster too, Ava. Never doubt that."

She didn't. Everyone had a dark side and could show anger or violence. But not everyone would take in an orphaned Maltese-Shitzu with OCD and strut around with a koala clinging to his back. He was a man who worshiped her like a goddess, who vowed to protect her, and who had a strong belief in Fate. He wasn't a man who would cause hurt for his own pleasure or gain.

But he could snap Blair's neck with a flick of his wrist, Ava was sure about that. He might have denied being some kind of secret agent, but there was something he wasn't saying. She knew him now. Knew him intimately. And a powerful warrior lurked beneath his beautiful skin threatening to pounce the moment it was called upon.

"But you've never killed someone," she whispered, her heart pounding against her ribs. "Have you?"

His gaze held hers. "I have never killed a human being, Ava. But if Blair lays his hand on you again, I make no promises."

Ava's breath caught. Fuck, he was serious. "But ... you can't!"

"Why not?"

"It's not right! The police—"

"The police won't stop Blair and Tyrone, will they?"

"No, but ... but ..." Shit, he was right. There might not be any other solution. But whatever Finn hid from her, whatever it was he wasn't saying ... would it be enough to protect him from the law?

Would he make it look like an accident?

Who *was* Finn Cassidy?

"You can't kill him," she whispered, terror coursing through her. "It'll darken your soul."

Finn's eyes softened as he reached across the table and took her hand. "It'll be okay, Ava. Trust me."

Her gaze fell to his fingers intertwining with hers as there it was again. *Trust me*. Fear and desire coiled inside her belly because, deep down, she did trust him. She knew he would do the right thing. What he fought for, she hadn't a clue, but she knew Finn would fight for what was right for him. What meant the most to him. And her.

"What's your plan to stop them?"

"It'll develop as the situation does, but I'll do what I must, Ava. I'm in a unique position to help Rain gain retribution for Shelby's murder. And to help his brother find peace."

"And will you trust me one day, Finn? To share with me the secrets that you keep?"

His lips quirked, but hesitation filled his eyes. "I will. I want to tell you everything. But the time must be right."

"Okay." She glanced at their empty plates. Dessert was waiting, but she feared she'd ruined the mood. Stupid of her, really.

As though sensing it too, Finn nodded out over the water. "Moon's nice tonight."

She followed his gaze, smiling up at the half moon hanging in the inky sky. "It's particularly big tonight."

"Yep. The moon size varies throughout the year, and the next two months will bring supermoons."

"What does that mean?"

"The moon's closer to Earth, so they appear bigger."

"Oh. That'll be nice. It's full moon in a week."

Finn grinned. "Yeah, it is."

"Are you looking forward to the party?"

"I think so, though I don't think I'll see much of it."

"Why not? I'd have thought you guys would be busy since it's the biggest night of the month. The hotel's booked out and Jam are one of my favorite bands."

He quirked his eyebrow. "They are?"

"Well, I know a few of their songs," she reconsidered. "They are pretty popular though."

"Yeah, maybe. But Rain has a whole separate crew to handle the Full Moon Party. It's his preferred night off."

"Probably wants to party himself. Not that I blame him. But I'm looking forward to it as I've never been to one."

His eyebrows shot up. "I thought the Full Moon Party was all the rage over in Townsville."

"It is, but it's not really my thing. I like music and dancing and concerts, but I hate the wild aspect of parties with people drinking and doing crazy shit."

"Fair enough, but I don't think our Full Moon Parties are like that. I'm sure you still get the few drunken idiots, but

Rain tries to be more dignified here. The original Full Moon Party is certainly crazy, though."

She frowned. "The original one?"

"Yeah. Rain didn't come up with the idea. Full Moon Parties occur all around the world, having started with the Koh Phangan Full Moon Party in Thailand. Thousands of people go there every month to dance and celebrate life beneath the full moon."

"But why?" She understood the whole lunar cycle and the long history of civilization worshiping the moon. When the Full Moon Party had started at Luna Views almost two years ago, she'd thought it was a fantastic way to bring people to the island. But it was still just a moon. "What's so special about it?"

Finn's face sobered. "The Moon is a powerful being, Ava, and harnesses a gravitational and mystical pull to all living creatures. She represents change with her process of disappearing and reappearing every month. She symbolizes death and rebirth. She can influence feelings, emotions, and controls Fate, so she deserves to be celebrated."

Ava's pulse pounded hard and slow as she stared into Finn's pale eyes, warmth spreading up her arm at the touch of his thumb rubbing over her radial pulse. *Moon forbid?* "So … you like the moon?"

He shrugged. "I'm quite captivated by it. But if people want an excuse to party beneath her full light, why should we deny them that?"

He released her hand and pushed back to stand.

"I suppose," she agreed, glancing up at the sky before standing too. "And it is pretty tonight."

"The most beautiful moon I've ever seen," he agreed, though his eyes were on her as he slipped his arm around her waist. "And now I want you to ravish me beneath her half moon light."

Ava grinned. Only Finn could say something like that and make it sound sexy, sinful, and majestic all at once. Curving her body against his, she trailed her finger through the hair in the center of his chest and down his stone hard abs, rocking her pelvis against his growing erection. "I think it's dessert time, Finn. And I'd like a bit of abs with my ice cream."

His hand hardened on her back. "Ice cream, huh? Bit colder than I anticipated, but all right. As long as I get to lick it from your spine afterwards."

Said spine tingled. "If that's what you want. But we'll have to open the windows if you want the light because I'm not doing it out here."

She turned and strode into the room, Finn following her as he closed the doors and pushed the curtains open, basking in the glow of the moon. Ava's chest tightened, mesmerized by the golden glint in his hair and the hue of his skin. He looked good in moonlight, especially as he slipped his fingers beneath the sideband of his boxers and dropped them to the floor. Two round ass cheeks flexed as his thighs tightened. Heat pooled low in her belly as she strode towards him, cupped his perfect glutes, and pressed her lips to his spine.

His hair swished over the top of hers as he glanced over his shoulder. "Strip."

She obeyed willingly, slipping the black straps down her arms and shimmying out of her dress. Then she pressed herself against him and explored another part of Finn that she loved. His back was a work of art with every muscle chiseled to perfection, creating round shoulders and a deep groove to mark his spine before tapering into a narrow waist. Running her hands up his sleek lats, she pressed her hardened nipples against his traps. Finn's hands fell to the glass, his breath escaping in a deep whoosh. She wrapped her hands around the front of his shoulders and pressed her lips against him. She kissed and sucked gently at his spine, relishing his salty taste until he peered over his shoulder again. Ava met his dark, sated gaze as his mouth curved.

He turned in her arms, placed his back against the window, and flexed every one of his abs as he pulled her between his legs. "What flavor ice cream are you having?" he asked, his voice husky as he looked at her with all the tenderness in the world.

Ava's fingers shook as they grazed down the bumps and grooves of his rectus abdominis, including the last, long bunch of muscle that attached to his pubic bone sporting his impressive erection. "Choc, caramel, and vanilla swirl."

"Mmm ..." His tongue darted out to lick his top lip, the hair above his mouth twitching. "You will share, right?"

"I don't know ..." Grinning, she stroked her fingers up his shaft. "Only good boys get ice cream."

That soft growl she loved so much rumbled from his chest. "Too bad I'm past that, but I do obey orders. Where do you want me?"

Ava let him go and stepped back on jelly legs. "Get on the bed, Finn."

She hurried to the fridge and dug the ice cream out of the small freezer compartment before reaching for a spoon. Turning, she found Finn propped on the pillows waiting for her, his hands resting behind his head while his cock stood to attention. He was the epitome of male godliness, and the sexiest thing she'd ever seen.

Moving towards him, the ice cream stuck and burned to her hand as she knelt on the bed. "So ... have you done this before?"

"Ice cream? No. Licking food? No, I haven't done that either." He brushed his hand through her hair. "You're the only woman I've ever wanted to play with, Ava."

She melted onto her haunches. "Really?"

"Really. Although …" His gaze fell to the container frosting in her hand. "I'd thought we'd do this with syrup."

Her cheeks heated. "I haven't done this either, so I googled because I thought there had to be something more appetizing than syrup or sauce. Ice cream was a suggestion, and I like ice cream, so—"

He pressed his finger to her lips. "It's fine, Ava. I like ice cream too and I'm sure it'll be pleasurable." Leaning back, he placed one hand behind his head and offered her his body with a wave of the other. "Enjoy my abs, honey."

Her mouth watered, desire pooling between her legs as she lifted the lid. She was sure their combined body heat would melt the ice cream before it caused him too much distress, so she scooped out a spoonful and placed the container aside.

She quirked her eyebrow. "Ready?"

He nodded, and she placed the ice cream in the center of the six bulging muscles of his upper abdomen. Finn hissed and flexed, the tricolors mixing as it melted slowly through the grooves of his belly. Grinning, Ava tucked her hair behind her ears, dropped down, and caught the chocolate with her tongue before it dripped over his obliques. Slowly, she licked the dessert up his tendinosis intersection.

Finn quivered and groaned, the sound vibrating beneath her lips and igniting her core. Her hands fell to her rippling plate as she reached the melting ball and sucked it into her mouth, moaning at the deliciousness of sweet mixed with salt.

"Good?" he asked.

"Delicious."

"Then have some more." He took the tub, scooped more ice cream, and dropped it before her eyes. "But this time, you must share."

Heart pounding, she swallowed the first bite and waited for the next dollop to melt. Then she licked and sucked at his glorious abs, delighting in the pleasure as his hand fell to her spine. Sucking up what was left of the solid piece, she lifted her head and kissed him, their tongues connecting in an explosion of chocolate, caramel, and vanilla as she slipped the ice cream into his mouth. Overwhelmed by the sensations, Ava's bones shuddered as her core clenched tight.

Breaths apart, her gaze connected with his and all thoughts evaporated. There was only Finn, the pleasure in his eyes, and the love in her heart. He could keep secrets from her if he wished. Kill for her if he wanted. She would live her life on the run as long as they were together.

The words were almost on the tip of her tongue, but they stuck. She might feel such things, but they'd known each other for a week. It'd been three days since their kiss. It was too soon to say words. Far too soon.

Wasn't it?

Finn's tongue darted out to lick her chin. "Chocolate."

She sank against his chest.

"Want some more, Ava?"

She nodded wordlessly. Moonlight illuminated his eyes and golden skin as he scooped a heavy dollop onto his abs, and she lowered her head, reveling in the fun as he continued to feed her until her blood buzzed on a sugar high.

When he dug the spoon in again, she grabbed his wrist. "No. No more. I need ... I need ..."

His eyebrow quirked. "What do you need, Ava?"

"This." She grasped the steel shaft that had been torturing her peripheral vision.

Finn stilled. "Not with ice cream."

"No," she said, and he fell back against the pillows on an exhale.

"Finally! Fucking hell, Ava. That was torturous."

"I could see. But I promise." She grinned. "I'll make it up to you."

She wriggled down the bed and while blow jobs might not

be her forte, Ava didn't hesitate to cup his balls and take his cock into her mouth. Finn hissed as his hand speared into her hair.

"Fuck, your mouth's cold!"

Her lips puckered as she withdrew. "Sorry, I—"

"No, keep going." His hand softened at her nape, and she pressed her lips to his hot, swollen tip, slowly opening and taking him deeper as she flicked her tongue over his pulsing vein. His hips bucked and her name escaped his throat on a growl, making her shiver as she sucked him with a smile.

She'd never felt stronger. *She* did this to him. She made this strong, virile, glorious man come apart. Brought him to his knees. Put the protective streak in him and the glow of darkness in his eyes. *She* did that and she loved the power it gave her as she withdrew to run her tongue up along the base of his truly spectacular cock.

"Ava ... Fuck, honey. You better climb on if you want to join in the fun."

Laughing, she straightened and tossed her leg over him. "I wouldn't want to miss that."

"No," he agreed as she slipped his tip inside her hot, pulsing warmth. "Ready?"

"Go."

Then she dug her palms into his chest and took him in one thrust, her back arching as they both cried out in the moonlight.

Chapter 39

Finn gunned his Sea-Doo towards West Point, power surging through his veins as water splashed up his legs. With Ava's arms around his waist and her thighs cradling his hips, Finn had enough energy to circumnavigate Australia. But today, he would settle for Magnetic Island as he longed to explore its shores and reefs with his beautiful mate.

Grinning, he twisted the throttle and turned the handlebars, her squeal and laughter melting through him like liquid chocolate. Or ice cream. Fuck, he wouldn't be able to look at ice cream the same way again after watching her lick the melting deliciousness from his heated body. It had without a doubt been the sexiest thing he'd experienced in his life. Three more nights had passed over the weekend, each hotter than the last, and still, Finn couldn't get enough. So, Ava could be horrified all she liked, but he would stay true to his word.

If Blair touched her again, he was a dead wolf.

Though he'd likely be killed anyway when Finn and Rain defeated the rogue pack.

Finn narrowed his eyes at the Townsville coastline and the headland that was Cape Pallarenda. Just how many wolves roamed that conservation park? How many were on the police payroll? And how many ransacked the town influencing young minds and creating violence?

How many rogue wolves preyed on young women like his mate, trapping them into abusive relationships or outright raping them?

Finn's mouth twisted in disgust as he tore his gaze away, focusing instead on the warm arms wrapped around him. Ava was safe, and that's all that mattered. That and ravishing her every night as they drew closer and closer. Not just physically, but emotionally, too. She'd told him about her family, her childhood, and it thrilled him to know she'd grown up happy. Ava deserved that. She also told him about some of her favorite patients she'd rehabilitated in hospital, including one who'd suffered an immobilizing stroke during a valve replacement and had spent months learning how to function again so he could safely return home.

Hearing her stories had helped him break down his barriers, too. He'd shared some happier memories from his youth, told her about completing his scuba diving training at seventeen—twenty according to his ID—and how he'd secured a job running jet ski tours on the Mornington Peninsula near Melbourne. Those years were easy to talk about, though he didn't divulge much about his childhood. Not yet. But opening up to her helped prepare him for the big moment, the one that would make or break them.

Chest tightening, Finn turned them in a wide arc. She giggled and squeezed him, her hands pressing to his abs. He would reveal his secrets. Soon.

Finn slowed the Sea-Doo offshore from West Point Beach and twisted to face her. "Having fun?"

"This is so much better than the jet boat. Or at least, a different kind of better. But can we do something more than a few little turns?"

His eyebrows lifted. "You want to do three-sixties?"

Ava's teeth sank into her lip. "Only if I don't fall off."

Resisting a growl, Finn kissed her. "Hold on tight, then."

"I won't let go."

To prove it, she interlocked her fingers and squeezed him even tighter, resting her chin on his shoulder. Finn's chest swelled, his wolf bursting to take the reins as he revved the throttle.

"Hold on!"

Her grip tightened and he spun the jet ski, adrenaline pumping through him at the sound of her delighted scream. Fuck, his little daredevil was growing bolder.

After rounding West Point, they cruised past the general area he and Rain had found Xena and Cookie, then idled into Rollingstone Bay. Finn recalled the night they'd found the koalas, and the first glimpse he'd caught of Sly. He'd wondered then what would drive a man to take on the wolf full time, even though he'd understood the pain of a lost mate. He might not have experienced it, but a lost mate was as terrible as having a mate you loathed, and he'd witnessed that pain firsthand.

But loathing led to anger, whereas loss led to something far deeper. Darker. And if he lost Ava ...

Finn glanced back at the beautiful woman once again caressing his abs. He couldn't bear to think about it. He didn't know what he'd done to deserve her, but the Moon Goddess had blessed him, and he needed Ava more than his next breath.

Her beautiful, creamy brow crinkled. "What is it, Finn?"

"Nothing," he mumbled, glaring into the bush again. Doubt washed through him like a tsunami. Could they really help Sly shift back? He and Rain might be able to bring an end to Tyrone and Blair's hold over Townsville, but would it be enough to bring Sly peace? Would he ever find the strength to lead again?

The charcoal wolf's words echoed inside his head. *An Alpha needs his mate, Finn. And I'm broken.*

Sly was right. An Alpha *did* need his mate. So even if they managed to lure him out of the bush, what would that mean for the pack? Rarely did a wolf get two mates in his lifetime, but it wasn't unheard of. Mates were human after all, and illnesses and road accidents happened all the time.

But a wolf mated for life and mating for a second time just felt unnatural.

Finn's heart sank as he mused on that for a moment, then shook the thought away. He'd discuss that with Rain later because right now, he wanted to enjoy his day with Ava.

He surveyed the rugged, windswept landscape, far wilder than the south-eastern part of the island where the protection of the bay and mainland had helped the wind and water form the majestic granite boulders. But the northern side had nothing to protect the landscape from the raging sea and boasted more weathered, hardened, flat rock battered by the ocean.

"This part of the island reminds me most of the Freycinet Peninsula," he mused as they idled along the coast. "It's famous for its dramatic coastline, having been withered away by the brisk and heavy Antarctic winds of the Southern Ocean. The cliff faces are one hundred and fifty feet high with amazing caves. And penguins."

"Fairy penguins?"

He turned to catch her grin. "Yeah. You'd love them. They're cute." Hell, even he loved the penguins. "So, what do you say we head up around to Huntingfield Bay and find a spot for our picnic?"

She nodded and he sped up, but only a little so they could enjoy the scenery. Finn had done the round trip a few times now, so he pointed out a few of his favorite aspects of the island before eventually weighing anchor offshore the private beach of Norris Bay.

He leapt into the ocean, turned to help Ava slip off the jet ski, then grabbed their picnic from storage. Wrapping his arm around her waist, they waded out of the cool water and onto the private beach, their own tropical paradise. The beach was tucked away on the opposite side of the island to any settlement or road, leaving the sand untouched and water pristine as they gazed out over the uninterrupted northern view of the Coral Sea.

"It's like a whole other world," she breathed.

He pulled her in close. "I'm glad I could bring you here. It's the best thing about having the Sea-Doo. I can go anywhere I want and cruise to all the secluded spots."

"Where's the best place you've been?"

"I enjoyed my time in Victoria. The Twelve Apostles and the Great Ocean Road is even better from the water."

"I always thought that would be a nice drive."

"It is. It's bloody cold on the water, but the landscapes along the Southern Ocean are unrivaled. However ..." Finn pressed his hands to her spine. "I think the best place of them all, Ava, has been here on Magnetic Island."

She blinked. "Really? Here?"

"Yeah," he whispered, brushing his lips over hers and delighting in the catch of her breath. He kissed her longingly, purposefully, but he didn't deepen it. He wanted soft. Wanted love. Just enough to prove what he was about to say before drawing away and gazing into her beautiful eyes. "It's been a long time since I felt like I belonged anywhere, Ava. I've been alone for more than half my life. But here, things are different. I have a job that I love, and a good friend in Rain and the other guys. And I ... I found you."

Though he'd been ready to say those words, Finn's heart

pounded nonetheless. He might have opened himself up to Ava, but the thought of telling her the truth still caused terror to shoot up his spine. She showed all the signs of completing their mating bond and he could sense her love for him through the energy that they shared. Through her gaze, her touch, and the way she'd screamed his name when she'd climaxed around him these past few nights. They had connected emotionally and mated physically in ways he'd only ever fantasized about.

But if he wanted her to truly accept both sides of him, he needed to let go of the proud, dominant, alpha wolf, and open his heart as a man with his fate in her hands.

And safe hands he was in as Ava's blue eyes glittered brighter than the sea behind her. "I'm so glad you came here, Finn. And that I did too. It might have been by some strange twist of fate like you said, but I guess that's the beauty of life, isn't it?"

Finn caressed her spine. "It is."

"But I'm glad we found each other because I've loved these last few days with you. I didn't think you liked me at first, but—"

He jolted back. "Didn't like you?"

"Yeah. But then I realized you'd just had your pride shattered after falling off your jet ski." Giggling, she pressed her hand to his chest.

"It wasn't one of my finer moments."

"It wasn't one of mine either when I raced to your aid. A man I didn't even know." She shook her head. "I still don't know what I was thinking."

Finn resisted a smile. "If it makes you feel any better, I fell for you right then."

She softened. "Really?"

"Yeah. You were adorable. And yes, I was peeved I'd stacked it in front of a pretty girl."

"Well ... if it makes you feel any better, you could show off for me?"

His wolf twitched. "Now?"

She nodded. "Show me your moves, big boy."

"Ooh, I have." He rocked his hips against hers and grinned as her eyes glassed over.

"Yes. And you will again tonight."

He chuckled. "By the Moon, woman. Can you ever get enough?"

"Of you? Never. It's been one of the best parts of our time together."

The growl radiated from his chest as he swooped down and took her lips with his. "Sex with you has been the best I've ever had."

"Me too. But right now, I'd rather see your moves on the jet ski."

"Your wish is my command."

He kissed her fiercely, then tore himself away and splashed back to the Sea-Doo. And indeed, he did show off for her as he pulled off all his best tricks with flawless ease, his wolf preening the whole time.

When he returned, he found her seated on the picnic blanket with their lunch unpacked.

"Wow. What even possessed you to learn to do a head-stand on a jet ski?"

Grinning, he flopped down beside her. "Tried to impress some girl?"

"Really?"

"Yeah. Worked, didn't it?"

Shaking her head, she swatted his hand and reached for a peanut butter sandwich. "I guess. Though yeah, I'll admit. You are impressive, Finn."

Grinning, he captured her mouth with his and reveled in the heat filling his chest. Fuck, he was one lucky wolf.

AFTER FINISHING THEIR SANDWICHES, they took a short walk into the untamed bush, then continued their trip around the island, cruising by Horseshoe Bay and taking in the beautiful rock formation that had named the strip of eastern beach White Lady Bay. But even though they'd returned to the accessible beaches, few boats were on the water as they cruised past Balding and Radical Bays before circling the marvelous Orchard Rock formation a few times.

Finn was surprised to find Florence Bay deserted when he pulled the Sea-Doo into the quiet cove. Not that he was complaining as he enjoyed having Ava to himself. They unloaded the snorkel gear, then explored the reef hand in hand, spotting coral, fish, and the *Magnet*, the small boat that had wreaked on the reef in 1917.

A cool afternoon breeze enveloped them as they sat on the beach enjoying a fruit platter. The sun had lowered behind Mount Cook, providing ample shade as they sat side by side and dug their toes into the sand. Finn slipped his arm around her waist and dipped his lips to her shoulder. She tasted of ocean, sunscreen, and the faint hint of pine.

"How about we dine out tonight? Like we planned?"

"Like you haven't wanted to any night because you've wanted to keep me naked?"

He bared his teeth. "You're sexy naked."

She scoffed, smiling. "You're impossible."

"We've established that." He kissed her again and bit gently at her skin. He needed to be brave. "So, dinner?"

"Dinner sounds lovely, Finn."

"Excellent." Drawing away, he pushed to his feet. "Do you want to stop at Arthur Bay, or would you like to go back to Luna Views?"

"We have time to check out the *Platypus* there, don't we?"

"Sure." He pulled her to her feet, admiring her gorgeous round breasts in her pink bikini. "If you're up for more snorkeling."

"I could check out one more shipwreck. Then we're going back to shower so we can eat early and go to bed."

"I like the way you think."

But as he bent to kiss her, Finn stilled, his ears twitching at the sound of an approaching motor. All his senses fired as he lifted his nose and drew in a breath. The tang of dirt and deceit rippled through his blood.

He spun around.

A small motorboat sped around the headland with Blair in the stern, one hand on the outboard engine while his other arm lifted. Finn's breath caught in his throat as the gun glinted in the dying sun. Ava gasped.

He turned and grabbed her. "Run!"

She stumbled but didn't hesitate as she ran up the beach. Finn held her close, shielding her as a shot fired.

Ava screamed and ducked her head.

"Stay down! Keep going!"

But the trees were too far away. They'd never make it. Sand flew up their legs as shots ricochetted through the air. Ava screamed again and Finn reached for her head, tucking her against him as heat scorched his arm. Then pain blasted through his side. His thigh. His knee exploded and he fell with a roar.

Ava spun around, her eyes widening as bullet after bullet plunged through his body. Blood spurted from his belly as he grunted in pain.

With a blood-curdling scream, Ava fell to her knees and caught him beneath his arms. "FINN! No! *No, no, no!*"

Her cries were unlike anything he'd ever heard, at a decibel that couldn't be human and filled with panic that tore terror through his heart. Swearing, he fell against her and rolled onto his back, her long golden hair haloing her face as she pressed her hands to his neck. Screaming. Crying.

He could barely breathe, his chest heaving as every nerve ending set on fire. Ava had to get the fuck out of there. Outrun the bastard. How, he didn't know, but she had to try.

He grabbed her forearm and squeezed. Her wild blue eyes met his. "Run, Ava."

"No! I can't leave you! We'll get you help. *Help!*"

Gritting his teeth, he squeezed her arm until her bones quaked. "Run."

She didn't listen, her shoulders shaking as fear wailed from her chest. "No, Finn. Don't leave me. Please. I love you, do you hear?"

Her hands pressed to his cheeks, his hair, her face inches from his as the words he'd longed to hear and to say himself wailed desperately from her lips.

Heart breaking, he gripped her hair and pulled. *"RUN, AVA!"*

But it was too late. Large arms snapped around Ava's waist and her screams took on a new kind of terror as her legs kicked and arms flailed as she tried to fight.

But his tiny mate stood no chance against Blair. Finn bared his teeth as the bastard strode into view, an ugly, victorious sneer twisting his mouth.

Finn growled. "You fucked up, Thorne. You didn't even use silver."

"Father wants you alive. But he never said anything about pretty."

Then his foot stomped down on Finn's face. Pain exploded behind his eyes, dulling the sound of Ava's shouts as they faded into the distance.

Chapter 40

Terror ripped Ava in two as she kicked and thrashed in Blair's hold. She couldn't stop screaming. Couldn't stop fighting. Her heart would never beat again as the figure of Finn lying on the beach grew smaller and smaller. But Blair hauled her through the water with an unnatural strength and tossed her into the boat. Her head clanged against the metal, knocking the breath from her chest and shooting pain down her spine, but it was nothing compared to the agony shattering her soul.

Finn. Shot. Bleeding.

Footsteps thudded into the boat, followed by the rip of a cord and rev of the motor. Gasping, Ava scrambled onto her knees and scorched her palms on the edge of the hot tin as she screamed. *"Finn!"*

His body twitched, knee lifting off the sand. But she could barely see through the tears streaming down her face as she cried out again. This couldn't be happening. He couldn't die alone. He wouldn't.

But as she prepared to jump, Blair grabbed her hair and pulled.

"Don't even think about it."

They sped away and Ava crumpled, dropping her head to the side of the boat as she gasped for air. "How could you? He's your brother!"

"He's no brother of mine. But Father still believes he's useful, so the lieutenants will come and collect him shortly."

She spun around. "You *shot* him!" Multiple times. The image of Finn's convulsing body would terrorize her forever. She didn't know how many hits he'd taken, but there was no way a man could survive those wounds. Not even one as strong as Finn.

Ava pressed her fist to her mouth and screamed. Her man. Her beautiful, strong, virile man. Dying alone on the beach.

"Oh, stop your blubbering," Blair snapped, turning the boat hard enough to send Ava falling onto her ass. "The fucker will be fine."

"How can you say that? He'll die before anyone gets to him! You murdered—"

Blair slapped her, snapping her head back against the hull. Then he grabbed her by the front of her bikini top, her boobs falling out as he pulled her towards him.

His face twisted in the vilest, cruelest sneer she'd ever witnessed. It wasn't even human. "Shut the fuck up! If I hear one more word about fucking Little Finlay—"

"He is *not* little! He is bigger in heart, soul, and strength than you'll ever be. And when he gets his hands on you ..."

A fresh wave of tears sent her crumbling to her knees as Blair dropped her with a sneer. Finn wouldn't be coming for her. Not this time. The murdering bastard had won. Even if by some miracle Finn did live, it would be months of rehabilitation before he was strong again. If ever. But dammit, she would help him. He might not be the same, but he would be hers and perfect in every way that mattered.

She couldn't give up on him. She needed to get back. Even

if she couldn't save him, he shouldn't be alone. No one deserved to die alone. She needed to escape.

But how?

Taking a deep breath, she strove for calm. She needed to focus. Distract Blair. Overpower him. Get off the boat.

Get to Finn.

Finn.

A vise wrapped around her heart, clenching until she couldn't breathe. Afraid to cry again, she stared at the headland as they sped towards Arthur Bay. A pulse filled her chest, a sensation that didn't feel natural, but one she'd felt before. It was the same energy that had drawn her to him the day she'd stepped off the ferry. The energy she felt when he smiled. Touched her. When they made love.

Her soul shivered and hope speared through her belly. *Get off the boat. Get back to Finn.*

Her gaze dropped to the ring he'd insisted she wear.

It worked once before. If you ever need to, use it again.

She didn't know how a silver ring could hold any power over Blair, but right now, she was desperate enough to try anything.

Ava straightened and spun towards Blair, her chest heaving. She almost halted when he gawked greedily at her still exposed boobs. Shit, she'd forgotten about those. But they also created the perfect distraction as she grabbed Blair by the shirt and hauled him to his feet.

"Touch them and die."

She punched him in the nose, then shoved her knee into his groin. Two sickening crunches echoed through the air, but Ava barely heard them over the sound of Blair's screams.

Then she dove into the water and swam. Her arms pumped, legs kicked, and she struggled to breathe after the agony her lungs had already sustained, but adrenaline was a powerful drug, and the current helped.

Bruised balls wouldn't keep Blair down for long.

She reached the shallows, her chest on fire as she scrambled to her feet, gasping. Ava stuffed her boobs back into her bikini top as she splashed out of the water and surveyed the beach. She almost wailed in frustration. Why was no one there to help?

But it didn't matter. It was a short run back to Florence Bay and if Finn didn't need shoes, neither did she. She'd find someone to raise the alarm and call for help.

If he wasn't already dead.

Ava's breath caught. No. He wasn't dead. She could feel it. Feel his heart beating, just as rapid as her own.

Not stopping to contemplate how that sensation could be real, Ava ran up the beach. The rumble of the motor approached, and she pumped her legs harder. But the soft sand slowed her down, her knees trembled, and Blair was too fast.

He tackled her.

Ava landed on her belly with a thump, but she managed to curl her fists around the fine grains before he flipped her over. He looked a fright with blood spattered down his face. Blair grabbed her and pinned her down with his hips.

She shuddered violently. "Let me go! You can't take me!"

"Oh, I'll take you, you little bitch. Right here on this beach."

Ava's eyes widened as she realized just how unclothed she was. How unprotected. Not that Blair's dick would work after the meeting with her knee, but … his hands …

Sex slave. Kill her.

Ava screamed and threw sand in his eyes. Blair squeezed them shut, grunting as his hands lifted, giving her the chance to throw him off her and punch him for good measure. His scream sent birds flying as she stumbled to her feet, shaking out her fist. Pain laced up her arm into her shoulder, but she barely noticed as she ran.

"Fucking bitch! I'll bite that ring right off your finger!"

Ava's hand tightened around the silver. What was with that man and the tiny hunk of junk? Sure, metal smashing into a nose would hurt, but—

He grabbed her forearm and yanked her backwards, spinning her until he stood between her and the trees, murder in his eyes as his teeth flashed in an animalistic snarl.

Ava backed up. Never mind, she'd take the boat. She would return to Finn, and Blair wouldn't stop her.

"Oh, I love frightened prey," he drawled, advancing. "Makes the hunt far more exciting to watch them wear themselves out."

Ava's knees shook. "I'm not afraid of you."

"Oh, really?"

She straightened her spine. "Really."

He halted and scoffed pitifully. "You don't even know what I am, do you?"

"You're a murdering cunt!"

Blair drew in a breath. "Ooh, such strong words for a little slut."

"I am no slut. But you are a disgrace! You and your father! Sadistic liars, the both of you! How many people have you killed?"

"I don't count."

Ava wanted to throw up. She'd kissed that man. Let him touch her. Hold her. "You should be locked up. Both of you. And after what you did to Finn, I'll make sure you are."

"I'd like to see you try."

"You and your father might run the underbelly here, but even you have enemies."

Blair's eyebrows shot up, then he tossed back his head and laughed. Ava stilled. She should have taken the opportunity to run, but shock rooted her to the spot as wicked delight flashed through Blair's eyes.

"Is that what Little Finlay told you? That we're mafia?"

"You kill people. You killed Shelby Blackwood. And you got away with it because you're a police officer. If that's not—"

"Oh, Ava." He shook his head, lips twitching for a moment before he stilled. His shoulders bulged and jaw hardened. "Little Finlay sure has kept you in the dark, hasn't he? Keeping secrets. Enjoying the pleasure of fucking you instead of the terror that your mating will bring."

Ava frowned, equally confused and disgusted. "You're sick."

"No, Ava. Finlay is sick. He's the one who contains the monster and believes in the will of the fucking Moon. But me? I fear nothing. I *am* fear."

He advanced again and Ava stumbled back. "I am not afraid of you."

"But you should be."

Then like a mirage, his body moved, warping and twisting before her eyes. His shoulders widened and bloody nose elongated. Hair sprouted over his skin, his eyes darkened, and with a roar, his clothes shredded from his body as he fell to all fours.

And Ava found herself face to face with what looked like a wolf-cum-Doberman-cum-monster. His jaw snapped, fangs dripping and eyes flashing with the kill.

Ava screamed.

Chapter 41

"Fuck, fuck, fuck!" Finn swore through his teeth as he dug into his calf muscle, the flesh popping around his fingers while blood oozed down his arm. The healing mechanisms of his body might be at work since Blair hadn't used silver, but that didn't mean the lead didn't hurt like a bitch as it cut through his muscles, severed his arteries, and pressed against nerves. The three flesh wounds had healed and the two through and throughs stitched closed with every pained, concentrated breath. But he needed to get the bullets out if he wanted to get to Ava in time.

And if he wanted to live. He might be invincible, but he could still bleed out.

Latching onto the bullet, Finn swore at the fucker and flung it across the beach. Then he took a deep breath and shoved his fingers into his side.

"Finn!"

"Thank fuck." Finn exhaled as Rain sprinted onto the beach. "Ava! He has Ava!"

Rain fell to his knees beside Finn, spraying sand into the air. "How many?"

"Bastard had a loaded Glock or something. At least fifteen

or more bullets. Six were lodged inside and I got three. I can't reach the one in my shoulder and another's in my thigh, so I'll need pressure."

He dug the third out of his side, then looked at Rain.

"Bloody hell. Hold tight," he muttered before pushing his fingers into Finn's back. Finn bit down on his lip and swore, but the pain was nothing compared to that squeezing his heart.

"We need to get to Ava."

"Where did he take her?"

"By boat, but I sense she's still on the island."

"I think I smelled wolf on my way here, but I needed to get to you."

Finn barely resisted grabbing Rain by the throat. "You should have gone to Ava."

"Don't panic, we'll find her."

Rain better hope they did. Finn gasped in relief as his friend pulled the bullet out.

"He's a bad shot for a cop."

"He wasn't aiming to kill," Finn muttered. "The lieutenants are on their way, so we need to get Ava and get off the beach."

Rain moved around to face Finn. "We will. Now, are you ready?"

Praying his body healed fast enough, Finn nodded. "Yeah."

"You grab the bullet. I'll hold pressure." Then Rain pressed his hands into Finn's hip joint, stemming the flow of blood from his femoral artery as Finn dug the bullet from his leg. Blood spurted once. Twice. Finn's head spun, but he held pressure to the wound. The bleeding slowed. The healing wasn't instant, but he drew breath until his internal systems settled and he bore nothing more than flesh wounds.

Then Finn leapt to his feet and sniffed. *Ava.* She wasn't

far. Tugging into the nearly formed bond, he sought her heart-beat. *Rapid*. Sensed her emotions. *Terror*.

Fuck!

His gaze met Rain's. "Gather the scouts."

Then he ran.

SHOCK RENDERED AVA SILENT, her lungs having screamed enough today as Blair bared his sharp teeth. His sinewy forelegs bowed, ready to pounce. She would never have believed it if she hadn't seen it with her own eyes. Werewolves didn't exist. But when his jaw snapped, Ava jumped and knew she wasn't hallucinating.

Blair Thorne was a fucking werewolf. And he wanted to kill her.

Heart thundering against her ribs, Ava backed up, stumbling in the sand. Terror coursed through her veins and shivered up her spine. What was she going to do? She hadn't been able to outrun Blair when he'd been human so it would be suicide to attempt it now. He would tear her to pieces.

"Blair—"

A howl shuddered through the air, rustling the trees as birds took flight. Ava's head lifted at the screech of the rainbow lorikeets. Blair's did too, which was just the second she needed.

She ran. Where to, she didn't know. Nor did she care. But she barely made it a few meters when paws slammed into her back. Ava fell onto the sand with a huff, then claws slashed her flesh. She yelled as he held her down, hot, putrid breath puffing against her neck. Drool dropped onto her shoulder. There was nothing she could do. He weighed a ton. This was how she would meet her death, being eaten by a bloody werewolf.

Then a familiar roar thundered in her ears, and the weight lifted. Ava's head snapped up as she rolled over and pushed onto her elbows, watching as Blair's hairy black body tumbled along the beach.

A golden wolf barrel rolled in the sand before leaping deftly to his feet between her and the monster. Ava blinked. And blinked again. No, it was definitely a wolf as it was too big to be a golden retriever, and far more menacing with his long snout and sharp teeth.

But while this wolf looked just as fierce, he was nothing like Blair. While Blair was ugly and mangy with his short, patchy fur, this wolf was nothing but majestic with his full golden coat blowing in the soft breeze, hair standing on end along his spine. Blair might be all brawn and sinew, but the golden wolf radiated power. Blair was terrifying but the other one ...

He was beautiful.

Blair stopped rolling and sprung to his feet. The golden wolf dropped his shoulders, lowered his head, and stalked forward. Blair side stepped, his murderous eyes flickering towards Ava. Her rescuer released a low, menacing growl as she shuffled onto her knees.

It seemed like hours as the two wolves stood off against each other, but it was only seconds before Blair lunged. The golden wolf leapt into action, his mouth open for a bite. But his back leg stumbled. Blood matted his fur at his hip, leg, shoulder ...

Blair's claws latched and swiped through his beautiful golden fur.

Gasping, Ava struggled to her feet as the wolf fell. "Finn!"

The air pulsed around her, knocking her breathless. Finn's fur shivered and Blair flew backwards as though hit by a wave of energy he could not withstand. Ava pressed her hand to her chest as everything she knew about werewolves—no, wolf *shifters*—from popular fiction flashed through her mind. She'd seen movies and read dozens of books, dazzled by the strong shifters with God-like bodies. The proud, dominant, sexy alpha males.

Finn.

Creatures bound to the Moon. Who believed in Fate. Men who loved and protected fiercely and with their entire being.

Also Finn.

Her heart pounded beneath her hands as his secrets, his immediate affection for her, and overpowering protective instincts suddenly made sense. Everything shifted into focus. The dirt in his hair as he clutched the koala, his lack of clothes on various occasions, and his hatred of shoes. She hadn't imagined the scratches on his arm disappearing that night or the devotion in his eyes when he called her "mine."

Finn Cassidy was a wolf shifter. And she was his mate.

With a gasp, Ava ran forward and threw her body over the golden wolf as Blair crawled back to his feet. That bastard wouldn't take Finn from her. Not again.

But Blair's eyes weren't on her. Or Finn. Instead, his gaze darted to either side of them, and Ava peeked behind her to see four more wolves emerge from the trees, charcoal stripes running down their backs as they snarled and advanced. With her arms around Finn's warm, furry neck, Ava watched them back Blair towards the water. Two moved on her right, the other two on her left. Then she spotted another wolf, pure charcoal, standing on the rock at the end of the beach, watching.

A splash sounded, and a black tail disappeared into the clear waters of Arthur Bay. A moment later, a naked Blair crawled into the boat, revved the motor, and sped away.

Shoulders softening, Ava glanced into Finn's crystal blue eyes, then buried her face into his soft fur, sobs shaking her body. Pain, horror, and relief came flooding out as his wolf moved and morphed beneath her. Her eyes peeked open to see his hair spiral into hot, smooth skin. She jolted back and there was her man, his chest heaving as a gash wounded his side. But there were no bullet wounds.

He reached up to cup her face, his wide eyes boring into hers. "Are you okay?"

"Me? *Me?*" Shaking her head, she examined the bloodied wound in his side, watching as Finn's skin drew closer with every breath until finally, the edges no longer split and his perfect oblique was perfect once again. Fascinated, Ava ran her fingers down his side. No scar. Nothing. All that came away was blood.

With a shuddering gasp, she pressed her mouth to his. "You're alive!" she cried, tears prickling her eyes. "Yourealivey-ourealiveyouralive."

Spearing her hands into his hair, she kissed him all over. His lips, his chin. Jaw, nose, eyelids. The terror she'd felt, the heartache, it had been like no other. She'd felt like she'd been dying alongside him and knew if he had, her soul would have been ripped from her.

But he hadn't died. Couldn't? She didn't know. Nor did she care. Finn was unharmed. His heart beat beneath hers and his warm hand caressed her shoulders, holding her against him as their relief poured through the magnetic connection that finally made perfect sense.

"You have so much explaining to do, Finn."

His lips quirked. "I know."

"I was so scared."

"I know that, too," he said, sitting up. Ava fell to her hip beside him, unable to tear their beating hearts apart. "I could feel you through the bond."

"Our mating bond?"

"Yeah." Smiling softly, Finn slipped his hand into her hair and brushed her cheek with his thumb. "I'm sorry, Ava."

She shook her head, not knowing what to say. How would he have told her he could shift into a wolf? Would she have believed him? Probably not. And if he'd shifted in front of her, she would have freaked out of her bloody mind.

But she wasn't scared. Not of him.

Exhaling, she pressed her forehead to his. "I thought you were dead."

"It'll take a lot more than a few bullets to kill me, honey."

"Clearly." Her hands fell to his side, his hip, and only then did she remember he was naked. Shit. He had nothing to cover up with, but Finn didn't seem to mind. Her eyes returned to his. "How many times did he shoot you?"

Finn sneered. "Eleven, I think. Three flesh wounds healed quickly, the two through and throughs were a bit more painful. But I had to dig out the six lodged inside me before I could shift and come for you." His eyes darkened as he looked her up and down. "He didn't hurt you, did he?"

Ava shook her head. "No."

"Good. I'm going to kill him anyway."

And this time, that intention didn't terrify her. In fact, she wanted to agree with him. Blair Thorne wasn't just a crooked, underbelly cop. He was a real monster straight out of a nightmare, and he didn't belong in this world.

But Finn ... he was different, and not just because she loved him. He possessed a different aura, a different kind of strength. He was nothing like Blair.

Finn had a soul.

"We can talk about it later," she said, as she realized the other wolves had vanished. She glanced over her shoulder and winced as pain shot along her skin.

Finn snarled as he examined her back. "I'll fucking kill him!"

"It's not that bad." She craned her neck but couldn't see the wounds. "Is it?"

His lips twisted until he almost resembled his wolf. "He hurt you, and he will pay for that. But no, honey." With a heaving breath that looked like it pained him, Finn's gaze softened. "It's not bad. I'll wash you when we get home and you will heal."

His beard brushed her skin as he kissed her shoulder, and Ava melted into his touch. Then a rustling sounded behind her and Rain strode out of the bush, his long hair in disarray over his shoulders as he smiled nervously at Ava. He moved towards them, pecs defined and biceps straining as he held a rock in front of his groin.

Ava was not surprised to see him.

"You guys want a lift back to Luna Views?"

Chapter 42

Ava sighed as she slid into the bubbling spa bath, warmth enveloping her aching body. Everything hurt. The scratches on her back. Her thighs that had tried but failed to run. Her chest from the cries. Her throat from her screams. She still couldn't believe the events that had unfolded and never wanted to experience that kind of terror again. Thinking that Finn was dead had almost destroyed her.

But she wouldn't need to worry about that. Her boyfriend was a wolf shifter and though he wasn't immortal, he was invincible enough to heal himself with pranayama breathing. She couldn't believe that she'd found herself part of a paranormal world where she was connected to him by some will of Fate, but at least it explained her attraction, their connection, and the way he seemed to smell and sense her even from the other side of the island. And Ava had meant what she'd said before Blair had torn her from Finn's bullet-riddled body.

Had he heard her?

Glancing over her shoulder, Ava watched Finn slide into the bath, slipping his strong thighs on either side of hers as he pulled her against his unscathed body. His bearded chin nestled on her shoulder and she snuggled in comfortably, knowing she would find no safer place in this world than Finn's embrace.

"I'd have died if I'd lost you," she whispered.

"No, Ava. *I'd* have died if I'd lost you."

He pressed his lips to her skin and her eyes fluttered closed.

"Are we really mated?"

"Yes," he said, wrapping his arms tighter around her belly. "You are mine if you want to be. But I am one hundred percent completely and utterly yours."

She frowned, confused. "So ... I do have a choice?"

"Yes, Ava. You do. But you already made it, hence why our mating bond is complete. The moment you acknowledged the wolf was me, my world righted itself."

Her heart pounded. "I don't understand. I mean, I do. From the moment I met you, I felt more than attracted to you. There's been this magical pull between us that I couldn't explain."

"Fate can't be explained, Ava. It just is. Sometimes, it's cruel. Tricky. And sometimes, Fate gets it right."

His lips pressed into her neck, and Ava grinned. "Like us?"

"*I* think so." He drew back. "Do you?"

Meeting his gaze, she swallowed nervously. He'd shown no indication that he'd heard her desperate confession earlier. She'd wanted to admit it for days but had been afraid of looking like a fool. She'd told herself it was just sex. Primal, visceral attraction. But now that their connection had been explained and the truth revealed, it didn't matter that they'd only known each other for a fortnight. They were soulmates.

"You ... you heard what I said on the beach, right?"

His gorgeous face stretched into a slow grin as he crushed her against his preening body. "Remind me."

Ava grinned too as she stroked her hands along his hard,

protective arms. "I love you, Finn Cassidy. Your cheek, your pride, your dominance, and your wolf."

Finn rubbed his nose against hers. "Yeah, I heard you, honey. And I've loved you since the moment I saw you on that ferry."

She jerked back. "What?"

"Why do you think I fell off?" He quirked his golden eyebrow. "Takes something mighty strong to throw me like that, Ava."

"But ... you didn't even know me!"

"Doesn't matter. My eyes locked with yours and it was like what you felt today on the beach. A pulse. Except for me, the world shifted, and so did my balance. So, I belly flopped."

Ava pressed her lips together, chest rumbling. It was not funny. It wasn't. But— "Really?"

"Yep. So, when you showed up fussing over me looking all perky and perfect, I wasn't nursing my wounded pride because I'd stacked it. It was because I'd stacked it in front of *you*."

Giggling, she squeezed his knees. "You sure were one surly beast."

"Yep." He pressed his mouth to hers. "What made things worse was that you terrified me. I was so not ready for you."

Her heart softened, her grin melting away at the tormented affection in his eyes. "What do you mean?"

Finn ran his hand down his face, wetting his beard before reaching for the cloth he'd laid on the side of the tub. "Lean forward, honey, and let me clean these scratches."

Shuffling her bum forward, she did as he asked, wrapping her arm around his bent knee as his hand brushed down her spine. Bubbles popped against her feet as she pressed her toes over the spa jet. But she needed to know. "Finn—"

"Wolves mate for life, Ava. And because we love and protect them so fiercely, we only get one mate. One great love in our lifetime."

The water stung the gorge in her back, though she felt no pain. "Sounds romantic."

"It isn't always. Fate can be cruel."

She glanced over her shoulder. "Are you not happy?"

Finn's eyes snapped to hers. "Oh, Ava, no." He pulled her back to him with a splash, dipping her and draping her over his arm. "Fate has been kind to us. I'm so fucking happy to have you as my mate that I'll strut with pride for the rest of my days."

Her insides softened again as desire flashed through his eyes.

"I adore you," he continued, drawing her close. "I worship you. My sole purpose in life is to protect you and honor you in every way I know how. I will forever be connected to you, feel your emotions, and want to bury myself inside you. And I'm so fucking happy about that. Like I said, I've been alone for a long time. To become vulnerable to another person, to open up to them, trust them, and let them in has been one of the hardest things I've ever had to do. But you are my home."

His jaw hardened as he stopped saying the most beautiful things. Eyes fluttering, she reached up to stroke her fingers through his prickly beard. "That does sound terrifying."

"It was. Because no matter what happened, I would have felt that way, Ava. Even if you didn't. And I'd have turned into a monster."

Ava stilled. "Like Blair?"

"No. Like Tyrone."

"I ... I don't understand."

Sighing softly, he shifted her upright, moving her back into position so he could run the cloth down her spine. "The wolf is a wild creature, Ava. Unchecked, we can do unspeakable things, which is why we are Fated to find one mate who would hold us in balance. Keep us human." His lips pressed to her neck. "Most of us wait for that right person. We believe in our Moon Goddess and the power of Fate. We long to find our mates. It might terrify us, but love is terrifying, especially when you have little choice in the matter. But I trust Fate. I've always known that when I find my mate, I will accept her. I will be kind to her, get to know her, and woo her into falling in love with me."

Grinning, she twisted her neck to look at him. "You did a spectacular job."

"I did." He captured her mouth and drew hungrily on her lower lip. "A mating bond needs to form on three levels, Ava. The emotional, physical, and paranormal. We sort of did the first two in conjunction, though I argue we felt more physical attraction before the emotional side truly set in."

Tilting her head, Ava considered that. She'd been hot for him since day one, that was for sure, and she'd found herself caught up more in his body than his heart for the first few days. If Blair hadn't arrived and Finn hadn't gone all alpha and bundled her up in his hut, she'd have jumped him with a little less feeling. Because it had been during those moments when he'd held her at Eucalypts Grove, when he'd been dark and mysterious at Rain's house, and when he'd vowed not to touch her while holed up in this room that she'd toppled head over heels in love with him.

"I think it all happened that night," she agreed. "And while I always suspected there was something different about you, I would never have guessed you could shift into a wolf. But I'd have recognized that beautiful hair of yours anywhere."

Wrapping his golden locks around her hand, she kissed him again, diving deep to quench her desire.

"And the moment you did, you sealed our fate. There's no getting rid of me now." He cheekily bared his teeth, and she laughed.

"I don't want to get rid of you."

"Good." He lifted the cloth again and gently washed her

back. "Because if you did, I would be alone forever, Ava. Not a lone wolf, but a rejected one. Depressed and a burden to the pack rather than an asset. There's no place for a rejected wolf except inside his own misery."

Ava's heart sank as she swirled his wet leg hair beneath her finger. "That's so sad."

"It is. That's why we need to work out what our mate wants, how to treat her, and how to win her heart to save ourselves from that torment."

"Is that what happened to your father?"

Finn squeezed water down her back. "No. Tyrone ... he's different. Like in any faith, we have those who believe and those who don't. Tyrone turned his back on the Moon Goddess. He actively rebels against Fate and leads a pack of rogue wolves who either don't want to be tied to the Moon Goddess or aren't tied to her at all.

"You see, wolves are only supposed to breed with their mates. It's to stop the power from spiraling out of control. Mates are Fated to create more wolves and keep nature in balance. So, when a wolf mates with someone he's not supposed to, he creates a creature, one who isn't tied to the fate of the Moon and who runs rogue with the other Unfated."

Ava stilled. "Blair."

"Blair." Finn's jaw twitched. "Tyrone had him to prove a point. He proudly produced an heir to stick it to the Goddess. Blair is his chosen son. The one he wanted. And then he met his mate. My mother."

Understanding dawned. That was the difference between them. "You're Fated."

"I'm Fated. My sire was meant to be with my mother, and I was meant to be born. And that just pissed Tyrone off."

Fire flashed through Finn's eyes and Ava's heart pounded. They'd talked a lot these past few nights, but he'd barely mentioned his childhood. Part of her didn't want to hear what he was about to tell her, but she had to know. "What did he do?"

"Tyrone didn't want her, but he didn't want anyone else to have her either. He hated what he felt for her, hated that she didn't want him. So he turned rabid. And he kept her."

Ava didn't move. "You mean ..."

"My mother was a prisoner, Ava. And I was not conceived out of love."

Her heart broke for him as she turned, water sloshing around them. "But you're meant to be here, Finn." Slipping her legs over his, she wrapped her arms around his neck. "Despite what Tyrone might feel, or Blair, you're meant for this world. And they aren't."

"Blair isn't," he snarled. "But I do know that, Ava. It's the only reason Tyrone kept me. I'm useful to him. That's why Blair didn't use silver bullets today because Tyrone wants me alive."

"So, silver does hurt a wolf." Though she'd already worked that out since—

Gasping, she lifted her hand and glanced at the ring on her finger. "Shit, I'm sorry! I didn't even—"

She tried tugging it off, but Finn closed his hand over hers and the ring, stopping her. "It doesn't hurt me, Ava. It can't when we're mated, and silver only hurts when it touches our blood."

Her spine relaxed as she eyed her clenched hand wearily. "Are you sure?"

"Yes." His fingers squeezed hers. "I'd buy you a silver ring for every finger if that kept Blair away. I'd adorn you with it. I still might have to."

Her belly clenched. "He'll be back, won't he?"

"Let me worry about that. Rain and I will devise a plan."

She nodded. "I wasn't surprised to see Rain is a wolf, too. Is he the Alpha?"

"No. Sly is."

She frowned. "Rain's brother?"

"Yep."

"But I thought he left? After Shelby ..." Her eyes widened as her hand lifted to her mouth. Oh, shit. Shelby hadn't just been Sly's wife. She'd been his mate. The other half of his soul. And the rogue wolves who rebelled against Fate had killed her. "Oh my God."

Finn heaved a sigh. "Sly didn't go anywhere, Ava. He's roaming the island, lost in the bush, and refusing to shift back into human form as the wolf mourns his mate."

Ava's heart broke. "Poor, Sly. That's just terrible. Does anyone talk to him?"

"Rain tries, but Sly refuses to engage much."

"So, what happens to the pack, then? I thought a pack needed an Alpha?"

"It does, which is why I'm here. Rain sent out a Call for help, and I answered."

"I thought you came for a job."

"That is my job. I work as a water sports instructor most days, but I'm here to help Rain bring Sly back. You see, a wolf in trouble can send out a Call, and a lone wolf who fights for the Goddess will hear it. During the last full moon, I was wandering the Freycinet Peninsula when I heard Rain's Call. So, I packed up the Sea-Doo and came straight here."

Ava blinked. "You mean ... did you drive your jet ski all the way from Tasmania?"

He grinned. "Yep."

"Oh my God, that's insane! And with Gracie on the back?"

Laughing, Finn drew her close. "She loved it."

Ava wasn't so sure about that. She'd enjoyed her time on

the jet ski today, but to ride it all the way from Tasmania? Only a wild wolf would attempt something like that.

"Is Gracie some kind of mini wolf? A weird part of your own lone pack?"

Finn chuckled. "No, she's exactly what I said she is. My neighbor's orphaned dog. Two lonely souls, we were. Besides, she's too chicken to be a wolf."

"Are all wolves daredevils?"

"Not all of us, but we have a fearless appetite for many things."

"Like breaking your necks?"

"Like *fun*. We also love eating wholesome food, spending time outdoors, and having lots of wild sex."

Heat surged through her at the way he grinned around the word "sex." "Well, I've certainly experienced that last one."

"You have, honey. But do know, I meant what I said the other night. You're the only woman I've ever wanted to play with. The only woman I've given myself to. The only woman I've trusted with my heart."

Ava melted against him, lost in the honesty of his eyes. "Because I'm your Fated mate. The one you love."

"Yes. The only person I will ever love."

Her hands dug into her shoulders. "Then make love with me, Finn. To me. Take me to bed and show me how a wolf loves his mate."

Chapter 43

Finn helped Ava from the spa and reached for a towel, raw, unrestrained desire surging through his vessels. From the moment she'd recognized him as a wolf and cried his name, everything had been perfect, and now he had the chance to do the one thing he'd wanted to since the moment he'd laid eyes on her. The many times they'd consummated their mating wouldn't even compare now that she knew the truth and fuck it, the primitive animal inside him wasn't going to hold back.

Dropping the towel onto the floor, Finn watched his beautiful mate as she squeezed the white terrycloth around her sunshine hair. Her naked body stood plump and ripe for the taking, her pink nipples round and engorged. Finn's mouth watered as he palmed her breast and lifted her warm, freshly bathed skin to his mouth.

Her hand slapped over the back of his shoulder as a wet plop sounded behind her and he pressed his tongue to her peaked nipple. Her body arched against his, her warm, slick sex rubbing against his straining cock. Finn growled as the magnetic connection between them latched onto his heart and he sucked harder.

She held him tight, hands spearing into his hair. "*Finn ...*"

He scraped his teeth up her flesh and nipped at her collarbone, inhaling her scent before bringing his gaze to hers. "I will make love with you, Ava, but a wolf doesn't like slow. We like to tease. Torture. I want to ravish your body and have you look at me as you scream my name."

Her teeth dug into her lower lip on a whimper. "Haven't we done that already?"

"Not like this."

Slipping his arms beneath her back and knees, Finn scooped her up and carried her to bed. Ava's fingers brushed down his chest as she placed a kiss over his heart. He shivered. Did she know their hearts now beat in harmony? That even if she lay resting while he was in a fight, her pulse would be an echo of his own?

But he'd shared enough about his world tonight, about Fate and the bond that connected them. There would be time to tell her more later as he laid her down and knelt between her legs. Her pale hair stuck to the white pillows, her breasts lifting with deep breaths as gravity dragged them apart. Her belly sank beneath her ribs and shivered under his gaze as he glanced between her legs, finding her wet, hot, and ready for him beneath her speckle of curls.

Finn slipped his hands beneath her firm ass and dragged her towards him, watching her arms slide up above her head. She honestly was the most perfect specimen of a human being. What he'd done to deserve her, he would never know, but the Goddess knew what she was doing so he would honor that. And honor Ava as he brushed his hands up her slender legs, lifted her knees, and placed her calves onto his shoulders.

Her breath shuddered out. "God, Finn. You're just ..."

Watching her eyes glaze over as she admired his body would never grow old. Her wanton desire perked his wolf with pride as her gaze roamed over his chest, abs, and strong thighs before arrowing in on his cock.

Circling his hands around her ankles, he tilted his hips suggestively. "Yes, Ava?"

Her lips quirked. "Your ego is unmatched."

"Yes, it is. But we wolves always enjoy seeing desire in our mate's eyes." Then he released her ankles but kept her legs in place as he leaned over her, bending her in half. Ava's hands flew up to grasp his shoulders. "Tell me if it's too much, honey. Tell me if I go too far."

"I will, but you won't. I bend easily."

"Good."

He nipped at her lips before moving down to her throat and collarbone. Then unable to resist any longer, he gripped her thighs, pushed her knees into her chest, and sucked her hot, puckered clit into his mouth. Ava bucked beneath him, but he held her still, gently massaging the back of her knees as he kissed the sweetest, most glorious part of her while his name shuddered from her throat. Every night, he'd made sure to warm her up, terrified he would hurt her. But even though she accommodated him perfectly, he always wanted to greet her this way as he fucking loved every second of kissing her intimate flesh.

Ava's hands speared into his hair again and tugged, spurring him on as he lowered himself, bending her up to meet him and running his nose down her center. Finn gave her what she wanted, loving her desire for beard burn as he drove his tongue deep inside her.

Ava came with a roar and almost ripped his hair from his scalp. Grinning, Finn lapped up her juices as though parched, rubbed his face against her thigh, then dug deeper into her core.

Her legs quivered. "Fuck, Finn. Don't stop. Don't ... oh ... *fuck!*" Her hand slapped his back.

Barely able to contain himself, he lifted his head and rubbed his prickly chin against her clit. The wild craziness in her eyes almost made him come against the sheets. "Got it, honey. 'Don't stop.'"

He dove again just to hear her scream. "*Finn!*"

But even he had his limits. Slipping up between her legs, he brought his face to hers, Ava's slender thighs still pressed to his shoulders. He lifted her up, opening her to him but protecting her from his weight as he angled his cock into her soft, wet folds. Tremors shot through his arms, but he held them firm as he gazed through her blue eyes into her soul. They were so close. Breaths apart. Her hands reached for his hips, then fell to her thighs as he nudged at her opening.

"This will get me deep, Ava." He'd never tried this position as it apparently created an intimacy he'd never wanted with anyone else. But with Ava, he longed to bury himself and get lost in the throes of passion.

"Good."

With his eyes locked onto hers, Finn dug his hands into the mattress beside her head and slid inside. Her cry almost raised the roof as she shuddered with the first stroke. Finn's wolf howled. Ho-ly *fuck* she was angled perfectly. He drew out, then sheathed himself to the hilt. Ava's nails grabbed his ribs and clawed. Finn roared, blood firing through his body as he moved, leaving her whimpering until she mumbled incoherently. He knew she'd given herself over completely, unable to move, and was at his mercy. He withdrew and thrust home once again, finding that special spot that had her eyes rolling back into her head as she screamed out his name.

"*Fii-ii-inn!*"

Shuddering, he shifted his weight to one arm and grabbed her ankle as he thrust again. Her whimpers were a balm for his soul while his wolf relished in her delight. In her body. She was so fucking perfect for him, clenching around his cock as her juices soaked him.

"Come for me, Ava."

"I – I ha-ave! Twice!"

Pressure built inside him, his balls tightening as he drove again. His throat strained and he struggled to breathe. "Do you want it harder?"

"Yes."

"Then hold on." He slapped his hand back down and threw all his weight into his arms. "And look at me."

Her wide eyes held his as he dug his knees into the mattress and drove into her. Again and again. She cried out, breath chugging from her heaving chest as her breasts bounced with every thrust. But the glorious view of her body remained only in his periphery as their gazes glued. Passion scorched through his veins, and her eyes lit up as she came in a flood of heat. Only then did he let himself go with a roar and empty himself inside her.

Together, they stilled. He could barely breathe. Neither could she. But Finn did what he had to as he lifted his body off her legs, and she dropped her feet onto the mattress. He hesitated as she wrapped her arms around his shoulders, but then she drew him close and he went willingly, laying over her while buried deep inside.

She pressed her lips to his jaw, her breath shuddering against his ear. "I love making love with my wolf shifter."

Grinning, Finn ran his nose through her hair before their eyes locked again. "I love making love with you. Ava ..."

Lifting onto his elbow, he just looked at her, soaking her in. She was his future. The most stunning woman he'd ever seen. Meek and kind. Bold and brazen. He'd literally die to protect her, as he'd feared he might for a moment today in Florence Bay. He hadn't known Blair only carried lead bullets when he'd shielded Ava's body with his. And he hadn't hesitated to show his true self to rescue her.

She was his mate and to see her harmed ...

An Alpha needs his mate, Finn. And I'm broken.

Finn stilled as Sly's words echoed inside his head, the Alpha's pain sinking deep into his bones. His mission had been simple—bring Sly out of the forest. He and Rain had agreed that his mating with Ava might help inspire Sly.

But now, Finn wasn't so sure.

Ava's creamy brow crinkled as her hands brushed down his shoulders. "What is it?"

"Nothing," he whispered, touching his mouth to hers. An echo of doubt vibrated through his head, but he would worry about Sly later as right now, all Finn wanted was Ava. "Let's get ourselves cleaned up, honey. Then we'll have ice cream."

Chapter 44

Ava winced as she knelt by the tree in Xena's room. Good God, she was sore. Her hips ached, thighs burned, and she might have pulled a glute, but she didn't regret it one bit after the multiple orgasms Finn had shuddered through her body. He was a fucking sex god and she could still feel his cock getting her so deep in her back as he hit her G-spot every, single, time.

Shivering, she placed her hand over the koala's back as Xena turned her adorably cute head from the eucalyptus leaves. "You're looking much stronger this morning. Are you ready to do some climbing?"

Xena turned her back in response, standing up to reach for another handful of leaves. Ava grinned. The koala was improving in leaps and bounds as she sat for prolonged periods and crawled around the room. She could pull herself up onto this small branch, but could she climb a whole tree? Ava wasn't sure. But the big mama had to try if she and Cookie were to return to the wild.

"Come on, Xena." Ava lifted the koala from the branch and bent one knee up, her muscles aching as she pushed to her feet. "Let's go get some fresh air."

Xena clung to Ava as she strode down the corridor and into a spare enclosure. From a few trees down, Cookie cried out, and Xena's ears twitched.

"That's right, Xena. Let's do this for Cookie. What if she was in trouble and you needed to climb the tree to defend her? So, let's give it a try." She placed Xena on the ground by the tree. "There are lots of yummy eucalypts up there. Your favorite."

It took Xena another moment and what looked like a tired pout, but with gentle encouragement, she clawed her way up the meter high branch and pulled herself onto the crossbar before slumping, exhausted.

Ava grinned and praised her, keeping her hand on the koala's back as she ensured the leaves were within reaching distance. If this kept up, Ava was sure Eden could release Xena and Cookie within the fortnight, a thought that made her heart swell and sink at the same time. It would be great for the koalas, but she would miss them. She could hardly believe it'd only been eleven days since Finn and Rain had heroically rescued them and she'd fallen for the big, brooding wolf. Recalling that night, Xena's injuries, and the many things Finn and Rain hadn't said, Ava now wondered if he'd tell her what really happened. She knew they hadn't been fishing. Had they been wolfing around when they'd stumbled across the injured mama and joey? But then what had bitten Xena? Had they ... hurt her?

Ava's gut clenched. No. Rain wouldn't hurt a koala because that would hurt Eden, and he'd never do that. But at least Ava now understood why Rain had resisted Eden all these years. He was a wolf shifter and out there somewhere, he had a mate. Toying with her friend's feelings wouldn't be fair as Eden would only get hurt. Ava respected Rain for that, even though her heart broke for her friend.

But perhaps it was for the best since Ava doubted that

Eden's scientific mind would embrace the paranormal world. She might have enjoyed the odd fantasy novel and movie in high school, but Eden had grown into the sweet romcom girl where everything was quirky, tense, but guaranteed a happily ever after, whereas Ava continued to enjoy a touch of magic and darkness in her fiction.

But now that Ava knew the truth, she could help her friend move on. So, she returned Xena to the ICU, checked up on Cookie, and found Eden tending Patches in the treatment room.

"Finn's picking me up soon. Is everything okay here?"

"Yeah, but I might stay tonight and watch this one."

"He's that sick?"

"His lungs aren't the best, but it beats being alone at Rain's house."

"Oh." Ava stepped into the room. "Well ... maybe after the Full Moon Party, you could ask for a room at Luna Views. I know it's still a few nights away, but you might feel more comfortable."

"Maybe." Eden smiled softly. "But don't worry about me, Ava. I'm fine. You just go and have fun with your man, okay?"

Ava nodded. Maybe she should talk to Finn and see if he knew of a way to ease her friend's heartache.

She strolled outside as he pulled into the parking lot. Finn pushed her door open and once she'd settled into the Jeep, he greeted her with a long, deep kiss. He'd trimmed and styled his beard this morning and the altered sensation sent heat prickling in her thighs.

"How was your day?"

Ava brushed her fingers through his whiskers and resisted a snort. "Whiskers" now took on a whole new meaning. "Great. Cookie's cheeky as always and getting more independent. And Xena climbed."

"Yeah?" He backed out of the car park. "That's fantastic."

"It was only to a crossbar, but it's progress. What did you get up to?"

"Cruised around Cockle Bay. I sense restlessness at Cape Pallarenda."

The balloon of happiness popped inside Ava's chest. "Oh."

"With the full moon approaching, the Unfated grow rabid. Their rational thoughts weaken and they become more wolf than man. We have no doubt that Blair will launch an attack on Friday night."

Ava froze, blinking as he gunned the Jeep up the hill. Finn's jaw set and even though tension radiated from every pore, he remained the epitome of calm, relaxed with one hand on the wheel as he navigated effortlessly up the range.

"Are you really going to kill him?" she whispered.

Finn shifted gears. "I'll do what I must, Ava. Blair doesn't belong in this world and now that we're mated, he'll want to kill you even more. That's Tyrone's mission—to destroy Fated mates."

"Like Shelby."

He nodded and fear coursed down her spine. There was no other choice and even though she hated the idea of the man she loved becoming a murderer ... would he really? As he'd said, Blair wasn't meant for this world. She'd known there was something dark about him from the moment he'd begun pursuing her two full moons ago.

"So ... explain something to me. If these wolves are indeed 'Unfated,' what is their connection with the Moon?"

"They have none. At least, not directly. Not like we Fated do. We're at our strongest during full moon."

"Are you weak during new moon?"

"We're never weak, Ava. We celebrate and revere the Moon Goddess and since we draw our power from her, that's when we find ourselves most connected with our wolves. Our strength is tied to the Moon, but we're not disconnected during the new moon. It's still there, we just can't see it. And she can't see us."

That was true. The moon, sun, and earth remained in continuous orbit with each other, it was just the angle to which the sun and the moon were at that depended on how much of the moon you could see. "Right. And the Unfated?"

"They are ... the opposite. They feel the Goddess's presence, but they hate, fear, or experience pain from her. So during the new moon, they are at peace with their wolves, almost human. But during the full—"

"They run rabid." Inhaling, Ava forced her fear aside as she watched the high tide roll in over Geoffrey Bay. "It makes sense."

Finn placed his hand on her knee. "What does, honey?"

"I thought about it, and Blair first approached me as the moon was waning. I must have agreed to have dinner with him during the new moon, because he seemed more of a gentleman all of a sudden. Then he grew snarkier. He must have been out wolfing during the full moon though because there were three days that he didn't contact me. Then he returned, we went to Paluma, and it all went to hell."

"He'd have been coming off his high."

"And I never want to see that again. He terrified me, Finn. If I didn't have my ring—"

"You had a lucky escape, Ava. Trust me."

She exhaled. "He'd have raped me."

"Repeatedly." He took her hand and squeezed. "And once you had born him a pup, he'd have killed you."

A shudder coursed through her. "That's horrible."

"That's how the Unfated do it. It's how they're made. That's what Tyrone did to some poor woman to have Blair, and why it grated on him to bond with my mother."

"But now that I understand the mating bond, that doesn't

make sense. Why didn't she leave? Their bond couldn't have formed like ours if she feared—"

"There's more than one way to complete the mating bond, Ava."

She blinked at his hard tone, the set of his jaw, and it took him a moment to continue. "You know what I said about the three levels? That's the way a wolf is meant to bond with his mate. To allow her free will. The two of us, we're complete." He smiled softly. "We're pure and in love and are happy. But Tyrone took the easy road, Ava. The dark one. He bit my mother, claimed her as his, and didn't give her a choice in the matter."

Ava's heart sank. "That's cruel."

"Not only is it cruel, it's forbidden," he said, fire flashing through his eyes. "Biting your mate is one way to rebel against the Moon Goddess, as that's not how she intended us wolves to act. We need our mates to bond with us by choice. To love us as much as we love them."

"But your parents didn't love each other."

"And because he'd turned his back on the Goddess, Tyrone took what he thought was rightfully his rather than earn it."

"Is that why he killed her? Can a wolf really kill his mate?"

"I wouldn't have thought so if I hadn't seen it for myself. But I don't understand it. I mean, I'd never ... if you ... it kills me to see you bruised, Ava. Those scratches on your back made me see red and alone warrant my desire to snap Blair's neck. So, I don't know how Tyrone did it, but I guess if your bond is dark and you hate your mate enough, you find the strength to do so."

"I'm sorry, Finn." She squeezed his hand, feeling his pain. But at least he would never need to be alone again. "So, now that I know about your mystical world, will you tell me the truth about what happened to Xena? Because I know you didn't just *happen* to find her."

"No." He turned down the hill into Nelly Bay, then spared her a glance. "Bat shifter."

Ava blinked. "*Bat* shifter?"

"Vampire."

"There are vampires here?" Ava gaped at him. "Oh God, that's just ... just ..."

He chuckled. "Are you scared of vampires, Ava?"

"Do they drink people's blood?"

"Yes."

Ava shuddered. "Vampires. Bat shifters." Her eyebrows shot up. "Was that why you were afraid of the bat at the Forts? Was that a vampire?"

"I wasn't afraid. I was angry and concerned that it was following us, because yes, it was a vampire. The bats are living with the flying fox colonies in Townsville and Tyrone uses them as spies."

Ava couldn't believe it. She might have accepted Finn as a wolf shifter, but vampires? What other creatures of the night existed? Ava wasn't sure she wanted to know.

"Are the bats still spying on us?"

"We don't think so. They've been back and forth spying on the pack, but I haven't seen any since Sly wounded the last bat shifter."

"I thought vampires and werewolves were sworn enemies?"

"We are. We wolves love humans, live with the humans, and protect them. Vampires don't. They like to feed on humans, control them, and use them for their own sadistic pleasures. But as long as they don't harm humans in our territory, then we wolves have little reason to fight them."

That was comforting, at least. But Ava couldn't think of anything worse than drinking blood. Hence she didn't eat meat. "Do you think the vampires in Townsville are feeding off humans?"

"No doubt about it," he said, and Ava's eyebrows shot up. "And it's concerning that Tyrone is working with them, so the sooner we kill him, the sooner the problems in Townsville will end and we can live in peace on the island."

"And bring Sly out of the bush?"

Finn paused, then nodded. "And bring Sly back. So, we're heading to Rain's to form a plan of attack as we only have three days until the full moon rises."

Five minutes later, they arrived at Rain's cliffside house and Ava followed Finn up to the second floor and into the open-plan kitchen, where three young resort staff gathered around the island bench. Ava blinked with recognition, though she wasn't surprised as it made sense that the other wolves who had come to their aid yesterday were the three young daredevils in training.

So that must mean the wolf on the rock—

"Afternoon, everyone." Finn greeted them with back slapping hugs, then wrapped his arm around Ava's waist. "You fellas have all met Ava?"

Nate, who she'd met a few times, flashed her a smile. "Yeah."

"Kinda," Chad said, scratching his head.

"Nope." The other man who Ava didn't know leaned his hip on the bench. "But you're certainly worth going to war for."

Finn's hand tightened over Ava's hip as a soft growl rumbled from his chest. "Watch it, Kai."

The young wolf grinned and lifted his hands. "Calm down, man. Just stating a fact. But we've waited a long time to go after these bastards, so bring it on."

Chad nodded. "Thorne has another thing coming if he believes his bastard will come out of this alive."

"Especially if he's going to invade our territory," Kai agreed. "He's lucky we didn't rip him to pieces yesterday. No one attacks our pack and gets away with it."

Ava's belly clenched as the young wolf shot her a pointed look. It had been twenty-four hours since she'd flung herself over Finn's fluffy body and accepted her fate, and these young men were willing to go to war for her. She didn't know whether to be flattered or terrified, though she was grateful to be welcomed as a member of their pack. The weakest member, but the most important to Finn. And because of their bond, they had a reason to fight the rogues. She was their excuse. Bait?

Ava shivered. No, she wasn't bait. She was prey. And these men were bursting to fight the demons who threatened their territory, faith, and future.

She was Finn's future, so while she didn't know what role —if any—she would play in their pack politics, she would protect their secret and fight alongside them.

Chapter 45

Finn placed his hands on the table and studied the large map of Magnetic Island. He'd started considering battle tactics when he'd been cruising the west coast this afternoon trying to sense the threat pulsating from across the high, choppy sea. Knowing his sire, Finn didn't doubt Tyrone's intentions. He wanted to crush Finn's belief and force him to rebel. Killing his mother had been step one and though it had hurt, it hadn't shattered him. But killing Ava?

Finn's fists curled. That wasn't going to fucking happen, so he and his packmates needed to devise a plan. Fast.

Rain stood beside him with his arms crossed over his chest while Nate, Chad, and Kai sat with Ava at the table.

"We'll wait them out here," Finn said, digging his finger onto the map. "Cockle Falls. It's hunting ground we're familiar with and is one of the closest points to Cape Pallarenda far from any residences."

"Are you sure he won't come by ferry?" Ava asked.

Finn smiled softly at his sweet, innocent mate. "I told you, he'll be rabid."

"He won't dare mix with people or have the patience for

the ferry timetable. He'll want to do this quick and dirty, so they'll pile into boats and speed across to land here." Rain rapped his knuckle on Cockle Bay.

"They could land anywhere along the west coast," Nate said. "They'll shift and race through the bush to hunt her."

"They?" Ava asked as she regarded the scouts.

"Blair won't come alone," Rain said. "He'll bring his lieutenants."

"Wolves," Finn clarified. "Not the cops. And they'll be out for blood."

Chad interlocked his fingers and flexed his arms. "Bring it on. We can take a couple of Unfated."

"They might be rabid, but they're still strong," Finn reminded him. "Whatever you do, don't get cocky."

"We won't." Chad sobered as he glanced at Rain. "We trained under one of the best."

"We might have waited a long time for this moment," Rain said, "and we've trained hard. But don't mistake the scenarios we've practiced for the real deal. This will be a real life and death situation. If you make a mistake, you might be killed."

Silence fell, except for the pounding echo around Finn's heart. Ava's.

He moved to stand behind her and placed his hands on her shoulders. "I know you're all skilled fighters, especially under Rain's tutelage."

"And Sly's before that," Kai said, releasing a low whistle. "That wolf knows how to fight."

Nate turned to Rain. "You think he'll come?"

Finn, too, cocked his eyebrow as Rain rubbed his chin. "I don't know. He's still the Alpha. Barely."

"He'll sense the rogues approach the island, though," Finn said, absently massaging Ava's shoulders to help ease her tension.

"And to him, all the rogues had a hand in killing Shelby," Kai said.

Nate nodded. "Sly wants revenge more than the rest of us. More than we want him back."

"He'll sense a fight and be out for blood."

"Yeah, but Sly's unpredictable," Rain said, doubt clouding his eyes.

"He reached out when he told us about the bats attacking Xena and Cookie," Finn said.

"And refused to speak to us during the rescue."

The scouts exchanged puzzled frowns. "Who?"

"The koalas," Ava said, quickly filling them in on Xena's attack and Finn and Rain's rescue mission.

Nate huffed and crossed his arms over his chest. "So, you're telling me that Sly's out there rescuing fucking koalas, but you doubt he'll come to our aid?"

"He's our Alpha!" Kai banged his fist on the table. "If we're going up against those he hates the most, you'd think he'd come."

"I don't know ..." Chad shook his head. "He came to welcome me into the pack and give me my pack stripes, but since then, he's been a ghost."

Finn's chest tightened. He still hadn't received *his* pack stripes.

"I haven't clapped eyes on him in months," Nate pondered.

"He was there yesterday."

Everyone's heads whipped towards Ava.

"What was that, honey?"

"Sly." She grasped Finn's wrist as she glanced around the pack. "When you forced Blair to retreat, Sly was on the rock, watching. I saw him."

Mixed expressions of surprise, doubt, and confusion were exchanged around the table. Rain was the first to concede.

"I'll reach out to him. If he comes, he'll be more rabid and more powerful than any rogue, but we need to prepare for the possibility that he'll be inflicted with pain like every full moon. He might not want to fight, so we need to base our tactics around Sly not being there." He nodded at Finn. "What's your plan?"

Clearing his throat, Finn resumed his position at the head of the table. Rain was right, they couldn't depend on Sly. But if Finn had learned anything since being mated, it was how unpredictable and powerful the bond could be. And while Sly might feel the loss of his mate greater beneath the power of the full moon, Finn could only hope that Sly's taste for vengeance would overpower his torment.

But Blair didn't know the strength of Fated mates and wouldn't count on Sly being there. He would view the pack as vulnerable without their Alpha, so Blair would come with just enough wolves to get the job done.

Finn placed his hands on the table and surveyed his pack-mates. Blair had a death wish if he thought he could get through these four wolves and himself to Ava. And Finn would not hesitate to kill him.

Blair, however, wouldn't dare cross Tyrone if their sire wanted Finn alive.

"He'll employ basic hunting strategy and send the weak in first. We'll be outnumbered, but remember, they are rabid, twisted beings who don't truly belong in this world. You are strong, powerful, Fated wolves with the Goddess on your side. They have no family, only kept women and pups who are no better than they are, so if you need to kill, do so without hesitation." He turned to the scouts. "You three will form the first line of defense and await the rogues in the creek. Look out for each other."

Nate, Kai, and Chad nodded, though Finn noted Kai didn't look as confident as the other two.

"Nate and Chad, you take the front and Kai, stand behind. Rain will back you." Finn glanced at the man beside him, who nodded. "Remember, you will heal given enough time, but protect your necks. And your eyes." Eye gouging was a common tactic and though they might be invincible, they couldn't regrow body parts. "I hope the fight won't last long, but they'll try to tire us out before going for the kill. *Try*, because they'll tire well before we do. If you need to heal, stay by Ava."

She straightened. "Me? Where will I be?"

"Up on the rocks," Finn said. "Beside me."

AVA GAPED AT FINN. Having been too caught up in their tactics and consumed by fear of these men going into battle, she hadn't even considered where she would be. For some stupid reason, she'd imagined Finn would tuck her away somewhere safe. Lock her up in their hut or at Rain's house or in a cage of silver.

But where else would she be other than beside Finn? It was her that Blair wanted. Her he hunted. He didn't give a flying fuck about the men surrounding her and if Finn did lock her up, Blair wouldn't go after the pack. He'd go after her.

Prey.

Ava slumped in her seat. "Of course, I will be."

"I'm sorry, honey." Finn moved to crouch beside her. "I didn't make that clear, did I?"

She shook her head. "No, it was me. I wasn't thinking."

"If there was any other way, we'd do it," Rain said, crossing his arms over his chest. If Ava hadn't known better, she'd have assumed he was the Alpha with his wide stance, steel-eyed determination, and hard-set jaw. "I'd love to leave you at Luna

Views, but we need to consider the lives of the other people on the island. Finn's plan is a good one, Ava. Trust him."

"I do. And it is a good plan. I'll be with you guys and help in any way that I can." How she'd watch them risk their lives for her though, she didn't know. "But ... can I ask a few questions?"

Finn nodded. "Shoot."

"What if he comes with silver bullets?"

A shudder ran around the table.

"He won't," Finn said. "Blair will be running off his animal instincts to hunt and kill. He won't resort to human weapons."

She accepted that. "But what if he tries to kidnap me again? You say he wants to keep me."

Rain snorted. "He's past that, Ava. Blair's rabid and he won't try to take you, sneer at you, or rape you this time. He'll just go in for the kill."

Finn's lips curled as he rose to his feet. "You don't need to scare her."

"It's the truth."

"Still." Finn strode around to face Rain, his chest heaving. "This is already terrifying enough for her. And besides, I'll kill him first."

Ava's eyebrows lifted as she watched Rain and Finn, her pulse softening as heat unashamedly rushed through her. Perhaps if she actually had to pick one, *Finn* seemed more Alpha than Rain.

Conceding, Rain inclined his head. "She'll still need a weapon."

Then he turned and strode down the hallway. Finn watched him go before facing the pack and eyeing them each individually. Including Ava.

"Any other questions?"

No. Only what weapon did Rain have in mind?

"We'll gather before sundown, I presume?" Chad asked.

"Let's say six," Finn said. "That'll give us time to stalk the perimeters and enjoy ourselves before the moon rises."

"Pity you'll miss out on the Full Moon Party, Ava," Nate said. "You were planning to go, right?"

"I was only going to check it out because I'm here. Though I was keen to see Jam play."

"Yeah, I convinced Rain to book them." Kai grinned. "They rock."

"But with any luck, we'll have Blair cleared out of here early," Chad said. "Then you'll make it in time for the main event."

Ava smiled. "That would be nice. I'll definitely be going to the next party—"

Though she didn't get a chance to explain about Isla as Rain returned clutching a black velvet bag tied off with a gold rope. Like the kind jewelry sometimes came in, only larger. Ava felt compelled to stand as he lifted the bag with two hands and tumbled it into hers as though burned. Ava's hand curled around the object as she untied the rope and withdrew a glistening silver dagger with rubies embedded in the hilt.

Three chairs scraped back while Rain and Finn cleared their throats.

"You just have that lying around?" Finn asked.

"It was Shelby's. So, take care of it, else Sly will have my head."

Ava nodded as she slid the knife back into the bag. "I will. But ... why would she have a weapon that could kill Sly?"

"It wasn't to use against Sly. There was no bad blood between them. Would you ever be compelled to use it against Finn?"

Ava clutched the dagger to her chest, twisting away to place her body between it and Finn. "No!"

"Exactly. It was to protect her against Tyrone."

Ava examined the black velvet in her hands. "Why didn't she use it?"

"She never even had the chance. They were too quick."

Ava's heart sank as she turned the dagger in her hands, thinking about that poor woman and the terror she must have felt. They said Tyrone had killed her, but had Blair played a part in that, too? The media had only been told so much about her murder and now that Ava knew it had been wolves who had killed Shelby, she could only imagine the truth about what the police had covered up.

But Ava wouldn't let the same thing happen to her. Clutching the dagger to her chest, she glanced up at Finn. "I don't know what to do with it."

He smiled softly and placed his hand on her back. "I'll teach you."

Chapter 46

Ava listened to Finn's stabbing advice with half an ear, distracted by the short, steel kitchen knife he aptly twirled between his fingers as he led her into the bush later that afternoon.

"Never hesitate. Maintain a solid stance, keep a firm grip on the handle, and throw your weight into it like you would a punch."

She nodded. "And where should I aim?"

"Try for high on the shoulder or low in the belly, though the neck will be optimal." They reached a clearing in the bushland, and Finn handed her the knife. "It'll be too difficult to reach a wolf's heart unless he has you pinned beneath him. If so, thrust upwards." He adjusted her grip on the knife, wrapped his hands around her fist, and demonstrated, sending a jolt through her shoulders. "Okay?"

She nodded. "It's common sense, I suppose. Overhand grip and thrust down. Underhand and thrust up. I just need to keep my nerve and remember it's okay to hurt them."

"If you don't, the wolf will hurt you. It's self-defense, Ava, and you've done it before."

"But that was a punch, not stabbing somebody."

"All you need to do is connect silver to the wolf's blood, and you'll wound him. It's just stabbing them is more effective than breaking their nose."

"All right." She changed her grip and thrust the knife through thin air. "How's that?"

"Good. Nice shoulder power." He took a few steps back. "Now, try it for real."

"What?"

Finn tore his shirt off and tossed it aside. "Stab me."

The knife clattered from her hand. "No."

Finn chuckled. "Come on."

Ava shook her head until her ears rattled. "Nuh-uh. No way."

"Do you want to learn how to defend yourself or not?"

"Yes, but there has to be a better way."

"Nothing's more effective than sparring."

"But I don't want to hurt you."

He spread his arms, chest heaving and abs rippling with barely controlled laughter. "I'll heal."

"I don't care! You'll still feel pain and I don't want to be responsible for—"

"Ava." Softening at her hysterics, Finn drew her into his arms. "It'll be okay. You trust me, right?"

She nodded against his chest. "You know I do."

"Then trust me when I say that you need to have confidence in battle. And to do that, you need to practice. You need to know how to stab a wolf."

"And I will stab one. Just not you."

His chest expanded and, strangely enough, she felt his calmness ease into her. His confidence. Ava lifted her head and sank into his blue eyes. Finn's face gentled as he wiped the tear from her cheek.

"None of that, honey. You need to be fierce. And I'll feel

more relaxed during battle if you've practiced stabbing a wolf. So, please? For me?"

Resigned, Ava's spine softened. "I'll do anything for you."

"And I'll do anything for you." Pressing his lips to her forehead, Finn squeezed her tight before stepping away. "But I'm trusting your knowledge of anatomy here, Ava. So, whatever you do, don't aim to kill."

Ava drew in a deep breath, then let it out slowly. She hated this. She didn't want to stab Finn, but she also didn't want to stand by helpless when the pack put their lives on the line.

"I'll be careful." Bending down, she retrieved the knife. It was lighter and smaller than Shelby's silver dagger and wouldn't mortally wound Finn if she didn't hit him in any major arteries. Except—"Wait! Aren't you going to be in wolf form?"

"Yeah ..."

"I don't know the anatomy of a wolf!"

Finn shrugged. "Pretty much the same, honey. This is just practice to boost your confidence, so avoid the areas you want to target tomorrow. If you hit my carotid, I won't heal in time, so aim for the shoulder, legs, and belly. All of that will be enough to bring a wolf to his knees with a silver dagger." Finn lowered his shorts and kicked them aside. "And if you want to play tonight, don't touch my balls."

She tried to laugh but failed. "Like I'd want to cut off that part of you."

He shuddered and grinned at the same time. "Many women would kill to have that chance. Or the opportunity to stab their boyfriend."

"But you haven't hurt me."

"And I never will."

No, but he was right on his way to pissing her off. Drawing in a deep breath, Ava gripped the knife and nodded. "All right. I'm ready."

"Stab high at the shoulder or a low undercut to the belly. Neither of those will mortally wound me."

"Okay."

Then with a shiver, Finn's body matter contorted as he morphed into a massive, golden wolf, hair rising along his back, tail in the air, and paws larger than his hands clawing into the soft soil. She could still scarcely believe it, but she thought him wonderful. Beautiful. Strong and powerful. A big, ferocious golden retriever.

Finn bared his teeth and snarled.

"Is that supposed to scare me?" Grinning, she leaned towards him like she would a puppy. "You're so cute and fluffy, I could just snuggle up and—"

He snapped at her fingers as she reached between his ears, and Ava straightened. Right. Training. She had to stab him.

She didn't want to.

But as Finn started circling her, Ava recalled the redness in Blair's eyes and the twisted, patchy, contorted body of his wolf form. He certainly wasn't as beautiful as the Magnetic Island pack. Rain and the scouts were stunning specimens of wolves, all reflective of themselves with charcoal markings stretched along their backs.

But Finn didn't have markings. Why? She'd thought he was—

He lunged and Ava yelped, clutching her arms tightly beside her body. He flew past her in a flurry of golden fur and growled.

Right. *Training*.

She spun around and pointed the knife, shoving all humorous thoughts aside. She needed to focus. It would not be funny in three nights time beneath the full moon when it wasn't Finn stalking her.

He attacked again, coming at her with his claws extended as though ready to tackle her. Clenching her teeth, she plunged her hand upward and connected with his belly. Ava screamed. He yelped. Hot blood seeped down her hand as she let go of the knife.

Finn fell to the ground. Gasping, Ava dropped to her knees, tears blurring her vision as he shifted back and pulled the knife from his abdomen.

"I'm sorry! I can't believe I did that! You—"

Her hands swiped through the blood to find nothing but skin, and her shoulders slouched. "Oh, thank God, that—"

Finn gripped the back of her head and pulled her close. "I'm so fucking proud of you." Crushing her mouth to his, he dragged her lips apart and drove his tongue inside. He kissed her deeply, passionately, nipping at her lower lip before drawing away and baring his beautiful but just as ferocious human teeth. "And I am *not* cute and fluffy."

Ava grinned. "Oh, yes, you are," she teased, pressing her nose to his and rubbing his head.

Finn growled as he dug his human claws into her waist and rolled her into the dirt. Ava lost her breath as she gave into his hard, demanding kiss.

Then his weight lifted and he jumped back onto his feet, extending his hand. "Round two. This time, go for my shoulder."

He made her stab him three more times. She hated it and still screamed, but her confidence grew and so did her determination.

After almost an hour, Finn slipped his shorts back on and threw his arm around her shoulders, grinning as they strolled to the Jeep. "You did well, honey."

"You didn't have to yelp every time, you know."

"It hurt," he said, rubbing his oblique. "You got me good that last time. Almost lost my kidney."

"Aww, poor baby." Leaning into him, she ran her hand

down his hard, smooth oblique. "Do you want me to kiss it better?"

"You're the one who stabbed me, Ava. It's the least you could do."

She stopped walking and ducked her head, kissing his warm skin where moments ago, she'd plunged the knife. And yet, not a mark remained. Remarkable. *He* was remarkable and this past week she'd spent with him had not only opened her heart, but helped shed her fears and unleash the strong, fierce woman she'd always longed to be.

Grinning, she stepped in front of him, heat rippling through her as she kissed up his glorious belly, sternum, and neck before capturing his mouth. Finn welcomed her with a growl, pressing his hands into her back and feasting on her awe. Her desire. Her gratitude.

Ava speared her fingers into his long, soft hair. "Thank you for teaching me, Finn. And I promise that come Friday, I will not falter."

Finn's lips curved as he brushed his nose against hers. "I have every faith in you, Ava. You wouldn't be a wolf's mate if there wasn't a fighter in you. But I do think we should practice again tomorrow."

She drew back to gaze into his azure eyes. "Okay. But right now, I'd like to do a bit of yoga and have a good stretch. Would you like to join me?"

"I'm not sure I'll be any good at yoga."

Grinning, she took his hand. "Don't underestimate yourself. I could show you many poses you might enjoy."

And she did, though they did not use happy baby and puppy pose the way they were originally intended.

The next two days continued to be riddled with tension and excitement as the full moon approached. Ava tried to stay calm and focused, keeping her nerves at bay as she sparred with Finn in the bush and discussed battle tactics at the packhouse while Rain ensured Eden was safely out of hearing range. Though that wasn't difficult when her friend spent most of her time at the hospital. Ava hated seeing Eden so withdrawn, but she supposed that's what Finn meant when he said Fate could be cruel. Rain wasn't in charge of his own destiny and once this battle was over, Ava hoped she could help her friend heal and move on.

After finishing her rehab on Xena, she found Eden in the treatment room examining Marco. "I'll meet you and Dee at the party tonight, yeah?"

Eden nodded. "Yep. We'll be there. Rain's insisted that I don't miss it."

"He just wants you to enjoy yourself." And be safe hidden amongst a crowd during tonight's showdown. "Besides, it'll be fun."

"Not as fun as next month's will be. Jam are cool, but Isla's better."

Ava grinned. "Next month is going to be epic," she said, hugging her friend. "I'll see you later."

Chapter 47

The sun hung precariously close to the horizon, casting pinks and golds over the mainland when Ava and Finn pulled the Jeep over on West Point Road. Ava unclipped her seatbelt and clutched the velvet encased dagger to her chest. She hoped she wouldn't have to use it, but if she could stab the man she loved, she could certainly stab a rogue wolf. Her ring had been enough to weaken Blair with a bloody nose, but it wouldn't help much tonight if Finn's plans failed.

Not that they would. With his hair tied back and muscles bulging in his tight black T-shirt, Finn oozed cautious confidence as he opened her door.

"Don't worry, Ava. They won't be here until moonrise at least as they'll want the cover of darkness to steal across the bay. We have plenty of time to have fun yet."

Two hours at best, but she would try her best to enjoy herself as she followed him along the sandy walkway towards Cockle Falls. The creek had been flowing when they'd driven over it a few meters back, and Kai had already reported that there was plenty of water running over the rocks for them to enjoy themselves and "warm up" before battle.

Taking a deep breath, Ava ordered herself to remain calm. If all went well, she'd be back at Luna Views partying beneath the full moon by the time Jam took the stage. She might not have been keen on the partying aspect like the hundreds of people who'd been gathering at the resort when she and Finn had left, but she'd rather be deafening her ears in that crowd than be waiting in the peace and quiet for rabid wolves who wanted to kill her.

Guilt swarmed in her belly. It was a terrible burden to be prey. But she could be in no safer place than with Finn and his glorious friends. They arrived at the waterhole where a small waterfall trickled between two large boulders into the pool before flowing down the sandy creek. Bush surrounded the clearing that opened to the darkening sky, where the soon-to-rise moon would provide light for their antics. Smaller rocks tumbled from the cliff face down either side of the swimming hole and across the creek.

A playful howl echoed through the air and Ava smiled as the auburn wolf chased the larger chestnut one up the rocks. A sandy colored wolf dragged himself out of the water and stood on the bank, shaking himself dry, while the black wolf lay on the highest boulder watching over everyone.

The tension in Ava's spine eased. Despite their plans for the evening, the wolves seemed to be at their height while remaining relaxed and enjoying themselves. At least, Kai and Chad were as Chad—who had to be the chestnut wolf—circled behind auburn Kai as though encouraging his friend to jump. Nate rolled himself in the sand on the other side of the creek. Rain spotted Finn and Ava, rose to his feet, and lowered his head in greeting.

This time, Ava knew they communicated telepathically as Finn nodded in return. He'd admitted that pack members could communicate wolf to man, but they couldn't use the power man to man, despite the long looks Finn and Rain had shared appearing to indicate otherwise.

"They look like they're having fun," Ava said.

"Yeah, but they're prepared. The scouts are preening for a fight."

She took another deep breath, but the squeeze of Finn's hand did more to calm her than any breathing exercise ever could. "I hope so. I don't want anyone to get hurt."

He placed a kiss on her forehead. "We'll be fine. We might be facing a vicious foe, but we're blessed with the power to defeat them."

Ava tried to share his confidence, but it was difficult when she was used to avoiding conflict and the notion that killing was wrong. And it was. In her world.

Her *old* world.

"All right. But—"

"Ava, honey." He bent to bring his gaze to hers. "Trust me. It's the full moon, the time for power to reign and miracles to happen. But it's also time to celebrate, so let's scout the perimeter, then have some fun."

Ava didn't want to deny him that. She might have found these past few days terrifying, but she hadn't failed to notice Finn's strength grow as the full moon approached. This was his time to honor and embrace his faith, and she wanted to witness such a celebration.

They walked around the waterhole, then stood at the base of the massive rock that Rain had been lying on. It was almost twice as tall as her and Ava agreed she would be safe up there when the rogues arrived.

Kicking off her shoes, she strolled into the water and slipped her feet into the shallows as she watched Kai leap off the cliff and splash into the water. Panting happily, he paddled towards her and strutted out onto the bank. Then shook himself.

Ava threw her hands up and laughed. "Kai!"

"Beat it," Finn growled, lunging at the young wolf.

Kai seemed to chuckle as he trotted away and clambered back up the rocks.

Ava wrapped her arms around her knees and smiled as Finn sat beside her. "I don't think you need to save me from Kai."

"A wolf shouldn't flirt with another's mate."

"He's just having fun."

"Don't care." Finn placed his hand on her back and kissed her. "You're mine."

"That's indisputable. But be nice to the young guys."

"I am. They're great guys and being here with them ..." Finn's chest expanded. "I mean, I've always hoped I'd find a pack, Ava. We're social creatures and we need to live among friends. The life of a lone wolf is ... well, like it sounds. Solitary, quiet, and very, very lonely."

She squeezed his hand. "You have a pack now, Finn. And you'll never be alone again."

"No. So come on. Swim with me beneath the full moon."

Ava smiled and together, they waded into the water, swimming across the creek to duck their heads beneath the cool waterfall. Finn grinned and her heart swelled as he kissed her, delighting in the Moon's power that Ava feared was getting too close as darkness fell far too quickly.

After splashing around with Finn and the wolves, she moved out of the water and shivered as he led her up onto the rocks. Water rushed beneath their feet as they clambered over the waterfall and onto the giant boulder.

Kai took another running leap off the cliff.

Finn laughed. "You going to jump, honey?"

"No."

"Scared?"

"Yes. I don't like jumping from heights. You could hurt yourself."

"Yeah, but we don't break that easily, remember?"

With a playful howl, Nate leapt off the cliff, his paws outstretched as he dove clean into the water.

"Show off," Finn muttered. "Then, are you okay up here?"

"I'm fine." She nudged his shoulder with hers. "You've hung out with me long enough. Go wolf with your packmates."

He dropped a kiss on her shoulder. "I'll return to you soon."

Finn moved back and kicked off his shorts, powerful thighs clenching as he ran and jumped off the rock. Ava gasped as matter contorted and Finn shifted midair before sliding his fluffy golden body effortlessly into the water.

Grinning, she sat and let her feet dangle over the cliff as she watched the wolves play, splashing and calling softly in the darkness. They sure were marvelous creatures. Strong, protective men with hearts of gold.

She could sit there and watch them all night.

Tyrone paced the veranda, his mind restless and body aching for a run as the cursed Moon beckoned. Despite having shunned the Goddess, he couldn't ignore the power that this time of the month brought or the strength that pumped through his veins. The wolves would wreak havoc tonight, keeping his police force busy with all sorts of unsavory behavior they called "criminal activity." But what was a celebration without alcohol, fast cars, and maybe a beat down or two on a weak-assed punk?

It was the ultimate night for it and all Tyrone wanted was to run in the bush with his son, feast on some unsuspecting wildlife, and finish the evening rutting with a whore at Night Bite.

And he would, as soon as Blair quit sulking and arrived to complete their ritual.

Tyrone ground his teeth. Blair might have failed in his mission, once again having let his dick steer his conscience when he'd gone after that bitch instead of effectively containing Finlay. But while Tyrone was pissed, he was willing to overlook it. Finlay might have forged a mating bond, but Ava would never be safe. Tyrone had more tactics up his sleeve, darker and nastier ones than the brutal death he'd given Shelby.

But none of those involved sending Blair back to claim her, and his son had been none too pleased. He wanted to be the one to kill Ava, and if he quit being so reckless, Tyrone would allow it. But first, Blair needed to swallow his wounded pride and show some restraint. There were plenty more women he could plant his seed in, and stepping foot into Blackwood's territory again would be nothing short of foolish.

Blair hadn't agreed when Tyrone had forbidden him to return, which was why he should have known something was amiss long before he sensed the putrid, bitter odor accompanying the black wings that glided into the tree. His mouth twisted as Eric landed on the ground in a cloud of black shadow.

"Boss, you need to get to the beach. Quickly. Blair's taken the boats and is heading for the island."

Tyrone's spine bristled. "He wouldn't."

"The rogues are going with him. I tried to—"

With a roar, Tyrone ran towards the bush, his muscles straining and bones cracking as he burst out of his jeans and shifted. His claws dug into the track as he raced up the mountain.

Fucking idiot! He'd told Blair to let it go. Leave her alone.

That he'd get his turn with her when they had her back in Townsville away from the Blackwoods. Away from Finlay.

But as usual, Blair hadn't listened, and Tyrone reached desperately through the pack bond as he sprinted up the cape.

"*Blair!*" He couldn't be too far away. "*Don't be stupid! Get your ass back here!*"

He jumped the creek and scurried up the loose pebbles onto the walking track while Eric flew overhead. "*Blair!*"

Only silence answered, and Tyrone bared his teeth. He knew Blair could hear him, but the reckless kid—

"*Blair, don't do it!*"

A cackle whispered through the bond. "*You can't stop me, Father.*"

Tyrone growled as he ran over the hill and past the first fort. Almost there. "*You'll get yourself killed!*"

Blair scoffed. "*You think I can't take Little Finlay? You think he's stronger than me?*"

Tyrone's pulse pounded faster, watching as boats sped off into the darkness. More motors fired up and the air filled with the metallic taste of the Unfated's lust for blood.

"*Of course not.*" It wasn't a complete lie. "*You're strong, Blair. You always have been.*"

"*And Finaly is a weak-assed pussy. He'll never turn his back on the Moon, Father. He won't join us, so it's time we end him once and for all.*"

Tyrone leapt off the track and onto the roof of his favored fort just as Blair's boat sped away from the beach meters below.

Shadow swirled as Lucas shifted to stand beside Tyrone and crossed his arms over his chest. "I tried to stop him, but he wouldn't listen to reason."

Clawing at the concrete roof, Tyrone threw back his head and howled. His son was a bloody fool. But what was worse, he was right. Finlay would never turn. Even if they killed Ava, the Goddess had taken hold of him heart, body, and soul. He wouldn't have become a Warrior otherwise.

But while he might have the skills to fight, could Finlay defeat dozens of bloodthirsty rogues with only a handful of inexperienced scouts and no Alpha?

Tyrone smirked. He'd love to see the whelp try.

Chest heaving, he arrowed his gaze in on his beloved son. *"Then stay focused, Blair. Forget the girl and go for Finlay. If you can't turn him, take him down."*

Blair stood from the boat and sent him a salute. *"I'll return soon, Father. And we will feast on Finlay's head."*

Chapter 48

The clearing brightened as the moon rose behind Ava, casting its shimmering reflection upon the water. As one, the wolves raised their snouts to greet the Goddess. Ava peered over her shoulder too, smiling at the sight of the giant, yellow September supermoon. It might not be officially full until two a.m., but that moment of fullness would only last an instant.

Paws padded over rock and Ava glanced up at Finn, the light shimmering in his golden fur before he shifted and knelt beside her. His strong thigh pressed against her back as he held her between his legs.

"It's almost time."

Ava admired the moon. "It sure is beautiful. No wonder you revere it."

"She's glorious," he agreed softly as his strength surged through their bond and into her spine. Turning her head, she ran her gaze up his thick thigh, his ripped abs, and his expanding chest as his fierce blue eyes fixed on the moon. He was beholden to it, drawing power from its light.

And Ava's fears eased. This was the true Finn. He was a warrior, and Fate was on his side.

She pressed her head to his belly and breathed in deep. "I love you, Finn."

Spearing his fingers into her hair, he held her close. "I love you, too, honey."

Ava lifted her face as he bent to kiss her. But their lips had barely touched when a howl echoed in the wind. Gasping, she tore her mouth away as Finn shot to his feet.

"Get in formation!"

Ava scrambled to her knees. "My dagger!"

"I'll get it."

Finn leapt nimbly off the boulder and onto the rocks below, landing in a crouch before grabbing the velvet bag. He tossed it onto the rock where it landed with a muted clang, and she snatched it up. Standing, she withdrew the weapon with a trembling hand.

Finn clambered up the rocks to join her. "Don't panic." With his hand on her hip, he urged her against the boulders.

Ava clutched the dagger to her sternum as she surveyed Rain and the scouts below. "Finn ..."

"Remember what we practiced."

She nodded. "I'll aim to maim, then aim to kill."

"Good girl."

His lips brushed her forehead, then he stilled. His body hardened, nostrils flared, and everything around them quietened. Even the trees seemed to stop moving.

Then Finn turned and moved to the edge of the boulder. His thighs, ass, and back tensed as he stood drenched in moonlight and fixed his gaze on the dark trees.

The eyes appeared first, then the sleek, twisted bodies of wild, rabid, Unfated wolf shifters.

Ava's palms sweated around her knife as Finn angled his chin towards his shoulder. "Don't be afraid, Ava. Stay right there where I can see you."

"I will. And Finn ... stay safe." *Stay alive.*

"I will." Then he shivered and shifted. Tall and proud, he stood over the pack, his golden fur gleaming as he arched his back, lifted his head to the sky, and released a battle cry of his own. Rain and the scouts joined in.

A growl vibrated in return, and the eyes kept coming. Ava's breath caught. Five Fated powerful wolves against at least two dozen rogues. Maybe more. That was hardly fair.

She pressed her back against the rock behind her as Finn's tail lifted. "*Where's Blair?*"

Ava jumped at the voice inside her head. "Finn?"

"*He's not here, Ava!*"

Holy shit! They shared a telepathic connection? How was that possible?

"*We're mated. We can communicate.*" He glanced over his shoulder, his ears perked in alarm. "*But Blair's not here.*"

"What does that mean?"

But Finn had no time to answer as with a roar, the rogues attacked.

Ava ducked on instinct, crouching by the rock as the animalistic snarl of wolves howled through the air. They didn't all come at once, but a few rogues broke away and ran up either side of the waterhole. The Fated didn't hesitate. Nate's wolf leapt into battle with two rogues and Chad was quick to follow as Rain clambered down the rocks and into the fray.

Finn remained where he was and prowled back and forth along the edge of their cliff.

Snarls quaked through her bones while whimpers ripped her heart to shreds. Rain leapt at a rogue and together, they fell into the water, jaws snapping and claws swiping as they paddled. Chad and another rogue circled each other, baring their teeth before Chad pounced and sank his jaw into the rogue's flank. The darker wolf yelped and fell to his side, jaws snapping at Chad's throat. But

Chad got there first as with a rip of his teeth, the rogue fell at his feet.

Only for two more rogues to tackle the young chestnut wolf.

Ava gasped. "You have to help them!"

"I can't leave you."

She was about to protest that he couldn't spend the whole fight protecting her when Finn's eyes darkened and he leapt over her shoulder. Ava ducked, turning to see him sink his teeth into a rogue. Her stomach churned as the wolf's jaws snapped at Finn, but Finn was too strong as he tore flesh from the rogue's neck and clawed at his belly. They broke apart, but the rogue didn't retreat. It wasn't Blair, but he was no less terrifying. Rising on shaking legs, Ava pressed her back into the safety of the rock.

The wolf leapt at Finn, snarling and sniping. Chests clashed as they rose onto their hind legs. The rogue nipped at Finn, but he twisted and brought the rogue down, sinking his teeth into him. They rolled once, twice, then Finn kicked him over the edge into the water below.

Ava released the breath she hadn't realized she'd been holding as Finn rolled onto his feet. Blood matted his right shoulder, the wound closing as his breath hissed in and out.

Then three more rogues flew out of the darkness. Ava screamed and with a roar of their own, all four wolves tumbled into the water.

"No!" She raced to the edge of the cliff. *Please be okay, please ...*

"Fuck! Ava, be careful!"

Gasping, she held the dagger to her chest as she turned in a slow circle to survey her surroundings. She couldn't see anyone, but her heart pounded nonetheless as she stared down at the water. One rogue hobbled onto the banks, blood streaming down his gray leg as he retreated into the trees. Two still had Finn in a battle of snapping teeth in the shallows, water splashing as they pounced and ripped into flesh. She couldn't watch. Couldn't tear her gaze away. Teeth sank into Finn's rump and she squealed. *God no ...*

He kicked the rogue away and took down the other until it lay still in the water.

A yelp pierced her eardrums. Glancing across the clearing, three rogues were on top of Nate. Teeth ripped into the young wolf's shoulder and Ava's hands shot to her mouth. One bite to his carotid ...

"Nate!"

No! No, no, no. Tears formed in her eyes as Nate lay motionless and Finn limped onto the bank. Chad leapt out of the fray and disabled one of Nate's attackers.

"He's fine. Hurt, but alive."

It didn't ease the turmoil raging inside her though as tears streamed down her face. Ava watched Finn as he shook himself like a dog.

Then a growl sounded to her left, and she stilled. Hair prickled on the back of her neck as she turned to find herself face to face with two massive, ugly wolves, their fangs twisted and eyes yellow as they stalked towards her.

She backed up a step and found herself pressed against the rock. Fuck. Chest heaving, she gripped her knife. But she was outnumbered. She and Finn hadn't practiced this. She might be able to take down one, but two?

Her knees buckled. "Finn!"

His telepathic cry deafened her. *"AVA!"*

Another pained yelp of one of the Fated shuddered through the trees, but Ava didn't get a chance to see who had fallen. The rogues lowered their shoulders and bent their knees, preparing to pounce.

Then a thunderous roar echoed across the clearing and a

shadow flew over her. Ava's knees gave out as she fell forward, her knife clattering over the rock.

The wolf before her wasn't like the others. Certainly not a rogue, but hardly like Finn and his friends either. He was large, fast, and powerful, so definitely Fated. And he was as angry as a cut snake as he ripped his teeth into the rogue's throat and came away with his jugular. Blood spurted. Flesh dropped. And the Unfated fell. Dead.

Ava screamed and scrambled back into the rock, horrified at the sight of the mangled wolf. But it wasn't fear that surprised her, not of the black wolf anyway, even when he ripped into the other rogue.

Sly had come.

Chapter 49

Finn's chest heaved, watching in equal parts relief and horror as Sly ripped into the second wolf and dropped him without a thought. Ava huddled in the corner, shaking.

"It's all right, Ava. It's Sly."

"I know!"

A cry of pain shuddered through the air and Finn turned to find Rain on his side, struggling to get up while two rabid wolves ripped into his legs. Finn scrambled over the rocks in an attempt to reach him, but Sly was faster. He bounded down the cliff towards his brother, knocking into the first rogue with his shoulder before attacking the second. He dropped him within seconds. Dead.

"That's for Shelby, you fucker."

"Thanks, brother." Rain stumbled to his feet, blood oozing from his hindquarters. Sly simply snarled and jumped on the wolf that was crossing claws with Chad. Finn watched, stunned, as Sly took him down too.

"Mate killer."

Sly pounced on another with the power of more wolf than man. Blood spurted. Wolves howled and whimpered. A rogue retreated from attacking Kai, but he didn't get far as Sly slaughtered him too.

Then claws scratched at Finn's shoulder, catching him off guard. Turning, he snapped his jaw and grabbed the wolf by the ear. But Sly knocked the rogue off him, ripping his teeth into his chest and pulling flesh away as blood seeped over the sandstone rocks.

Sly backed away from another dead rogue, blood smearing his snout and salivating canines as he glared at Rain. *"Where's Thorne? I sensed him."*

"Tyrone Thorne is not here," Finn told him, and Sly snarled. *"But Blair ..."*

Finn stilled, his ears twitching as he sniffed. He hadn't stopped hunting the bastard during battle. Blair had been close, but he hadn't approached. Not that Finn was surprised as he'd expected Blair to send in the lieutenants to weaken the guard before attacking. But now—

Finn spun around. Ava stood on the other side of the waterhole, watching them with her hand pressed to her mouth, her eyes wide. With their bloodshed and Sly's menacing snarl, they didn't paint a pretty picture.

But then bright red eyes appeared behind her, and Finn's world stopped as Blair's twisted body emerged from the trees, his teeth bared.

And for the first time in so long, Finn knew fear. *"AVA!"*

She turned, froze, then released a terrified scream that sprung his body into action. Finn raced up the rocks even though he knew he wouldn't make it to her in time. Ava backed up. Blair lowered onto his front legs, ready to pounce. On the other side of the waterhole, Rain ran too, but she was too far away. So even though it went against all his instincts, Finn stopped running. He looked at her, down, then reached through their connection and bellowed, *"Jump!"*

She didn't need telling twice. Turning, Ava launched

herself off the cliff. Finn dove in after her, barely breathing a sigh of relief when she broke through the surface on a gasp. Paddling towards her, he looked up to find Blair glaring down at them, his body straining with rage.

"*Thorne!*" Sly growled as he attempted to approach the rogue, but Rain blocked him.

"*Don't, Sly.*"

"*He killed Shelby!*"

"*Tyrone killed Shelby, and you will get your revenge. But this is Finn's fight.*"

Grateful for Rain, Finn came up alongside Ava, though he doubted he'd want to leave Tyrone to Sly when the time came. He had his own vengeance to seek after what the bastard had done to his mother, but that was a score he would settle another time. Right now, his focus was on Ava as he swam with her to the rock edge, her panic vibrating inside him.

"*I've got you, honey.*"

"*Swim all you want, you whore! You're mine!*"

Clambering onto the rock, Finn growled at Blair while Ava lifted herself out of the water. "*Touch her and die, Thorne.*"

Blair lowered his shoulders again and growled. "*Should have known you'd take her, Little Finlay. You always wanted to play with my things.*"

Finn snarled and shot daggers at Blair. "*She was never yours.*"

"*Yes, she was. I don't wait for the Moon to tell me who to fuck. That bitch was mine first.*"

With rage pounding through him, Finn glanced at Ava to ensure she was okay, then started up the rocks towards Blair. "*I mean it. Fuck off home or suffer the consequences.*"

"*Of what? You're no match for me, Little Finlay. I'll take your whore down and drag you back to Father. He'd rather you alive, but I'm no fool. You'll never rebel. And I'd rather have the pleasure of killing you myself than listen to you whine like a little bitch over your lost mate."*

Over Finn's dead body. *"You're an animal, Thorne."*

Blair smirked. *"We're all animals. It's what we're meant to do. Claim and fuck and kill. You didn't even mark her."*

Snarling, Finn leapt up onto the next rock. *"Marking is barbaric. She's mine by choice. Not force."*

Blair cackled and stalked across the rock. *"You Fated pussy. You're a slave to humanity."*

Rain and Sly backed Finn up on the other side of the waterhole while his bastard brother awaited him like one awaited prey. Fucking cocky wanker.

Finn stepped up onto the top rock. *"I'd rather be a slave than a monster. Rather have Fate guide me than run rabid and blind. You will never understand the blessing I have, Blair. Father might have killed his mate, but if he wants mine dead, he shouldn't send someone as piss weak as you to do it."*

Snarling, Blair lunged. But Finn was ready as he lifted onto his hind legs and swiped Blair with his claw, sending his brother rolling. He lunged after the bastard, ready to sink his teeth into Blair's neck, but the wolf's legs got to him first and kicked Finn away.

He landed with a grunt and quickly regained his feet.

"You Fated believe such shit. You're just threatened because I'm the son he wanted. You were forced *on him."*

Finn stood tall. *"By Fate, Blair. He might have wanted you, but I am the son he was* meant *to have, and I am not afraid of you."*

"Yes, you are," he scoffed as they circled each other. *"Father and I are everything you fear, Little Finlay. It's why you ran from us. We believe in everything you don't and nothing is going to stop me. I'll show you just how weak I am when I bring you down and force you to watch as I rut with your mate."*

Finn roared and ran at Blair, sinking his teeth into his

flank. Blair yelped, his legs kicking as his claw gashed Finn's shoulder.

Then a weight fell over Finn as an Unfated lunged out of the trees and tore into Finn's rump. Pain seized his body as a yell strangled from his throat.

Sly pounced and ripped into the Unfated's neck.

He fell. Dead.

"Thanks."

Sly snapped his blood-soaked teeth. *"Finish the bastard."*

Breathing life back into his body, Finn jumped to his feet as Blair hobbled to his. It was no contest who would regenerate faster, and Blair seemed to know that as he backed up a few paces.

Then Finn froze, sensing the mistake before he saw it. Blair, Ava, and nothing in between them.

Blair turned and scurried down the rocks. Finn raced after him, Ava's scream echoing in his ears as he flew through the air and sank his claws into Blair's back. This time when they rolled, Finn didn't let go. Until his head hit a boulder.

Everything fuzzed. Then he blinked and found his feet, positioning himself between the rabid beast and his beloved.

"You and Tyrone should know better, Blair. Killing Ava won't make me give up on the Goddess. You know what happens to wolves who lose their mates."

To prove Finn's point, Sly growled.

"They don't all turn piss weak like Blackwood. Being released from the burden of Fate makes you stronger. Fiercer. Like Father. I helped him prove that."

Finn froze at the gleam in Blair's eyes, the smugness of his tone. The air grew colder as his heart pounded hard and low. *"What did you say?"*

Blair snorted. *"You believe in Fate, yet you don't understand it. Do you really think that Father killed Cassidy? Even a wolf as powerful as him doesn't have that kind of strength. But when she was going to take you and run, we had to stop her. So I ripped my teeth into that slut and ate her screams for dinner."*

Pride flashed in Blair's eyes to accompany his smug confession, but Finn barely registered any of it. Every muscle in his body corded as the animal inside him lunged through the air and snatched Blair Thorne around his shoulders. With violence unlike any he'd felt before, Finn shoved him to the ground and didn't hesitate. He sank his teeth into Blair's throat and ripped.

Silence fell as the rogue stilled beneath him. Rage pooled in Finn's mouth until he could bear the foul taste no longer, and he spat his brother's flesh in the bastard's face.

Only Ava's cry could pierce through his red haze. He turned his head to find her hands pressed to her mouth, her eyes wide. Chad and Nate flanked her while Kai lifted his head and struggled to his feet.

Finn stepped away from Blair and moved towards his mate. *"It's over now, honey. You're safe."*

Trembling, she fell to her knees. Finn quickly shoved his face in the water, doing his best to wash away the blood before shifting and dropping beside her to take her into his arms.

Ava dug her fingers into his shoulders and lifted her teary, awe filled eyes to his. "I've never been more terrified in my life. But thank the Moon you're okay."

She pressed her face to his chest, her breath heaving in shuddering gasps as he held her close and felt her fear slowly ease.

Chapter 50

The scouts crept towards them while Rain clambered down the rocks. Sly didn't move from his perch.

"*We did it!*" Chad cried, equally elated and exhausted. "You *did it, Finn! You killed the fucker.*"

"*Good job, Finn,*" Rain said, moving into their huddle.

Finn shook his head, his limbs weary with fatigue and shock. "I can't believe I didn't realize before ..."

"Realize what?" Ava asked.

Finn brushed his hand down her wet hair, his chest constricting. "It was Blair. He was the one who killed my mother."

Her eyes widened. "What? But I thought—"

"He was right, I should have known better." Finn darted a glance at his dead brother. "I *did* know better, but I'd never have thought ..."

Finn shuddered, anger and guilt creating a sour cocktail in his gut. His poor mum. Finn didn't doubt Tyrone had hurt her that awful night, but he wouldn't have been able to carry out the final deed. So, he'd unleashed his teenage son full of pent-up rage and hatred. The adolescent wolf who had completed the job with delight.

Finn grimaced as his insides constricted, but as he pressed his face into Ava's hair, peace accompanied the old, painful memory. He knew the truth now and had gotten his revenge. Blair was dead, and he had saved Ava. She never had to fear again.

Although Finn knew that wouldn't be true for any of them while Tyrone remained at large.

"*So, what now?*" Chad asked. "*Blair's dead and we killed at least half of the rogues.*"

"*Thanks to Sly.*" Rain turned to the wolf up on the rocks. "*Thanks for coming to our aid, brother.*"

Sly inclined his head. "*Rogues have no business entering our territory. I'll always be here to help the pack.*"

Hope shimmered in Rain's eyes. "*Does that mean—*"

"*You made a mistake, all of you. We may have won this battle, but the war is far from over, and the two of you are fools to think that your mates are safe. Tyrone will seek revenge for the death of his son. When he does, I'll be back.*"

Then Sly turned and scurried up the rocks.

"*No!*" Rain raced after him. "*Sly! Get back here!*"

But the wolf had gone, disappearing into the trees and shutting himself off from the pack bond. Up on the boulder, Rain lifted his head up to the moon and howled, his pain shuddering through Finn as the rest of the pack released soft howls in commiseration.

Sadness filled Ava's eyes. "He's not coming back, is he?"

"Not tonight," Finn said, releasing her as she sat up out of his arms.

Nate sat back on his haunches. "*Bloody hell.*"

"*Well, we did only kill a few rogues,*" Chad pointed out. "*There are still the Fated rebels and Tyrone himself.*"

Rain's shoulders sank as he sauntered into their circle. "*He'll be back when we face him.*"

"*But what are we going to do until then?*" Kai asked,

resigned. "*Tyrone is the darkest rogue Alpha out there, and he knows our Alpha's abandoned us. He knows we're vulnerable. And Sly said himself that Tyrone will come for us now that Blair's dead.*"

"*We're not vulnerable, though.*" Chad's chest puffed out as he surveyed the carnage around them. "*Look what we did tonight.*"

"*Yeah, thanks to Finn.*" Nate's gaze turned to him. "*Sly did come to our aid, but this was Finn's fight. And none of it would have happened if it wasn't for him.*"

Finn's heart rate spiked as four sets of eyes filled with pride, gratitude, and hope turned to him.

"No, it's you guys I should be thanking. You were incredible tonight and only thanks to you do I still have Ava."

She smiled at him, then at the wolves. "Yes. Thank you." She reached out to rub Kai's head because he was closest. Or the flirtatious wolf had inched forward. He closed his eyes, enjoying the scratch, and Finn let it go. This time.

"*You know we'll always fight to protect our own.*" Rain glanced at Finn. "*And even though Sly failed to stripe you, you are still part of the pack. And I'm incredibly grateful that it was you who answered my Call.*"

The other wolves nodded in agreement, and Finn's chest expanded to twice its size. "Thanks, guys. And I promise, I will uphold my vow. I'll help you bring Sly out of the bush, help him shift back into a man. But maybe before we can achieve that, we need to continue to reduce the power of the Pallarenda Pack."

"*The only way Sly will truly return is if he has the chance to kill Tyrone,*" Chad said, glancing sheepishly at Finn.

"*I think so, too,*" Rain agreed. "*So, how do you think we can do that? What's the plan to bring Tyrone down?*"

Clutching Ava tight, Finn's breath caught as the wolves stared at him, eagerly awaiting a response and directions on what to do next. Of course, he had ideas. They'd been stewing inside his head all week.

But before Finn could voice them, the Moon's glow intensified and bathed them all in a warm, bright light. Ava squinted, but Finn didn't move as the charcoal pack stripes on Rain, Kai, Nate, and Chad's coats shimmered.

And turned gold.

Ava gasped.

"*Holy shit!*" Kai cried, circling Chad.

"*Unreal!*"

"*Wow.*" Nate chased his tail as he tried to get a better look. "*Did that just—*"

"*It did.*" Rain lowered onto his haunches, bittersweet pride in his tone as he dipped his head. "*Finn has become Alpha.*"

The wolves glanced at him, lowered their ears, and uttered a low, harmonious howl. Muscles cording, Finn released Ava and rose to his feet as a new power pulsed through his body. Unable to resist the urge or the call of the Moon, he leapt onto the small boulder, shifted, and studied the men who had become his family. His team. And the woman who had filled his heart and whose love made him stronger than any wolf on the island.

Strong enough that the Goddess had blessed him once again. As Alpha.

And beneath her golden light, Finn lifted his head and joined his pack in their howl of victory.

Chapter 51

Ava dropped Finn off near the lookout before returning to Luna Views. Finn had washed most of the blood off in Cockle Creek, but he'd been in no state to walk through the five-star resort. Neither was she, but she looked far better than he did.

The Full Moon Party was in full swing as the gardens overflowed with people mingling beneath the low music playing from the DJ. Ava weaved her way along the path through the quiet huts with a skip in her step. Watching the wolves fight had been terrifying and when Blair's teeth had sunk into Finn, her heart had almost stopped beating.

But her man had won, and she hadn't even been horrified when he'd ripped Blair's throat out, as he'd often vowed to do. Truthfully, all she'd felt was relief that it was finally over.

At least for now. Sure, they had more battles to face, but the pack could take on any challenge Tyrone threw at them now that their strength had been restored.

Finn was the Alpha.

Ava couldn't be prouder as seeing those pack stripes shimmer gold had brought her joy like no other. After everything Finn had been through, how he'd fought for her and the way he'd instilled belief into the pack, Finn deserved every such reward. He was strong, a born leader, and perfect to assume the role of Alpha.

If anyone could bring Tyrone down, it was Finn.

But as she leapt onto the veranda of their hut, all Ava cared about was thanking him for keeping her safe. She pulled open the door, and found him already in the shower.

Perfect.

Stepping into the steaming bathroom, she pulled off her shirt, kicked away her shorts with her bikini bottoms, and unclipped her top with a flourish.

Finn blinked. "Ava—"

Grabbing his shoulders, she kissed him fiercely beneath the spray. He didn't need any encouragement as his tongue sought hers and hands grabbed her hips. They needed to be quick. Finn had to go and lead his pack on a run beneath the full moon as in the throes of victory, they wanted to celebrate.

But she wanted her own private celebration first so tearing her mouth from his, she pressed her lips to his throat, chest, then dropped to her knees where his cock stood proud, waiting for her.

Finn's thighs clenched. "Ava—"

Taking him in her hand, she pressed her lips to his swollen tip and swallowed him whole. His hands speared into her hair as his back sank against the shower wall.

"Fuck!"

She grabbed his firm ass, pressing her lips tight as she drew back, lapping her tongue around him. Finn's hips thrust and she moaned. Heat flooded her thighs as she peered up at him, every muscle pulled tight as his jaw strained and eyes met hers. She took him deep again, then drew all the way back, stroking his throbbing cock with her hand.

With practice, she seemed to be getting better, and thoroughly enjoyed the way he felt and tasted as she licked the vein pulsating down the side of his shaft. She loved the way he surrendered, how his thighs tensed and quivered, and how she could bring such a powerful man to his knees with only her lips, tongue, and talented fingers. So, with that pride powering her, Ava cupped his balls and delighted in the warmth of his cock. Finn thrust and grunted, pulled at her hair as she squeezed his ass, and cried out her name.

"I'm—I'm gonna—"

She let him pull out and tug her to her feet, his mouth capturing hers as he came against her belly. Grinning, Ava's bones melted as she sank into the kiss.

Breathless, he pulled away and pressed his lips to her forehead. "I know you said you were hot for me, but fuck. Ava. That was just—"

"I wanted to thank you."

His arms tightened around her. "You never need to thank me. I did what I had to do. What I'll always do. Because I love you. Though I'll never say no to having your beautiful mouth around my cock."

She grinned. "I just hope I'm getting better at it."

"You're amazing." He nipped at her lips. "You blow my fucking mind."

She laughed as he reached for the loofah and started washing her. Once they were clean, they dried off and returned to the bedroom, where Gracie lifted her head from her snuggle bed.

"I think we made good time," Finn said, pulling on his shorts. "Jam hadn't taken the stage when I came in."

"I might make it for their opening song," she agreed, tugging on her knickers before reaching for the ivory dress she'd chosen for tonight. "And you're going to ..."

She couldn't say it. The scouts had remained at Cockle Falls and awaited Finn and Rain's return, but Ava didn't want to know what they planned to do with the bodies of the Unfated.

"We'll clean up our mess and it'll be like it never happened."

She nodded and tucked her hair over her shoulder. "Can you zip me up?"

Finn tugged the zipper up her spine before placing a kiss on her nape. "I won't be long, honey. You go enjoy the party, and I'll be back to ravish you some more."

She turned, smiling softly. "Take your time. Enjoy this night, Finn. It's amazing what has happened and I'm so proud of you." She squeezed his forearms. "You're the Alpha."

He shook his head, wonder in his eyes. "It's strange. I never thought something like that would happen to me after a lifetime of having nothing. But I'll admit, it's ..." His shoulders straightened. "It's a great honor."

Beaming, she wrapped her arms around his neck. "It is. And you don't think Sly will mind?"

"Honestly? I think he approves. He never gave me pack stripes, even though he had two perfect opportunities. And there was something he said to me once. 'An Alpha needs his mate.' I don't think he believes he's strong enough to lead anymore. It might be why he abandoned them. He probably hoped Rain would assume Alpha if he mated, but ..." Finn shook his head, his eyes dulling. "Never mind. But yeah, in a way, I think Sly let this happen."

"Well, he's one smart wolf because he picked the perfect man to take over."

"You think so?"

"I do. You're strong, Finn. Strong in heart and soul. You'll make a fantastic Alpha. I know it."

His eyes crinkled as his mouth stretched into a grin. "That's because I have my mate."

"Yes, you do. A mate who loves you very much. Who

knows that this time, she picked a good man. A kind, loving, powerful man who will never hurt her and who loves her deeply."

He brushed his nose against hers. "Who will stop at nothing to ensure her every happiness."

"Who will protect her and keep her safe."

"And rip the throat out of anyone who dares threaten her."

"Who no longer doubts that after seeing it for herself. And who will forever be indebted to him."

He straightened, blue eyes hardening. "You owe me nothing, Ava. It is my job to protect, love, and cherish you. So, what do you say?" He squeezed her tight. "Will you stay on the island with me?"

Ava grinned. "Do I have a choice?"

"You always have a choice."

"Then I choose to be wherever you are, Finn. However ..." She glanced around the hut. "We could get a bigger place."

"Yeah, we can't stay here forever. We need to form our own packhouse."

Her knees weakened. "I've always wanted to buy my own home. I only have a small deposit, but as a physiotherapist, I'm entitled to a waiver on low-deposit insurance."

Finn shrugged her suggestion away. "I have savings, Ava. There's enough for a deposit."

She drew a deep breath. "Finn, you know I love your macho, alpha, dominant attitude, but this is still the twenty-first century and I will contribute financially to our home."

His mouth twitched. "Yeah, okay. But I would love to buy a house with you, Ava. See your dreams come true. And mine, too, as we build a home together."

She grinned. "Me, too. And when it's safe to do so, I will return to Townsville and work again."

His gaze softened as he brushed his hands up her back.

"Then that gives me extra incentive to eliminate Tyrone, so that you and Eden can return to work safely."

"Thank you. And speaking of Eden, I should join her at the party to celebrate the full moon human-style while you run with your pack."

He grinned. "All right." He touched his lips to hers. "I love you, Ava."

"I love you, too."

He kissed her deeply, longingly, but briefly before letting her go. Ava walked him to the door and after ensuring no one was watching, he dropped his shorts, handed them to her, and shot her a grin before running naked into the bush.

Ava's heart fluttered as she closed the door and turned to Gracie. "Aren't we the lucky ones, Gracie Belle?"

She folded Finn's shorts, placed them aside, then slipped on her shoes and grabbed her purse. After rubbing Gracie's adorable head, Ava left the hut in the opposite direction to Finn, skipping towards the crowd who were chanting Jam's name.

She found her friend as the band ran on stage and wrapped her arm around Eden's shoulders.

Eden's eyes widened. "You made it!"

"Yep!" she cried over the strum of electric guitar and the thumping of drums. "I'm ready to party!"

Throwing her arms into the air, Ava swayed her hips and sang along with Eden and Dee to one of Jam's biggest hits, reveling in the glory that was the full moon.

The Goddess who had blessed her.

Chapter 52

In human form, Finn and his pack loaded the dead Unfated wolves into the awaiting boat, getting no help from the bat shifter who sat at the helm sucking on a possum. The death toll hadn't been great, but it would be enough to shift the power balance and enrage Tyrone.

Finn took care to lay Blair's body in the boat last. He might have taken a life, but it was kill or be killed in their world, and Blair had made his choice. Finn had no feelings of kinship towards him and the bastard had caused him unsurmountable amounts of hell. He'd threatened his mate. Killed his mother. Finn would sleep easier knowing Blair no longer wandered this world.

Tyrone might have always wanted Finn to join him, but now that his pride and joy was dead, Finn doubted Tyrone would rest until he had Finn's own mangled body resting at his feet.

Jaw hardening, he stepped away from the boat and nodded at the bat shifter. The pale man tossed the bloodless possum into the water with a plop, revved the motor to life, and took the dead back to Pallarenda.

Finn regarded the lights across the bay, drew a deep breath, then turned his back. Tyrone's revenge would come swiftly, but it would not come tonight. So, he joined his packmates on the beach, slapped Rain on the back, and glanced at the scouts. With the beat of the Full Moon Party echoing in the air and entertaining his mate, Finn smiled.

"We have five hours until the flash of the full moon, boys. Let's make the most of it."

"All right!" Chad pumped his fist in the air as he, Kai, and Nate ran ahead up the beach. Finn and Rain exited the mangroves at a slower pace.

"Are you okay?" Finn asked quietly. "With the turn of events? I know it's not what you planned—"

"It's exactly what I planned," he said, and Finn's eyebrows shot up. "I mean, I didn't expect you to become Alpha, but I'm not surprised. I called for help. We needed a strong leader, and the Goddess gave me what I asked for. And honestly ..." Exhaling, Rain gazed up at the moon. "I think this is for the best. I'm okay with that."

Finn's shoulders relaxed. "You really think so?"

"Yeah."

Finn clapped Rain on the back. "Thanks, man. And I promise we'll get Sly back. I'm sure of it. But you know ... I think you were right."

Rain frowned as they crossed the road towards the bush. "About what?"

"We need to prove to Sly that we can protect our mates at any cost."

Exhaling, Rain glanced at his feet. "Don't start, Finn. You might be the Alpha, but that doesn't mean you can tell me what to do."

Finn chuckled. "Actually, it does. But I'm not telling you, Rain. Just advising you to think about it."

"Yeah, well ... I don't think Sly will care either way. He's already lost his mate. Securing our own will only remind him of what he's lost."

"But who's to say Fate's that cruel, Rain? Sly's young. Would the Goddess really expect him to be alone for the rest of his life?"

Rain scratched his head, contemplating that as they joined the scouts waiting in the trees. "I don't know."

"Neither do I. But honestly, Rain, stop worrying about Sly for once and think about what you want." Finn poked him in the chest. "That *is* an Alpha order."

But Finn didn't push it any further as he grinned at his pack. "Let's run, boys, and bask in her glow."

Together, they shifted and with a howl, Finn led them for a run beneath the September supermoon. Their paws pounded and hearts raced, their golden stripes shimmering in their various shades of fur as they darted in and out of trees along Cockle Creek. Passing the falls now washed free of blood, they clambered up the rocks and deeper into the national park.

It was pure freedom. A rush of fresh air. An exhilarating moment of power as they reveled in the light. Once their tongues sagged and breaths panted, they stopped to play. Leaping into the creek, Finn relished in the cool water as he rubbed his back over the smooth pebbles. Magnetic Island was wild, beautiful, and it was home. He had native bush to run in, a pack to protect, and a woman who loved him for everything that he was. He'd never been happier.

Tyrone, he could deal with. He'd killed his brother, the true villain of his nightmares, so he could face his sire after half his lifetime. Finn was stronger and wiser now. An Alpha. His pack were by his side and Tyrone the dark rebel wolf stood no chance.

But one thing remained missing, one vital strength, and that task lied with Rain. He wanted Sly back more than any of them, and his resistance against mating was cracking. Finn could feel it.

Rain wouldn't let the pack down.

But as for Sly ...

Finn flipped onto his belly, stretching out in the creek as he watched the pack leap, roll, and celebrate their goddess. Panting, he enjoyed the water flowing over his body and the soft breeze rippling through the trees.

Then his ears twitched. Finn rose to his feet, sensing him before he turned and glanced up at the granite cliff overlooking the creek.

Sly stared down at him. He said nothing, but his pain ... it speared Finn in the chest, knocking the breath out of him. Deep, gnawing, gut-wrenching pain. Pain Finn never wished to feel. Pain he wouldn't have to now that Blair was dead.

But Sly's enemy still lived, and his anguish wouldn't vanish so easily.

Finn watched the former Alpha, his dark coat blowing in the breeze. Then Sly's nose dipped, and his shoulders slumped. Turning, he sauntered back into the bush.

Finn's heart clenched for the broken wolf.

Don't worry, buddy. We'll help you find your way back to us.

Because now, that was Finn's job. He was the Alpha.

And Sly was the Lone Wolf.

Epilogue

Tyrone paced back and forth inside the fort, his heart pounding.

The rebels had come, awaiting the return of the rogues beneath the painful glow of the full moon. Their pack. Their sons. The unhinged idiots who'd rushed into battle without thought or preparation. But Tyrone tried to remain calm. Blair was strong. He'd trained the boy himself and for thirty years, Blair had been his right-hand man. The one he could rely on. For most things.

But when the first boats returned filled with taut, angry men, Blair wasn't among them. While enraged fathers greeted their bloodied sons with a mix of scorn and relief, Tyrone watched. And waited.

Then the final boat arrived with one ghostly pale bat shifter steering, its passengers unmoving, and everything inside Tyrone bunched and blew apart.

With an anguished howl, he leapt out of the fort and down the hillside, dodging the rocks along Shelly Beach.

As the boat moored in the shallows, he saw the body of Blair's wolf lying atop the cargo of twisted fur.

Lucas morphed beside him as Tyrone shifted back into a

man, his chest heaving as he approached the boat, reached out, and placed his hand over his son's cold shoulder.

Wrath unlike any he'd ever felt surged through his veins.

"Finlay ..." Growling, Tyrone shot his gaze across the bay, the moonlight dancing off the glistening water. That Fated cunt. He should have drowned the tyke at birth, but no, Tyrone had thought he'd be useful. Had given into Fate for one moment with the belief that he'd been given the useless brat for a reason.

But as usual, he'd been wrong. The Goddess was nothing but a bitch and Tyrone would not rest until Finlay lay dead at his feet.

Lucas slipped up beside him and Tyrone cleared his throat. "A deal is a deal, Lucas. You want a bride? I know of the perfect woman."

Author's Note

Inspiration is a funny thing. When I moved to Townsville in 2009, the Magnetic Island Full Moon Party was all the rage among my university peers. As a non-drinker, it was of no interest to me. But I did think, 'Hmm. That's just a coverup for werewolf activity!' This idea stayed in the vault until 2023, when I decided to write a paranormal romance and drew on aspects of the local community to create *Island Wolf.*

Magnetic Island is a sleepy suburb of Townsville and famous for majestic rock formations, beautiful bays, and koalas. I took little creative license with this book, so everything in the story actually exists. You can stay in Finn's hut, snorkel the shipwrecks, and rent a hot red Jeep or topless pink Mini. You can also observe Magnetic Island from Tyrone's favourite fort at Cape Pallarenda. However, the hospital is not open to the public, Cockle Falls was exaggerated for my plotting needs, and unfortunately, the once famous Full Moon Downunder Party no longer runs.

The tagline 'Don't eat the koalas' popped into my head and loving it so much, I built a subplot around Australia's famous marsupial. Koalas were introduced to Magnetic Island in 1935 to sustain the population after they were almost hunted to extinction for their fur. Now, the island is home to the largest wild koala colony in Australia were they are safe from most natural predators. The hospital is a real place, though not as described in the book, where the dedicated vet treats injured koalas and volunteers raise orphaned joeys all while protecting the natural habitat. Maggie's koalas are free from the serious chlamydia virus, but they do have koala retrovirus, making them susceptible to illness in the dry environment. The Forts Walk is famous for spotting koalas in the wild, though I'll believe that when I actually see one there!

Luna Views and Eucalypts Grove are based on two real backpackers resorts. Rain's hotel is a far grander version of Base Backpackers, who once held the Full Moon Party and where huts really do jut out over the ocean. However, Eucalypts Grove is based exactly on the koala retreat on Magnetic Island where, yes, you can have breakfast with the koalas.

But while koalas receive a lot of love, flying foxes get a lot of hate. They have invaded Townsville parks, cause a ruckus at night, and they stink. However, they pose little threat to locals, are only trying to survive a changing world, and are actually vital to the koala's survival by pollinating the eucalypts. Not to mention they make the perfect cover for vampire covens and I loved mixing the bat issues and Townsville's out-of-control crime to create *Island Wolf's* dark villains.

Crime is a hot topic of concern in Townsville. Dozens of car thefts and break-in's occur weekly, and everyone has been or knows someone who's been affected. I haven't intended to imply the police are to blame by creating a corrupt force in this book as they do their job to the best of their ability, but I've thoroughly enjoyed mixing aspects of my home to to bring my paranormal world to life.

Acknowledgments

This book would never have come to be if it wasn't for one person, my stepfather Ian. Thank you for being intrigued by the idea of wolf shifters on Magnetic Island and therefore motivating me to plot and write this book. Finn and Ava would never have come to be without your unwavering support. Thank you for brainstorming with me every day before writing time and your never-ending encouragement as you made these characters as real in your head as they were in mine. I had a lot of fun on our recipe to Magnetic Island as we found the *Moltke*, scoped out Cockle Falls, and traced Finn's footsteps through the bush after bat shifters.

As I wrote this book during NaNoWriMo 2023, a big thank you goes to the wonderful ladies at the *How to Write Academy* for creating the group that kept me accountable that month. Granted, I got a little competitive, but 107000 words in 35 days would not have happened without this initiative. So thank you Amy Andrews, Ally Blake, Clare Connolly, and Jennifer St. George, and everyone who participated in the event for your encouragement. It was an intense writing sprint that I never plan to repeat.

And of course, I'd never have been able to do this without the encouragement from my friends and readers, even though I switched subgenres. Thank you to Deeanna West, my fantasy-loving friend who helped me ensure my mystical elements made sense. You are my best buddy and I love having someone to be book crazy with!

But the final elements wouldn't have come together

without my fantastic editor Nicola and cover designer Danielle. Nicola, thank you for your invaluable insight and suggestions that not only improved this story, but fixed the trouble I had with book two! The wolf shifters certainly wouldn't sparkle without you. Nor would they look so fantastic without the remarkable skills of Danielle. Thank you for sending me four amazing covers to painstakingly choose from. Though I'll always regret not having all four, I think I made a solid choice. Your work is stunning.

As always, I'm forever grateful for the support of Romance Writers of Australia for building the network and tribe that help us all succeed. You are my home and my family. Thank you to all of my writing friends who I've turned to for advice and support. I love that we're all in this together.

Last but not least, thank you so much to the adorable Gracie Belle! The idea of giving Finn a dog as cute and crazy as you was too funny to resists. Thank you for being quirky, hating change, stealing socks, and just being so freaking gorgeous that I needed to immortalise you in this book.

But the biggest thank you goes to you, dear reader! Whether you're a fantasy/paranormal junkie who has read my work for the first time or jumped ship with me from contemporary, each and every one of you make my life worthwhile as I strive to continue bringing you more stories. I hope you love my paranormal twist on Townsville and Magnetic Island as much as I do and are keen for the next book. And if you're local, don't be afraid of the bats. They're not actually vampires and won't bite. Much...

About the Author

Rachel Armstrong has always loved making up stories and is now living her dream of being an author. She writes romantic fiction about rural small towns, stirs up the suspense with terrifying villains, and places paranormal shifters in our every day world. Her novel, *The Man from Shadow Creek*, was awarded the 2024 Romantic Book of the Year Award by Romance Writers of Australia.

Rachel lives in Townsville, Queensland, with her border collie, Jacob, where she helps people live their best lives as an exercise physiologist. In her spare time, she is either reading on her treadmill or plotting out her next novel while grooving at Zumba. Rachel's a keen traveller and has enjoyed many holidays exploring historic London, flying through the Grand Canyon, and hiking volcanos in Bali.

Rachel loves to connect with readers and fellow writers through Facebook and Instagram.

www.rachelarmstrongauthor.com.au